In Dangerous Waters

In Dangerous Waters

Jack Russ

Alamo Hills Press
Alamo, California

Interior and cover design by Pete Masterson, Æonix Publishing Group,
www.aeonix.com

ISBN: 978-0-9830149-0-4
LCCN: 2010914918

URL: www.JackRuss.com

Alamo Hills Press
Alamo, California

Printed in the United States of America

To my wife, Arlene, for her patience and continued support through multiple rewrites.

Acknowledgements

SPECIAL THANKS GOES TO ELISABETH TUCK for her superb editing, encouragement and persistence. Her edits always contained a welcome explanation. To my teachers Camille Minichino and Charlotte Cook. And to the talented California Writers Club members of my critique group, Susan Berman, Fran Cain, Nannette Carrol, David George, Jill Hedgecock, and Cheryl Spanos for their skillful editing, astute comments, imagination, and encouragement.

1

Mike Kinkaid had to admit he'd run out of options. The well-worn wallet in his pocket held his last twelve dollars. The driver's Jeep-chase proposal, a gamble at best, offered Mike the last possible way to carry out his Navy orders and report for duty by the deadline, tomorrow, June 26, 1951 to a ship he couldn't find.

The lanky, gum-chewing soldier floored the war-weary Jeep, scattering sand and gravel across a barren stretch of South Korea's Pusan Air Base. A trailing dust cloud lingered in the hot and windless afternoon. Next to him, Ensign Kinkaid's right hand grabbed the bare metal handgrip and hung on. His other hand reached behind him and fought to restrain his two battered canvas-and-leather bags that, with every bump and pothole, threatened to flee their precarious backseat perch.

"Chasing a convoy to find a ship must seem crazy to you, soldier." Mike raised his voice over the engine's erratic coughs and backfires, serious tune-up distress calls. "Thanks for your help. This is not how I wanted my career to start, but maybe your idea will work. I've got to make it on time." But, would the elusive supply party they raced to intercept provide the information he needed? Where was his ship?

A sudden, sharp turn onto a rutted pathway forced Mike to release his grip on the bags. A quick grab for the rusty, seat frame prevented him from being tossed from the Jeep. His smaller bag wedged itself behind the driver. Mike snatched the larger one moments before it would have departed.

"So, you just got your commission, Lieutenant?" the soldier asked over the engine's knocking, the Jeep now steady again. "When're you supposed to report to your ship?" The soldier's high-speed shortcut plowed through another patch of knee-high, dead grass.

"Not later than tomorrow," Mike said. If he didn't find the ship by then, he would fail to comply with his orders. Missing his ship, his first active duty assignment, would land him in serious hot water.

"Gotcha, sir." The soldier's foot on the gas pedal urged greater speed. "Like I said, you ain't gonna find no Navy ship 'round here, sir. Only Army and Air Force." He bounced the Jeep across a shallow, dry rain gully onto an airfield taxiway and picked up speed.

"Don't make sense to me, for sure," the soldier continued. "Seems like them Navy guys would tell you where your boat is. You check with the colonel's office, did you?"

"No, and I couldn't even find a Navy rep on the base," Mike said.

"Those Navy thieves I told you about were over at the supply base this morning," the soldier said. "Their rag-tag convoy comes for a refill from time to time. No real schedule. If they're still there, maybe we can see what they know about your boat."

The Jeep left the aircraft taxiway and crested the raised embankment that ran alongside it, a sidestep maneuver that cleared the two Air Force fighter planes that had been rolling toward them. The planes reawakened Mike's nagging disappointment. He would have been in Pensacola to begin flight training now if the Navy had kept its promise.

"One day I'll be flying one of those," Mike said, his pointing finger bouncing with the Jeep's motion. His dream, for as long as he could remember, had been to fly. Not yet, the Navy's orders stated.

"You said you was Navy," the soldier said and stared at Mike. "Them's Air Force. How you gonna do that?"

"The Navy promised me flight training," Mike said, "but the orders were changed. A shortage of officers they said. Now I have to do a shipboard tour and qualify at sea first." The switch still grated, but he had no choice. "After that, I'll go to flight school. Anyway, I'm curious about life on a destroyer. My father was a Navy lieutenant commander. I'll have a chance to see what life was like for him."

"What're you gonna do if those supply-store raiders we're trying to meet up with can't help?" the soldier said.

"Don't know," Mike said. An even worse scenario filled his mind, one that had harried him for several days. Since he hadn't found anyone in Pusan who knew where he could find the ship, perhaps it was at sea. How would he reach it then? There'd be no way for him to make his reporting deadline. This trip felt like a fiasco, not the romantic adventure the instructors had touted in his Midshipman training.

The Jeep avoided the worst bumps along the embankment then left the higher ground where an access road merged. The soldier took a short-cut behind four aircraft hangars and cut off another half mile. A sharp right turn headed them toward an unfenced storage area.

The soldier swerved, the Jeep's tires screeching, onto another access road toward the base's supply depot. Slow movers ahead blocked their way, the nearest loaded with shifting, empty wooden pallets.

The soldier down shifted. He drove part way off the road to the right as if to pass, but veered back behind the truck. He tried a similar brief foray to the left. A pause, then he floored the gas pedal and swung farther left to pass the pallet carrier.

Mike turned to the back seat reaching to wrestle with his bags. The soldier sounded the Jeep's horn, swerved, then jammed on the brakes, the shrill horn still screaming. Mike swung around to see an oncoming truck closing fast. The first of four stake trucks were less than thirty yards away.

A screeching skid caused the Jeep to wobble. The soldier fought for control. The truck's brakes shrieked, and its blaring, low-pitched horn joined the racket. Mike watched, entranced as both vehicles slowed, but would it be enough? He held on.

At impact, the Jeep's right front wheel hit the truck's right front bumper and fender. The smaller vehicle spun onto the roadside but remained upright. Mike's white-knuckle hold on the seat, and his legs braced against the doorframe kept him from vaulting out. The soldier's death grip on the steering wheel saved him from an equally ungraceful exit into the dirt.

The daring young soldier's stunned, open-mouthed expression soon became a wide grin, then a roaring laugh. He turned to Mike.

"Looks like this little buggy is bound for the junk heap now," the soldier said, "but she's still running. Don't make 'em like this any more." He side-slapped the steering wheel, let out a loud, "Whooee," and turned to Mike. "You okay, are you, sir?"

"Sure," Mike said. He matched the soldier's grin. "That's some ride you gave me, soldier."

A slim, bare-chested man about twenty-two, Mike's age, jumped from the driver's seat and stomped around the front of the truck through the settling dust.

"What the hell were you trying to do, soldier?" the man yelled at them. "You both okay?"

"Yeah," the soldier said straightening up under the trucker's tirade. "Sorry about that, driver. You and your rig okay, are you? Bessie, here, is gonna need some time in the shop." He stroked the dashboard as though petting a dog.

"Where you going so damned fast anyway?" The angry truck driver ripped off his cap and beat it on his thigh. "We're headed out. Your joy-riding is holding us up."

"Got a new Navy officer for you thieves," the soldier said and pointed his thumb over his shoulder to Mike.

Mike scrambled from the Jeep, retrieved his uniform cap, and picked up his two bags that had been ejected onto the dusty roadside. He scanned the convoy's three other trucks. Each held four or five scruffy men along with a cargo of crates and cardboard boxes.

"Who's your boss-man this trip?" the soldier asked the truck driver. "Maybe you clowns can give this officer a ride if you're going his way."

"The lieutenant, back there," the driver waved a hand, gesturing to the second vehicle, "ain't going to like this. We're running late already." He beckoned to the truck behind him.

A man jumped down from the second stake truck and approached. His John Wayne swagger caught Mike's attention. A holstered .45 caliber pistol hung low on his hip, reinforcing the Wayne image. The likeness ended at the man's gigantic, jet-black, handlebar mustache. Mike ran a hand across his own clean-shaven face then hoped no one noticed.

"Hi." The olive-skinned man glanced at the battered Jeep and eyed Mike then the driver. "You okay, young man?" he asked the soldier.

"Bessie here needs fixin'," the soldier said. "Could use a tow, too."

"Helo," the man said to Mike. "I'm Riley. You Kinkaid?"

Mike raised his eyes to meet the man's black ones. Six foot three? A relief rush filled Mike. Riley had to be from the *USS Bartley*, his destination. What other stranger would know his name?

"Yes, sir," Mike said, grinned, and dropped his bag. "Ensign Mike Kinkaid." Mike held out his hand. "Are you from *USS Bartley*?" A big hand grasped his.

Surprised that an officer would lead a supply party, Mike noted that the man had the bearing, but not the appearance of a naval officer. He wore no insignia on his sleeveless khaki shirt. His ragged and stained, wash khaki uniform pants were cut off to about four inches above his knees, appropriate in this humid heat.

"You sure make your entrance the hard way," Riley's deep voice continued, "Where the hell have you been?"

"Trying to find *Bartley*," Mike said and grinned.

"We got your orders about two weeks ago," Riley said. "Expected you to show up earlier but didn't know when. Glad you made it. C'mon. We're headed for the ship now." Riley turned to the soldier. "Thanks, soldier. Good job. We'll take care of Mister Kinkaid from here. And about that junk heap," he said, and pointed to the Jeep. "When we get to the west gate I'll let them know you're out here with a flat, bent wheel, and need a tow."

The sun forced Mike to squint as he studied the men in the trucks dressed no better than Riley. Mike envied their cooler attire. All but one was shirtless in the oppressive heat. Some wore blue dungaree pants. Others wore Marine greens. Mike sweltered in his full summer uniform including black tie, khaki outer blouse, and cap. He'd followed the protocol drummed into him in training that dictated that he report to his first duty assignment in full uniform.

"C'mon," Riley said. "We'll take you to the ship." He grabbed Mike's smaller bag, pointed toward the second truck and motioned Mike to follow. "You ride with me." Riley's words seemed congenial, but contrasted with his furrowed brow and pursed lips. Mike lifted his remaining bag and followed.

The first two trucks' condition puzzled Mike. The drivers' doors on each had been lost in previous incarnations, leaving the cabs open to wind, rain, and the ever-present dust. The first truck had a windshield panel missing in addition to the newly-twisted fender. Were these typical of US equipment in Korea? Except for the drivers, each man held either an M-1 or a Browning automatic rifle. This had to be more than a supply convoy, else why were they armed? His stomach tightened.

Riley tossed Mike's bag onto the second flatbed's crowded platform then waved Mike toward the cab. Mike hefted the larger, battered, war-surplus, B-4 bag next to the first, pleased that it had held up this far. He climbed into the cab and laid his crumpled blouse and dusty cap on the narrow shelf behind the tattered bench seat, then sat next to the diminutive driver. Mike opened his top shirt button, loosened his tie, and flapped his shirtfront away from his chest in a vain attempt to pull in a bit of cooler air. June in South Korea sure wasn't necktie weather.

"I'm Finetti, Fingers Finetti." The driver extended his hand. "Welcome to the fleet."

Mike's involuntary glance at the man's fingers revealed nothing of significance. Unusual nickname.

"Move it, Fingers," Riley said. He stood on the makeshift running board and waved a move-out signal to the other trucks before he swung in and landed on the seat beside Mike. "We don't have all day. Let's get this crew back to the ship before somebody starts shooting."

"What's up, Lieutenant?" Mike asked. Mention of shooting came as a surprise. He'd been told the Army and Marines had secured this part of South Korea and had pushed the Chinese and North Korean forces well north. If that was the case, why were they armed as though expecting trouble?

"The name's Riley, Mike," the mustached man said. "We don't do formal on *Bartley*." He glanced back at the two trucks that followed. "The ROKS warned us some Gook raider teams have slipped through the lines again." Riley turned forward and, one by one, pulled each of the three

M-1 rifles from their rack, checked their ammunition clips, and returned the guns. "I'm not about to get our butts shot off."

"Rocks?" Mike said scanning his brain for a meaning and his surroundings for boulders.

"Republic of Korea soldiers, ROKS, the local South Korean cops," Riley said. "Tough little buggers. Glad they're on our side. They run ambush patrols to catch the Gook bastards that sneak back after dark." Riley pointed to each rifle. "We always come armed anyway." Mike's eyes followed Riley as he again looked back through the rear window where the men in the truck bed also held rifles. "We team with the Marines on these supply runs. It's still hunting season around here."

Mike mopped his face with his sleeve. Had he stepped into a nightmare? Maybe a potential firefight? He hadn't pictured reporting to his ship waving a rifle.

2

R ILEY'S REFERENCE TO HUNTING SEASON resonated in Mike's mind
while the convoy continued toward the military base's west gate. He
sat uneasily between Riley and Fingers in the second truck of the four.

"*Bartley's* in Masan," Riley said, "about fifty miles west. That's at least
two hours, unless we have some problems along the way."

Problems? What sort of problems? The battered trucks certainly didn't
appear reliable. Could they fix a breakdown? Or did Riley's comment refer to a hunting season sort of problem?

The convoy passed through the security gate and drove along the adjacent Korean community's narrow streets. The squalid conditions outside
the base surprised Mike. He couldn't attribute any of the damage to combat. Many families and small businesses were crowded together in shacks,
some roofless, some missing all or parts of walls, and some with fabric or
sheet metal rigged as awnings. Random, tattered tents squatted between
buildings. Several, mostly naked, children watched from among the hov-
els. The convoy drew little interest from the adult Koreans in the streets.
The strong and unfamiliar smells bespoke disease, decay, and sewage. The
lack of any breeze added to Mike's discomfort. He'd encountered slums
before, but had never seen such extreme poverty. Tension eased after the
supply convoy escaped the odors and lethargic citizens of Pusan's ghetto.

Farmland marked the western edge of Pusan better than any fence
or road. Beyond the city, Riley scanned the fields with a strange intensity. What was he looking for? Finetti's fingers maintained a tight hold on
the steering wheel. Mike turned again to the truck bed. He had expected

some of the crew to nap on the drive to Masan. Instead, each man faced outward from the truck. They leaned on boxes or bales, guns ready. The arrangement wasn't casual. They had full visual coverage of their surroundings, ahead, behind, and to either side.

Mike again used his shirt's long, khaki sleeve to dab sweat from his forehead. This time he noted dark blotches on his once-clean uniform. He glanced at the rifle rack in the cockpit. The guns certainly weren't decoration. They gleamed, ready for trouble.

Twenty minutes after leaving the cultivated area, the trucks approached two Korean civilians on fat-tired bicycles headed back toward Pusan. After the riders had passed, the four trucks became the rutted road's sole occupants. An ominous silence blanketed the humid and windless countryside, an area where one might normally expect to see farm workers or field animals.

"How long were you in Pusan?" Riley interrupted Mike's musings. He continued his methodical scan.

"Three days," Mike said, relieved to have Riley's question break the silence. "I'd have been here sooner except I couldn't find anybody who knew where to find *Bartley* or how to contact the ship.

"You were lucky to run into that crazy soldier." Riley said. Mike tried to read Riley, but couldn't. The man wasn't unfriendly or cold. Preoccupied for sure.

Riley stood on the truck's running board to get a better view of the area. After about five minutes he sat down in his seat again and said, "We figured you'd be here sooner. Your orders didn't say when to expect you."

Why didn't Riley make eye contact when he spoke? Instead, he maintained an unbroken search of the surroundings.

"I'd have been here sooner," Mike said, "except for the flight interruptions." He expected Riley to ask for more, but Riley scanned in silence. The John Wayne likeness flashed through Mike's mind again. "Ten days after graduation I left Carol in Seattle," Mike said, thinking Riley would chat, "then I reported to the Navy office in San Francisco for a flight."

"Carol?" Riley said. "Girlfriend?"

"My wife."

"New bride?"

"Yes," Mike said. "We were married the day after my graduation and commissioning."

Mike's mind flashed to petite, blonde Carol and how well she'd handled the disappointment after his flight-school orders were changed. The thought of her brought a familiar, warm glow.

The new orders had come as a shock. Instead of the anticipated flight school, he had been sent to a ship. He wanted to fly. He'd dreamed of flying from a carrier. The Navy had promised immediate flight school, a promise in writing. He had to admit he hadn't taken the change in their plans well at all. Carol had been more accepting.

Mike expected some comment, maybe another question from Riley, perhaps something from the silent Fingers, too. He didn't understand why neither spoke. If he described the rest of his journey, it might break the ominous tension.

"I managed to finagle an Air Force flight from San Francisco to Hawaii two days later," Mike said. Talking helped to brush away his growing anxiety. All the men in the truck seemed tense. Did they sense danger that he should recognize? "They wait-listed me for two days in Hawaii. A military-chartered TWA plane dumped me in Guam to sit for two more days then I spent several days cooling my heels in Tokyo."

Riley's attention was elsewhere. He'd only attempted small talk up to now and damned little of that. The convoy traveled another five or so, barren miles before Riley spoke again.

"Where did you get your commission?" Riley asked. The lines in his face had eased somewhat, although his eyes remained locked on the countryside. "You were Navy ROTC, right?"

"Right," Mike said. "I went to the University of Washington in Seattle."

"We hoped you might be Naval Academy," Riley said. This time he looked directly at Mike.

"Why?" Mike couldn't hide the surprise in his voice. The ship had received a copy of his orders. They would have seen that the orders were addressed to the NROTC unit at the University, not to the Naval Academy.

"Watkins hates the NROTC," Riley said. His eyes pierced Mike's, his chin lowered. "Don't be surprised if you get some heat from him about it."

"Who is Watkins and what's his problem?" Mike asked. Without thinking, he flexed his left fist. He didn't intend to be impertinent, but Riley's comment came as a warning with a tinge of challenge.

"Watkins is our executive officer, our XO," Riley said. "He says the Navy ROTC program produces lousy officers, a bunch of playboys he calls them."

How should he take this comment? Did Riley share the antagonism? Probably not. His tone came across as friendly advice, perhaps only a warning concerning *Bartley's* executive officer. Maybe Riley exaggerated. He didn't appear to be in a mood to go into detail.

Mike's uneasiness grew. Riley and Fingers kept searching for something. Mike hadn't seen any structures or evidence of people, animals, or agriculture for several miles. Fewer potholes in the last ten miles of road had made the ride less jarring. Dry, shallow ditches along both sides of the narrow road would permit one vehicle to pass another or might carry rain runoff. The low hills to the south steepened as the trucks moved farther west toward Masan. The hills had an odd closeness about them, or maybe his imagination played tricks.

"What should I look for?" Mike's dehydrated throat caused his voice to crack. "Things seem peaceful enough." The words didn't come out with the self-assurance he had intended.

Riley's frown and non-response added to Mike's foreboding. Had the day suddenly become hotter? Riley leaned out the doorway and again stood with one foot on the truck's running board, the other still in the cab. He shielded his eyes against the intense afternoon sun.

"It's quiet, too damned quiet," Riley muttered shaking his head. Mike tensed at the concern in Riley's voice. "On most trips we see at least a few people along here. About a week ago the ROKS caught a Gook raider team nearby." Riley glanced at the two trucks that followed. "Grabbed the bastards trying to get through the air base fence before sunup." He shifted his attention to the hillsides. "Damned Gooks are clever. Dangerous as hell."

Mike rubbed his hand over his crew cut. How had he gotten into this predicament? Sure, his orders said go to sea, to a ship. They didn't say take a convoy ride through the South Korean countryside, and maybe encounter enemy gunfire. The picture didn't fit anything he'd imagined. If he'd wanted that sort of life, he would have applied for the Marine Corps option during Midshipman training.

The lead truck slowed to a stop ahead. Riley's raised hand cautioned Fingers to slow down. A Marine in the lead truck waved and pointed to the roadside on the right. Grim-faced, Riley reached into the cab and grabbed a rifle from its rack.

Mike sat taller, straining to see what the Marine had noted. A large, truck-size green bush partially obscured something on the ground.

"What is it, Lieutenant?" Mike asked. He'd said to call him Riley. Maybe later?

"Close it up," Riley said to Fingers. The sharpness in Riley's voice heightened Mike's discomfort. "Let's take a look-see." Riley leaned out the cab's doorway. "Keep your eyes peeled."

The truck slowed. Mike twisted toward the two trucks that followed. They also slowed but kept a planned interval. Mike recognized that the technique would keep the trucks from becoming a bunched target. His apprehension increased a notch. They expected trouble.

Fingers stopped the truck alongside the shielding bush. Mike's heart pounded. An old man lay sprawled over his bicycle in the ditch next to the bush. Vegetables had scattered from his basket. Swarming flies veiled his bloody face and the missing scalp. Whoever had killed him wasn't out to steal a bicycle.

"A civilian," Riley said. "He wasn't here when we came through this morning." He jumped down and circled the figure.

Riley raised a cloud of flies when his rifle prodded the torso. An involuntary shudder shook Mike. If the dead man had been wired with explosives, Riley could have been killed. He and Fingers might have died or been seriously injured. Carol would never have known what happened to him.

The term "combat zone" flashed through Mike's brain. Until now, he had associated the words with aerial combat, one plane versus another, pilot against pilot. Here, a dead man lay in the hot dirt, evidence of a different kind of battle. Despite his fear, Mike admired Riley's take-charge manner, a man he could welcome as a friend. However, he didn't admire Riley's apparent carelessness in nudging the body.

"Hasn't been dead long," Riley said. He brushed aside branches of a nearby bush with his rifle. "No booby-traps this time." He scanned the area again. "All clear here. Let's move on," Riley said climbing back into the cab. "Pick up your interval with truck one. It's getting late."

As the trucks rumbled west, the small trees and bushes on the left gradually gave way to larger trees and thicker underbrush that covered the steepening hillside. The afternoon sun, through intermittent clouds, draped random shadows over the narrowing valley.

Riley's hand jerked up startling Mike. Riley grabbed an M-1 from the rack and shoved the rifle at Mike. Two ammunition clips followed.

"You know how to use that?" Riley barked.

A shiver ran through Mike. He let a nod answer for him. He checked the rifle. It held a full ammo clip and the safety was on. He shivered again. What should he fire at? He didn't like the way things were developing. He flipped the safety off.

Mike looked out into the looming hills. He strained to hear any unusual sounds. He could hear nothing above the truck engine's steady drone. What had Riley heard that he'd missed?

The rifle felt heavy. Mike had last held one at his brief session with the Marines during his second Midshipman summer at Little Creek, Virginia. Sure, he'd proven to be a pretty good shot then. He'd been shooting at a stationary target and could take his time with each shot. Nobody shot back. This could be different. Would he actually have to shoot someone? Could he?

"Slow the truck," Riley said to Fingers. Riley leaned forward and appeared to listen. He looked to the rear at trucks three and four.

Mike followed Riley's gaze through the cracked rear window. The attentive men in the truck bed held their guns ready. One man offered Mike a thumbs-up, then returned his attention to the hillside.

Since things seemed quiet, Mike reached to replace his rifle in the rack.

Shots and a single explosion came from an area ahead beyond the bend in the road. Mike's shoulders hunched up as he ducked at the unexpected sound. He gripped the rifle tighter in a surge of anger. Who had shot at them, and why? He hadn't even reported to his first ship and now someone wanted to end his career. No thanks. He had a lot more living to do.

"Take cover," Riley screamed. "Move it." Riley jumped down to the roadside ditch and scooted behind the nearest bush.

Mike twisted in the seat, prepared to follow. The driver's windshield panel exploded. A second bullet splintered the passenger-side windshield. A sting registered on Mike's left shoulder. He leaped from the truck, taking what shelter he could from the shallow ditch. He'd held on to the rifle, but the two ammunition clips had slipped from his hand and disappeared.

3

THE TRUCK ROLLED TO THE right into the ditch and stopped against a shed-size, old bush with a sturdy trunk. Mike crouched and followed alongside the truck to block the shooter's view. He squatted next to the truck's right front wheel and took in the surroundings. Riley remained prone behind a bush twenty yards away. Neither moved. The lead truck had also drifted off the road into the ditch. Two Marines jumped down and sought the modest protection provided by the underbrush. Others took advantage of the cover provided by the truck itself.

The third and fourth trucks had closed their interval to about thirty yards and pulled into the ditch. The men in them sought what shelter they could or huddled near their respective trucks. The silence that followed offered a dramatic contrast to the earlier gunshots. With no visible target, no one from the convoy returned fire. The shooter had chosen his cover well.

Mike scanned the hills. Because the shots had echoed through the canyon, he couldn't determine exactly where they had originated. The compact growth of bushes and scrub trees on the hill across the road to his left offered the gunman the best place to hide and an unobstructed view of the roadway.

One gun-crazy Gook? Could there be more concealed somewhere on the rocky hillside to the right or maybe behind them? Nothing obvious. The scattered, smaller trees and bushes on Mike's side of the road offered far less cover. No, the hill across the roadway to his left offered a sniper the best position for an ambush.

Anger and apprehension swirled through Mike. Right now he should be in Pensacola learning to fly, not providing target practice for some lunatic Gook. He hadn't signed up to be a Marine, or a shipboard officer for that matter, especially not a shipboard officer after his father's agonizing experience. For now, he'd focus on staying alive.

"You okay, Mike?" Riley called in a stage whisper.

"I think so," Mike said.

"Can you tell where the shots are coming from?" Riley said.

"Can't tell," Mike called back. "Maybe he's in the shadow area over there." Pain pierced his left shoulder as he lifted that arm to point to the largest foliage clump on the far side of the roadway. He glanced at his hand. The blood on his sleeve and hand hadn't registered. It had to have been that devil's second bullet. Odd. The arm didn't hurt if he kept it down. He did feel some stiffness, though.

Mike checked the rifle again, thankful for his midshipman training with the Marines. He looked around for the ammunition clips he'd dropped. Nothing. The single clip in the rifle would have to be enough.

"Dammit, there's no cover around here," Riley said, his frustration evident. "That bastard has us bore-sighted. We have to get him." He stayed low and crawled along the ditch to a bush closer to Mike. A shot rang out. Mike estimated it had come from the larger group of low trees and shrubs across the road.

"Missed me, you bastard," Riley yelled.

Mike had to grin at Riley's challenge to the gunman. The man had guts but was it a wise move?

A groan came from the truck. Mike and Riley exchanged glances. At the truck's rear, a sailor and a Marine hid from the shooter. Both shook their heads. The sound hadn't come from them.

"Where's Fingers?" Riley said, alarm evident in his voice. He started to rise. Mike's right hand cautioned Riley and pointed to where he thought the shooter hid. Riley nodded and squatted again.

Another moan, softer this time. Mike couldn't pinpoint the sound.

"Fingers," Riley called. "Fingers, dammit, sound off." No response. "Dammit, truck two, sound off," Riley hollered again, louder this time.

Mike rose from his crouch behind the right front wheel. A shot pinged into the truck. He ducked. That shot removed any doubt. The sniper had to be in the bushes and trees on the hillside.

Kneeling below the missing right door, Mike rose a few inches and peered inside. Fingers lay on the bench seat, his right arm stretched toward Mike. His head rested on the worn leather among glass shards and a puddle of blood. More blood from an eyebrow-length cut across his forehead trickled into his eyes, down his nose and onto the tattered seat. Mike could reach the outstretched hand and maybe the top of Finger's head. Could he pull him from the truck? Would he be too exposed? The shooter had to be watching them, maybe through the magnification of a sniper scope.

"My eyes," Fingers muttered but didn't move. "I can't see. Help me."

Mike grabbed Fingers' arm and pulled. The man didn't budge. Mike squirmed between the seat and the dashboard to see what held him. The leather laces of Fingers' boots had become entangled in one of the truck's low gearshift levers. Could he reach that far without exposing himself? He had to stay below the truck's silhouette to avoid another sniper shot. That wouldn't be easy.

"Hold on," Mike said controlling the quaver in his voice. "I'll get you." Mike reached to free Fingers' foot, careful to avoid injuring him further. He tugged at the leg of Fingers' dungarees to pull the foot free. The foot wouldn't give. He stretched farther toward the boot. He could only touch the end of one leather lace. He wriggled for another inch and grasped the lace but couldn't get a good grip. Angry, he lurched himself again. Something in his uniform ripped, but the lunge let his right hand seize the laces. He fed one end through a loop and pulled. The bootlace came free. Another shot banged into the cab. Mike hunched lower, but held on to Fingers' boot. A final yank freed it. Mike slid backward on his belly to the doorway. He expected another bullet at any moment.

"Can't see," Fingers muttered again. "Help me."

"Easy there," Mike murmured. "I'll have you out in a jiffy." He knew facial wounds bled profusely but that didn't always mean serious injury. He had to get Fingers out first. He'd clean him up and go from there.

Mike's right arm swept the splintered glass from the bloody bench seat. He pulled Fingers toward the door, wrapped his arms around his chest, and lowered him to the ground.

A Marine worked his way from the truck's rear toward Mike. Together they propped Fingers against the truck's rear wheel.

"Got anything to stop this bleeding?" Mike asked.

"The first aid kit," the Marine said. "It's under the seat."

Mike moved back toward the truck door, careful to stay below the truck's profile and, he hoped, hidden from the attacker. He fished under the bench seat, glass shards klinking. His hand came away with a gash from broken glass, but no kit.

"On the driver's side," the Marine said.

Mike knocked away the worst of the remaining glass and wiggled across the bench seat on his belly. He twisted to peer below the seat and froze. Automatic weapons fire mixed with single shots came from somewhere ahead but in no particular pattern. Did the gunfire grow closer? He couldn't tell.

Another swipe with his hand found worn and dusty boots that wedged a cardboard box between a metal container and the seat frame. He freed the flimsy box and tossed it and the boots out the driver's side. He gripped the metal box hoping it was the first aid kit and inched backwards out the passenger side.

"Hold still while I clean this," Mike said as Fingers raised a hand to his face. Mike grabbed the hand. "Keep your eyes closed until I'm done." Water from the Marine's canteen washed off the worst of the blood. Mike took off his black uniform necktie and fashioned it and his pocket-handkerchief into a makeshift bandage. So much for his plan to report to *Bartley* in a squared-away uniform.

"I can see, a little anyway," Fingers whispered. "Thanks." Fingers touched the temporary bandage.

Mike pointed to a second red gash above Fingers' left ear. Nasty. A bullet must have creased him, or maybe flying glass. Mike and the Marine fashioned another crude bandage for the injury using the Marine's t-shirt.

"Hey, truck one," Riley called. "What's up ahead?"

"We can't see from here," a man hollered. "Sounds like a firefight around the bend. All we can see is one of them ROK APCs, you know an armored personnel carrier."

A Marine who had been squatting next to the lead truck's rear wheels rose to a crouch. Two more shots brought the Marine down with a scream. He rolled into the ditch.

"Help him," Riley hollered to the first truck, "but stay low." Two of that truck's crew started toward the downed Marine.

The sniper fired again. Both Marines dived into the scrub brush. They squirmed on their bellies until they reached the cover of a small boulder among a clump of bushes.

"Dammit," Riley screamed. "Got to get that bastard."

"I can't pinpoint him." Mike said. "Too many shadows."

"How's your arm?" Riley said. He pointed to Mike's bloody sleeve. "Can you use your gun?"

"I'm okay," Mike said. He touched the blood-soaked fabric. The afternoon's escapade had made a mess of his khaki uniform. Nothing he could do about it. First, get that bastard. Then get the hell out of here. Worry about uniforms later.

"Okay, we can't sit here forever," Riley said. "Cover me." He stayed low, camouflaged behind bushes, and worked his way toward the lead truck. He made it to within twenty yards without drawing fire. Then, more shots could be heard from beyond the curve in the road. "Take cover," Riley ordered. He dived face first behind a clump of brush.

Mike could hear yelling from ahead that he couldn't understand. He rose from his crouch to follow Riley. He stiffened. Was there a flicker of movement on the far hillside? The shadows were deceptive. He suspected the trees hid the gunman. He couldn't detect movement, reflection, or color contrast. The shooter had hidden well.

"Stay put, Mike," Riley hollered, then rose to a crouch and ran in a staggered pattern toward the heavier growth closer to truck one.

A rustle of movement part way up the far hillside grabbed Mike's attention. His eyes locked on the spot. A figure in the trees aimed a rifle toward Riley.

"Riley. Get down," Mike called. He fired three quick shots at the shadowy figure. A yelp signaled that one of the rounds had found its mark.

"Got him," one of the crew yelled. The others cheered.

An engine rumbled. An armored personnel carrier with South Korean markings crawled toward them around the bend in the road. Two ROK soldiers, hidden from the shooter's view by the bulk of the APC, moved alongside it. Riley ignored his own risk and shouted to the South Korean soldiers. He pointed to the sniper's probable place on the hillside. This time Riley's exposure drew no fire.

The machine gunner in the APC fired several bursts into the wooded area. Mike peered around the truck to watch. The ROK soldiers moved in cautious spurts and advanced up the hillside toward the gunman's position.

A single shot resounded from the hillside's wooded area. A ROK dragged a limp, camouflaged body out onto the open ground and down to the road where he left it. Mike gulped at the sight. Had his shot killed the sniper?

The APC turned and drove back toward the curve in the road. The lean ROK soldiers followed, while scanning the surrounding hillside.

"Get the injured in the truck," Riley called. "Follow the APC."

Mike held his rifle at the ready, his heartbeat rising, unclear of Riley's intentions. Mike gripped the rifle tighter, angry that he'd been unable to find at least one of the dropped ammo clips. What if there were other snipers? Or worse? Would following the road put them in the middle of an ongoing firefight? He'd intended that his shots would distract the shooter. Hitting him had been sheer, dumb luck.

A Marine crawled into the truck replacing Fingers at the wheel and drove in low gear toward the bend in the road. Fingers rested in back. Mike matched Riley's cautious pace alongside the truck, both ready to fire if necessary.

A small cul-de-sac, perhaps fifty yards deep and heavy with low growth, came into view around the curve. The first convoy truck and the APC had stopped in the middle of the road among some ROKS. Three bodies lay alongside the roadway. Several soldiers probed for raiders in the clumps of heavier brush scattered along the walls of the cul-de-sac.

"The Gooks must be cornered," Riley said. He moved ahead but dropped to a crouch at the sound of a shot from the closed end of the cul-de-sac.

Mike dropped face down following Riley's lead. More snipers? The shot had sounded near. They were all exposed now. No cover nearby.

Mike raised his head. A bloodied man with his hands over his bowed head stumbled toward the roadway, prodded by the rifle barrel of a South Korean soldier. Once in the clear, the butt of the soldier's rifle knocked the prisoner to the ground.

An unintelligible yell came from the far end of the cul-de-sac. Four more soldiers walked toward the road. Moments later Mike's head snapped toward the source of a nearby shot. The prisoner lay in a pool of blood. A ROK officer shoved a pistol into his belt. Another soldier bent to search the body.

In a stunned semi-trance Mike stared at the scene. He'd seen people shot in the movies, but never up close like this. He'd become part of a three dimensional scene with sound, color, and the smell of gunpowder. Curiosity surpassed apprehension for a moment then an uneasy sensation forced him to turn away.

Riley and the ROK officer conversed for a minute then waved to the convoy crew to gather around the lead truck.

"Our South Korean buddies tracked this bunch for a couple of days," Riley said. He stroked the monster mustache. "The Gooks meant their ambush for us. Keep your eyes open. We may face another Gook team before we reach the ship."

4

THE CONVOY ROUNDED THE FINAL bend in the roadway and began a gentle descent toward the harbor giving Mike his first view of the coastal village. Masan had been only a name until then. Riley had called it a fishing village, but a village in near ruins came as a surprise. Many of the outlying buildings had been leveled. The nearby farmland looked barren.

A single-lane bridge that crossed a dry riverbed ahead appeared to lead into the town's narrow main street. The bridge offered the lone evidence of repairs. A ROK, incongruous in a starched, white jacket, directed the one-way traffic. The soldier halted a single small truck on the Masan side of the bridge. His arm signaled to give priority to the convoy.

The battle-weary stake trucks traveled Masan's dusty, unpaved, and potholed street into town. Mike counted fourteen adults alongside the road, all silent and unmoving, resembling mannequins. Only their eyes moved. However, two small groups of shoeless and naked children waved to the passing convoy. No smiles though.

"The fighting," Riley said, "left Masan a mess by the time the Marines stopped the Gooks here last fall." Riley gestured to a nearby building. "Our crew repaired some of the damage. We send out cleanup and repair crews when we can. The Marines do, too. They fixed that bridge into town. The Marine encampment is down that way." He pointed toward the low hillside.

The first and last convoy trucks pulled off at a damaged sign that hung at an angle, held by one bolt, the "USMC" letters weathered. The middle two continued along the narrow, main road. The Marine driver pointed ahead, a silent signal that he'd drive to the ship.

The two trucks entered the town's main harbor area and headed toward its largest feature, a wide, concrete causeway that extended to the bay. Mike guessed it to be about a quarter mile long, and wide enough to accommodate a football field laid sideways with ample end zones. A hill of damaged military equipment and miscellaneous junk, as high as a three-story building, ran the length of the causeway. No color stood out in the bland mass of grays, greens, and browns. Where did all the stuff come from? Some of it could be combat residue, but some looked like pieces of people's homes. Why pile this garbage in the middle of a major harbor pier? He'd ask Riley later. The Marine driver turned onto the causeway down a narrow lane wide enough for a single vehicle.

Mike searched for a glimpse of the USS Bartley. Based on Riley's few comments, Mike had expected to see the ship alongside a pier, or maybe anchored in the harbor. Instead, he could only see the ship's gray mast and uppermost, staggered superstructure at the far end of the causeway, the rest hidden by the intervening mountain of debris.

The truck halted twenty yards from Bartley's gangway. Mike's once-clean uniform was now filthy, blood stained, and incomplete. He retrieved his outer blouse and cap. Getting squared away wasn't easy with his arm in the temporary sling that the convoy crew had fashioned for him.

"I'll never pass inspection on these size thirteens," Mike stage-whispered to Riley. He pointed to his shoes.

"Relax," Riley said. The monster mustache flexed to reveal a smile. "The captain doesn't fuss about uniforms." Riley's failure to don a shirt or take steps to improve his appearance confirmed the policy. The apparent lax dress code didn't ease Mike's discomfort.

Riley led the way to the ship. He strode across the gangway and dropped Mike's bags on the deck next to a bulkhead. Mike followed the traditional Navy ritual.

"Request permission to come aboard, sir," Mike said to the man lingering on Bartley's deck at the end of the gangway. An officer? An enlisted man? Or a civilian? Each of the few ships Mike had seen during his training had a minimum of one petty officer in uniform at the quarterdeck when in port. He had expected a petty officer, maybe an officer, and in uniform. The man he faced wore only khaki shorts and Japanese thong sandals. Nothing matched Mike's expectations. At the end of the gangway, he turned toward the ship's stern and saluted the American flag to complete the ritual.

"Permission granted, and welcome aboard," said the slim, short man. He reached out his hand as Mike approached. "I'm Captain Clark. You must be Ensign Kinkaid. Glad to have you aboard." Mike tried not to gape at the lone welcomer.

"Yes, sir," Mike said and saluted. "Ensign Kinkaid, sir. Glad to be aboard at last." It felt strange to be met at the quarterdeck by a captain who dressed like a sunbathing sailor. What manner of ship had he joined?

"What happened?" The captain pointed to the makeshift, ragged sling and Mike's bloody uniform. "That looks fresh. How—"

"It's one hell-of-a-story, Captain," Riley interrupted. "Young Deadeye, here, saved my ass and got winged in the process. We patched him up best we could." Riley waved toward two other crewmen who helped Fingers up the gangway. "Fingers took some flak, too. Messy, but probably not serious."

"Okay, Mike. Let's get something cool into you for starters," Captain Clark said motioning to Mike and Riley to follow him forward along the main deck. Mike reached to grab his bags, but Riley beat him to it. An unexpected wink from Riley came as a surprise.

Mike followed the captain through the main deck hatch and into a compartment that had to be the officer's wardroom. One lieutenant in summer wash khaki uniform, standing next to the coffee service at the far end of the wardroom, held a coffee cup. A moment later a second officer in similar uniform appeared through a green and gray, heavy-weave curtained entrance.

"This is our operations officer, Lieutenant Powell," the captain gestured toward the officer with the cup. "And this is Swede," he added and pointed to the blond, balding officer. "Swede is today's duty officer."

Mike shook hands with each man. The contrast between the pudgy, blond Swede, the athletic Riley, and the reed-thin Lieutenant Powell couldn't be missed.

"I'll get Doc Webster up here after he's finished with Fingers," Swede said opening the door to leave, "and we'll get the Marines' doctor, just to be sure."

"Please, be seated," the captain said to everyone. He waved Mike to an aluminum frame chair with a tattered seat cushion at the near end of the wardroom table. The others took adjacent seats. The wardroom steward on duty poured five glasses of lemonade.

Mike hadn't been in an officers' wardroom before. Few of his midshipman classmates had been privileged to visit or eat their meals with officers during training.

Mike made a quick scan of the room. More crowded than he'd been led to expect. Pale green bulkheads. A traditional dark green cloth he'd been told to expect covered the wardroom dining table that dominated the room. Fifteen chairs placed around it. Mike had expected fewer officers for a ship this size. Several tattered magazines occupied a wall-mounted rack next to the settee. Did *Bartley's* mail come through the military system any better than those battered magazines? He'd been told mail often took weeks.

The three-pot coffee service on a low built-in cabinet contributed to the pervasive, acrid odors of long-boiled coffee, cigarettes and the stench of fuel oil. Mike could hear the whir and low-pitched whistle of the ventilation system that did not deliver cooled air as he had expected. Mike guessed that the curtained entrance Swede had used led to officer staterooms.

"Okay, let's have it," Captain Clark said to Riley. "What's this Dead-eye business? Ensigns are hard to come by around here, you know. What did you do, try to kill him off before we got him aboard?"

Swede rushed back into the wardroom, as though not wanting to miss a word of Riley's story. He picked the seat next to the captain.

"This has to be one for the books, Captain," Riley said. "I'll bet Mike's the first Navy officer ever to report to his initial duty station by overland truck convoy and earn the Purple Heart along the way."

Riley's abbreviated but exaggerated account of the ambush that followed tempted Mike to interrupt. He watched the reactions of the others instead.

"Mike, looks like you joined your assignment the hard way," the captain said. "So, tell us a little about yourself, your training, your background."

"As you know, sir," Mike said, "I got my degree and commission from the NROTC Unit at the University of Washington in Seattle. I made the normal summer training cruises. We were on the USS *Springfield* my first summer."

"That's my old ship, *Springfield*," Captain Clark said. He nodded to Mike to continue.

"We spent the first half of the next summer with the Marines at Little Creek, Virginia," Mike said. "Pensacola followed for aviation indoctrination." He paused and examined the faces of the others. Did his mention of aviation or Pensacola raise any interest? Apparently not.

"What did you study in college, Mike," Captain Clark asked. He pulled a crumpled cigarette pack from his pocket. Swede held his lighter to the captain's cigarette.

"A general management course, sir," Mike said. He hesitated to add details. "I received a degree in personnel management."

"How about the Navy classes? How did you do in those?" Clark asked.

"I graduated number one in my Navy class, sir." They didn't need to know that he hadn't done quite as well in the other subjects. He wouldn't mention that unless they asked. Mike rubbed the bandage over his aching shoulder, realized his mistake, and rubbed the bloody hand on his shirtsleeve.

The captain's approach had been casual but he listened carefully and considered each reply before he continued. When the captain finished, the others asked a few questions. The topic of flight training did not come up. Instinct told Mike to keep it that way if possible.

"Now that you're aboard, Mike," Captain Clark said, "we'll put you to work. You are our new communications officer. You're Smitty's relief."

Mike's stomach tightened for a moment, confused by the unexpected assignment, but he didn't want to let on. Certainly the ship had to communicate, but the topic of communications hadn't been addressed in his classes. Why? Or had he missed it somehow? He had no idea what the task required. How would he manage the assignment without making a fool of himself? He'd have to learn fast.

"I had hoped you'd have a face-to-face turnover," the captain continued, "but we needed to send Smitty to Tokyo for treatment before you got here. Instead, Riley and Swede," he nodded to each of the two officers, "can help you with the classified message traffic and get you started. When the doc's done with you, Riley will get you settled and show you around."

Mike glanced at Riley. He had expected a sign of welcome similar to what he'd received from the others. Riley didn't return Mike's gaze. His sour expression, aggravated by the drooping black monster on his lip, and a hand run across his close-cropped dome, seemed to reveal displeasure at the order.

"But, Captain…" Riley said. The captain ignored him.

Riley's objection confused Mike. He thought of Riley as a friend, perhaps a close friend in time. How badly had he misjudged? Riley seemed reluctant more than inhospitable, a resistance Mike didn't understand. Riley had been congenial enough on the trip from Pusan. Why did he object to helping?

Bartley's medical corpsman, carrying a bag with a Red Cross emblem, entered the wardroom and interrupted Riley's plea. Captain Clark slid his chair away from the wardroom table and introduced Mike to Hospital Corpsman First Class Brian Webster, known as Doc to the crew.

"He's all yours, Doc," Captain Clark said. "Fix him up. We need him. Swede has sent for the Marines' doctor, too."

Webster cleaned the wound area, did some minimal probing, and applied a snug bandage. "That will hold you for the moment, sir. A nice, clean puncture." Webster said with a grin. Mike relaxed when he realized that Webster knew his business.

"Afternoon, Captain," Doctor Jenkins said when he threw open the wardroom door and said, "Understand we have a damaged sharpshooter on board. You sure you haven't snatched one of my Marines?"

Doctor Jenkins nodded to Webster then examined Mike who focused on the green table cover while the doctor worked on him. He certainly could feel the probing. He'd never been shot before. How would it limit his use of the arm and for how long? He gritted his teeth at the three injections. He'd prefer a lifetime without shots.

"You're lucky," Jenkins said a few minutes later. "The bullet missed the bone. Went clear through." A fresh dressing followed. "You're mobile. You can have something to help you sleep tonight if you need it." He stood back and appraised Mike. "From the look of you I'd say you won't need it. Don't lift with that arm for a few days. It will be stiff for a week or so. You may have a scar, but you'll be good as new in a couple of weeks." Webster stepped in and fashioned a proper sling.

"Come on," Riley said and nodded to Mike. "We'll bunk you down in The Pit. That's our junior officer's bunkroom. Follow me."

Riley picked up Mike's clothing and the larger of Mike's bags then led off along the inboard passageway. Mike stuck his hat on his head, grasped the leather handle of his smaller bag in his good hand and scrambled to catch Riley. Keeping up with Riley in the narrow corridors proved more difficult than he'd expected. Twice he had to stop and retrieve his hat when he neglected to duck to avoid the cables, brackets and other items attached to the dim passageway's low overhead.

Why had Riley become so abrupt now that the captain had told him to help? *Bartley* was quiet, almost lethargic from what he'd seen so far. Riley didn't appear overworked.

Riley led Mike along the long, narrow passageway and opened a door near the aft end of the ship. "You'll bunk in here," he said. "We call this The Pit. It's for the four junion officers. Yours is the top one," Riley said. He tossed Mike's bag onto the bunk. "The head's across the passageway. Get cleaned up best you can." He glanced at his watch. "I'll come by in half an hour for you. Summer khaki uniform for dinner." He left without further comment.

Mike tried to reconcile his impressions. The few officers he'd met on *Bartley* so far seemed friendly, but what had Riley said about someone on board hating NROTC graduates? And why was Riley suddenly unfriendly? Here, halfway around the world, he'd been assigned to do a job he didn't know existed until a few minutes ago, and it certainly wasn't flying.

5

"M IKE, COME IN AND MEET the rest of us," a smiling Captain Clark
said. Mike followed Riley into the crowded wardroom his first evening aboard *Bartley*. "You've met Riley, Powell, and Swede already. This
is Ensign Davis, one of your bunkmates." The captain nodded toward the
nearest officer. Mike extended his hand to the porky ensign in glasses.
"And Ensign Stevens," the captain nodded indicating the grinning, six-
footer next to Davis. Mike and Stevens shook hands. Captain Clark led
Mike around the table to introduce each officer. Their hearty welcomes
reassured Mike. He noted three lieutenants, four lieutenants junior grade,
and six ensigns in addition to himself and the captain.

Then Captain Clark introduced Lieutenant Gene Watkins, the ship's
Executive Officer and second in command.

"Welcome aboard," Watkins said. A soft handshake. A sweaty palm,
removed quickly. Shifting eyes that would not look Mike in the face.

Watkins, referred to as XO by everyone, wore his stringy, blond hair
longer than regulation, and combed over his bald spot, in contrast to the
close-cropped or balding heads of the other officers. His neatly pressed
uniform, at least one size too large, added to the anomalies. Watkins' slim
frame, at about five feet nine, put him among people Mike might meet
in any gathering and soon forget.

During dinner Mike watched the XO preface his comments with a
quick, caressing swipe of his hand to smooth his blond, pencil mustache,
not at all in the same league as Riley's showstopper. Nervous? Covering
something? Mike tried to remember Psychology 101 from his freshman
year at the university.

Over a spaghetti dinner, Riley's Irish story-telling rendition of the ambush made him the evening's headliner. All the officers around the table, except Watkins, roared and some slapped the table in glee at his embellished account of the ambush. Mike winced at Riley's frequent exaggerations and the occasional addition of pure fiction.

"So Mike here sticks his head up to spot the Gook varmint knowing damned well that bastard had him bore sighted," Riley said. "So the sniper got in one lucky shot. Does that faze Mike? Hell, no. The other shots miss him, like Mike, here, had an invisible shield around him. Does it bother Mike? Not by a damn sight. 'Stay down Riley,' he hollers to me. 'I'll get him', he says." Riley stroked his mustache. "Guts, there, I tell you." Riley twisted the end of his mustache in a dramatic pause.

Being treated as some sort of hero in Riley's performance made Mike uncomfortable. A hero? He'd just reacted. But, the humor in Riley's delivery did help him ignore his aching arm.

"Handled that M-1 like he'd been born with it, he did," Riley said. "Didn't even break a sweat." As the new kid, Mike knew he should listen, enjoy the story and observe until he had a better feel for the group.

"Riley," the XO said, "what loot did you bring back from Pusan this time?" A pronounced shoulder tic accompanied the XO's grab for attention.

Riley turned to the XO sitting at the far end of the table.

"The usual, XO," Riley replied. His sparkling eyes, sharp tone, and raised jaw sent a "don't interrupt" message. "Food and toilet paper. No booze this time." Riley winked at the others. "So, as I was saying," Riley flashed anger at the XO, "here we are in this ditch—"

"Where'd you learn to shoot, Kinkaid?" the XO asked Mike, his voice louder than Riley's. The question was reasonable, not the tone or interruption. Mike tried to understand the exchange. Didn't the XO recognize Riley's body language? Or, perhaps he didn't care.

"Dammit, XO," Riley said, both hands on the edge of the wardroom table as if to push himself up. "I'm just coming to the best part. "Deadeye he is, I tell you," Riley said. "Better than any Marine. Single shot. That's all it took to drop the bugger."

"Didn't know they let you school kids handle grownups' weapons," the XO said to Mike even louder this time. The sarcastic, bullying tone surprised Mike. "Where'd you learn to shoot?"

Mike shifted in his chair, puzzled. How should he respond? Could this be some sort of hazing ritual for the new man? Some humor might help, but nothing seemed funny at the moment. He tried a deep-breathing, temper-control trick. He was new, the junior man. Instinct warned: Don't do anything hasty, and watch your mouth. Stick to simple and direct answers. Learn the politics of this group first before mouthing off.

"We received some small arms work from the Marines during our second summer training cruise, sir," Mike replied. Mike glanced at Riley, who appeared interested in the exchange, but gave no clue as to how to deal with the XO.

"Lucky shot, huh?" The XO crossed his arms in a pompous, judicial pose.

"Guess so, sir," Mike said. Was the XO testing him? Testing for what? And why?

Mike's quick scan around the table detected general curiosity and a tinge of discomfort from the other officers. What bothered them? The XO's manner? No, the XO's interruptions seemed more likely.

"Lucky or not," Riley half rose from his seat and faced the XO, "he saved my ass."

Lieutenant Powell sitting next to Riley placed his hand on Riley's arm and eased him into his chair. Riley snatched his coffee cup and downed what remained before he resumed. Riley's words had approached open defiance of the ship's second-most-senior officer. Puzzling behavior. Mike would have expected swift censure. The others accepted the XO's conduct as normal. What was going on?

"Kinkaid." The XO's hand wiped across his mustache. "The name's familiar. Was your father in the Navy, Mister?"

"Dammit, XO." Riley scowled and half rose in his chair again.

Mike feigned a casual calm he didn't feel. He set down his coffee cup before answering. He needed time to swallow the flash of panic raised by Watkins' question. Did his quick glance at Riley reveal a slight nod? Could the nod have been a warning or a sign to proceed? Instinct told him to be careful. This wasn't the time or place for details about His father's war experience.

"Yes, sir," Mike said.

"Was he an officer?" The XO leaned forward in his chair, palms of both hands flat on the table.

"Yes, sir," Mike said. Keep it simple. He remembered Riley's caution about a potential problem with the XO. This had to be an example of what Riley meant.

"Is he still on duty?" the XO said.

"No, sir," Mike said. He took a sip of his coffee and looked away. He couldn't let this continue, but how could he stop it?

"Maybe not the same man," the XO mused. "Did he serve on convoy duty in the North Atlantic, on a destroyer or escort ship?"

Mike's stomach tightened. The possibility that he might have to resurrect his father's agony threatened to break his composure especially after the tension of the day. His father's episode was history. Probably none of the officers had even heard of the tragic wartime incident.

"I don't know, sir," Mike said. He tried to keep the tone conversational. "I was just a kid then." The XO's questions had become dangerous. How could he deflect the man?

"The name 'Dunleavy' mean anything to you, Mister?" the XO said. He leaned forward again, a sly grin forming as though he had cornered Mike.

Mention of the name of his father's ship clinched Mike's suspicion. The XO must have known the connection, or at least suspected. Mike didn't want to fight the lies about his father's experience again. He'd try a ploy. Play innocent.

"I believe an Admiral Dunleavy served in World War One, sir." Mike replied in the manner of a good student.

"I mean a ship named *Dunleavy*."

"I might have heard of it in one of our history classes." Mike clamped his jaw shut and returned the XO's glare. Would he back off?

"I wonder if you might be related," the XO said, the sarcasm in his voice evident.

"Sorry, sir," Mike said and shook his head as though mentally reviewing his family history. "Nobody in my family is named Dunleavy."

"No. I meant—"

"Drop it, Gene," Captain Clark interrupted.

"But, I just wanted—"

"I said drop it."

6

MIKE LAY NAKED ON THE upper bunk in The Pit, his bedding damp from sweat. A single three-inch-diameter vent trickled humid air into the room, twelve feet from his toes. A red emergency light encased in a protective metal mesh basket cleared Mike's head by six inches. The eerie glow couldn't be switched off.

Riley hadn't gone into any detail when he introduced Mike to the tiny stateroom, the domain of the four most-junior officers. Mike had expected austerity but not The Pit. Two double bunks, a double wardrobe closet, one eight-drawer cabinet with a fold-down desktop and a sink provided the minimal amenities. Only one person could dress at a time. An upper, and the least desirable, bunk had become Mike's.

Mike couldn't sleep. The hot and sticky air left him tossing. He wanted to choke off Ensign Dixon's snoring. It punctuated those few periods of rest he did manage. He also had to find, and eliminate if possible, whatever made the periodic loud rumble and heavy flushing noise from below, sounds the others probably slept through. Maybe he'd become accustomed to them in time. He tried a second shower. It didn't help.

Mike's mind replayed the dinnertime exchange with the XO. The man suspected a family connection but didn't know the full story. A confrontation might be avoided for a while, but somehow he knew the XO would persist.

Mike reached for the small, kidskin pouch his sister had made for him years before just after his father had died. The bag held his father's lieutenant commander rank insignia, a gold, oak leaf medallion. He had carried it with him ever since. The emblem brought him luck. A tap on the leather before a big move or decision had always provided support, as though his father perched over his shoulder, coached him, or warned of dangers. Would the talisman help him deal with the XO?

Carol's pink letter, postmarked three days after he left her in Seattle, rustled under his pillow. Mike pulled it out and carried it and the bunk-room's single chair into the passageway where he could read by the, dim overhead light. He wanted to savor her words again.

The background odor in the passageway wafted up from the ship's fuel tanks, located below where he sat. He held Carol's letter close to his nose to relish its faint perfume, a scent that brought quick memories of their private times. She had included a photo taken on their honeymoon in San Francisco. He loved her long, blonde hair and how it had flowed in the breeze that afternoon as they walked across the Golden Gate Bridge. He'd always carry that image of her in his mind. He'd have to fix a place for the photo next to his bunk where he could see her and remember better nights.

Now in this barren corridor he reread her words.

Dear Mike,
I miss you so already. I love you very much as I've told you so many times. Our honeymoon was wonderful, a memory always. Let's plan to do it again sometime. The sooner the better. Is it too soon to tell me when you will come home?

A silent vow reaffirmed that he would do his best to make her proud, and be the best husband and eventual father he could be. Her words reflected her usual bubbly self, but more upbeat than he'd expected. Earlier in the spring, their plans had been different when his assignment to flight school seemed imminent. He'd expected the crinkly pages in his hand to tell him she had moved. Instead, she'd written:

I've enclosed that favorite picture of your father that you misplaced. It was clipped in with the papers you left me. I have good news. The university's head librarian told me today that my part-time job has been upgraded to full time. My duties won't change much right away, <u>but I'll earn forty-five cents an hour more.</u> Now that I'm working full time, I've decided not to move to Mother's. I'm going to share Lisa's apartment with her.

Mike could imagine Carol's excitement as she wrote. She'd underlined the pay raise sentence. She and her older sister Lisa were close. Carol enjoyed her job. Her move meant a two-block walk to the campus. He needn't worry about her for a while at least.

Mike opened his mail folder. The first sentence of his note to Carol, started the night before at the Pusan air base, remained incomplete. What did he have to share with her other than that he missed her? He didn't want to tell her that he was hot and anxious, or that, without a miracle, he'd have missed the ship.

He had to be cautious with what he wrote. Carol could read him as though she looked through clear glass. She would catch his mood and worry.

Mike closed the folder. He'd answer her after his first full day on board. Perhaps he'd uncover something less frightening than gunfire to tell her. He had to be upbeat. She'd be amused to learn of *Bartley's* casual atmosphere. He'd tell her how the officers spoke and behaved toward each other. What he'd seen so far didn't follow the protocol or the strict standards drummed into him in his four years as a midshipman. He'd tell her how Captain Clark didn't match the image of a ship's commanding officer. He'd add how *Bartley's* juniors offered little deference to seniors. The relationships he'd seen so far resembled a fraternity house. The ambush would become an interesting trip. Details could come later, when he could tell her in person. Riley would become a new friend who would help him get started in his assignment as communications officer. He'd omit that Riley didn't volunteer for the role. He wouldn't mention his wound, either. It would be healed by the time he got home. He'd let her find the scar.

Mike considered the day ahead. He'd have to keep his eyes open from now on as the junior officer aboard. Riley had said meet him before breakfast, but he hadn't said why and Mike hadn't asked. He viewed Riley and the XO as unexpected mysteries, possible adversaries, and perhaps dangerous. He couldn't afford to step out of line. His gut told him that the more serious threat was the XO. An unresolved conflict with him could become a barrier to his shipboard qualification and even kill all hopes for flight training after his shipboard assignment. And that job as comm officer. How in hell would he master that one? Where would he start? Riley's attitude suggested he would provide little help.

Mike, showered yet again, and in a fresh, wash khaki uniform, followed Riley up the pierced metal steps of several narrow, steel ladders to the port side of *Bartley's* signal bridge. The wardroom officers' overall lack of urgency at dinner had puzzled Mike. Had they been tied to the causeway too long? Weren't they eager to get to sea, too? He wanted to start his new assignment right away, get in his qualification, then reapply to fly.

How should he deal with Riley? He hadn't decided whether to be open or reserved with him. First impressions could be misleading. He'd be wise to weigh what he observed. He had one chance to get it right.

The morning's high tide raised *Barley's* signal bridge fifteen feet higher than the causeway's junk mountain. The added height provided an excellent view of the small, crowded fishing village of Masan. At this early hour, serene, but the slight breeze off the water failed to overcome the ever-present shroud of heat and humidity. The odors of fish, decayed seaweed and fuel oil filled the air. The ship's machinery provided a near-inaudible, low rumble.

"You get the best view of the harbor from here," Riley said. Perfunctory. No enthusiasm. What's bugging this guy?

"What's all that junk, and why is it dumped here?" Mike pointed to the mountain of trash on the causeway.

"We pulled in last winter and most of it was already piled here," Riley said. "Leftovers from the fighting. Never learned why they left it here. Haven't added to it for more than two months now. A bunch of scavengers salvage stuff, over there," Riley pointed to his right, to the far side of the junk hill. "Interesting what they find and what they do with it. Kids' toys made from beer cans, for example."

Mike saw no activity around the junk hill.

"We'll tour the town tomorrow," Riley said. He gestured at parts of the devastated village awakening with the rising sun. "The place still looks worse than our farm did after the tornado came through in '48. That brown building is our officers' club." Riley pointed to a wooden structure at the far end of the causeway. "It's the last two-story still standing in Masan. We use the upper room. It's dinky. Can't get more than eight of us in the club at once. Nine, if you count Sunny, but she stays behind the bar."

"Who's Sunny?" Mike asked. Riley had referred to a she.

"A refugee," Riley said. "She keeps the place clean. Tends bar. We feed her and let her live in the room on the ground floor. She's like a little sister to all of us." He paused and stared at Mike. "And don't get any ideas. We've all agreed she's off limits. Nobody messes with Sunny, understand?"

"She speaks English?" Mike asked.

"Fair," Riley said. "She learns fast." Riley leaned against the rail. "She'll pester you on how to say things. Does that to all of us. It's fun." Mike paused to consider Riley's comment.

"Sunny doesn't sound like a Korean name," Mike said.

"We had some trouble with her name," Riley said. "It's something like Kim Soon Yee. The Captain called her Sunny. Fits her. She likes the name."

Riley pulled a pack of cigarettes from his shirt pocket and offered one to Mike.

"No, thanks." Mike shook his head. He scanned the harbor. Eight small, net-fishing boats shared the harbor with *Bartley*. "How long has the ship been here?"

"Since the second week in January," Riley said. Six months. Mike tensed.

"You mean we don't go to sea? I understood a seagoing ship needed me to fill a vacant billet." Unspoken words flashed in his mind. He should be in flight school now. Had he been lied to? It would be impossible for him to qualify if the ship didn't get underway. He had to have that qual before he could reapply to fly. How long a delay would it be?

"When is the ship scheduled to return to the States?" Mike said. Riley gazed toward the nearby hills for a moment.

"We left San Diego two days after last Thanksgiving," Riley said. "They said we'd be home by May, June at the latest. Here we are, the end of June. No return date even scheduled. We'd be at sea now except for those damned things." Riley pointed aft to the boat deck, to two weathered pieces of equipment, each the size of a house trailer.

"What're they?" Mike said. He hadn't seen similar structures on other ships.

"Transformers," Riley said. "The Gooks' attack last summer knocked out the power plant north of here." Riley pointed toward the distant low hills. "The Marines stopped the Gooks just over that ridge. You heard of the Pusan Perimeter, have you?"

Mike nodded.

"Masan was the western end of the Pusan Perimeter. After the Marines pushed the Gooks back, the Navy sent us here to provide power. We're one of four tin cans in the fleet with turbo electric drive and transformers. We're an emergency power plant." He took a final puff and flipped the cigarette into the harbor. "That's on top of our standard tin can capabilities, of course."

"How much longer are we stuck here?" Mike asked. "When do we go to sea?" He clenched his jaws and flexed his left fist in frustration.

"Don't know," Riley said. "We're all damned sick of this place. Our relief is a civilian ship. We expected her today."

"Today? What changed?"

"She's delayed," Riley said. "Some sort of engineering problem."

"That explains the twenty-sixth," Mike said. It all made sense now. His orders had said to report no later than June twenty-sixth. He'd scrambled, investigated all options, and cut some corners to make it to the ship on time. Damn. All his worry and lost sleep had been wasted effort.

"What about the twenty-sixth?" Riley said.

"My orders said to report no later than today," Mike said. "I figured I'd be in deep trouble if I had missed the ship."

"You should know schedules are made to be broken." Riley grinned and stroked his mustache. "Anyway, her message yesterday said her repairs should be done this week, maybe sooner if the parts come in. She's coming from the States. Be here in maybe a month, two at the outside."

"So we sit here until then, right?" Mike said.

Riley nodded.

"Okay. I'm ready," Mike said. "The captain said I'm the new communications officer. How do I start? I'll have to learn the comm job from the ground up."

"There's good news and there's bad news," Riley said. He reached for a fresh cigarette, lit it, and faced the bay as though his mind were on something else.

Mike had to bite his tongue to hold back the angry comment that formed in his mind. This wasn't the guy who took center stage at dinner last night. Does he think helping me is beneath him?

Riley took another puff then flipped the cigarette into the water.

"The good news is you have a solid radio gang." Another pause, expressionless.

"And?" Mike tried to ignore Riley's teasing. Or was he teasing?

"The bad news is you don't get a normal turnover. Smitty left about two weeks ago," Riley said. "You get to learn the ropes the hard way."

"I wondered about that," Mike said. That he'd replaced a departed officer came as no surprise. The fleet's officer shortage had been common knowledge among his midshipman classmates. It explained why Mike, and all his classmates, went to ships to fill the holes, and, in his case, not to the promised flight school.

Two boats of local fisherman cast their nets a half mile from the ship.

"We're at the end of the food chain out here," Riley said.

"What do you mean?" Mike said. He'd concluded Riley's behavior wasn't teasing. Perhaps evaluation? No, he was testing again and watching Mike's reaction.

"Our supply officer keeps us fed," Riley said. "All our info comes from your radios. Without the radios we're out of business. Your job is to keep us informed. You better learn damned fast." He turned and headed to the down ladder. "Let's go get some chow."

7

"FOLLOW ME," RILEY SAID TO Mike and nodded toward the wardroom door after a scrambled eggs and bacon breakfast. "Time you earned your pay."

Mike followed Riley up a narrow and surprisingly steep inboard ladder to the boat deck level, then along a dim, gray interior passageway toward his first exposure to his new domain, the radio gang and the radio shack. Mike had a vague idea about what the communications officer's job entailed and was eager to meet his crew. How many radiomen would he have? Would they help him learn the job? If not, he'd handle the challenge somehow.

Sweat beaded on Mike's his upper lip. The passageway was sweltering. *Bartley's* quarter-inch steel hull behaved as a sponge absorbing the morning sun. Would he ever adjust to the heat and humidity? His left arm, confined in the bandage and temporary sling, soon became sweat-soaked.

"Riley," Mike said, "You picked the right name, you know. That bunkroom really is the pits. I figured the ship would have air conditioning."

"Get used to it," Riley grumbled. He climbed another steep interior ladder to the deck above.

"Not much cooling gear to go around when they built this bucket back in forty-three," Riley said pausing at the upper deck landing. "Only two compartments are cooled. CIC, our Combat Information Center, houses the radar control equipment. Has to be kept cool to protect the electronics. The other is the sonar control station forward of the open bridge.

Same reason. The rest of the ship swelters in weather like this. We freeze in winter, too. Get used to it."

Riley disappeared to the right into a compartment. Mike followed two steps behind. A rumbling voice from inside called, "Attention on deck."

Mike squeezed into the small room packed with a dozen sailors. Electronic boxes in multiple shapes and sizes, speakers, cables and equipment covered all the bulkheads. Three stations occupied one end of the radio shack, two of them manned by radiomen wearing headphones. One typed, the other clicked a telegraph key. Fuel oil fumes mixed with the sweaty smell of bodies. Mike marveled at the electronic gear. How could he be in charge of men who understood all this if he didn't?

"Somebody here I want you to meet, Chief," Riley said to the man nearest to Mike. "Ensign Kinkaid, our new communications officer." Then to Mike, he said, "Mister Kinkaid, this is Chief Petty Officer Pops Dietrick who runs your radio gang." Riley patted Mike on the shoulder. "He's all yours, Chief. He needs to learn fast." Riley tossed a semi-salute to Mike and left the radio shack.

"Glad to meet you, Chief," Mike said stretching his good arm out to Dietrick. Mike shook the chief radioman's hand and noted the firm grip, long fingers and huge smile.

The chief's modest belly and graying, red hair matched Mike's image of a seasoned sailor: stable, experienced, and, he hoped, good-humored. The chief's sandy beard, covering all but his upper lip was trimmed like Abe Lincoln's. It highlighted a round face that Mike imagined might belong to an aging leprechaun.

"Welcome to *Bartley*, sir," Chief Dietrick said. His cheery eyes and wide grin radiated good will and a sincere welcome.

A surge of relief destroyed any of Mike's lingering apprehension about how he would fit in with an experienced crew. He should be able to work well with this man.

"And this," the chief said gesturing to the eleven other men crammed shoulder to shoulder into the tiny compartment, "is your radio gang. We're damned glad to have you aboard, sir." A murmur from the men reinforced the chief's welcome. "They're top notch, Mister K. All rated radiomen."

Mike could see he had seasoned sailors. Chief Dietrick epitomized all he had hoped for. He shook hands and chatted with each man as Dietrick made the introductions. Mike searched for a feature in each man: height, eye color, hair, scars, any identifier to link to a name since sometimes names eluded him. Mike relaxed as each man's smile and words reinforced the warm welcome.

A movement in the corner caught Mike's attention. He turned to see a bandaged head peeking over an adjacent shoulder.

"Fingers," Mike said. "I didn't know you were a radioman." Mike reached out a hand to share a firm handshake with Fingers.

"How's your arm, sir?" Fingers replied

"Better than your head, from the looks of that bandage," Mike said.

"He's doing fine, sir," the chief said. "We all appreciate what you did for him. Doc Webster said it's messy but not serious. Good as new in a couple of weeks."

"Looks like you – no, now it's we — have a seasoned team," Mike said to the chief.

"Problem is," the chief said, sweat obvious on his forehead, "your radio gang are all recalled reserves. They're due to head stateside over the next six months, back to civilian life, all except for Fingers and me, that is. No idea when we'll see replacements."

Mike caught the warning. How long would his experienced team be in place? Would some replacements be delayed? More important, could he learn fast enough to maintain an effective communications team?

"Let me show you around the shack, Mister K," the chief said. "We can get around to the details in due time." He pointed out the three radio operator stations, the regular and classified message file cabinets, Mike's safe for classified documents and codes, and the tiny crypto closet barely large enough for a man to sit at the small console inside.

The chief lowered a fold-down, student-size desktop from the bulkhead, and pulled over two chairs. He motioned Mike to sit. From the nearby coffee maker he poured two cups and set them on the wooden tabletop.

"You are a coffee drinker, aren't you Mister K?" the chief said with a twinkle.

"Yes," Mike said and noticed that the radiomen were paying close attention. He expected their initial curiosity, but something else was afoot.

"To a good cruise and a good team," the chief said raising his cup toward Mike's. The cups clicked. The chief took a swallow. Mike drank some of his hot coffee then lurched back in his chair spilling some of the brew onto the desktop and the deck. He set the cup down and checked to see if he'd spilled any on his uniform.

"You passed, Mister K," Fingers said from the nearest operator station, sporting a wide grin. "Welcome to the team. Pops' Poison goes with the job."

Mike turned to Chief Dietrick expecting an explanation. Pop's Poison had to refer to the ultra-strong coffee he'd swallowed. He realized he'd been the victim of one of the radiomen's jokes. Instinct said there would probably be more.

"It's my own special blend, Mister K," the chief said. "Super extra strong. Nobody else but me messes with the coffee pot. I have to keep the men alert, you know. Easy to dope-off with long hours at the operator stations, little exercise, stuff like that. Hope you can handle it."

"Okay, Chief," Mike said. He might even get used to Pops' Poison in time. He realized a warm feeling inside, probably not from the coffee. He hadn't expected teasing, especially so early in his assignment. This would be a good crew to work with.

For much of the day Mike paid close attention to the chief's briefing, covering a wide range of information in simple terms. Dietrick reviewed their equipment, the tactical and administrative radio circuits they monitored, and some procedures. Mike appreciated the chief's candid and sometimes humorous, comments on each man in the radio gang, including himself.

By mid-afternoon Mike fought information overload. The chief had talked as though speaking to an experienced comm officer. Mike's discomfort grew. Did Dietrick realize he wasn't knowledgeable about the comm world? He didn't want to mislead the man. He nodded to the chief to follow him to the outer deck for a private chat away from the other radiomen.

"I'll level with you, Chief," Mike said. "I only have a vague understanding of the technical stuff you've covered, the circuits and procedures and all, but I want you to know I'll learn."

A grin twitched the corners of the Chief's mouth.

"My classes at the university didn't even mention the communications job," Mike said. "I'll need your help until I can carry my weight."

"No need to fess up, Mister K," the chief said. "All tin can comm officers start out green. I've known a few over the years. I'll see you get on top of this job fast." Pops cocked his head and peered at Mike with a slight squint. "You asked some good questions for a man new to the comm business, you know. You sure you ain't pulling my leg?"

"My father was a chief radioman before he was commissioned," Mike said. "I didn't pay much attention as a kid, but parts of what you told me rang a bell."

"The crew calls me Pops, Mister K," the chief said. "I like it that way." The tension Mike had carried eased. He'd found a friend, some support in this all-new world.

"Pops it is, then." Mike offered his hand.

"Another thing, Mister K," Pops added. "We all appreciate how you saved Fingers during the ambush. He'll never tell you, though. The men are talking like you can do no wrong. But my gut says watch out for the XO. He started bad-mouthing you even before you got here. We sure don't know why. I'd keep my eyes open if I was you."

Mike sat between Riley and Swede over toast, corned-beef hash and coffee at breakfast the next morning enjoying Swede's story about his adventures on his recent R&R trip to Tokyo. Swede's story-telling talents rivaled Riley's.

The XO hesitated at the wardroom table and glared at Mike before he sat. Swede paused and stared at the XO. The other officers at the table followed his gaze.

"I see our boy-hero's on his feet this morning," the XO said in a voice higher pitched than Mike recalled from the night before. The comment's sarcastic tone silenced Swede for no more than a moment before he continued. Mike ignored the XO, pretending to be engrossed in Swede's story telling. The XO focused on his breakfast when the captain joined the table.

Riley excused himself and gave a nod to Mike to join him on the main deck. Mike followed, relieved to be away from the XO. What did Riley intend?

"The XO seems to be down on me," Mike said as soon as the wardroom door to the main deck closed. "Did I do or say something out of line?"

Riley didn't answer. He led Mike to a quiet spot along the starboard side of the deck. He leaned against the rail, thumbs jammed into his belt.

"Remember, I told you before that the XO might be a problem?" Riley said. "My advice? Ignore him whenever you can. We tolerate him. The captain, and now you, have regular commissions. The rest of us are re-servists, recalled to active duty last year when this damned war started. The XO's an Annapolis grad. He turned in his regular commission for a reserve commission after the last war ended in forty-five."

"I don't understand," Mike said. "Why is my commission an issue?"

"Remember, I also told you the XO says Naval Academy grads are the real professionals," Riley said. "The rest of us are short-timers, amateurs in his view. He's bad-mouthed the Navy's NROTC program for months. He calls them playboys and lousy officers. Then you come aboard with a hero story. Makes him look like a damned fool. Incidentally, the whole crew's talking about the ambush, Deadeye."

Mike caught the hint of a twinkle in Riley's eye. The nickname made him uncomfortable. So far no one but Riley had used it. He hadn't been any more a hero than Fingers or Riley. The ambush had scared him. He'd simply made a lucky shot.

Riley leaned against the railing and gazed out across the water for a time, watching fishermen recover their nets at a pace that left the harbor's calm surface unruffled. To Mike the scene seemed somehow out of place in wartime.

A baby's cry interrupted the serenity of the rag-tag community at the foot of the causeway. People appeared one by one from the huts and shelters in the shantytown along the harbor's edge. Mike scanned the scene to find the child whose cry came from the huddle of refugee family shelters near the base of the causeway.

Riley turned back toward Mike and leaned against the rail. He pulled a cigarette from his shirt pocket and lit up.

"Another thing," Riley said, "the business with the XO at dinner last night, I mean the part about your dad. Guess the XO's jibes didn't make much sense, but I could see his petty crap was getting to you. You played it smart."

Mike nodded and waited for Riley to continue. He hadn't realized anyone else had noted his distress. His assessment of Riley grew a peg.

"When your orders came in," Riley said, "the XO went into a wild story about how, during WWII, a captain named Kinkaid deserted his ship after a collision and sinking on a North Atlantic convoy run. None of us had ever heard of the incident. I have a hunch he wants to connect you with it, somehow."

"Just because the name's the same?" Mike said. His throat tightened. Must he replay history? This had to stop. What could he do?

"Claims he lost a brother in the sinking," Riley said.

8

MIKE PAUSED OUTSIDE RILEY'S TWO-MAN stateroom. He held a classified message, received minutes earlier, that read as though he might
already be in trouble. He would rather not ask Riley for help so soon after taking on the communications job, but the message had him baffled.
With his predecessor Smitty gone, Riley had become the resident expert
on communications matters. Mike knocked on the passageway bulkhead
then parted the green, heavy fabric curtain that covered the entry. Riley
raised his head from the automobile magazine he'd been reading then
tossed it onto his desktop. Mike had an uneasy sense that somehow he'd
been expected, although Riley said nothing.

"This is one you'd better look at," Mike said. "It's from Washington.
I don't understand it." Mike handed Riley the message.

"Hmm, Washington," Riley muttered as he read parts of the message
aloud. "No receipt records… no destruction reports… inventory report
not received." Riley paused and stroked his mustache. He licked his lips.
"Serious stuff. The captain will have a fit with this one." Riley was now
open and business-like. Mike felt more comfortable.

"Why?" Mike asked. "What reports?"

"Washington says Smitty didn't do his job." Riley handed the paper
to Mike. "I suspected that might be the case before we sent him to the
hospital. This message says our classified publications management is
all balled up. Washington wants to know why, and pronto. I've heard of
problems like this before. First time I've run into it, though. Bad news."
Mike's throat tightened. The communications responsibilities were his
now, regardless of the shape they were in.

"As comm officer, Mike, you're the custodian of our classified pubs and code stuff," Riley said. "You sign for them, keep them safe, keep records of who signs for each one, destroy the outdated stuff, and make the regular reports to Washington. You know, filing and stuff. Smitty did all that – or was supposed to."

Mike hadn't realized the scope of his assignment. He understood paperwork in general, but not the way the Navy wanted it done. Where would he find the rules? He had a premonition. A problem serious enough to have Washington send the ship a detailed discrepancy list could bring high-level attention. The last thing he needed now was to be in hot water.

The trace of a grin escaped from under the black monster on Riley's lip. Mike straightened his shoulders. If Riley didn't volunteer more, he'd do the best he could to unsnarl the problem on his own. Riley at least knew the regulations. What better place to start.

"Okay," Mike said. "How do I begin?"

"What comes to mind?" Riley replied.

Five minutes later Captain Clark read the message Mike handed him. Riley stood behind Mike, close to the door. Pops stood next to Riley. The XO sat in the spare chair.

Clark tossed the sheet onto his desktop as if it were contaminated. He slumped in his desk chair and shook his head. He traced his hand over his crew cut.

"I'll draft an answer for Washington on this one, XO," the captain said. An eyes-closed, slow headshake followed. "Riley," Captain Clark continued and stabbed a finger in Riley's direction. "You help Mike start on a thorough inventory. I mean all the documents we're supposed to hold, codes, tactical pubs, everything." He paused before he scanned the message again. "In the past, a lost classified document has been a career-breaker. Washington shows no mercy in matters like this." His hand ran over his close-cropped skull. "This is a priority for each of you. Get on it. Now."

Mike followed Riley from the cabin. A few steps along the passageway, Riley paused. His furrowed brow and uplifted chin spoke serious business. No nonsense this time.

"You heard what Captain Clark said about no tolerance for missing classified stuff," Riley said in a stern voice. "The captain is in serious hot water if we've lost anything. In case you haven't figured it out, a lost classified pub could translate to a mighty short career for you, too, even though you're new on the job."

Three days later Riley, Pops and Mike reported to Captain Clark in his stateroom. The XO glowered. Riley let Mike make the report.

"Sir," Mike reported, "we checked all our records and publications against what Washington says we're supposed to have. We found a locker full of unopened document bags that Smitty must have stowed. We inventoried them all."

"How do we stand?" The captain's eyes pierced Mike. A taut, no-nonsense scowl and narrowed eyelids replaced his usual cheerful demeanor. A smirk appeared on the XO's face. Mike's instinct signaled trouble, a possible trap.

"We found the last three this morning," Mike said. "One is still missing. It's identified on the inventory list as AGF-1440. No title listed. It's classified secret." At the word "secret", Captain Clark flinched as though struck. He looked at each officer. A small bead of sweat appeared on his upper lip.

"What's the pub for," Clark asked, "and who had custody?"

"We don't know for sure, sir," Riley said. "Based on its number, my guess is the pub contains contingency codes for shore bombardment, or maybe gunfire support for operations like MacArthur's landing at Inchon last fall."

"Who had the pub last?" the captain's face reddened. He looked at each man in turn for a reply.

"We've never seen the pub," Riley answered. "Smitty's records don't show that anyone signed for custody, either. His records are trash. Mike's already started a housecleaning."

That evening at dinner the Captain Clark covered the missing document problem with all the officers.

"I want you to go through everything," Clark said. "Let me stress everything. No exceptions. Consider this an emergency. We have to find that pub. I have a week at most to get our answer to Washington."

At breakfast the next morning, speculation about the lost document dominated the sparse conversation and confirmed a shared worry. The captain's silence, in contrast with his normal, chatty behavior, reinforced the somber mood.

"Well, hotshot," the XO said to Mike as he joined the wardroom officers. He focused a prolonged glare at Mike before he unfolded his cloth napkin. "Found your lost pub yet?"

All conversation stopped. Heads swung toward Mike. He wasn't misled by the XO's superficial congeniality. Another XO harassment appeared in the offing. He resisted the urge to give his own quick comeback. Instead, he chose to follow Riley's earlier guidance and ignore the XO's behavior. After all, the XO might be able to help.

"Not yet, sir," Mike said. "We're still looking. Riley and I checked all our related pubs. We think the missing one deals with gunfire support missions. We don't have its title though. I understand you were gun boss before you became XO. Any chance you might have—"

"Not a chance," the XO snapped. "Haven't seen your pub. And, don't expect me to bail you out, Mister. You sure it's not buried in that rat's nest you call a radio shack?" He leaned back in his chair with a smug grin and stirred three spoons of sugar into his coffee.

Two days later Mike rapped on the door to the captain's cabin and said, "Sir, may I speak with you?"

"Mike, come in," Clark said. Slumped in his chair, he offered a listless wave at the spare chair. A cigarette smoldered in an ashtray full of butts.

"Found the pub, sir," Mike said. He opened a large envelope, withdrew a four-page document, and laid it on the captain's desk. The word secret, in bold, black print, emblazoned the solid red cover page.

Captain Clark slammed back his chair, jumped up and raised both arms over his head like an excited fan at a ball game. He reached across his desk, grabbed Washington's threatening message form that had come earlier, tore the wrinkled thing to pieces, and threw them into the wastebasket as though he held contaminating filth. He picked up a draft message from his desktop and waved it at Mike.

"Washington won't need this now, will they?" Clark said. He crumpled it and tossed it into the wastebasket as well.

The captain's broad grin banished what Mike imagined must have been three days of a personal hell. Captain Clark took the recovered document from Mike, scanned it, and handed it back. "Okay, where did you find it?"

"Fingers found the pub when he routed the morning messages," Mike said. "He toppled some magazines from the XO's desk by accident. When he picked them up he discovered the document."

"You believe Fingers' story?" the captain challenged. Concern lines wrinkled his forehead. Clark's sudden change of attitude puzzled Mike. Why question him or Fingers on something like this? Neither of them had a reason to lie.

"Yes, sir," Mike said. "Why wouldn't I, sir?"

"Fingers handles your classified stuff, doesn't he?" The captain's stern voice revealed an underlying anger.

"Yes, sir," Mike said, "but only the comm stuff."

"Does the XO know you found this?" Anger punctuated each of Clark's words like gunshots.

"I came to you first, sir," Mike said. He had expected the rejoicing but not this rapid swing to anger.

"Okay, Mike," the captain said. A lengthy pause followed while he stared at the calendar on his desk. He drummed his fingers on his desktop. He ran his hand over his scalp then shook his head. "Okay, Mike, and thanks. Carry on and keep me informed."

"How'd it go with Captain Clark, Mister K?" Pops asked when Mike stepped over the six-inch transom into the radio shack. Pops offered a fresh cup of Pops' Poison.

The phone rang. Fingers grabbed the handset.

"Yes, sir, Captain. He's right here." Fingers glanced wide-eyed at Mike. "Yes, sir. Right away." Fingers hung up the phone. "Mister K, Captain wants to see you and me in his cabin. Both of us. Now."

Mike checked his watch. He'd left the captain less than five minutes ago. What had he overlooked? He stowed the recovered document in the safe, twirled the combination lock, and led the way up the nearby ladder to Captain Clark's cabin on the deck above.

Clark opened his door at Mike's knock and motioned to the two men to step in. The XO stood next to the desk, glaring at Mike and Fingers.

"Settle down," the captain said to the XO. "Mike, I want you and Fingers to get to the bottom of this lost pub business. Fingers, Mister Kinkaid tells me you found the pub this morning in the XO's stateroom. Is that true?"

"Yes, sir, Captain." Fingers said, standing at attention.

"How did you happen to find it?" Clark said, his brow furrowed, eyes squinting.

"I leave the XO's message copies on his desk if he's not in his stateroom," Fingers said, "same as I do yours, sir. This time, when I pulled his message copies off the clipboard, I bumped the pile of girlie magazines on his desk and spilled them. When I picked up the magazines, I saw—"

"The hell you did, sailor," the XO shouted, his face flushed. Spittle traces appeared at the edge of his lips. "It wasn't there. I never—"

"Enough," Captain Clark snapped at the XO. "I'll get to you in a minute."

"But this man is—" the XO said.

"I said enough." The captain growled tight-jawed at the XO. "You'll get your turn."

"I saw the pub poking out of the spilled pile," Fingers said. "The cover's bright red, you know. I didn't mean to spill his stuff. I picked everything up and put it all back on his desk."

"Captain, he had no right to—"

"XO, I'll tell you for the last time," Captain Clark interrupted. "You'll have your turn."

"Fingers," Clark said, "were you responsible to Pops for this missing document?"

"No, sir," Fingers said. Both hands were balled, knuckles white. He flashed an angry glance at the XO. He stood taller, his eyes on Clark, chin raised. "Never saw the damned thing before this morning, sir. Pops gives me just the comm pubs, and damned few of those. I don't see any other classified stuff."

"Do you have anything else to tell me?" The captain paused and inclined his head slightly at Fingers as though encouraging him to say more. His stare didn't waiver.

"No, sir," Fingers said. He returned a steady gaze. "I found the damned thing just like I told you, Captain. I don't lie." Fingers then glared at the XO.

"Okay, Fingers," Captain Clark said. "You're dismissed." The captain stood and closed the cabin door behind Fingers.

"Okay, Gene," Clark said to the XO, "I told everyone to check all their material. Everything. A misplaced secret document is no joke. How come Fingers found the pub in your cabin?"

"He's lying, Captain," the XO said. "It wasn't in my cabin." The XO's shoulder tick accompanied the statement. "I've never seen the pub. Still haven't. His wild story is crap. It's something to make me look bad. I wouldn't be one damned bit surprised if our young hotshot, here, put Fingers up to it." The words came with little pause for breath. "Fingers owed Mike for saving his butt in the ambush. I wouldn't be surprised if our college boy hero pulled this stunt to cover his ass. And how do we know we had a lost pub in the first place?"

Did the captain recognize that the XO lied? The lies ignited a flash of temper in Mike. Somehow he had become the culprit. He couldn't ignore the venom in the XO's accusations. The man was a serious threat, unscrupulous and with the power to damage his career. He would have little chance of flight training after his *Bartley* tour if Washington held adverse reports.

"You have anything to say, Mike?" the captain asked.

Mike looked first at Clark. The narrowed eyes reflected the captain's intense but controlled anger. Mike turned next to the XO's gloating smile and raised chin that signaled caution.

"I don't understand all this, Captain," Mike said. "I told you what happened." He made an effort to speak slower, a struggle against his rising anger. A quick, deep breath helped him regain control. "I first saw the pub when Fingers handed it to me this morning. I believe him. He has no reason to lie." He glanced at the XO's gloating face. "Pops says all the classified tactical documents go straight to Lieutenant Powell after we receive them. He distributes them where they're needed. Fingers gets certain communications pubs. I keep the rest in my safe. Fingers has no reason to invent a story."

"Like I suspected, you—" Watkins took a step toward Mike.

"Shut up, Gene," the captain interrupted and jabbed a finger at the XO. "I'll handle this." The XO flinched and retreated, the gloat gone.

"Classified documents and codes are your responsibility, Mister Kinkaid." Clark's words carried an unexpected severity and restrained anger. "Their management requires precise, careful, attentive handling. No exceptions. No excuses. We won't have any more missing documents. Do you understand? Your inexperience is not, nor will not, be an acceptable excuse, if we have another incident. Do I make myself clear?"

9

I NEED THE LIST." *BARTLEY'S* supply officer said and held out his hand to Mike in the radio shack.

"What list?" Mike had no idea what the supply officer wanted.

"You know, the booze list," the supply officer said. "The club manager builds the booze list. That's part of your new job. Riley didn't tell you?"

Then Mike remembered the conversation. He had set himself up when he'd admitted to Riley that he wasn't a drinker. That goof resulted in one more job added to the odd duties he'd already accumulated, like postal officer, and manager of the ship's single copy machine. He attributed it to the curse of being the junior officer. He should have kept his mouth shut. He hadn't expected Riley to blab. The others had voted him the new officers' club manager. Unanimous. He'd learn.

"Job's easy," Riley had said on their walk back to the ship that night. "As O-club manager you are also Sunny's English tutor, you know. That's part of what we agreed to pay her for keeping the place in shape. She's a quick learner but can be a pest. "

The task came as a complete surprise to Mike. He'd never thought of himself as a teacher. Would it be a chore or fun? He spoke no Korean.

"Another thing you should know," Riley added. "We rotate the officers on space-available flights to Tokyo on R&R from time to time. It's a way to get away from this stink hole and get some good booze. That reminds me. Whoever goes takes the booze list. That's the real reason for the trips. No other way to get booze around here." He paused to light a fresh cigarette. "That Air Force bunch at the Pusan O-club won't sell theirs. That means near empty luggage outbound, full luggage on return. Now that you're club manager, it's up to you to maintain a current shopping list."

"I'm on a run to Pusan tomorrow," the supply officer said, his grin widening. "Davis and Edwards go along too. It's their turn for R&R. Add two more vodkas to the list, Mike. And check the captain's brandy bottle, too. He may need a refill."

The O-club job had proven to be simpler than Mike had anticipated. He kept the tally of the drink chits and calculated who owed the club how much. Sunny's diligence handled the rest. But, he'd forgotten to monitor the booze inventory. Another lesson learned.

Mike strode the quarter-mile trek along the causeway to the O-club, this time to build the booze list in addition to his daily check with Sunny. His arm sling had come off two days before. That allowed him to swing his injured arm and work out the stiffness.

The daily ten-minute, mid-afternoon break provided a welcome change to an increasingly busy routine. He'd said he needed to check on things. He didn't add that it also gave him an opportunity to get to know Sunny better. Riley's imposed schedule, designed to accelerate Mike's qualification, left limited opportunity for exercise. Most mornings all Mike could manage was five minutes of calisthenics in the cramped passageway outside The Pit.

Mike passed seven naked Korean children, approximate ages three to seven, playing in an open area of the cluttered causeway. The children kicked an old, partially-inflated soccer ball, ignoring Mike while he paused to watch their game. Squeals of delight and anger were part of their game. They jostled and pushed each other as they vied to kick the ball. The kids looked healthy, although all were long overdue for baths. Mike remembered when he and his brother had played similar games years before with a good ball and an open field without a trash pile.

Mike glanced up and noticed a movement at the officers' club. Someone inside closed the shutters over the single second story window. Why? Sunny always kept the shutters open for ventilation.

Mike paused at the club's threshold to remove his shoes, a routine Sunny insisted upon. He stopped short. The sliding shoji screen at the entry to Sunny's tiny, ground-level room was off its track. Two of its paper panels were broken. Yesterday the screen had been undamaged.

"No. No." A woman's scream and sounds of a scuffle came from the clubroom above. The thump of a heavy object crashing to the floor followed.

Mike's pulse peaked. Sunny was the only woman allowed in the clubroom above. Was she hurt? The cry sounded fear-driven.

Shoeless, Mike raced up the narrow stairs two at a time. He paused for a microsecond one step inside the clubroom. He'd expected to find that Sunny had fallen. She hadn't. She grappled with a different danger.

Sunny stood with her back pressed against the far wall next to the shuttered window. Her wrinkled, pink-flowered blouse hung outside the waist of her black skirt and off one shoulder. Only one button remained fastened. Shaking hands covered her face while her arms tried to cover an exposed breast.

The XO confronted Sunny, his back to Mike and the toppled table. His arm rose as though to strike her.

"You little—" the XO gasped.

"Stop it," Mike yelled. He lunged toward the XO, his path blocked by the table. "Leave her alone."

Sunny's head snapped up at Mike's yell. She dropped her hands to her throat, showing wide tear-filled eyes. He read relief in her dropped jaw and surprise in her eyes. Her brief sigh followed.

The XO spun around, red-faced. His arm dropped at the sight of Mike. Sweat stained his collar and shirt front. A shoulder tick racked his body as if struck by a lightning bolt.

"What the hell are you doing here?" The XO's words fought their way between gulps and heavy breathing. A quick tongue chased spittle from the corners of his mouth. The agitated stance and the touch of fear in his voice belied his challenge.

Mike took two steps toward the XO. His fingernails dug into the palms of clenched fists. Senior officer or not, he would not let Sunny be hurt.

Sunny gasped when Mike stepped forward. He glanced at her. A drop of blood oozed from the corner of her mouth.

"Scram," the XO gasped and backed away from Mike behind the

fallen table. His eyes searched the room. "Nothing happened. Get out of my way." He scampered past Mike keeping the overturned table between them. Mike grabbed for the XO, but a moment too late. The XO bounced off the doorframe and stumbled down the narrow stairs.

Sunny stood silent and still. She peeked at Mike between her fingers as if she were a terrified, yet curious child. Mike's stomach tightened as he realized what he'd prevented.

He opened the shutters in time to see the Korean children scatter as the XO stormed by. His arms flailed and accented his hustling stride. He appeared to be talking to himself.

Mike righted the table and two chairs. He wanted to help Sunny, but how? She might misunderstand his intentions. His outstretched hand encouraged her toward one of the chairs, and urged her to sit. The offer drew no response at first. A modest nod of thanks followed moments later. Sunny kept her eyes averted. Mike offered his handkerchief so she could blot the few drops of blood from the corner of her mouth. She accepted it. In silence, he urged her recovery.

Sunny sat, head bowed, hands over her face. Her soft crying soon stopped. Her eyes wouldn't meet Mike's and she made no attempt to watch his movements. Mike read deep embarrassment mixed with fear. Then, Sunny stood, adjusted her clothes, and began to tidy the room. She appeared to dismiss the incident, but continued to avoid Mike while she worked.

"I clean. Soon happy hour," Sunny said in a hesitant, hushed voice.

No comforting words occurred to Mike. What else could he say or do? Maybe she needed time alone.

Mike hustled the quarter mile along the causeway back to the ship. His mind replayed the encounter with the XO. Sunny didn't deserve abuse. The XO might try again. His priority had to be to shield Sunny from another attack. But how could he protect her? It would be pointless to confront the XO. And who would believe him if he told the others what had happened? Would his word, the new man, the junior ensign, outweigh the XO, the second senior man on board? Not a chance.

"Mister Kinkaid." Petty Officer Gomez, on watch at the quarterdeck, waved to Mike when he walked aboard. "The XO wants to see you the minute you come aboard, sir." Gomez shifted his weight from one foot to the other. "He said you better see him first thing. No delays. Said if I didn't make sure you got your, ah, butt aft to the fantail, I'd be scrubbing pots in the galley in the morning." Gomez pointed aft.

"What's he want?" Mike preferred not to speak at all, afraid his temper would take over.

"Don't know, sir," Gomez said. "He didn't say, but he looked mad as hell."

Mike strode aft. He balled his fists and swung his arms in an effort to control his anger. He rounded the aft deckhouse and stopped within inches of a collision with the XO. The XO jumped back, drew himself up and puffed out his chest. His hand made a quick swipe across his face.

"There you are, Mister," the XO said. The frightened inflection in his voice didn't match the belligerent stance. "I want to talk to you." He glanced around as if to ensure they were alone. A stabbing finger pointed at Mike. "Nothing happened up there, Mister. Understand?" The XO, chin up, took a menacing step toward Mike.

Mike held his ground. He locked his mouth shut and strained to focus on self-control. He stared at the XO's darting eyes that refused to match his own. Mike flexed his hands open and shut. Sweat trickled down his chest. He willed himself to slow his breathing.

"Forget everything you think you saw," the XO said. "Understand?" His eyes darted from Mike to the nearby deck area. "If you don't, you can kiss your career goodbye. You'll never qualify while I'm aboard." Repeated stabs of the XO's nervous finger never touched Mike's chest. "And I'll see that your fitness reports kill any hope you have of promotion." The XO's shoulder tic punctuated the harangue as though a second being, trapped beneath his shirt, fought to escape.

Despite the turmoil in his head Mike refused to move or flinch from the stabbing finger. His gut said to smash the bastard for attacking Sunny even though he's a senior officer. His eyes remained locked on the XO who avoided Mike's gaze. The XO's shaky voice and stammer told the story. Here stood a frightened man.

"I know your kind, Mister," the XO said louder than before. "Smart-ass. That's what you are. Do-gooder. No guts. No discipline."

In an unconscious action, Mike eased his weight forward to the balls of his feet. His forearms tightened. His left fist flexed in his struggle to maintain control.

The movement didn't escape the XO who took a quick step back, stopped by the gray metal bulkhead of the deckhouse. The XO's right hand wiped his face.

"I've got your number, Mister," the XO said, the volume now almost to conversational level. The XO continued to stab his finger, but beyond Mike's reach. "I won't take any crap from you, Mister. Understand?"

A deep breath prevented Mike from losing his control. Keep your mouth shut. Let him rant on. You won't gain anything by arguing.

"A Captain Kinkaid killed my brother," the XO said. "Had to be your father. I swear, I'm going…"

A sailor carrying tools came around the corner of the deckhouse. He stumbled in surprise at the near collision with the XO in this usually un-occupied area of the main deck. His quick sidestep avoided them.

"Oh, sorry, sir," the sailor said. "Excuse me."

"Watch where you're going, sailor," the XO snapped. The XO snapped back to Mike once the man passed from sight.

"You mark my words," the XO said, hands on hips. "Understand, Mister? Now get back to your job."

The long route along the main deck to the bow and back to the mid-ships ladder, gave Mike time to calm down. The situation felt impossible. He really needed Riley this time. Someone had to know about the danger Sunny faced. Could he trust Riley with an incident this sensitive? His gut said yes. He couldn't protect her by himself.

"We need to talk," Mike said with a quick, directive head nod when he found Riley alone in the operations department office. Riley pushed the desk chair out, rose and followed Mike through the hatch to the main deck. Mike led the way forward toward the gun mount where they could be alone.

Mike related what he had witnessed between the XO and Sunny, and the face-off that followed with the XO. He tried to be as unemotional as he could, but he paced the deck, made a fist and swung his arm while he told Riley the details. He omitted the part about the XO's brother.

"That bastard scared the hell out of Sunny," Mike said. "Good thing I happened to come along. How can we protect her?" Mike's responsibility as club manager had to include Sunny's welfare. He wouldn't let her be hurt. Orphaned, she'd been through enough already.

"This isn't the first time he's tried to mess with Sunny," Riley said. "I stopped him a couple of weeks before you showed up. He was drunk that night." Riley reached into his shirt pocket for a cigarette. "You lay low. Let Swede and me bird-dog the XO if we have to. Won't be for long. Our relief's on the way. Getting caught in the act this time should hold him for a while. Too bad you were the one to catch him."

10

THREE DAYS LATER MIKE PARTED the curtains to Riley's stateroom. Riley sat on the bunk's edge, in skivvies and bare feet, not yet dressed for the day.

"The decoding procedure you showed me doesn't work," Mike said holding out a message form for Riley. "I need help with this one."

Riley's bleary-eyed gaze confirmed that his attempt to go drink-on-drink with the XO the night before probably had been, at best, a draw. It had been Riley's turn to monitor the XO to keep him away from Sunny.

"Later," Riley muttered. He flipped his hand at Mike to wave him away then held his head in his hands, elbows on his knees. "Maybe I'll live 'til noon," he said in a semi-whisper. After a lengthy pause he added, "See me then."

"No can do," Mike insisted. "This one's marked priority."

"Go see Swede," Riley said. Another listless wave followed. "Let me die in peace."

"Swede went with the supply team to Pusan to see if he could round up some more booze," Mike said. "I thought you told me to decode priority messages right away. I need your help to do that."

"Dammit." Riley raised his head and frowned at Mike, but dropped his forehead back into his hands. "I thought you rich college geniuses knew it all. Read the damned manual. That's how I learned."

Mike stifled a heated retort. He chose silence instead. With Swede gone, only Riley could deal with the code. No others knew how to use it.

He'd make it a point to get checked out on this new code first thing. He couldn't risk a bind like this again.

Riley raised his head after a prolonged silence. A glance, followed by raised eyebrows, registered surprise to see Mike hadn't moved from the doorway. Riley's extra-slow negative headshake followed.

"You don't take no for an answer, do you?" Riley mumbled.

Mike let his grin answer for him. He took the empty coffee cup from Riley's desk then returned from the wardroom with a fresh cup. He set it on the desktop within Riley's easy reach. He folded his arms and leaned against the doorway again.

Riley raised his head and opened one eye. "Get lost."

Mike held the message in one hand and motioned to the paper with the other. He appreciated that Riley and Swede had volunteered to drink with the XO to keep him away but Mike had a job to do. The priority, encrypted message couldn't wait until he could give it to a sober Riley.

"Okay. Okay." Riley made an unsuccessful attempt to stand. "I knew this nursemaid job would be a pain in the ass."

"Hey, smart-ass," Mike snapped, louder than intended. "I didn't ask for a crybaby nursemaid. In case you haven't noticed, I don't need one. Will you help or not?"

Riley's hands snapped to cover his ears at Mike's outburst.

"And what's this about rich college kids?" Mike continued. "Forget it. I held jobs along with my classes and counted every damned penny. I earned my degree and my commission. No free rides in my family."

"Okay, you win," Riley said. He uncovered one ear and motioned, palm down, "But not so loud, okay?" He stared at the coffee cup for a moment before he reached for it. He snatched his hand from the hot cup. Riley's flash of anger passed. He shrugged, and took the message.

Riley held the message on his lap, his chin on his chest. He didn't move or speak for over a minute.

"Oh, hell, I see why," Riley said. He looked at Mike through bleary eyes. "It's a different system. Not the one we worked with before." He handed the message to Mike, a grin evident under the monster mustache. "It's probably more of the routine admin junk like the ALNAVs, stuff the paper pushers in Washington think are important. Stateside stuff. Probably doesn't apply to us out here." He stretched. "Let's get some coffee in me first." Riley finished his first gulp of coffee then stretched again.

"Guess I sized you up wrong," Riley said. "We all liked the way you didn't give ground to the XO your first day. Gutsy. Don't think I'd have done that as a green ensign. Guess it's your expensive ring, or maybe the way you talk and handle yourself." A brief shudder wracked Riley's body. "I figured your folks were rich. Back home we used to call them uptown folks."

"It's my granddad's ring," Mike said. "I inherited it when my father died."

"You said you worked in school." Riley finished the coffee with another gulp, drops glistening on his mustache. "What'd you do?"

"I had a couple of jobs," Mike said. "I took the late shift at a local gas station and garage my last two years. That gave me enough to pay for what the scholarship didn't cover."

"What's the story on your Navy ROTC scholarship?" Riley stretched again. "Didn't have them when I was in school."

"My father died just after the war ended," Mike said. "Left Mom with damned little money to feed my kid sister and me. We all worked to help pay the bills. I needed a scholarship to get to college. I applied for the new Navy NROTC program Congress authorized when the war ended. The program offered the best way for me to get to flight school. I made the cut."

"Flight school?" Riley said. He ran his right hand over his scalp. "I don't understand. How come you're out here?"

"I passed all the tests and the physical for flying back in April," Mike said. "The Navy sent a letter saying I'd been accepted for flight training and to expect orders to Pensacola after commissioning. Instead, my entire class got orders to ships. No exceptions. We had to fill the holes."

"I don't understand." Riley picked up the empty cup but put it down with a frown. "How are you going to fly out here?"

"I can't reapply for flight training until I qualify at sea and finish this tour," Mike replied.

"Sorry for riding you, Mike." Riley stood with deliberate care. He grabbed the upright bunk frame and paused.

"Do me a favor," Mike said while Riley stretched and reached for his pants. "Keep the flying thing to yourself. My gut tells me the XO will find some way to derail me if he knows I want to fly."

"I need another refill." Riley handed his cup to Mike then reached for his shirt.

"Sit down," Riley said after Mike returned with another full cup. He pointed to the spare stateroom chair. Riley eased himself onto the bunk and leaned forward, hands clasped, elbows on his knees. "It's time you faced facts. The XO has a bug up his ass. He blames you for his brother's death somehow. He won't drop it."

Mike hadn't expected the concern in Riley's voice.

"What can I do?" Mike said. Did he dare tell Riley the whole story? He already knew some of it, the XO's version anyway.

"For starters," Riley said, "you can tell me what's behind the XO's game. You haven't leveled with me up to now, maybe for good reason. I haven't pressed you. It's time to rethink this one." He rubbed his hand over his mustache. An even softer tone emerged. "Maybe I can help, but first I need to know what I'm dealing with." Riley focused on Mike.

How much should he disclose to Riley? The accident happened over eight years ago. That made it history. Why reopen it? The XO's retaliation was the issue. The XO believed he knew what happened. He was wrong. But could Riley help?

Mike returned Riley's stare. His left hand fingered a piece of paper on Riley's desk, moving it about as he contemplated. He had to trust someone. Riley had been a friend. The story had to come out sometime.

"I want your assurance that this stays between us," Mike said.

Riley's "Of course" carried a tinge of anger.

Mike settled in the chair. He couldn't avoid the XO forever. He rubbed the back of his neck while he decided where to start the painful recollection. How much did Riley already know, or surmise?

"You mentioned a story the XO had given the officers before I reported aboard," Mike said, "a story about his brother's loss during the war in a collision at sea? From what's been said since, I know his version is wrong."

"Oh? Let me be the judge, okay?" Riley said.

Mike's memory of his father's disfigurement and slow decline after the tragedy remained all too fresh. How could he talk about it and remain unemotional?

"Here's what my father told me." Mike leaned back in his chair, clasped his hands across his lap, his chin uplifted. "I've verified the details."

"In World War II, my father commanded a destroyer escort similar to *Bartley*, the *USS Dunleavy*, his first command. In January 1943 in the North Atlantic, a merchant ship convoy escorted by Navy ships steamed in dense fog at night, in waters known to have German wolf pack subs. Those subs ganged up on the convoys. In my father's convoy, a merchant-man turned the wrong way on a defensive, zigzag pattern and rammed *Dunleavy* broadside. The collision cut *Dunleavy* in two. Both ships sank. Eleven men from *Dunleavy* and seven from the merchantman survived." Mike's hand rediscovered the now-rumpled paper on Riley's desk.

Riley's eyes locked on Mike, questioning eyes, eyes that said go on.

"None of the convoy's civilian ships had radar. They steamed blind," Mike continued. "Two other Navy ships had the only radar equipment in the convoy. *Dunleavy* was scheduled for radar installation on return from that convoy run."

Mike paused for Riley's reaction. Riley didn't move.

"My father suffered major injuries. He had a broken jaw and lost his left eye, part of his left ear, and his left arm from just above the elbow. He suffered a serious concussion, and a broken hip in a couple of places. The doctors told us he'd broken some other bones and was pretty messed up inside. He almost died from blood loss."

The familiar tightness in Mike's throat and the unbidden dampness around his eyes had returned. The survivors' accounts melded into a mental kaleidoscope of horrors. His father's image, his body mangled, even after several surgeries and months of recovery, flashed in painful memory. Mike raised his head. He pushed aside the crumpled paper. His reluctance to speak passed.

Riley's eyes urged Mike to go on.

"The ship's chief quartermaster saved my father. Got him into the one lifeboat that survived. My father was unconscious when a ship found them the next day. They took him to a British hospital."

"Why a British hospital?" Riley asked, surprised.

"The convoy was two days steaming from England."

"Go on," Riley said.

"A British nurse wrote a letter about the collision for my father and sent it to us. The next months were hell."

"I can imagine." Riley reached in his shirt pocket for a cigarette.

"The Brits patched him up as best they could," Mike said. "After they released him, he came back to the States on a hospital ship and spent thirteen more months in the Navy hospital before his medical retirement. Then things started to go sour."

"Sour? Seems to me things were pretty bad already," Riley said.

"They got worse while he was in the hospital," Mike said. "Charges were brought against him for the merchant ship's loss."

"Why?" Riley snapped. "The ship's in fog, at night, with no radar, and limited communications. Hell, I read about those convoy runs. Most were lucky to have any survivors."

"The merchantman's owners wanted compensation for their lost ship and cargo," Mike said. "They filed suit against the Navy. They claimed *Dunleavy* was at fault, therefore, my father was responsible."

Riley stroked his mustache, the cigarette smoking in his other hand.

"The Navy held a formal inquiry," Mike continued. "The charges were ruled unfounded and dropped."

Mike looked away. He couldn't shake the painful images of his father's efforts to retain his self-respect. He recalled his father's torment, and his belief that he had failed his crew. Mike's fist squeezed the crumpled paper into a tight ball. Would he ever be able to shed his feelings of helplessness, a son unable to find comfort for his father?

Riley sat motionless, eyes fixed on Mike.

"Word of the charges against my father got around," Mike added. "He got angry letters and phone calls. Lots of them. The kids at school learned of the collision and gave my kid sister and me a bad time, too. Mom gave me hell more than once for the fights at school. I got more information on the collision a couple of years later. It confirmed what my father told me before he died."

Riley cocked his head and toyed with his mustache in slow motion then stabbed his cigarette into the ashtray.

"I guess I understand why you kept mum," Riley said. "What I don't understand is how the XO fits in."

"That's easy," Mike said and tossed the paper ball toward Riley's wastebasket. "We met the man who rescued my father on one of our family's visits to the hospital. He was *Dunleavy*'s chief quartermaster. Later I attended the ceremony where my father pinned a medal on the chief for heroism in the rescue."

"And…" Riley leaned forward.

"*Dunleavy*'s chief quartermaster was Frank Watkins, the XO's older brother," Mike said. Okay, so now Riley knew. Somehow he was relieved, and surprised at the sensation.

Riley seemed puzzled. He started to say something, but clamped his mouth shut and waved to Mike to go on.

"I knew this man," Mike said. "I had a long talk with him."

"What did he say?" Riley cocked his head.

"He told me what led to the collision," Mike said, "and what he did to save my father and the others. Chief Watkins had the foresight to bring along the ship's log and quartermaster's notebook when the survivors piled into the lifeboat. The entries in those documents supported my father's testimony of what led to the incident, and convinced the investigation board that the charges against him were without merit."

Mike stared at the desk for a moment while the painful imagery slipped back into its cave, deep in memory.

"Even though the Navy dropped the charges," Mike said, "the episode took its toll. In his final days, we had several long talks. My father told me he loved the Navy and would be pleased if I joined as well, but that it was my choice. I told him, then, that I had a dream to fly from an aircraft carrier. He told me to follow my dream. I promised him I would. He gave me one of his rare smiles after his injuries, one I'll never forget.

I hoped my service would erase any lingering issue with his record or the kind of man we was."

Riley shifted in his chair.

"His personality changed," Mike said. "The loss of his men ate at him." He leaned forward in the chair, elbows on his knees, eyes down. The memories tormented him.

Mike paused. He swallowed. "Father died about eighteen months after he left the hospital. Mom died two years ago."

The telling relieved a significant burden for Mike. Now that Riley knew, could he help deflect the XO?

Riley sat motionless, head down for a full minute. He raised his head, sighed and reached into his shirt pocket for another cigarette. He crumpled and tossed an empty pack into his wastebasket.

"The XO's story was phony," Riley said, "or at least part of it. He claimed he lost a brother in the sinking, but didn't go into detail. That's not normal for him. From what you've told me, I doubt he ever knew the details."

"Chief Watkins told me he had a younger brother at the Naval Academy," Mike said, "but I'd forgotten that until the XO started in on me. At dinner, my first night aboard, I realized the XO was the younger brother."

"But, what you tell me still doesn't account for the XO's story," Riley said. "What happened to his brother?"

"I don't have an answer," Mike said. "I only know that Chief Watkins survived the sinking uninjured. When my father pinned the medal on him at the hospital, I shook Chief Watkins' hand."

11

Six weeks to the day after Mike had reported to *Bartley*, he handed the captain the message that all hands had waited to receive. *Bartley's* replacement, the civilian ship *MSTS Ulysses*, would arrive the next day and release *Bartley* to return to the fleet for normal operations, and, if all went well, soon head home to San Diego.

A half hour later, the captain's impromptu meeting in the wardroom to read the message to the officers brought a raucous response. *Bartley* had been deployed for almost a year. For some, the good news came as if they'd received a governor's pardon. For all aboard it raised hope for Christmas with families.

When the hilarity subsided sobering thoughts crept in.

"Who breaks the news to Sunny?" Riley asked the group when the hilarity subsided. Heads swiveled and fingers pointed to Mike.

Mike trudged, head down, toward the officers' club. He ignored the children at play, even the shoeless little one who saluted as Mike passed. Mike had enjoyed the daily language sessions with Sunny, but not this one. He'd have to tell her that this afternoon's session would be their last. He'd avoided similar emotional situations in the past whenever possible.

Mike had explored ways to tell Sunny the ship would leave the next day. He wanted to be gentle. All the words he'd considered seemed somehow wrong. None conveyed how he thought of her. He had grown fond of her, more than merely liking her. He'd found the teaching fun and challenging. To the other officers she remained pleasant, quick, competent, but reserved. In those afternoon sessions, intended to help her master English, she relaxed. As her ease grew she had revealed much of her history, her fears and her dreams. The sessions passed all too quickly. Each class had ended when the first happy-hour patron arrived. A twinge of guilt flashed through Mike's mind. No, they were friends, good friends.

Sunny always waited for Mike inside the O-club's entry with a wide and excited smile, a lemonade or tea ready for him. She had treated him as both an honored guest and a close friend.

But today Sunny wasn't in her usual place in the shaded entryway. Where was she? Was she all right? The XO had been on the ship when Mike left. That eliminated one possibility.

"Sunny. Are you here?" Mike called through the open doorway. She didn't answer.

No response came from Mike's light tap on the repaired shoji screen shielding Sunny's small room. He slid the screen back a crack on the chance she might be napping. No Sunny. He climbed the stairs, two steps at a time, to the bar above. Again, no Sunny.

A rustling fabric sound came from below. Someone had arrived.

"You early today, Mister Mike." From the bottom of the stairs, Sunny tilted her head up at him and smiled. "I shopping." She held a small package at her side. Her fingers rattled the paper wrapper. "We have class, yes?"

Mike nodded. Tell her now, an inner voice said. Don't risk an unwelcome interruption by the happy-hour crowd.

Before Mike could find the words, Sunny darted into her room and brought out the notebook Mike had given her weeks before. She joined him in the bar area above. Both sat in their usual seats across from each other at the small barroom table. Sunny opened her notebook. She laid the written English homework exercise next to the notebook, ready to report on her assignment.

Their more recent sessions often opened with some gentle teasing, a flirtatious comment or a sly look Mike had come to enjoy. Not this time. She sat silent, her face impassive as she waited for him to begin.

"I have something to tell you, Sunny," Mike said. He searched her eyes. He couldn't put it off any longer. How should he say it? The hoped-for, gentle words refused to come. "Sunny, we—"

"You leave." Sunny bowed her head then looked up into Mike's eyes. "No come back. You go States." She made no effort to hide the moisture in her eyes. "Everybody know."

Mike reached in his pocket for a handkerchief. Sunny closed her eyes and made no move to accept it. Mike stepped around the table. He tipped her head with a gentle touch under her chin and dabbed her tears. She didn't resist. His throat tightened. He wanted to comfort her, to hold her close.

"We leave tomorrow, Sunny," he said after he returned to his seat. "To-morrow afternoon. The Marines will care for you after we go. You can stay here. They'll pay you and give you food, as we have. Whatever you need. Colonel Peters has promised. And, he has the spare key to the door."

"No more class, Mister Mike," Sunny said after a period of stoic silence. She exhaled a deep sigh and said, "Thank you for teach Sunny."

Before Mike could think of what to say, she closed her notebook, rose, left the table, and scurried down the stairs. Mike followed her to the entry. She disappeared into her room.

Mike's anxiety peaked. She must realize he had no control over the ship's schedule. How could he make amends?

A moment later she returned to the tiny foyer with a small package.

"You good man, Mister Mike," Sunny said. "Good to Sunny. Teach me much English and about America. I get good job when war is over." She paused. Her somber tone changed to a child-like excitement. "For you." She handed Mike the package. Her unexpected move and sudden change in demeanor surprised Mike.

"You open. Please, Mister Mike." Sunny's smile reminded Mike of his sister's excitement Christmas mornings past.

Mike opened the wrapping to reveal a small red lacquerware box slightly larger than a deck of cards. Gray silk with the South Korean and the United States flags embroidered in delicate stitches covered its top.

"For you to remember Sunny, and for thank you," she beamed. "I make sewing."

Mike put his arms around Sunny and pulled her close. She looked up at him. His gentle kiss lingered as she returned the kiss. Sunny pushed away. Tears welled in her eyes.

"I fix for happy hour."

"Eat up. We have a busy day ahead," Riley said the next morning. He clapped Mike on the shoulder before taking the seat next to him at breakfast.

The somber atmosphere in the wardroom surprised Mike. He had expected excited chatter about the orders to get *Bartley* underway. The ship would leave its incarceration in Masan within the hour and head to sea. All hands had hoped the orders to depart Masan would also include a date to head home. Instead, *Bartley's* orders and the thirty-day operating schedule, gave no hint of an overdue return to the States. To a man, each officer had expressed anger about the delayed return to San Diego and to their families.

Riley nodded to the wardroom steward for a refill of his coffee. He swallowed half of it in one gulp, and nodded to Mike to follow him out of the room.

"Gonna get your feet wet today, young man," Riley said pausing on the main deck. He lit a cigarette, and leaned against the rail. "The captain has okayed five open bridge watch teams again, like we had before Masan, a one-in-five rotation, so I'll have every fifth watch. He's agreed to put you on my team as J-O-O-D, Junior Officer of the Deck. We'll relieve Swede and Sanders for the 1200-1600 today."

Mike attempted to hide his excitement. To his knowledge, the makeup of bridge watch stander teams hadn't been discussed since he'd reported aboard. He could have been teamed with any of the qualified OODs, but he preferred Riley. Riley's tutoring sessions had often carried some teasing and occasional humor, but always included sound substance and guidance. At times Mike had to slow Riley when he spewed out information faster than Mike could assimilate it. He had decided his best approach with Riley was to admit his limits at the start. The upcoming, relatively short run, from Masan to Yokosuka, Japan would be Mike's first active exposure toward the vital shipboard qualification. It had to go well.

"Are we going to talk about ship driving pretty soon?" Mike had asked in one of Riley's tutorial sessions the week before. "My midshipman training didn't cover watches procedures, ship handling, tactical communications, things like that."

"We'll cover all that and more once we get underway," Riley said adding a mischievous twist of his mustache.

Mike wasn't satisfied. He was the only officer on board who wasn't accustomed to the routines and underway watch standing requirements. Driving a ship, conning as Riley termed it, had to be far less exciting than flying, although he had never done either. He couldn't wait to tackle the ship-driving business. He had to get that vital underway qualification as soon as he could so he could reapply to fly.

Mike reported to the open bridge fifteen minutes early, ready for his first underway watch with Riley. *Bartley* had left Masan at 0830 that morning. The ship steamed independently at fourteen knots along a route to the naval base at Yokosuka, Japan, a trip expected to take three days. Mike made no attempt to hide his exhilaration or broad grin. He was underway at last on a beautiful day in good weather. He'd try to describe the day to Carol in his next letter.

Riley joined Mike five minutes later, chatted with Swede for a few minutes, then relieved him as OOD for the afternoon watch.

"You ready to go to work, young man?" Riley said to Mike. Mike's grin and nod were all the response necessary.

"In this job," Riley said, "the conning officer—that's me for now, and you later—instructs the helmsman and lee helmsman through the voice tubes here." He tapped the pair of three-inch diameter brass tubes at chest level on the forward bulkhead. "We'll tell him what course to steer, when to turn, and what speed to signal to the engine room."

Mike already knew that much, but decided this wasn't the time to smart-mouth Riley.

"For independent steaming, we follow the navigator's directions, the course to maintain, the speed to maintain, things like that," Riley said.

"The XO is also our navigator. That's one of the few things he's usually good at. Once we join the task group, after our Yokosuka pit stop, we maneuver the ship to follow the flagship's orders, follow tactical signals, and conduct exercises, you know, whatever we're told to do. You'll see plenty of action. I guarantee you won't be bored." Riley paused to light a cigarette, then crossed the bridge to the gyro repeater and checked the ship's heading.

"We'll run some drills on the trip to Yoko," Riley said. "I'll see that you stay busy. No doping off on my watch. Understand?" Although he said it with a wink, Mike detected an unmistakable undertone of the no-nonsense teacher. "Consider this run a warm-up," Riley said with a smile. He twisted his mustache, a signal Mike had learned to recognize as teasing. The glint in Riley's eye could mean anything. He'd be tested and teased. That's Riley's way. Okay. Mike was ready.

Their first watch that afternoon proved busier than Mike had anticipated. Riley kept up a steady chatter interspersed with penetrating questions and assignments for Mike to complete before they teamed up again for the 0400-0800 in the morning.

Midway through the afternoon, Riley took a cigarette break. Mike chose the opportunity to dig through the publications stack in a locker next to the navigator's table. The homework Riley had assigned would require him to read selected parts of several documents. Mike stood at the navigator's table intent on reading the portion of the operation order for *Bartley's* next assignment. A few minutes later, instinct warned him he wasn't alone. He swung around. The XO stood three feet behind him, silent, watching.

Mike glanced at Riley. Had he forgotten something Riley had asked him to do?

Riley twisted his mustache.

The exchange puzzled Mike. What in hell was going on? What did the XO want?

The XO left without comment.

On subsequent watches, episodes of uneasiness puzzled Mike. He tried to isolate the cause. He couldn't link his discomfort to anything about Riley or his drills and demands. Those were fun. He hadn't been seasick. He had enough sleep, although more would have been welcome.

"The XO's been up here at some time on every watch we've stood since we got underway," Mike said to Riley in a quiet period. "He hangs around for a while. He doesn't say a word. Is that normal?"

"He's nosing around. Looking for trouble," Riley said. Something he can hang you for and get the captain to support. You're sand in his shorts."

"I don't talk to him if I can avoid it," Mike said.

"Keep it that way, and keep your eyes open," Riley said. "When you stand watches with me, you're okay."

"What if I'm teamed with someone else?" Mike asked.

"If you are," Riley said, "and you make even the slightest mistake, you can bet the XO will hound you. He can block your OOD qualification. No qual means you don't fly, remember?"

Mike flexed his fists, angry with himself. He'd forgotten Riley's earlier caution. He'd recognized the XO's antagonism, but had failed to connect the threat the man represented. No more. He had to find a way to end the harassment.

12

BARTLEY MADE A BRIEF STOP at the Yokosuka Naval Base in Tokyo Bay for provisions, refueling, supplies and minor repairs. The size and complexity of the former Japanese base impressed Mike. Four days later, the ship joined an eight-ship, carrier task group off Korea's east coast.

Mike liked standing watch as JOOD with Riley "chasing the flat-top" as Riley termed it. In that frequent assignment, *Bartley* served dual roles as plane guard during flight operations when planes were landing or taking off from the carrier *USS Valley Forge*, and as rescue destroyer for the task group.

Bartley maintained station one thousand yards astern of *Valley Forge* during the carrier's flight operations. The carrier, voice radio call sign Fearless, launched and recovered planes each day and most nights in support of the ground fighting in Korea. *Bartley*, voice radio call sign Postman, shared the task with the seven destroyers and destroyer escorts that constituted a protective screen for the aircraft carrier. From where he stood, Mike could see the carrier's fighter and attack planes take off and land, much like having a prime seat at a ball game. He dreamed that some future day he, too, would join the carrier aviator fraternity.

"This job looks easy," Riley had said on their first night assignment as plane guard, and rescue destroyer. "It's not. It's worse at night. Hard to see when the carrier starts to turn, and it turns often. You maneuver as necessary to stay in position whenever Fearless changes course. You have to anticipate a change and notice telltale signs."

Mike relished the challenge of maintaining station behind a maneuvering carrier. He had accepted Riley's guidance and learned the clues.

The task was simple in concept. Stay in a defined position relative to the carrier. That sounded easy enough at the outset, but he soon learned that the carrier had an annoying habit of changing her course when planes were launched and recovered. She would not announce these course changes until after she had steadied on a new heading, and sometimes not even then. Night or bad weather aggravated the challenge because the carrier's movements often couldn't be seen in time to make prompt corrective maneuvers to remain on the assigned station.

"The secret is to stay alert and keep your eyes open," Riley had repeated on each watch of *Bartley's* plane guard assignments. "Captain Clark raises hell if you get off station. He's damned sensitive about our professional performance."

Riley's parting shot was often, "Gotta get you smartened-up if you want to fly some day." Mike appreciated that he didn't say it when the XO was nosing around on the bridge.

In one of his letters to Carol, Mike noted:

> *Riley's worse than a top sergeant. If I don't do everything exactly right, I hear about it. He never lets up. I know that sounds like complaining, but he's right. How else would I learn? Driving a ship is more difficult than I imagined, but fun. It's probably easier than flying, however. I'm intrigued by Riley's ability to include something new in every watch. He answers most of my questions on the spot, but sometimes he'll postpone his replies until our next watch, or add a homework assignment. He demands excellence. Okay. I'll deliver excellence.*

On the plus side, Riley's diligence had managed to keep the XO at bay.

❀

"I see an early winter ahead, probably a hard one," Riley said two weeks later from his hunkered-down position behind the windscreen on *Bartley's* open bridge. For five days a storm had dogged the carrier task group with no sign of letup. "It's too early in the fall for a storm like this." He pulled up the hood on his parka as did Mike squatting beside him. "We get any message traffic about maybe heading home?"

"Pops would come screaming up here himself with something like that," Mike said. "No such luck."

"Too bad we can't change heading," Riley said a few minutes later. "It wouldn't take much to keep us from plowing into the wave tops and kicking up this spray. I'm sick of getting drenched." He rose and crossed to the cabinet that housed the barometer and the thermometer. "Temperature's down another three degrees in the last hour," he said. "That's twelve degrees since we came on watch. Wind's picking up some, too. This is more like Siberian November weather than the end of September."

Mike stared into the night, his mind on Carol. He missed the sparkle in her eyes, her easy laughter, and the way she teased. She could change despair into delight with a smile. What he'd give for a day at home with her right now. He'd been gone from her longer than either of them had expected.

Carol had written regularly, but the mail system delivered her much-anticipated letters at odd intervals. At least she took the extended separation well. On nights like this he wanted to be with her, to cuddle and to love her. Instead, he sat on an icy steel deck, halfway around the world, wet and near freezing, only able to think of Carol, unable to talk with her or to hold her.

A routine call from the wheelhouse for a minor matter banished Mike's reverie.

"Bridge. Aye," Mike replied to the wheelhouse, ending the exchange. Then to Riley he said, "Haven't seen the XO for several watches now. Suppose he's given up on me?"

"Fair weather sailor," Riley said. He reached for a cigarette, held it for a moment then tapped Mike on the chest with the unlit cigarette. "You ready to take the conn, young man?"

Mike's wide grin provided the response.

Mike scanned the radar repeater to check *Bartley's* position two thousand yards on the carrier's starboard quarter, their station when the carrier wasn't conducting flight operations.

"I'm ready," Mike said. He welcomed Riley's confidence in his ability and exalted each time Riley turned the conn over to him. He relished being in command of a warship and one hundred seventy six men, albeit for a limited time. No other assignment would give him this much control, except flying.

"Okay, you have the conn," Riley said. "Since Fearless has cancelled tonight's flight ops, we'll stay on this station. Good practice for you. It should be a quiet watch. I'll have to find something to keep you on your toes." Riley settled back in the captain's pedestal chair and picked up his cup. "Damn coffee's cold," he muttered and settled in observing Mike.

"I'll take the conn now," Riley said a quiet half hour later. "Time to check on our boat crew. Make sure they're on their toes and stay night-adapted. Remember, red lights only in their space and no smoking this time. If we ever have to launch the crew, their eyes will need to be fully dark-adapted for a pickup."

Mike climbed down four ladders to the main deck for the chore assigned to the junior officer-of-the-deck on each watch. Not much chance they'd need the boat for a rescue during this watch since the carrier's planes weren't flying. He didn't blame them. He wouldn't be eager to fly on a night like this either. One day he'd learn how the pilots managed to get back aboard the ship in the dark. It looked like black magic when viewed from *Bartley's* bridge. But if those pilots could do it, so could he.

Mike paused at the main deck level and gazed to starboard before he turned aft toward the boat station. The quarter moon provided little light. Scattered low clouds let enough moonlight through to reveal an endless expanse of wave tops that broke into lacy white foam. A shudder raced through him at the thought of survival in a cold and angry sea.

"Time to check out the boat, Dutton," Mike said to the whaleboat coxswain, snug inside the boat crew's shelter. Dutton, a short and wiry, high-energy man had become one of Mike's favorites, a seasoned, first class petty officer with unlimited sea stories to relate to any willing listener. "Hope we don't need the whaleboat tonight. It's nasty out there. But in case—"

"Yes, sir," Dutton said. "We're ready. Looks pretty bumpy." Dutton scratched his head then ran the back of his sleeve across his face to wipe away wind-blown spray. "And, uh, Mister K, I forgot to tell you earlier." Another quick stroke followed. "I meant to tell you before. Anderson's my new engineer on this crew. He joined us in Yokosuka."

"Why didn't you say so on our first watch instead of now, two weeks later?" Mike said. "How come you let him join the boat crew if he isn't qualified? Come on, Dutton, you know better."

"Oh, he's qualified," Dutton said, "or at least his record says he is. He qualified on his last ship. Said their whaleboat's a little different. Newer engine. Things like that."

"The question is does he have any experience?" Mike said trying to control a rising temper. It wasn't like Dutton to be evasive.

"Some," Dutton said. "Crivelli's my regular engineer. You remember we left him back in the Yokosuka hospital. Andy's the backup." Despite his words, Mike caught some discomfort in Dutton's answer.

"My point is can he do the job?" Mike said, fists clenching. He didn't appreciate surprises, particularly one with negative safety overtones. Maybe Anderson did know his job, but Dutton should have told him earlier that the new man had joined the boat crew. "Has he ever operated this engine before?" Unblinking, Mike eyed Dutton.

"Yes, sir," Dutton said. "We took him out on the bay our first afternoon back in Yokosuka. He ran the boat then. Crivelli checked him out, said he'd be okay."

Mike paused to consider the situation then asked, "Do we have another engineman?"

"No, sir," Dutton said.

Mike returned to the bridge to tell Riley of the crew change.

"We have a new engineer in the boat crew," Mike reported to Riley. "Dutton says he'll be okay. He doesn't have a backup anyway, so we can't replace him. Don't know why Dutton waited until tonight to tell me. I'd prefer some experience in this weather."

"Damn," Riley said. "May not be a problem tonight with flight ops cancelled. I'll have words with Dutton and his division officer in the morning." He went to the radar repeater, scanned the display, then checked *Bartley's* heading. "Okay," Riley said, "You can have the conn. We're still on course one six five, making turns for twelve knots. The radio's been quiet. I ran a radio check with Fearless after you went below. They said to expect better weather to the southeast."

"Okay, I have the conn," Mike said following the protocol. He checked *Bartley's* heading and position relative to the carrier. Things were as they should be. Mike expected a quiet watch. In that case, Riley could be counted on to come up with another what-if drill.

"Postman, this is Fearless," blared from the radio speaker on *Bartley's* bridge. "Man overboard port side. I say again, man overboard port side. We are maneuvering to stay clear. Stand by to recover."

13

Mike froze at the emergency call. The carrier's flight deck flood-lights exploded out of the darkness two thousand yards ahead on *Bartley's* port bow.

"Sound man overboard port side. Captain to the bridge," Mike called through the voice tube to the quartermaster in the wheelhouse. He shifted to the other voice tube. "Combat, conn. Mark our position. Fearless has a man overboard. Stand by to maneuver."

Riley joined Mike.

Mike grabbed the radio handset.

"Roger, Fearless," Mike said. "We're maneuvering to search. What can you tell us? How many and their condition? Over."

"Postman, wait one. Out," Fearless replied.

Mike considered what action *Bartley* should take. Riley had drilled him on many events and potential emergencies. Before Mike stood his first watch on plane guard station, they'd talked about plucking an unlucky pilot from the water. A man overboard incident had to be similar, but was it? Why had that scenario been overlooked?

Bartley's crew raced to their assigned emergency stations. The six-man motor whaleboat crew donned life jackets and prepared to lower the boat into the storm-tossed sea when directed. Once the man in the water had been sighted, Mike, as JOOD and therefore boat officer, would be the last to board the whaleboat, then the boat would be lowered into the sea for the recovery.

Captain Clark stepped on the bridge. The XO followed.

"Fearless reported a man overboard port side," Riley said to Captain Clark. "CIC has a plot on the man's approximate position. He should be off the port bow about eighteen hundred yards ahead."

"Come left to course one five zero," Mike ordered. His stomach tightened. He glanced at the captain but there was no sign that he intended to take over. Would the captain let an inexperienced man conduct the search and rescue?

"Looks like Mike intends to pick up the carrier's wake," Riley said to the captain in lowered tones.

"Are you crazy?" the XO said to Riley. "Why did you give him the conn? This is serious business. He doesn't know how to handle a man overboard. Has he ever been through a rescue drill? He'll blow this one I promise you." Riley shook his head but ignored the XO. The captain did too.

Would Riley intervene if the captain didn't? Riley watched Mike but didn't move or speak. The captain made no move to take the conn. The XO was right this time. One of them should take over and run this rescue. Mike didn't know the proper procedure to conduct a rescue. More important, he didn't know what to avoid. He might make a mistake, maybe a deadly one. The man in the water wouldn't survive in this weather unless they picked him up fast.

"Postman, this is Fearless," the radio call interrupted. "We have one man in the water. We believe he does not, repeat does not, have flotation gear. We dropped two life rings and one floating light. The light failed. At least we can't see the light from here. Over."

"Roger, Fearless." Mike replied. "We're closing on the man's estimated position. Will keep you posted. Out."

"Tucker," Mike said to Seaman Tucker, the sound-powered telephone circuit operator, "any word from the lookouts?"

"No, sir," Tucker said. "I'll check with 'em again."

Mike moved to the port wing to scan the waves. He hoped to spot the carrier's disappearing wake. If he could put *Bartley* in the wake it would put them closer to where the man fell in.

"We're in the wake. Come right to course 165," Mike said ordering the helmsman to keep *Bartley* in the carrier's wake. "All engines back one third." Mike judged the maneuvers should put the ship about where the unfortunate sailor had gone overboard.

"Bridge, combat," the CIC watch officer called on the squawk box. "Six hundred yards to go. Fearless is manning the spare helicopter for a pickup if we can find the man in the water. The regular helo slipped over the edge of the flight deck while they were parking it. It's hung up on a deck edge gun tub. The helo's crewman fell overboard. That's all the info we have."

"Bridge, conn. All stop," Mike ordered to allow the ship's momentum to coast *Bartley* into the approximate position where the man had fallen.

"Signal bridge, conn," Mike called on the squawk box. "Are you manned and ready?" The survivor would be tough to find in the dark in these seas. Would the signal bridge's twelve-inch searchlights, designed to exchange signals by flashing light, be strong enough? Those lights were all *Bartley* had for the search.

"Yes, sir," the signal bridge replied.

"Okay," Mike said. "Illuminate to port and starboard and keep a sharp eye out. We have one man in the water without flotation gear. Try to spot a couple of life rings, and maybe a floating light."

"Captain." The XO tugged at Clark's arm. "You aren't going to let him run this. Are you, sir? The kid's green. Doesn't know what he's doing. He'll blow the job for sure. We might miss the man. We'd look like fools or worse. At least let me get someone else to take the boat officer duties. Hell, I don't even know if the kid can swim."

The captain ignored the XO and moved alongside Mike.

"What's your plan, Mike?" Clark said.

"I figure we're about where he went in," Mike said. "If we can spot him, or a life ring, we can recover him. I hope this wind eases some, though. Those whitecaps are damned confusing. Can't tell a life ring from a break-ing wave top."

Captain Clark clasped his hands behind his back but took a step closer to Mike. His slight nod made clear that Mike should continue.

Mike realized that instinct had carried him while he'd expected Riley or the captain to take over the recovery. This time a man's life depended on his actions. A tinge of panic flew past and disappeared. He tapped the gold insignia in his pocket for guidance.

"Combat, bridge," Mike called into the voice tube. "How far are we from where the man went in, from your datum?"

"Bridge, combat," the CIC officer replied. "We figure the man fell in about a hundred yards ahead."

"Sir," Seaman Tucker reported. "Bow lookout has something off the port bow. Can't be sure what he saw. Might have been another whitecap. They're everywhere."

"Signal bridge, conn," Mike called on the squawk box. "Bow lookout reports something in the water off the port bow. Put some light on it."

"Aye, aye, sir," the signal bridge responded. Searchlights swept the area. They illuminated nothing but roiling sea.

Bartley's forward movement stopped. The waves worsened the ship's rolling motion. The carrier steamed on ahead, its lights dimmed further by the blowing spume.

"Fearless, this is Postman," the captain called on the radiophone. "We're at datum. Nothing yet. We're still looking."

"Roger, Postman," the carrier replied. "We don't think he's injured, but can't be sure. A crewman reported he thought the man was swimming before we lost sight of him."

All the lookouts and the watch team peered into the gloom. The whitecap from each breaking wave seemed to flash a sighting, then disappear into the swell like a pop-up target in a carnival shooting gallery.

"Sir," the bridge-talker yelled, "bow lookout reports a life ring off the starboard bow. Says he thinks he can see the guy hanging on to it."

"Mike, I have the conn," Captain Clark said. "Get down to the whaleboat and stand by to launch."

"He'll blow this one, Captain," the XO said. "I know he will. Send an experienced officer. This is no time for amateurs."

"Gangway," Mike yelled, heading for the ladder. He slid down four deck levels hitting every third or fourth step. Sailors along the way flattened themselves against the bulkheads to avoid a collision with two hundred pounds of charging ensign.

Mike reached the motor whaleboat and jumped in as the boat crew lowered it into the waves and cast off. Dutton steered where *Bartley's* searchlight pointed. The whaleboat, once clear of the ship, took on icy water from the breaking wave tops. The boat pitched and gyrated like a rodeo bronco released from its chute. In seconds, the whaleboat's motor coughed once and died. Engineman Anderson stared at Mike, momentarily frozen.

"Get the damned thing running, Andy," Coxswain Dutton screamed. "This is no time to screw up."

"What's the problem?" Mike yelled at Anderson over the wind.

Anderson squatted behind the whaleboat's engine control console and jiggled some levers before he threw his hands up in exasperation. "I think it's flooded," he hollered over the noise of the wind and the sea.

"Fix it, dammit," Dutton screamed.

Anderson tried two restarts. Nothing.

"Try again," Mike hollered. His anger flared at the debacle. The motor had to run or any chance for a successful recovery would be lost. What could he do?

The motor turned and coughed, hesitated, then roared at full throttle. The whaleboat jumped ahead into the breaking waves. Dutton steered toward the illuminated area.

"Mister K, your life vest," Dutton yelled over the engine's roar. He pointed to a kapok vest under one of the boat's thwarts. Mike reached under the wooden bench for the vest never taking his eyes off the turbulent seas.

"I see him," a whaleboat crewman shouted and pointed to their right. Mike dropped the life jacket and craned his head toward he ocean. He spotted the survivor on an up-swell. The sailor in the water held on to the life ring with both arms, his back to the whaleboat. Mike shuddered. The man had been in the icy water at least ten minutes. In another five, maybe sooner, he would be helpless to aid his own rescue. Mike offered a silent prayer for the man to hold on. They would reach him soon.

The whaleboat, broadside to the wind, closed in on the life ring. Both boat and life ring bobbed in the waves. A crewman did his best to keep a hand-held battle lantern pointed at the waterlogged sailor.

The man in the water reached for the light. A wave broke over him. His hold on the life ring released.

Mike's stomach wrenched. He dived into the blackness taking in a mouthful of salty ocean when he hit the icy water. He spit out the sea water and fought for the surface and a gulp of air. He reached toward the disappearing hand. Another wave broke in his face. His foot hit something. He sucked in a quick, deep breath then doubled over, reached down and around him. Nothing. One more try. Mike swung his arm in an arc. Clothing. His hand gripped clothing. The struggle back to the surface, pulling the limp body, seemed endless.

Mike raised the survivor's head above water in a wave trough and swam as best he could to keep them both afloat. The cold numbed him.

A serene sensation as if floating well above the scene overtook Mike. He seemed to be looking down at the ocean below, at a swimmer struggling toward a life ring that grew no closer.

The brief otherworld vision vanished when Mike's hand hit the life ring but knocked it away. Again waves bobbed the ring away from his cold fingers. He swallowed another mouthful of icy ocean. He couldn't hold on to the man much longer. He needed rest. Then, his hand hit something solid. He gripped the ring.

A blinding floodlight exploded from the enshrouding world of black. Startled, Mike had forgotten the possibility of rescue assistance from the helicopter crew. He hadn't recognized the helo's engine and rotor roar above the raging wind and breaking seas.

The helo hovered over Mike and the sailor. A rescue crewman, silhouetted against the helo's floodlight, slid down a cable into the maelstrom of swirling salt spray from the helo's downwash. Mike needed all his concentration to maintain his hold on the life ring and the man.

"I've got him. Let him go," the rescue crewman yelled in Mike's ear over the roar of the helo's engines. "You okay? Can you hang on for another minute or two?"

Mike gazed through salt-stung eyes at the helo crewman. The man's shouted words were indistinct. He nodded. Another wave top broke over them.

"Hold on to the life ring," the crewman yelled in Mike's ear. "I'll get you in a minute."

The helicopter lifted the survivor through the swirling spume. Mike lost sight of him, blinded by the helo's floodlight. He tried to kick. Had his legs even moved? His fingers wouldn't. He could see his right hand gripping the life ring but he couldn't feel it. He spit out some of the next wave that washed over him. His breathing slowed. Then, the helo's rescue crewman was beside him again.

The crewman helped Mike into the horse-collar-shaped rescue sling. Fuzzy and disquieting sensations followed the man's solid pat on his shoulder ... the pull of the sling around his shoulders ... being lifted ... distant voices ... words he didn't understand. Someone pulled him into the helo's open hatch, onto a solid floor. He couldn't feel his hands or feet. Mike glanced at a hazy image. Another man was pulled through the helo's hatch and sat next to Mike on the vibrating deck in a dripping exposure suit. He leaned close to Mike's ear.

"How're you doing?" the rescue crewman said above the tumult of engine noise and the rotor's throbbing beat. Mike's eyes registered multiple images. A sudden vile taste signaled his stomach might lose its contents. Someone threw a blanket around him. Time lost all measure.

A mild jolt, then the quieting of the helo's engine followed. Two men helped Mike onto the carrier's flight deck. He stumbled. Another man grabbed him, threw a fresh blanket around him and led him, staggering, toward the protection of the carrier's island structure. The man he'd helped rescue was lifted onto a stretcher.

Mike spent the night in the carrier's sick bay. Dry clothes, a warm shower, a solid night's sleep and a good breakfast restored him. The doctors and several of the carrier's officers and crew visited him and thanked him for his efforts for one of their own. The sailor he recovered wasn't able to offer gratitude. He didn't survive.

14

BEFORE HE WAS FLOWN TO *Bartley* the next morning, Mike watched the carrier's first launch cycle from his seat in the hovering helicopter. Minutes later, the helo lowered him in a rescue sling onto *Bartley's* fantail. He waved his thanks and scrambled into the ship's aft superstructure.

Neither Mike's second cup of coffee nor the warmth of *Bartley's* wardroom relieved his depression at the outcome of the rescue attempt. He welcomed the compliments of Riley and the other officers, but their comments didn't cheer him. The supportive wardroom atmosphere changed when the XO joined the luncheon table.

"I see our would-be hotshot's back," the XO said in a derisive voice. "Those fly-boys treat you right on the flattop, Mister?"

The words might have been congenial enough in an exchange between friends. The XO's smirk and the taunting inflection in his voice told a different story. Mike knew the pattern, a precursor to another belittling tirade.

"Yes, sir." Mike flexed his fist.

"I understand the sailor didn't make it thanks to your sorry performance," the XO said. "Your amateur screwing around in the boat—"

"Lay off," Riley said. "He made a damned good effort."

"Little slow getting to him, were you, Mister?" the XO continued. "I'm not surprised. And jumping into the water has to be the dumbest move I've seen. Only an idiot would pull a stupid stunt like that in this weather. The man would have survived if you hadn't—"

"That's enough," Captain Clark snapped with a scowl and a tone that said shut up. "Mike made a tough decision. He risked his life. I'm proud of him. He's earned our respect, not some cheap crap from you. Understand?"

"Yes, sir." The XO withered in his seat at the captain's stern words, but flashed a sour glance at Mike.

Writing to Carol that evening, Mike had been tempted to include the cartoon Fingers had drawn of the rescue. The crew had nicknamed Fingers' frequent drawings "Fingerprints." Fingers' hobby had become an irregular, humorous addition to the bulletin board in the crew's mess whenever an incident prompted him to draw. The cartoon depicted Mike as a hero. Mike didn't feel like a hero, but he enjoyed the drawing.

If he included the cartoon he'd have to do some explaining. He wanted to describe the stormy seas, the problem with the whaleboat, the helo lift, and his treatment on the carrier. He didn't include the cartoon. He chose words to minimize any threat there had been to him. He hoped Carol didn't read between the lines.

Mike reread what he had written one final time before he sealed the envelope. He couldn't change the facts. He'd tried to save the man. He'd failed.

The images and sensations of his struggle in the water persisted unbidden. His mind relived the cold, the thrashing to stay afloat, and the struggle to reach the elusive life ring. The images faded. He sat back and relaxed in a way he hadn't experienced before. The many years of frightening dreams with long-imagined scenes of his father's wartime tragedy, that had so often awakened him were no more. Was he now free to be his own man?

15

LESS THAN A WEEK REMAINED in *Bartley's* third extended-operation period with the seven-ship carrier task group. Mike, as officer-of-the-deck in training, had run each of their joint watches, while Riley observed his every move and injected random and unexpected tests of Mike's skill and knowledge.

The subtle contest with Riley inspired Mike. He tried to anticipate what Riley's next gambit would be in their unspoken game. Often, Mike could guess what Riley would throw at him next. About ninety percent of those tasks were successfully accomplished.

Mike hadn't expected the captain to allow Riley to be his only coach. Any one of the several other OOD-qualified officers could have trained him. Their "teaching" consisted of teasing Mike about the mistakes he made. He didn't mind being the target for their random jibes and enjoyed the attention.

Captain Clark joined them on the open bridge and settled into his pedestal chair on the port side. He braced himself against the ship's motion and wedged his coffee mug in a corner next to the windscreen. Like Mike, he seemed to enjoy watching the planes land on the aircraft carrier. He waved Riley over to him.

"I signed your letter this morning," the captain said to Riley. "Don't know how fast Washington will act on it. Soon, I hope."

"Thanks, Captain," Riley said. "I appreciate it."

The captain motioned Riley closer and, in a subdued voice, continued their brief conversation. Mike moved to the starboard wing where the wind's constant roar put him out of earshot.

Mike maneuvered *Bartley* to remain on plane guard station behind the carrier through another course change and subsequent aircraft launch-and-recovery cycle. At one point it seemed to Mike that Captain Clark paid more attention to his ship handling than to the landing aircraft. He dismissed the thought as overactive imagination.

"What devious test have you two planned for me this time?" Mike taunted Riley after Captain Clark left the bridge. His smile belied the irritation in his words.

"You wanted to get qualified. You have to prove you can do the job." Riley's stern words failed to mask the smile that twisted his monster mustache.

"It's none of my business, of course," Mike said, "but what letter was the captain talking about?"

"Captain's been on me to stick around, you know, stay on active duty instead of shifting to civvies next spring when my Reserve time's up," Riley said.

Mike knew little of Riley's previous civilian life. Riley had made only brief mention of what he did before being recalled to active duty when the current war began, no girlfriend tales, and no family stories.

"I had the impression you weren't eager to head home, like the others are, after your active duty is up," Mike said. "You damn near never mention, what is it? Iowa? A farm? Or something like that?"

"The family farm is not for me," Riley said. "I like this life better. Let my brother take over. Besides, I like trying to pump some smarts into youngsters like you," he said with a twinkle in his eye. "With luck by this time next year I'd probably be a lieutenant, that is, if Washington accepts my letter."

"Why not go all the way?" Mike said. "If you want to make this life your career, ask Washington to swap your Reserve commission for a Regular one? You could—"

The phone rang. Riley picked up the handset.

"Bridge, OOD," Riley said. "Yes, sir." He frowned and handed the phone to Mike. He mouthed the word "captain."

"Ensign Kinkaid, sir." Mike paused to listen.

"See me in my cabin after you get off watch," Captain Clark said.

"Aye, aye, sir." Mike replaced the phone. The unexpected call puzzled him. A solo summons to the captain's cabin was rare. His first. Had to be something important, something that Clark wouldn't talk about earlier.

"Captain wants to see me in his cabin when I get off watch," Mike said to Riley glancing at his watch. "Twenty minutes to go. What do you suppose he wants?"

"Don't know." Riley shrugged. "You lose any more classified pubs lately?" The overgrown mustache could not hide Riley's teasing grin.

After Mike was relieved from the watch, he gripped the handrails on the ladders for stability as *Bartley* rolled in the stormy seas and hurried down the two decks to the captain's cabin. He paused outside the door. His mind cycled through his activities for the past several days to uncover some omission, error, or oversight. He wanted to be prepared. As far as he could tell, none of the events warranted a summons. All the radio equipment worked. He knew of no classified publications issues. Any new documents or changes to *Bartley's* current collection would not be available until the ship returned to port. All message traffic had been handled without a hitch. All bases were covered. What did Captain Clark want?

"Come in," Clark said at Mike's knock. "Sit down." He pointed to the chair next to his desk.

Mike hadn't anticipated an invitation to sit, and hesitated before he moved to the chair. Riley's jest about a missing document flashed through his mind. Another problem? If so, this was a strange way for the captain to raise the issue. Maybe Washington had sent another critical message? No, Pops would have made sure Mike had seen it first.

The captain placed his pipe in the ashtray before he picked up the top sheet from a small paper pile on his desk. He appeared relaxed. No evident anger.

"You've seen the recent message traffic about the fleet's officer shortage," Clark said. "As you know, three of our reserve officers leave in the next month. We've heard no word about their replacements."

"Yes, sir," Mike replied. "I've read the traffic." What did the other officers' departure have to do with him?

"I doubt we'll see face-to-face turnovers," the captain said. "We can expect to deal with empty billets for a while. Some may stay vacant for months. When replacements do arrive, chances are good they'll be green, inexperienced. We'll have to train them."

"Yes, sir. I understand." Mike leaned back in the chair. The captain's congenial lead-in indicated he wasn't upset. Still, why had he been invited to a private session?

A sudden caution caught Mike. This wasn't the captain's usual, concise, no-nonsense manner. Some recent message traffic to other ships and stations in the past six weeks contained orders for officers with special qualifications to transfer to fill vital holes. Had he been an unlucky one selected for transfer to fill another ship's vacancy? He held no special qualification that would warrant such a move.

"Most new officers," the captain said, "take anywhere from six months to two years to qualify as an officer-of-the deck underway."

"Yes, sir, I know." Mike's anxiety grew. Could his vital qualification be in jeopardy? He'd worked hard to qualify. Riley said he'd made good progress. Had the XO's constant harping prejudiced a decision?

"I've decided to make an exception in your case, Mike." The captain picked up his pipe, saw that it was dead. After a casual refill with fresh tobacco, a relight and a couple of puffs, the captain continued.

Mike held his breath.

"I've been impressed with how fast and how well you've learned the OOD business," Captain Clark said. "We've recently lost some good ship handlers. We lose more in the next few months. I need to fill the void. I can qualify you today, earlier than normal, with a clear conscience." The captain pointed to the document on his desk. "A qualification letter will go into your record tonight, with a copy to Washington when we hit port. Congratulations." Clark extended his hand. A broad smile followed.

Mike was speechless, open-mouthed. He had known he would qualify as officer-of-the-deck in time, maybe in six months or so, but not this soon.

"Thank you, sir." Stunned, and at a loss for what else to say, Mike stood and reached out to accept the handshake. The captain motioned him to sit again.

"Riley tells me you're ready," Captain Clark said. "I agree. I plan to give you your own watch team. You'll begin with our next underway period in about two weeks, after our in-port period in Yokosuka. Keep in mind that during your OOD watches you're second only to me in command of this ship and its operations. You'll have the mission and the lives of 176 men in your hands. Call me if you're ever in doubt about anything. Don't hesitate. Delay can cost lives in some instances and embarrassment in others. It's a big responsibility. I'm convinced you can handle it."

Mike nodded. Second in command while OOD on watch? He half rose from the chair but the ship rolled, he lost his balance and fell back into the seat. The captain smiled and motioned him to stay.

"I've observed you with some interest, Mike," Clark continued. "I know your duty obligation is four years. I want you to think about a career. You have the makings of a superb surface force officer, and someday your own command."

Mike's stomach twisted. He appreciated the compliment. His father would have been proud. But he couldn't accept shipboard life as his future. Somehow he would fly.

"Thank, you sir," Mike said. "I appreciate your confidence in me. I won't let you down."

Mike sat alone at the quiet wardroom table after his mid-watch, a second cup of coffee at his elbow. Carol had to know the good news. At last he had something positive he could share. He stared at the far bulkhead and saw visions of Carol. He chewed on his pencil's eraser for a moment envisioning how he would have shared the excitement with her had she been here. His mind drifted to the motivation within him. His dream was closer now.

His letter to her that evening was an easy one to write.

The captain approved my qualification as OOD tonight. It came as a shock. It's effective immediately. I've worked hard for the OOD qualification. It's the best thing that has happened to me since you said, "I do." The paperwork goes to Washington once we get into port. They'll have it when I reapply to fly. So, Honey, the major barrier to flight training is behind us. Wish I were there to celebrate and hold you close. We'll have our special celebration after I get home. It's been too long already. We expect a return to the States soon, I'm told, but nothing firm yet...

The XO said little at dinner that evening, a welcome respite from his usual barbs and sarcasm. At the end of the meal he motioned to Mike to follow him.

Mike flashed a glance at Riley. Riley's raised eyebrows and slight sideways head tilt signaled the move surprised him, too.

Once in his stateroom, the XO spun around to face Mike. "I see the captain qualified you," he said, the words spoken in a rush, evident strain in his voice. "Didn't ask me first." The shoulder tick emphasized the statement. "Let's get this straight, Kinkaid. I told the captain he's made a mistake. You're not qualified. You aren't ready. For my money, you will never be OOD material."

Mike stood silent. Tight jaw muscles and a flexing left fist helped to control the defiance that rose within him. He'd earned the qualification, despite the XO's hurdles and bad-mouthing. Did the captain share the same dim view of the XO that the other officers held?

"I'll watch," the XO said and shook his finger at Mike. "You screw up, even a little bit, and you're dead meat."

16

THEIR FIRST NIGHT IN PORT, Mike joined the other *Bartley* officers for a raucous Sunday night farewell party back at the Yokosuka Naval Base Officers' Club. Two more of *Bartley's* reserve officers would be released from active duty the next morning to return home to civilian life. Two others had been released earlier, also without replacements. Mike envied their opportunity. He wasn't interested in returning to civilian life, but would welcome some time, even as little as a day, to be with Carol again. The departure of the two reservists resulted in both bad news and good news for Mike.

On the negative side, Mike and the other officers would absorb the workload of the officers being detached. On the positive side, the departure of these two made possible a welcome move for Mike from The Pit's tomb-like environment into the smallest stateroom in forward officers' country, the series of sleeping quarters forward of the wardroom. Until other replacement officers reported to *Bartley*, he'd have the smallest of them to himself.

Mike moved into the new stateroom Monday morning. The room had the usual double bunk, one chair, a small wardrobe locker, a cabinet with six drawers, and a pull-down desktop. The cramped forward officers' head, three paces away across the narrow passageway, held a toilet, a shower, and a washbasin. Best of all, the new quarters on the main deck level, had a porthole and an eight-inch air-supply duct in the overhead. The air duct proved to be noisy, but Mike considered the greater air volume a positive trade-off. Daylight and ample fresh air in the room raised his spirits.

Describing his stateroom to Carol he included, "...*the pale green paint on the bulkhead and overhead matches the wardroom, a big improvement over the deadly gray of The Pit. It's small and cozy. Needs a woman's touch...*" Cramped, equivalent to a closet, would have been more accurate. He'd also have to get used to the new array of sounds, especially the 1-MC speaker, mounted in the passageway about six feet forward of his stateroom and used around the clock for general ship announcements. For now, at least he had no snoring bunkmates.

Mike didn't expect to see Riley until noon or later. About 0930, a bleary-eyed Riley shuffled through the flimsy green curtain at the doorway to Mike's new quarters and sat on the lower bunk. He rested his head on his hands, elbows on his knees, to shade his eyes from the brilliant sun that streamed through the porthole. His extended silence puzzled Mike.

"I suppose you noticed the way the XO fell into the rum at the party last night," Mike said to jump-start the conversation. "I'm surprised he lasted through dinner." He paused for a reaction from Riley.

Riley didn't respond. Had Riley heard his comment? Slow breathing confirmed Riley still lived.

"Too bad Washington won't listen," Mike said. Still no reaction from Riley.

"What?" Riley's head raised in slow motion as though from a deep sleep. He shielded his eyes with his left hand to block the sunlight.

"Washington won't send us another XO," Mike said.

"Oh, that." Riley's hand wandered over his hair, his face vacant. His head dropped back on doubled fists. "Washington doesn't care," Riley mumbled. A long pause followed. "They could find somebody if they wanted to."

"Not this time," Mike said. "The captain asked Washington for a replacement for the XO again. Washington turned him down again."

Riley's head came up, faster this time.

"What? You holding back on me?"

Mike tensed. He'd promised to keep Riley informed. This time he'd neglected to tell Riley about the message from Washington, received as the ship arrived in port the day before. He'd given the message to Captain Clark. Pops had been the only other man on board who knew of the rejection.

"Dammit, Mike." Riley grabbed the bunk railing in an effort to stand. He sank back down, hands over his eyes. "Dammit, Mike, we agreed. No secrets. Don't do that again. Understand?" Riley's head lowered before he spoke again. "I had trouble following the XO's jabbering last night. Tuned him out after dinner. Couldn't get him to shut up about his brother, and the collision, and—"

"Wish he'd drop it," Mike interrupted. "He's convinced my father caused his brother's death. He didn't."

"Suppose you tell him what you know?"

Mike caught a hint of anticipation in Riley's bleary eyes.

"He won't believe me," Mike said. "His mind's made up." How could he get Riley to drop the subject?

"What did you expect?" Riley said. "You've managed to make him look stupid a time or two, you know."

"What do I expect?" Mike snapped. "I'll tell you, dammit. I expect a fair shake, measured on my own performance. He tried to block my OOD qualification. He sure as hell won't support a request for flight school. It's another no-win."

"Sit down." Riley pointed to Mike's chair. "Yelling at me doesn't help your case."

"Riley, drop it. It's my problem, not yours."

Mid-morning the next day Pops handed Mike a message form containing unexpected orders for Captain Clark. Mike's jaw dropped at the first line of the brief message. He folded the sheet and hurried to find the captain.

Clark opened his cabin door at Mike's first knock. Mike handed him the message, impatient for a reaction.

The captain glanced at the brief message as though it would be something routine then did a double take. He moved to his desk chair, sat, and studied the orders. He flipped the message form over as though more information might be on the reverse side. He seemed to check his desk calendar. His pencil scratched some notes on a pad.

"I'll have to scramble to make this deadline reporting date." The captain held up the message form. "Leave by Monday at the latest." He gazed at Mike in an apparent daze then waved Mike away.

"Orders for the captain just came in," Mike said to Riley who was reading at his stateroom desk. "He told me he had to be on his way by Monday. He'll have to be relieved before he can go, won't he? I guess that means we'll see a new captain before long."

"Damn," Riley said. "I hope it's good news for him. He deserves it. But it's bad news, for us for sure. He's the best." Riley rubbed the back of his neck. "Where is he going next?"

"Newport News. To the shipyard," Mike said. "I didn't recognize the ship's name."

"New construction, I'll bet," Riley said, his mustache dancing over his wide grin. "Great. He's earned it. That's a damned prestigious assignment, maybe even better than a promotion." He'll be able to have his family with him too.

Mike felt a brief tightening his throat. When would he see his own family?

Mike and Riley joined the other officers in the wardroom for an impromptu meeting. Captain Clark read aloud the message about his pending transfer, and told them the orders surprised him, too. He had no reason to expect orders until sometime after *Bartley* returned to her home port in San Diego, estimated to be in about six weeks. Because of frequent and unpredictable changes, any "schedule" had become a standing joke.

"What about your relief, Captain?" Riley asked.

The captain focused on Mike. Did he expect him to hand over orders on a replacement? Mike didn't respond. Captain Clark sighed and shook his head.

"We'll just have to wait and see," Clark said, and waved his hand to dismiss the officers.

"This is crazy," Riley said to Mike leaving the wardroom. "Someone has to be in the pipeline to relieve the captain. A commanding officer can't just leave without a replacement. We can. He can't. Whoever is coming to relieve him had better hustle."

Wednesday morning, Mike pushed aside one of Riley's paper piles to make room for some new mail, a fresh mug of coffee, and two of the four oatmeal cookies he'd liberated from the wardroom pantry.

The XO had assigned a paperwork blizzard to the officers to prepare for an imminent command turnover. Mike considered himself lucky. He had only two reports to complete along with the required classified publications inventory.

"Is the XO all over you, too?" Mike said. "What's his hurry with all these reports anyway? We don't even know who the new captain will be, let alone when we'll see him."

Riley ran his fingers over the lined, yellow tablet on his desk. In the past weeks he had become both sonar officer and assistant operations officer after other officers had departed without replacement. The reports for both jobs were now his. He ran his palm over his close-cropped head, slammed his fist on the desktop then swung around in his chair.

"I don't get it," Riley said. "There's nothing wrong with the last sonar report. The XO rejected that one too. 'Do the damned reports over,' he says. 'Not good enough,' he says. The gutless bastard doesn't know enough about our installation to even spell sonar." Riley ripped the top sheet from the tablet. The wadded page joined scattered yellow-paper balls on the deck near the overflowing wastebasket.

Mike bit into a cookie and chuckled to himself at Riley's well-known disdain for paperwork. He had to admit Riley wasn't alone in chafing over what appeared to be the XO's make-work effort. All the officers griped.

"If Captain Clark wasn't due for orders," Mike said, "this command change is a bit sudden, isn't it?"

"Don't know," Riley said. "Doesn't really matter. It's a boost for Clark's career. Command of a new ship under construction is a real feather in his cap."

Mike leaned against the doorframe, sipped his coffee and munched his last cookie. He had expected to stand his first watch as a new OOD while Captain Clark was in command of *Bartley*. What would the new captain be like? The officers and crew worshipped Clark. Whoever replaced him would have big shoes to fill.

"Why haven't we heard a word about a new captain?" Mike said. "I'll bet that new ship has been under construction for at least a year, probably more. Washington had plenty of time to find a replacement captain for us."

"I'm stumped, too," Riley said and gobbled his cookie. "If you allow for travel time, the Captain Clark has to leave before we get underway on Monday or else he'll have to kiss the new command goodbye. That's five days, dammit. That's too quick."

Radioman Fingers dashed into Riley's stateroom and avoided by a millimeter spilling Mike's coffee. "Figured you might be here," Fingers gasped. "Here you are, Mister K," he said and waved a message form, "orders on the new captain."

Mike read aloud that Lieutenant Commander Louis Cavallo, USNR, would become *Bartley's* new commanding officer. He handed the copy to Riley.

"Damn, There's no reporting date on these orders." Riley shook his head. His slight frown reflected Mike's own concern. Would Cavallo arrive in time to conduct a command turnover and let Captain Clark be on his way on Monday?

"Clark can't detach without a relief by someone designated to be in command," Riley said. "No one on board is qualified to command, certainly not the XO."

"What happens if this new captain doesn't report before Monday?" Mike said.

"Clark has no choice. He has to stay," Riley said. "A delay could cost him his new assignment."

Mike took the message orders about Cavallo to Captain Clark's cabin. The captain read the message twice. He stared at is desk calendar for a moment, scribbled a note on a pad then reread the orders. His brow furrowed with signs of strain around his eyes.

"Anything else?" the captain asked, a subtle search for more information in his voice.

"No, sir," Mike replied. "Not yet."

Friday after lunch, Mike checked the latest messages in the radio shack before he left the ship. Nothing had been received regarding Cavallo's schedule. He headed ashore to the Navy Exchange for some personal items.

On his return to the radio shack, Mike asked Pops if there was any word on the new captain."

"He's on board now, Mister K," Pops said. "Came aboard just after you left. Sure surprised us. Captain Clark had gone ashore. I understand today's Duty Officer, Mister Riley, is touring him around. Don't know when Captain Clark will be back."

That evening after dinner Mike moved aside some of Riley's paper piles and plopped on his lower bunk.

"Spill it. What happened? I'm surprised he didn't stay around and talk with the rest of us," Mike said to Riley. "What kind of man is he?"

"Don't think he's the chatty type," Riley said. "Too bad the captain was ashore. Cavallo said he expected Clark to be at the quarterdeck to meet him. Being the duty officer, I ended up herding him around. As much as he wanted to see, that is."

"How would you describe him?" Mike said."

"Short, about the XO's height, but porky. Olive skin, balding. And, gruff." Riley seemed to weigh his words as though unsure. "He's no talker. Couldn't figure him out. I'm uneasy. He has a tic in his right eye that has me curious. He said nothing about his background. I'll hold off on any judgment for now."

"I presume Cavallo knows Captain Clark has to leave before we get underway on Monday morning," Mike said "They don't have much time for a turnover. Did Cavallo say anything to you about that?"

"Not a word," Riley said.

"What did you show him? Mike asked. "Did he meet any of the other officers? Is he professional like Clark?"

"We headed for Mount One up on the bow first," Riley said. "He asked damned few questions. Most were about our armament. Not a word about the officers or crew. He wouldn't answer my questions so I quit asking. Fortunately, Captain Clark came back and took over."

"What about the change of command?" Mike said. "I heard it's in the morning. Isn't that damned quick? I figured turnover would take at least a day or two."

"About a half-hour after they left the wardroom," Riley said, "Captain Clark called me. 'Pass the word to all hands,' he says. 'Change-of-command ceremony is tomorrow morning at 1130.' Guess we better get into the habit of saying Captain Cavallo." Riley grimaced.

A chill October overcast threatened rain Saturday morning. Mike, along with all officers and crew not on watch, stood in formation in dress uniforms on the pier, attentive and curious. The ceremony provided their first good look at Captain Cavallo. The short, overweight man who would lead them appeared unkempt in his ill-fitting, dress uniform.

Captain Clark gave succinct and complimentary comments then read his orders aloud in keeping with the traditional format. Captain Cavallo read his orders next. He faced Captain Clark, spoke the critical words, "I relieve you, sir," and thanked Captain Clark.

Contrary to the normal practice for new commanding officers, Captain Cavallo made no additional comments to the gathered crew. "XO, Dismiss the crew," he ordered ending the all-too-brief ceremony.

The expressions of the officers and men as they crossed the gangway from the dock to the ship gave Mike no indication of what they thought. As if by common agreement, they maintained silence. The first opportunity for ship's company to witness the new commanding officer had proven to be a non-event.

"The entire crew are keepin' an eye on this new boss," Pops said to Mike that afternoon, "lookin' to see what sort of captain we've got, and what changes he's going to make. Nothing to report yet, but my gut is a bit queasy."

Mike and the other officers exchanged quiet comments about the captain's every action and utterance to get some sense of how to deal with him. What sort of man was he? What could the crew expect from him in the months ahead? Riley had described him as prickly and blunt. The signs were not encouraging.

Riley pulled Mike aside in the wardroom before dinner. "Have you heard?" he said in a low whisper.

"About what?" Mike said.

"About the new watch-standing plan."

"Dammit, Riley. Quit stalling," Mike said. "Have I heard what?"

Riley motioned to hush Mike.

"Our sour-puss, new captain," Riley said "has decreed we form three watch teams and go to a one-in-three rotation for the rest of the deployment. That's both in port and underway. That means we stand the regular four-hour hitches, but at the same times each day instead of the staggering plan we've used up to now. Starts tomorrow."

"But…" Mike stammered. His stomach tightened. He'd expected to have his own team as Captain Clark had promised. Where would he fit with only three teams? Had his new OOD qualification been disregarded?

"So I talked with the XO," Riley said, "you know, about the new team makeup. Made a suggestion or two." Riley's voice carried an upbeat note. He paused as though expecting to be interrupted.

"He's formed the three teams for the captain's okay," Riley continued. "You know, the same bridge and CIC duty team each watch instead of the constant mix we've worked with until now. Each team stands one in three. He's eliminated the two-hour dog-watches we used to have. Since I'm the senior watch stander, I'll have a team. Sterling and Davis each will have a team. I picked the afternoon and mid-watches for starters."

Mike experienced a moment of panic. What about his own recent OOD qualification? How come he didn't have a team? Mike's jaws clenched at the realization he might be paired with someone other than Riley.

"Who's your JOOD?" Mike asked. He made no effort to hide his anger.

"My guess is the XO will assign Ensign Brooks since he's the newest junior officer." Riley's grin confirmed that he'd read Mike's disappointment. "So I suggested he put you and me on the same team."

"Thanks," Mike said, irritated that Riley had succeeded once again in giving him a hard time.

"We alternate bridge and CIC watches. Sterling will do the same. I haven't talked to Davis yet."

Mike checked for Riley's penchant to kid him. This wasn't a time for kidding or a topic to joke about.

"And? Now what?"

"The XO said no."

"Why not?" Mike's flash of anger died when he recognized the sparkle in Riley's eyes.

"He says you're not qualified," Riley continued as though not aware of Mike's reactions. "Says he told Captain Cavallo early on. You know he'll still try to find some way to kill your qualification. But don't worry. He'll see things our way," Riley paused while stroking his mustache, "after I mentioned it might be difficult to keep my mouth shut about the Sunny incident."

17

THE FOLLOWING MONDAY, *BARTLEY* SAILED mid-morning. Mike stood the 1200-1600 watch on the bridge, his first underway watch as a qualified officer-of-the-deck. Riley opted to take the supporting duty in the combat information center (CIC) to begin Cavallo's new one-in-three duty rotation plan.

Mike vowed to be extra attentive and stand an error-free watch. Sunday, he'd studied the governing operation order and memorized the procedural changes required by the new task group *Bartley* would join off Korea's east coast on Wednesday. He went over the notes he'd taken in the past months under Riley's tutelage.

Mike realized an unexpected thrill as he gave his first maneuvering orders. He'd worked for this qualification, a key step in meeting the Navy's requirements.

Midway through the watch, Captain Cavallo appeared.

"Good afternoon, sir," Mike said. "We're on course 042 making turns for seventeen knots. We join the task group Wednesday at 0515. We change course at 1710 to—"

"I know all that." The captain's jaw up-tilted like someone ready to pick a fight.

The curt reply to Mike's report raised a warning and contrasted with the congenial responses Captain Clark had given to similar routine reports. Did this captain want status reports omitted in the future? Mike's instinct told him not to ask. Just keep mum.

Cavallo heaved his bulk into the captain's chair, opened a folder, put on his glasses, and ignored the others on the bridge.

Mike remained uneasy although the afternoon passed without incident. Captain Cavallo had stared at him for several lengthy periods, however. Mike re-checked everything each time. All was as it should be.

"Mister Kinkaid," the captain said with fifteen minutes of the watch remaining.

"Yes, sir?" Mike crossed to the captain.

"The XO tells me you got your OOD qualification a week ago," Captain Cavallo said. "One of Clark's parting shots, I understand. The XO says he objected. Doesn't think you're ready. Are you?"

The unexpected challenge, spoken as an accusation, jarred Mike. His throat tightened in a momentary panic at the possibility that his qualification might be revoked. Whatever the XO said must have been damning.

"Yes, sir," Mike said in as confident a manner as he could muster. "Captain Clark qualified me."

"You're not listening," the captain snapped, his right eyebrow twitching. "Pay attention. That's not what I asked you, Mister."

Mike squared his shoulders. He wouldn't be intimidated.

"Yes, sir. I can handle the responsibility and stand a good watch." Mike straightened himself up a little taller and focused down into Cavallo's black eyes. "I'm ready, sir."

"We'll see," the captain said and went back to his papers.

The next day, Mike stood on the bridge on a quiet 1200-1600 watch. He relaxed as *Bartley* steamed alone in fair weather toward the rendezvous with the carrier task group. The meager warmth and the ocean's calm surface with a gentle swell offered a pleasant change to the early winter weather of recent weeks.

Mike looked around at the others on the open bridge. Each man displayed the same hypnotized reaction to the ship's gentle rolling motion and the unexpected warmer weather. He shook his shoulders and circled the open space twice to stay alert. Mike couldn't let the XO catch anyone on his team lax in any way.

Ensign Brooks had been assigned as the new Junior Officer-of-the-Deck for Mike and Riley's watch team as Riley had predicted. Brooks stared at the ocean in a semi-trance.

"Mister Brooks," Mike said to break the spell. "Take a tour around topside. Be sure the watch standers are on their toes. We might get one of the XO's sneak peeks any time, you know."

Brooks yawned, offered Mike a grin and a thumbs-up, then descended the ladder to the wheelhouse to begin his rounds.

"Tucker," Mike said to the enlisted man who controlled the sound-powered phone circuit, "give the lookouts another wake-up call. I want them to stay alert."

"Where are we going, Mister K?" Tucker asked after he'd completed the call to the lookouts.

"We'll join a different task group up north," Mike said, "off Korea's east coast. Don't know what's next. Guess we'll find out after we get there."

"Sounds like the same old stuff," Tucker said. "I figured you knew that me and the crew want to see some action. We're tired of this steaming around in circles chasing flattops like we been doing these past few months. If the admiral won't let us go home, we all want to get on with doing our part to stop the Commies."

"Let's wait and see, Tuck," Mike said with a grin. He shared Tucker's attitude. "We're bound to get some action soon." But would they? *Bartley's* assignments so far had been more of the same with little hope for change.

"Bridge, aye," Seaman Tucker said into his phone set fifteen minutes later. "What's it like?" He ambled toward the bridge's starboard wing to see what the lookout had reported.

"Sir," Tucker called to Mike, "Bow lookout reports something in the water dead ahead. Says he can't make it out from here. Some dark trash bobbing in the water, covered with gunk, maybe seaweed."

Mike strode the ten feet to the bridge wing and brought up his binoculars. Even a small diversion on an otherwise quiet watch helped to pass the time. The mystery item came into view. The object rode low in the water. It alternately appeared and disappeared in the slight swell. Mike judged it to be bathtub size, maybe an oil drum, black.

On an up-swell Mike picked up a glimpse of protrusions from the object, possibly detonator rods.

"Emergency left full rudder," Mike yelled into the voice tube to the wheelhouse. "All engines stop. Sound general quarters." The blaring alarm immediately engulfed the entire ship. He spun around to Brooks. "Get the captain up here. It's a floating mine."

The ship's bow swung to port in response to the rudder order. Mike held his breath. The forward momentum in the turn put the stern on a path that could strike the mine sideways, a reaction similar to a skid on a highway. Did he have enough time to avoid the threat?

"Shift your rudder," Mike ordered. "All engines emergency back full." Mike didn't wait for the required confirming response from the helmsman in the wheelhouse.

Bartley closed the mine fast like opposing freeway traffic. Mike could see the menace approach now without the aid of binoculars, its protruding firing rods clearly evident.

Bartley's twin rudders and twin propellers took effect but far too slowly for Mike. The bow hesitated before it started a casual swing to starboard as might a reluctant teenager avoiding a distasteful chore. Mike held his breath and prayed that the sidestep maneuver would work.

"Rudder amidships. Steady as she goes," Mike ordered.

He couldn't take his eyes off the mine less than one hundred yards ahead. The vibrations from *Bartley's* engines, in reverse at full power, shook the ship like a wet dog after a bath. Mike held his breath. He willed the engines to stop the forward motion.

The closure rate slowed.

"All stop," Mike ordered. The mine had closed to a position about twenty yards off the starboard bow. If *Bartley* maintained the present heading, the mine would pass clear but close aboard to starboard, too close to make a safe turn and far too close for safety. He had no remaining option but to pray.

"Out of the way, Kinkaid," the XO yelled. His presence startled Mike.

He hadn't noticed the man's arrival. The XO elbowed Mike aside on the starboard wing. "Gotta get that mine." He grabbed the M-1 rifle and an ammunition clip from the gun rack.

The XO made an amateurish attempt to insert the rifle's magazine. Mike gasped, stunned by the realization of the XO's intent. If the shots detonated the mine, an explosion close to *Bartley's* hull would cause serious, if not fatal, damage to the ship and crew.

"What the hell's going on, Kinkaid?" Captain Cavallo called from the top of the ladder, barefoot, his jacket thrown across his shoulders, disheveled as though he'd jumped up from a nap.

Mike snapped a glance at the captain, and pointed to the mine, close aboard, unmistakable and deadly.

The XO took aim before Mike could stop him.

The rifle didn't fire.

"Why won't this damned thing…" the XO yelled.

The rifle's safety hadn't been released. Mike reached over the XO's shoulder and snatched the rifle.

The startled XO spun around.

"What the hell are you doing?" The XO reached to grab the rifle from Mike, but froze when he saw the captain.

"We're too close," Mike said. "You'll sink us."

Mike and the others gaped in stunned silence as the mine approached ever closer. Sea growth that resembled a green bridal veil clung to the mine and floated on the surface. Its color and density obscured the mine's true shape. No one moved.

The backing engines had slowed the ship to a near stop, but *Bartley* continued to close the mine at the pace of a cat stalking a bird. Mike offered a silent prayer for the mine to pass clear of the ship's fragile three-eights-inch, steel hull plates.

Mike's call to battle stations had scrambled the crew to seal all compartments against possible flooding. He knew the precaution would be of limited value if the mine struck *Bartley* or exploded nearby. He pictured what might happen should an unsuspecting ship encounter this near-invisible threat in bad weather or at night.

The mine drifted aft of the ship about half the length of a football field during five of the longest minutes Mike had ever experienced.

"Break out some rifles," Captain Cavallo ordered the XO. "We'll have to sink this one. Can't leave that damned thing for someone else to run into."

The XO gave Mike a venomous look before he reached for the phone, but he made no effort to take back the rifle.

Mike tracked the retreating mine, expecting riflemen to appear at any moment. The XO, his shoulder tick in action, fidgeted and glanced repeatedly at the captain who wandered the bridge mumbling to himself.

"G'dammit, XO," the captain bellowed after five minutes of the crew's apparent inaction, "What are you waiting for? We can't sit here all day." Four men armed with rifles scrambled onto the aft main deck's fantail area. The XO called the fantail phone where the riflemen stood, coached them on the mine's position, and gave them permission to fire at the mine. The riflemen fired several shots without effect.

"What a sorry bunch of amateurs," the captain growled after a couple of minutes. "Dammit, XO." The captain stabbed his finger at the XO, who had been *Bartley's* gunnery officer before becoming XO. "You were supposed to train these men. You did a lousy job of it."

A wide-eyed and silent XO cringed at the criticism. They both turned back to the shooters on the fantail. The riflemen, holding their guns at ease, waited for further orders.

"I have an idea, Captain," the XO said glancing at Mike, his mouth twisted in a cruel grin. "Let's let our Deadeye here show us how it's done. You remember how he claimed some fame as a marksman in that June ambush. Let's see if he can do it again."

Trapped. Mike alternated between anger at the XO's attempt to embarrass him and the problem of hitting the mine with a rifle bullet at the extreme range. The shot would be difficult even in a dead-calm sea.

The captain cocked his head and stifled what might have been a grin. "Okay, hotshot, your turn," Captain Cavallo said to Mike. "Let's see you do your stuff."

Mike moved to a signal searchlight mounted on the wing, a firing position where he could rest the rifle. He needed to adjust his aim for the ship's slow roll. The range to the mine would have to be a guess. Mike patted the gold emblem in his pocket for good luck.

A small splash marked Mike's first shot, short by about twenty yards. His estimate of the range to the mine was at least in the ballpark.

A second shot from Mike splashed long, beyond the ominous black shape. No splash followed the third shot. The round must have hit, but no explosion. Mike fired all the remaining rounds in the ammo clip.

"I thought so," the XO said with a derisive laugh. "Your shot with Riley's convoy was pure dumb luck. I knew it all along."

An angry retort formed in Mike's throat but he choked I back. He'd made his best effort. A successful shot at this distance would be luck for anyone.

On the XO's orders the riflemen on the fantail fired several more rounds. Within three minutes one of the shots found its mark. The exploding mine shot a geyser of water into the sky and sent out expanding rings of shock waves. The ship shook and wiggled as though it had experienced a major earthquake. The crew's cheers followed the muffled underwater explosion.

"Mister Kinkaid," the XO said, hands on his hips, "the mine was big enough for you to see long before we got that close. Why didn't you and the lookouts see the damned thing sooner, much sooner? You're supposed to be a qualified OOD. You didn't stand an alert watch, did you? You weren't doing your job. Maybe doping off runs in the family."

Mike's temper flared. He almost said what flashed through his mind, but better judgment won out. What could he do to stop the XO's belittling? How could he fight back? He had done all he could under the circumstances and the XO knew it.

The clock ticked as Mike waited for a reaction from the captain. Surely the captain understood that the sidestep maneuver had saved the ship. The mine was barely visible, even during its passage a few feet from the *Bartley's* hull. Mike had no way to convince the captain that he'd stood an alert watch and had made sure all watch standers remained alert as well. They were lucky the lookout spotted the mine when he did.

The captain ignored the XO's tirade. The water disturbed by the mine's explosion held his attention for a full minute.

"Get a report out on this," the captain said to the XO. "And I want to see some practice for those amateurs of yours. They're pitiful."

"Kinkaid," the captain said, chin raised and eyebrow tic in action. "You stood a pretty sorry watch, Mister. You weren't paying attention. You damned near ran into that thing. Why didn't you alert me sooner? Can't you maneuver this ship better? The XO warned me you're not qualified. He's right. I'm pulling your qual."

Dumbfounded, Mike stood rigid and silent, his fist flexing.

"What else could we do?" Brooks said after the captain and XO had left. "We're damned lucky we could see that monster at all. I hate to think what might have happened if we had come this way in the dark."

"I have no idea." Mike's temper wouldn't allow him to say more. The surprise loss of his vital qualification had come as a shock, unjustified, and devastating. No one had given the XO credit for that much clout with the new captain.

"What did the XO mean about running in the family?" Brooks said. "I don't understand."

"Drop it," Mike said white fisted.

Within an hour, the wardroom officers learned the details of the incident on the bridge. From their comments to him, Mike judged that the captain's acceptance of the XO's bias had pushed the morale of the other officers to a new low.

"So much for rotating watches," Riley said. "At least you'll be warm on your future watches in the CIC compartment. Looks like I get to freeze on my bridge watches from now. Winter's on its way. It's going to be an early one, too."

Mike appreciated Riley's efforts to cheer him, but the unexpected loss engulfed him. He could see no avenue to regain his OOD qualification. Earning qualification from a man like Cavallo bordered on impossible. He tapped the emblem in his pocket and recalled his father's guidance to fight for his dreams. But how?

Mike tried several approaches in his letter to Carol. He didn't want to send her more bad news, but he didn't want to keep secrets. She would have to know eventually that Captain Cavallo had revoked his qualification. He trashed his first try before he'd written a page. Carol didn't need to hear of his troubles again. How could she understand if he couldn't explain the circumstances to his own satisfaction? She'd have questions he couldn't answer, the sort that needed his quick, personal response and reassurance. Nothing would be hurt if he delayed telling her.

Still angry at the bias and the captain's unfair decision, he vowed he would not accept the setback. He would regain the qualification somehow.

18

THE UNEXPECTED PRIVATE MESSAGE FROM the task group commander gave Mike an uneasy feeling when he delivered the envelope to Captain Cavallo in his stateroom. He shrugged off his premonition as tiredness. The captain waved him out of his stateroom without acknowledgement.

At lunch, Mike daydreamed of Carol.

"We have a new assignment," Cavallo muttered to the officers between bites of a salami sandwich. "We detach at sundown, back to Yoko."

The captain's words shattered the atmosphere of the near silent wardroom. The unexplained announcement surprised Mike. Curious glances confirmed that the officers expected someone to provide a reason for the schedule change. The XO remained mum. The captain continued to eat. The apparent secrecy sparked Mike's curiosity, but he held his questions so as not to risk another of Cavallo's temper outbreaks. Maybe Riley could provide answers.

"What do you suppose this is all about, this schedule change?" Mike said when he entered Riley's stateroom after lunch. "If it's a new assignment, why won't the captain say more? And what's so secret? We haven't done anything secret up to now."

"We're jinxed," Riley said. "Living with the old man is like living with a coroner. Nothing comes out of his mouth but bad news."

Pops told Mike later, in a quiet aside, that wide-ranging speculation about *Bartley's* new assignment had saturated the ship. The rumors during the two-and-a-half day return transit to Yokosuka ranged from *Bartley's* future involvement in a possible new assault landing, to chasing subs, to escorting a peace delegation.

After their watch, Mike shared coffee with Riley in the wardroom the day before they expected to tie up in Yokosuka.

"Have you found out why we detached early?" Mike said. "What mission could the admiral assign this bucket that's so damned secret?"

"I'm puzzled." Riley crossed to the coffee service for a refill. He swung back to Mike. "And Powell's pissed. As our operations officer he should be. His job is to plan all details of our operations. How in hell can he do that if the captain doesn't tell him? And why not tell all of us? We're going to do whatever it is together."

"You don't suppose we're headed back to Masan, do you?" Mike said. "Maybe home?"

Riley turned to Mike, frowning. A negative headshake answered for him.

Mike shared the somber mood that pervaded *Bartley* when the ship tied up at the Yokosuka Naval Base for a brief resupply visit. At lunch, the other officers joined the wardroom table for another meal in near-total silence, a pattern the men had adopted to avoid the captain's disdain, or, more often, his wrath. Few conversational topics were acceptable.

"Do you have the charts we need, Powell?" The captain's growl broke the silence. He remained hunched over his plate.

Lieutenant Powell swallowed a mouthful with a single gulp. He gagged, grabbed his cloth napkin and held it to his mouth, head lowered. A pause, another swallow then a sip of his coffee followed. "Uh, well, umm, yes, sir," Powell stammered.

"They'd damned well better be the latest," Cavallo muttered between forkfuls of food. Again, he didn't look at Powell when he spoke. A wave of his cup signaled the need for a coffee refill.

Mike shared inquisitive glances with Riley and the other officers. Some feigned indifference; others concentrated on their meal. The blank stares and shoulder shrugs from the other officers seemed to be confirmation that all were equally in the dark. Powell's napkin blotted his mouth in slow motion, his face slightly flushed.

"We have a complete set of charts for all the Korean coastal waters, sir," he said. "Any special ones we need?"

"Where are we headed for this next assignment, Captain?" Mike asked. Nearby officers nodded approval. "You said it's special. Special in what way?"

The officers gave their full attention to the captain. Riley's winked and offered a slight nod.

"I figured you'd know, Mister Kinkaid." The captain's eyebrow twitched. "You're the comm officer. Don't you read your messages?"

"Of course I do, sir," Mike said, "but not your personals."

The captain took his time to chew his next bite, then the next. The officers waited in silence, their eyes locked on him. "The northern patrol," Captain Cavallo said through a mouthful. "Out twenty-five to thirty days." Powell sat back in his chair. Cavallo ignored Powell and concentrated on his lunch. He raised his coffee cup to the steward again.

Powell rolled his napkin in a slow, deliberate manner, slipped the silver ring over the linen, and placed the cylinder next to his plate with an exasperated sigh.

"Captain," he said, "if you have time after lunch, can we go over the mission details? We don't want to overlook anything."

The captain grunted, downed the last of his coffee, and left the wardroom.

"What's this northern patrol business?" Mike asked Riley after lunch. "I haven't heard about it. And why is he keeping the details to himself?"

"Can't say I know the answer to that," Riley said, "but the twenty-five to thirty day part of it is what I don't like. The patrol assignment means we steam up and down the coast and freeze our butts off trying to find fishing boats."

"Why?" Mike asked. Looking for fishing boats didn't make any sense. Antisubmarine protection of the carrier task group was one of *Bartley's* missions, not chasing Gook trawlers.

"You remember the news from a couple of weeks ago, the one about the threat to our ships in Wonsan harbor?" Riley said. "They talked about floating mines endangering our ships anchored in the harbor. That mine you dodged was probably one of them. Gooks drop the mines into the coastal current north of Wonsan. The current carries the mines down into the harbor area to hit our ships. The Gooks are a sneaky bunch. I've heard some of their boats are armed. Ships like us assigned to coastal patrol are supposed to intercept and sink them."

An hour later Powell came into the radio shack and waved a message slip at Mike.

"Gimme the reference on this message," Powell demanded. The blustery, out-of-character behavior from a man noted for his calm puzzled Mike.

Mike handed the message to Fingers to get the reference from the files.

"How'd you get this one, sir?" Fingers held the message to his chest, his head cocked, squinting eyes locked on Powell. Mike and the entire radio gang had strict orders not to reveal the captain's personal messages without his express permission.

"From Cavallo," Powell said. "He gave it to me." "I don't want to miss a detail. Still don't understand why the old man didn't let me know about this change sooner. He should know by now that we do thorough pre-planning for all our operations."

"The message is one of Captain Cavallo's outgoing personals, Mister K," Fingers said. He held the message sheet to his chest. "Do we have permission to show it?"

Mike and Powell exchanged glances.

"I guess we do," Powell, said. "Cavallo gave me this message that approved one he'd sent earlier, and ordered me to make the necessary preparations." Fingers handed the message to Powell.

Powell read. His face darkened. His hands shook and his mouth worked as though unable to spit out the words.

"That bastard," Powell said. He ripped off his glasses and waved the message slip at Mike. "I don't believe this."

"What's the matter?" Mike took the paper.

"He volunteered us," Powell said. He grabbed the message from Mike's hand crumpling it.

"Volunteered?" Mike said, "Volunteered us for what?"

"You remember the message about three weeks ago?" Powell said. "The one from the Seventh Fleet commander? The one that asked ships to volunteer to extend their deployment out here?"

"You mean?" Mike took a quick intake of breath.

"That's right," Powell replied. He jammed his glasses back on and threw the message on Mike's desk. "That bastard volunteered us for an indefinite extension out here. Hell, we've been gone damned near a year already. Doesn't that old fool realize the crew will revolt? That means we won't head for San Diego for at least another month and probably a lot longer."

19

MIKE LOOKED UP FROM READING Riley's tattered, coverless copy of the Zane Gray novel, *West of the Pecos,* when the petty officer of the watch poked his head through the wardroom door.

"The captain's comin' down the pier, sir. Looks a little wobbly."

Mike, as the day's duty officer, tossed the book on the table, grabbed his cap and hustled after the petty officer to the quarterdeck.

The other officers were at the naval base officer's club for a farewell sendoff of two recalled reserve officers whose obligated service was over. They would depart in the morning and return to civilian life.

Captain Cavallo paused at the pier, raised his head to look up at Mike, shrugged then stepped onto the gangway. His stride paused once when he grabbed the railing, apparently to steady himself.

"Reporting my return," Cavallo said. Mike could barely distinguish the captain's grumble but noted his bleary eyes.

"Nothing to report, sir," Mike said. "No new messages. Crew's liberty is up at 2300. The officers are—"

"I know all that g'dammit," the captain said, louder this time, and ran a hand over his balding scalp. He headed for the hatch, staggered, caught himself and muttered, "Losers, all of them."

Mike looked toward the unlighted section of the pier to see if others were returning. Riley's John Wayne gait identified him even before he strolled into the floodlit portion of the pier.

"Figured I'd let the old man navigate for himself tonight," Riley said when he came aboard. He stretched then clapped Mike on the shoulder. "I could use some coffee." He motioned to Mike to join him in the wardroom.

"How was the party?" Mike asked. He pulled out a chair and sat opposite Riley. They sipped their coffee in silence. Mike knew not to press Riley. He'd talk about the party when he was ready, and not a moment before.

"Bad booze. But cheap. No women. And the captain." Riley got up, refilled his cup at the coffee service, and sat back down. "You didn't miss anything tonight. Couldn't shut the XO up. He passed out early, thank God. The captain was his usual obstinate grump. Don't think that bastard knows how to smile." Riley pulled a cigarette from his shirt pocket, lit it then took a gulp of his coffee. He set the cup on the table. "Did any significant message traffic come in tonight?"

"Nothing," Mike said. "Were you expecting something?"

"Just wondering about replacements for our departing shipmates," Riley said. "Guess we won't see any new faces for a while."

"You know," Mike said after a pause, "Detachment of Atkins and Perry tomorrow leaves us short on bridge watch standers."

Riley grinned. He twisted the ends of his monster mustache seeming to mimic one of the 1920's silent movie villains seen in the previous night's film.

"You're right, young man," Riley said and ground out his cigarette. "That gives me an idea."

Mike made his nightly visit to the radio shack after dinner, part of his in port routine. He wanted to be on hand when the duty radioman returned from the base's communications center with the day's collected message traffic and, more important, their mail.

The evening's mail would be the last assured delivery for a month while they were on the northern patrol. He longed to hear from Carol. A week had passed since he'd received a letter from her. Mike had planned to write before he turned in although he had little to say other than he missed her.

The radiomen sorted the ship's mail for delivery to *Bartley's* various divisions. Officers' mail went into a separate pile.

Pops handed Mike two pink letters. "Looks like this is all we have for you tonight, Mister K," he said.

Mike had read the first letter from Carol, and was on the third page of the second one, when Fingers handed him one more pink envelope. He finished the second letter and opened the third.

"I can't believe it," Mike yelled and ran from the radio shack clutching the crinkly sheets of paper.

Mike dashed into Riley's stateroom waving Carol's third letter and slammed it on the desk.

"I don't believe it," Mike said louder than intended. "I'm going to be a father."

"Good news," Riley said with a grin. He handed the letter back to Mike. "When's the baby due?"

"Don't know for sure," Mike said. "Sometime in the spring, probably March after we get back home, if we ever get back, that is." The captain's volunteering of *Bartley* for an extended deployment to the war zone had become a blanket of depression.

But when would *Bartley* go home? Return to the States was even more important to Mike now with the baby on the way. The indefinite extension meant just that: indefinite. The ship had sailed from San Diego at the end of November 1950, over ten months ago. Would the Navy keep *Bartley* and crew deployed to the combat zone over a year?

"I need to get a reply off to Carol now, before we get underway," Mike said.

Back in his stateroom, Mike settled at his desk and pulled his folder from a drawer. He gasped. Oh, no. Yesterday he'd mailed his latest thoughts to Carol about losing the vital OOD qualification, one of the more difficult letters he'd ever written. It would reach her before anything he might write now. Even if he could send a congratulatory telegram, his news would arrive soon thereafter, and spread disappointment and confusion.

Maybe it would be better to be upbeat now and put his delight and encouragement in tonight's mail. At least he could tell her how happy her news made him, and how much he regretted upsetting her with the previous letter's bad news.

You can't imagine how proud and pleased I am with the news, Honey.

I'm walking on a cloud of excitement and love for you. I've always loved children and having ours has been my dream for as long as I've known you. Bless you. Didn't expect it to happen so soon, but believe me I couldn't be more happy..."

He urged her to take good care of herself, let him know how things progressed, and asked what he could do for her.

Mike paused and stared at the bulkhead. A mixed sense of euphoria and helplessness engulfed him. The high vanished when he remembered he'd promised Carol on their honeymoon that he would be with her when their children were born. Would he be able to honor that promise?

Riley stepped into Mike's stateroom late that evening with coffee for both of them. Mike put away Carol's three letters. He welcomed Riley's unexpected interruption and the hot coffee.

"Just had a little one-on-one with the XO about the watches up north into icing country," Riley said. "Finally got him to listen."

"What are you talking about?" Mike said. Why did it take Riley forever to get to the point?

"Atkins and Perkins are on their way home before we sail in the morning. That leaves a hole in the bridge watch teams, right? We're down one qualified OOD with them gone, right? So how do we fix it?"

"Keep talking," Mike said. He took another swallow of his coffee.

"Okay, I'll keep it short," Riley said. "You're back on the watch bill."

"What's different about that?" Mike said. "I've been standing watches ever since we got underway months ago."

"No. You don't understand," Riley said. "You'll stand OOD watches again." He paused for Mike's reaction. "You'll alternate with me instead of being holed up in CIC like you've been these past few weeks while I freeze on the open bridge." He paused again. "This is your chance to share the frostbite game again." Riley took his time. "And," another pause, "the XO said go ahead. The captain said okay. Starts when we get underway for the northern patrol."

"So..."

"If you didn't get it," Riley said jabbing a finger at Mike, "that effectively reinstates your OOD qual. That's what you've been working for, isn't it?"

20

A SINGLE SUNNY AFTERNOON BROKE the northern patrol's monotony, ending *Bartley's* fourth week of isolated boredom. The assignment to search for and eliminate mine-laying fishermen in a huge expanse of remote ocean off the North Korean coastline had proven not only monotonous but also fruitless. The inactivity and bitter cold added to the collective depression of all on board.

Mike huddled behind the windscreen on *Bartley's* open bridge to escape the bitter late November wind blowing across the choppy seas from the nearby Siberian coast. Mike's sound-powered phone talker, Seaman Tucker, had wrapped himself in a blanket in his favorite corner, the one place on the open bridge to offer even a hint of protection from the elements.

Bartley had turned southwestward to once again transit their search sector. For a month of patrolling in this frozen hell, they had encountered not one mine-laying fishing boat, nor seen a North Korean train running enemy supplies south along the coastal rail line. Without those targets why couldn't they at least shoot up the rail line itself? The carrier's planes bombed the tracks from time to time, usually to stop a train. Too bad *Bartley* couldn't do that too and be part of the real action. He knew the officers, his radio gang, and probably all hands were bored to death, tired of freezing and angry because the damned captain had volunteered them without consulting a single crewmember. Mike vowed he'd never be that kind of leader.

Mike negotiated the few icy steps to the radar repeater at the navigator's station and removed the protective weather cover. He studied the radar picture longer than normal. The scope was clear, no contacts, the same as the last time he'd looked at the blank screen. Frequent checks were a waste of time, but he had to do something, move around, and do anything to keep his mind from stagnation.

"Combat, bridge," Mike called to CIC on the intercom. "Any radar contacts? Anything at all?"

"Same-o, same-o'," Riley replied. "Nothing. I'd even settle for a warm beer right now."

"Tucker," Mike said, "give the lookouts another wake-up call. See if they're still with us. We need something to investigate. Don't know how much more of this joy ride we can handle."

Ten minutes remained in Mike's twenty-minute stint under the cold weather watch rotation plan Riley had negotiated. Two open bridge teams alternated. Mike and Tucker, dressed in multiple keep-warm layers and fur-lined boots, stood twenty minutes segments on the open bridge then twenty minutes to attempt to thaw in the enclosed wheelhouse one deck below. Brooks and the duty quartermaster alternated with Mike's team.

Bartley's apparent design flaw puzzled Mike. Why hadn't the architects considered that the ship might operate in cold weather? The unprotected conning station was the topmost platform of the bridge structure, open to the elements. Safe operation required a conning officer and an enlisted, sound-powered phone talker to be on watch on the open bridge at all times whenever the ship was underway. That was okay for warm weather. Not for winter. The damned designers probably operated from cozy, heated offices.

Numbed by the cold, the boredom, and the unending wind, Mike's mind drifted to thoughts of Carol. He wrote to her at least every third day. After two weeks on patrol, his brain had gone dry. He re-read each of his letters searching for telltale signs of his boredom and frustration before he sealed it.

After the Navy replenishment ship failed to bring any mail midway through the patrol, writing to Carol became even more difficult. But, at least two weeks of his outgoing mail to her was on its way with the re-supply ship.

November in Seattle had been his and Carol's favorite season, a time to relish the colorful leaves, the football games, parties, the holiday preparations and just being together. He told her often that he wanted to be with her, to hold her and pamper her. He didn't want to send details of the isolation and cold, not at this delicate time in her life. Did she realize how deadly boring these last twenty-eight days had been for him? At least some of his news was on its way and she would know he was still alive, that he loved her and longed to be with her.

"Bridge, combat." Riley's call from CIC interrupted Mike's daydreams. "We may have some action here."

Mike's reverie vanished at Riley's unexpected mention of action. Alert now, he stepped across the deck to the squawk box, eager for any activity that would change the deadly routine.

"Bridge, aye," Mike answered. "What's up?"

"We just received a report from our patrol plane buddies," Riley said. "Some carrier aircraft stopped a North Korean supply train outside one of the coastal tunnels. They reported that the coordinates put the stopped train bearing 294 at eighteen miles from our position. Suggest we go have a look-see."

Finally a break, an opportunity to make a real contribution, something he and the crew could write home about. Mike moved to the voice tubes. This better not be a false alarm.

"Mister Brooks," Mike called to the wheelhouse. "Combat reports we may have a stopped Gook train in our neighborhood. Alert the captain then get up here. Let's go hunting."

Mike skidded across the icy bridge to the navigator's table to examine the chart of the nearby North Korean coastline. Much of the railway used to resupply enemy forces had been constructed at the water's edge along the sector *Bartley* now patrolled. The tracks passed through a series of tunnels cut into the many arthritic-finger-like ridges that stretched to the sea.

"Do we have a real target, maybe some actual action this time?" Brooks peered at the chart over Mike's shoulder. "Maybe we can fire the guns? I'm sick of just circling out here, and I'm not the only one."

"Maybe," Mike said. "Won't know until we get closer."

"Hope we find one to shoot up this time," Brooks said. "That's what we're supposed to be here for, isn't it? I'm tired of false alarms. So is the crew." He shivered and took a swallow of his cooling coffee. "Suppose we do find a train this time. No one on board remembers the last time we fired one of those three-inch peashooters of ours. And if they do fire, I wonder how much damage those pop-guns would do to a train, anyway."

"Don't be too sure," Mike said. "If I know our gun crews, they'll make those babies work. Anything to get some action. And don't forget," Mike added, "some of those trains carry guns. We'll need to consider counterfire if we find one."

"C'mon, Mike," Brooks said, "you're as eager for a good fight as I am. All we need to do is get in range and we can wax them."

The captain stepped onto the deck, his breath fogged from the exertion of the climb to the bridge.

"Kinkaid," Cavallo said, "did you tell the XO and Powell about the train?"

"Not yet, sir," Mike said.

"Why not, g'dammit?" The captain's bellow didn't hold the usual tinge of anger. Instead, Mike read the captain's words as grumpy excitement.

The XO appeared on the open bridge with Lieutenant Powell just behind.

"How close can we get to the shore?" Cavallo's question to the XO halted the uneasy man. He looked to Mike for information.

"Combat picked up a report about a stalled North Korean supply train at one of the tunnels," Mike said. "It's reported near our position." Mike gestured toward the navigator's table to suggest they consult the chart. "We're headed that way."

"We have good water in to about two thousand yards," the XO said squinting at the chart, "sometimes closer, along this stretch of coastline. And along here," his finger drew a line, "we can get in as close as one hundred yards. I don't recommend it, however."

"Did you get a good fix on the train's position, Powell?" the captain said. "Do we know which tunnel the train's in, or are we on another squirrel hunt?" Despite his evident excitement, Cavallo's eyebrow twitch signaled his irritation.

"The Navy pilots reported their estimated grid coordinates for the tunnel," Powell said. He rolled out a larger-scale chart of the area. "This shows four tunnels along this stretch of track. The train could be in any one of them."

"I know that, g'dammit." The captain stabbed his finger at an area on the chart. "We'll start with this one, here." His gloved finger touched the southern-most tunnel's chart position, "and work north. I want all the lookouts briefed on what to be alert for. I'll order general quarters in about forty-five minutes, after we're closer. Tell the gun boss to get ready. Be prepared to fire a couple of rounds to test all systems."

Twenty minutes later Captain Cavallo ordered Mike to set a modified, cold-weather version of general quarters, sending the crew to battle stations. The crewmen manned their stations with unexpected speed, despite the temperature and the ice on all topside surfaces. Mike and Brooks stayed in place since their general quarters stations were as OOD and JOOD on the bridge.

"Bridge, combat," Riley called from CIC. "We can't find any planes in our area. We'll have to spot our own gunfire unless we can get some air support. If we get in closer we can spot our shots better. I recommend we move in closer. There's deep water along here."

"Close in to four thousand yards from the beach, Mister Kinkaid," the captain ordered.

Mike stopped. Four thousand yards? About two miles. Even though all the bridge team and the lookouts had binoculars, how could they reliably spot their shots at that distance? Since the coastline had deep water near shore, why wouldn't the captain permit them to approach the coast? No opposition lurked there. If it were up to him, he'd go further to be assured of some significant hits.

"Captain," Mike said, "we could spot our shots better if we go in closer. The XO says we have safe water."

"Do what you're told, Mister," Cavallo growled and turned to the chart table.

"Tucker," Mike said to his phone talker. "Pass the word. I want an immediate report of any sighting by the lookouts or anyone topside, a train, a work party, anything significant."

"Will do, Mister K," Tucker replied. "Everyone with glasses wants to be the first to spot the Gooks."

Mike maneuvered *Bartley* northward at ten knots on a course parallel to the rugged, North Korean coast. Soon, the southern end of the first tunnel came in sight.

"Sir," Seaman Tucker reported to Mike five minutes later, "the officer in the fire control station reports he can see some debris along the track south of that tunnel, but nothing else. No train."

"Captain," the gun boss called on the squawk box, "recommend we put a couple of rounds into the area around the tunnel entrance. It'll give us a chance to check Mount One's readiness."

"Very well," the captain grunted. "Make it so."

Mike jumped when *Bartley's* three-inch gun fired the first round. The guns hadn't been fired since he'd been on board. He hadn't expected the shot to be so loud, nor had he anticipated the sharp jolt and movement in the deck plates under his feet from the gun's recoil. The wind blew a wisp of smoke from the barrel. The sight brought excitement and a brief smile to Mike. At last, they had taken some action. Would he feel differently if *Bartley* received return fire from Gook gunners? The thought died in the excitement of the moment.

"Wow, it works," yelled the helmsman from the wheelhouse.

Mike could see through his binoculars that Mount One's first round hit the bluff above the tunnel entrance. A second round landed in the water, short of the track.

"Two rounds fired, sir," the gun boss called over the squawk box. "Request another round."

"Okay, one more," the captain said.

The next shell hit above the track bed, a short distance from the tunnel opening, and produced a small rockslide. At that distance Mike couldn't determine if the debris blocked the track. If they were going to really do the job, the ship needed to move much closer to the shore or, better yet, get an airborne spotter. When they find the train, will the captain move *Bartley* in closer for a better shot? Mike would if he were running the show.

"They'll have to do better than that," the captain barked to the XO. "What a sorry bunch of amateurs."

The short span of exposed track between the second and third tunnel revealed no train and no activity. *Bartley* continued northeastward paralleling the coast.

"The train," came an excited call from a sharp-eyed spotter atop the fire control director station. He pointed north.

Anticipation filled Mike. A quarter mile of track lay between the northern end of the third tunnel and the southern opening of the fourth tunnel. He could see a southbound steam engine and three flatbed rail cars exposed outside the opening of the fourth tunnel. The engine leaned away from the water, perhaps resting against the sheer cliff beside it.

"Sir," Seaman Tucker said to Mike, "the port lookout reports people along the track. He thinks they've seen us. They're running for cover."

"Or maybe they're going for guns," Mike mumbled to himself.

Mike scanned the train with his binoculars. Scattered rubble and broken hillsides covered portions of the exposed track, damage that aircraft bombs might have created. Intact cargo crates lay on the ground beside the train's exposed flat cars. *Bartley's* arrival must have interrupted a work crew's attempt to right the engine.

"I don't see any guns, sir," Mike said. The ship they had relieved had reported that some of the North Korean supply trains carried mounted artillery apparently for self-protection. "No steam either. The train looks dead."

"I can see that g'dammit," the captain growled in reply. He swept the scene with his binoculars. "Take us out to about five thousand yards, Mister Kinkaid."

"Even further away? If we stay in closer, sir," Mike said, "we can get a better shot."

"Do what you're told, g'dammit," Cavallo ordered. The captain studied the situation for a couple of minutes, then said, "Kinkaid, reduce to six knots. Parallel the coast. No closer, though."

"Combat, bridge. This is the captain," Cavallo said into the squawk box to Powell in CIC. "If Mount One is ready they are free to open fire on the train. No more than fifteen rounds. Make each round count. Give yourself time between rounds to record your spots. We'll have to make a detailed report to the admiral on this action."

Mike viewed the impact of the first two rounds through his binoculars. The first fell into the water short of the rail line. The second brought down more of debris from the cliffside, possibly onto the rail tracks.

"G'dammit, XO," the captain bellowed after the first two round, "those clowns of yours couldn't hit the side of a barn at a hundred paces." The XO's shoulder tic jumped as he spun to pick up the hot line to fire control.

Neither of the next two rounds produced damage that Mike could identify. The second of the following two rounds struck the train's engine. Mike thought he detected pieces of machinery kicked up by the explosion of the shell, but no smoke and no fire.

Between rounds Captain Cavallo strode back and forth across the bridge muttering and pounding a fist into an open palm. He turned toward the shore as each shot was fired, paused to spot where the shell landed, then repeated, "Damn. Damn. Damn." No one crossed his path.

The next four rounds appeared to land on the train engine or on one of the cars. Mike couldn't assess the damage except that the last shell's impact appeared to be just inside the tunnel's opening.

"Sir," Mike reported to the furious captain after the last round, "combat reports we've fired the fifteen rounds you ordered. The lookouts report they think we got some hits on the train and exposed cars. They can't determine the damage at this distance."

The red faced, angry captain just stared at Mike.

"Captain," Mike said, his temper rising, "let me take us in closer so we can do this job right."

"G'dammit, do what you're told," the captain bellowed. "No closer, I said."

Mike fumed at the captain's caution and lack of imagination. If it were up to him he'd carry out the mission and be sure the train was destroyed. Their guns could also damage the tunnels adding to the Gook's problems. The ship might receive some small arms fire if they got in too close, but probably not. The lookouts had seen no evidence of any defenses around the train. Until now *Bartley* hadn't been able to claim any accomplishment for the month-long patrol. The crew deserved to know they had significantly damaged the enemy.

"Captain, combat," Powell called from his station in CIC. "Sir, we have voice radio contact with one of our patrol planes. With your permission, I'll ask them to round up some bombers to come in and work over the train. Some of the carrier's planes operated south of here earlier. It's worth a try."

"Permission granted," Cavallo replied. "Kinkaid, secure the crew from general quarters. I'll be in my cabin." He left the bridge.

Ten minutes later the squawk box announced "Bridge, combat. Good news. Two of the carrier's birds are headed our way. Should be here in about half an hour. I'll switch their radio channel for you to monitor up there."

Mike slid across the icy deck to the small radio speaker by the navigator's station. The chance to listen to pilot's chatter in an action situation became an unexpected bonus. How long would it be before he would join them and fly?

Two Douglas AD Skyraiders arrived over *Bartley* thirty-five minutes later. Mike's wide grin and cheering wave welcomed the single-engine planes passing low overhead, their wings loaded with bombs and rocket pods. The roar of the planes' engines brought the captain and XO back to the bridge and alerted everyone that air support had arrived.

The planes circled below the broken clouds to search for gun positions or troops. Mike and the other bridge watch standers gathered around the radio speaker to listen to the pilots' conversation. Their chatter revealed they hadn't spotted anything suspicious. Mike smiled at one of their encouraging comments. "...better than our original mission. It's a sitting duck."

Each Skyraider flew a series of shallow dives and dropped two bombs on the exposed train on every run.

"We even have a peanut gallery," Brooks joked. He pointed to the ship's excited off-duty crewmen gathered on deck to watch the planes finish off the stalled train.

"Mister Kinkaid," the captain called to Mike who had moved to the conning station for a quick check of their heading.

"Yes, sir," Mike said, and wheeled around to see Cavallo near the top of the ladder leading down to the wheelhouse. Their eyes met, the captain's eyebrow twitch working overtime.

"I'll be in my cabin, g'dammit," Cavallo growled. He paused with his foot raised over the low coaming and aimed at the ladder's first step. He looked at the XO standing next to his plotting table, then added, "XO, get a message out to..."

The captain slipped on the icy first step. He reached for the railing to steady himself.

"Mike, we need to..." Brooks said, his arm rose as he swung around at the same moment.

Mike's stomach tensed. He viewed Brooks' movements in slow motion as the outstretched arm struck the captain's upper back. The captain teetered forward, his foot searching for a purchase.

Mike gasped, frozen, helpless to intervene.

The wide-eyed captain flailed in his effort to grab for the rail. His right hand found the ice-covered rail. His gloved fingers slipped. He grabbed again. Too late. He tumbled down the ladder head first.

21

THE SICKENING THUD OF BONE against steel stunned Mike. The entire bridge crew stared in silence at the ladderway. Apprehensive glances flashed among them.

"Oh my God," the XO wailed, and scrambled down the ladder after the captain.

"Damn. I didn't mean to..." Brooks moaned.

"Quartermaster," Mike yelled into the voice tube, "Get Doc Webster to the wheelhouse on the double." At the other voice tube to CIC, he hollered, "Combat, bridge. The captain—"

"Mike. Look," Brooks interrupted. "Tracers."

Mike turned to where Brooks pointed. Tracer shells followed Buckeye-Two as the plane pulled out of a bomb run.

"Buckeye-Two," the radio speaker crackled with a call from the flight leader, Buckeye-One, to his wingman. "You're taking fire from the ridge."

Buckeye-Two pulled out from its dive. More tracers followed. To Mike, the tracers appeared to pass behind the plane until...

"I'm hit," Buckeye-Two's pilot called. "Got the engine. Doesn't look good, boss."

"Oh, m'God," Brooks said and pointed toward a trail of smoke streaming from the damaged plane. Then, flames erupted. A river of fire flowed along the plane's fuselage.

Mike stood, momentarily stunned.

"Head for the ship," called Buckeye-One. "I'll cover you." Buckeye-

One made a diving left turn toward the gun's position.

"Steve," the strained voice of the Buckeye-Two pilot broadcast, "I'm bailing out. Cover me."

Buckeye-One, circled behind the damaged Buckeye-Two. Mike checked for following tracers.

Engulfed in flames, Buckeye-Two rolled left, silhouetted against the low clouds. The plane's nose staggered, appeared to stabilize, then dropped. The Skyraider rolled left and begin a dizzy spiral toward the frigid sea.

Mike, riveted, witnessed the pilot of Buckeye-Two separate from the plane and free-fall. A shiver of mixed excitement and dread ran through him. He offered a silent prayer for the pilot. He might have been the pilot in that plane had his original orders sent him to flight school.

The entire bridge team, apprehensive and silent, watched the figure tumble from the plane through the scattered wisps of low cloud. The pilot's parachute streamed, and a moment later, blossomed into a full canopy seconds before he splashed into the water.

Mike's eyes widened at the image in his binoculars. The parachute canopy floated, but he couldn't see the pilot.

A splash, too big for a bullet's impact, appeared next to the parachute. The pilot's helmet surfaced. Mike couldn't detect any movement. Maybe the pilot had been injured or otherwise incapacitated. A moment later, the yellow Mae West flotation vest blossomed. The survival raft popped up next with a slight splash and inflated immediately.

The pilot scrambled to climb into the raft. Mike squirmed, his body language attempting to help the pilot whose thrashing pushed the raft away on the first try. The raft flipped over on the second try. Mike held his breath. The pilot slowed his movements and eventually worked his way onto the unsteady, yellow life raft.

Mike recalled his own recent exposure to the frigid seas. The pilot would have to be recovered fast or he'd freeze. In the meantime the life vest and raft made a good target for snipers. Too good.

Should he order the whaleboat? Could the boat get to the pilot before he succumbed to the cold or was shot? Why not take the ship in closer?

The captain had said no closer. With the captain out of the picture, authority passed to the XO. The XO could give permission to move closer to shore for a pilot pickup. But, the XO was gone.

"Postman," Buckeye-One called. "Get my wingman. I'll fly cover for you."

Mike grabbed the radiophone. "Postman, can do. Moving out."

"Brooks, saddle up," Mike yelled. "Take the whaleboat and get the pilot. Move it."

The alert whaleboat crew had tracked the circling aircraft, spotted the pilot's parachute, and lowered the boat on their own initiative. Brooks jumped into the whaleboat as it was being lowered into the sea. The whaleboat, its engine at full throttle, pulled away toward the downed pilot.

In moments Mike knew that he needed a better solution. The motor whaleboat was too slow. He couldn't let the pilot be captured or killed. Somehow he had to get him out of the water fast. The ship would have to pick him up. But, the captain had ordered no closer.

"XO, dammit, get up here and take over," Mike muttered to himself. He paced the narrow bridge. He flexed his fists in anger. Waiting for permission to go closer to shore added to the pilot's danger. He couldn't just wait for the man to be shot or freeze. He had to get the pilot. He had to do it now.

"Bridge, conn. Right full rudder," Mike ordered. "Come right to 260. Emergency all ahead full. Make turns for eighteen knots. We're going after our pilot."

"Postman, Buckeye-One is out of bombs," the Skyraider pilot called. He maintained his low orbit overhead, below the clouds. "I have Zunis and twenty millimeter left, guys. Put some rounds on that gun on the ridge to keep them quiet." Buckeye-One paused. "And, I see your boat. Tell them to move out. That water's cold as hell."

"Bridge, conn," Mike ordered the quartermaster in the wheelhouse. "Pass the word. Man Mount One. Prepare to fire."

The fire control officer waved a thumbs-up to Mike from his station above and behind the bridge, to confirm that the gun crews, eager to view the activity, had remained at their posts.

"Combat, conn," Mike called to CIC, "I want three rounds on the ridge top. Use proximity fused shells if you have any." If they were lucky, the shells would keep the enemy gunners' heads down long enough to accomplish the pilot's rescue.

Mount One fired its first round almost immediately. Two more rounds followed at fifteen-second intervals. Mike exchanged wide grins and told-you-so glances with Tucker as the explosion of each shell blanketed the enemy gun position, exactly on target. He waved an excited thumbs-up to the gun crew.

Mike sent a series of brief orders to the helmsman. His mind created a clear plot of where and when to turn, when to stop, and the allowances he must make for the ship's momentum to avoid overrunning the pilot. He also had to avoid the shallow water. In the brief pauses between orders to the helmsman, he worried about the captain's condition. He couldn't deal with that now and save the pilot at the same time.

"Postman," Buckeye-One called in the circling plane. "Good shooting. The gun's quiet. I'll hang around until you get my wingman."

"Mike," Powell called three minutes later from the top of the ladder. "The captain's out of it. Hit his head pretty bad. Big gash. Lots of blood, but he's breathing." Powell's breath formed steam clouds as he spoke. "The old man's cold weather gear must have padded his fall. Doc Webster doesn't think he broke anything. Doc gave him a shot."

"We're going to get our pilot," Mike said. He pointed toward the land ahead. Powell, as next senior after the XO, could countermand the rescue effort. Would he?

Powell paused, cast a quick look toward the coast, and gave Mike a thumbs-up. "The old man's asleep. Doc says he should be up and around in a couple of days."

"Where's the XO, dammit?" Mike said. Mike's fists clenched. "Why isn't he up here? He's second in command. He should be running the ship."

"I left him with the captain in his cabin. You know the XO, Mike." Powell shrugged. "It's all yours," he said over his shoulder. "Go for it. I'll be down in CIC if—"

"Sir," Seaman Tucker interrupted, "Starboard lookout says he can see the pilot in his raft, and from here he seems pretty close to shore. He reports splashes in the water near him, like the Gooks are shooting at him. The whaleboat crew might take some hits, too."

Mike grabbed the microphone for the aircraft's circuit.

"Buckeye-One, your wingman is taking small arms fire," Mike said. "Can you see where they're shooting from?"

"Wait one," Buckeye-One replied.

Buckeye-One completed a tight search turn and rolled in again. Two rockets flashed toward positions atop the bluff above the train tracks hidden from Mike's view.

"Combat, bridge," Mike called. "How close can we get to the shore?"

"Bridge, combat," came Powell's reply from CIC. "You have deep water out to about two hundred yards from the beach along here."

"Bridge, Conn. Pass the word." Mike ordered. "Clear all topside stations on the port side. We're within range of gunfire from the beach." He turned to his phone talker. "Tucker, pass the same word to all stations. Our port side will be exposed to small arms fire. Everyone take cover. No exceptions. That includes the gun crew in Mount One."

"You take cover, too," Mike added after Tucker relayed the orders. "I'll put our pilot in the ship's lee long enough to get him aboard. Then let's get the hell out of here." Mike glanced toward the whaleboat *Bartley* was overtaking. The boat was still too far from the pilot to help his recovery. "Tell the aft gun crew to stand by to snatch the pilot from the starboard side. Make it quick. We need to get out of here fast."

"Combat, conn," Mike called down the voice tube. "I'm going in for the pickup. It'll be tight. Shallow water ahead. Give me Fathometer readings every fifteen seconds and when any rapid changes occur. And, don't expect a reply."

The charts said he had deep water up to 200 yards from shore. How far out was the pilot? The old charts had been reliable so far. He might run the ship aground if they were wrong. He had to take that chance.

Mike maneuvered *Bartley* to stop within ten yards of the downed pilot. The ship's mass shielded the pilot from the scattered gunfire from the shore.

"Sir," Tucker called, "port lookout reports splashes in the water. Says he thinks some shots hit the ship's port side. He can hear what sounds like hammer blows, too."

"Dammit," Mike yelled, "tell him to take cover. You too. Now."

"Buckeye-One, this is Postman," Mike called the circling plane. "We're taking small arms fire. Can you see where it's coming from? We can't."

"Roger, Postman," came the call about twenty seconds later. "The Gooks are behind some bushes at the crest of the bluff. I'll get 'em."

The circling Skyraider turned in toward the bluff. Buckeye-One passed low over the ship in a slight descent. A stream of rounds from the Skyraider's 20mm guns walked up the side of the bluff and concentrated at the crest.

"Think I got 'em, Postman," the pilot called back, "but I'm ammo zero now."

Mike slid across the bridge to the starboard side in time to see the aft gun crew lift the downed pilot aboard and hustle him into the safety of the deckhouse. They let his raft drift away.

"He's aboard, sir," Seaman Tucker reported.

"Bridge, Conn. All ahead full," Mike ordered. "Come right to 085. Let's move it. We'll pick up the whaleboat."

"What in hell is going on here, Kinkaid?" Mike spun around to the voice of the red-faced XO. Powell followed the XO up the ladder.

"Are you out of your mind, Mister?" The XO shot nervous glances at the receding shoreline. "Who in hell gave you permission to steam into enemy fire?"

"We had to…"

"And who gave you permission to fire? That's a court- martial offense. I intend to see you answer for it."

"We had to recover our pilot," Mike said. Mike's fists balled and flexed. "Dammit, XO you didn't expect me to let him get shot or captured while we sat here and just watched, did you?"

"Like hell. You've overstepped your authority, Kinkaid," the XO yelled. "You put us in jeopardy. You dumb smart-ass college kid. Dammit, Mister. You risked the ship and put the crew's lives in danger. That's more than irresponsible, Mister. That's criminal. Seems to run in the family."

Mike's fists clenched and unclenched. He locked his jaws to prevent the furor in his brain from exploding. Didn't this damned fool realize he'd saved a pilot from captivity or possible death? Didn't that count for something? This is a warship. It has a mission. It isn't expected to run from danger. A quick, deep breath ended the microsecond of internal fury. His brain warned: Don't let that bastard bully you. You were in command as OOD. You had the authority. You took the necessary, and yes, the proper action.

"And where would I get the authority?" Mike said in as deliberate a manner as his anger would permit while he fought the urge to match the XO's tirade.

"From the captain, or from me." The XO glanced again at the retreating shoreline.

"And where were you? Sir." Mike said. He leaned forward on the balls of his feet, his intense stare fixed on the XO. He couldn't keep the sarcasm from his words. "As second in command you should have stayed on the bridge." He leaned toward the XO. "Why didn't you? Sir." the last word spoken louder.

A shudder racked the XO's entire body as though he'd been struck. He shivered, wide-eyed and slack-jawed. His tongue wet his lips while he appeared to search for words.

The moment he'd uttered the words Mike regretted the public challenge. Too late. The incident would spread throughout the ship within an hour. His stomach roiled. He'd allowed himself to be provoked. It wouldn't matter that saving the pilot was the right thing to do.

"Don't get smart with me, Mister," the XO said after a pause for two deep breaths. He blinked and wiped his mouth. "The captain will get you for this one." He wiped his mouth again.

"Do I understand I'm relieved, sir?" Mike snapped back. He struggled to keep his words civil. He'd had enough of the XO's vendetta and constant belittling.

"Not by a damned sight," the XO said. The steam had gone out of his voice. He turned to leave, but paused on the ladder's second step and added, "You'll stay up here and freeze if I have my way."

22

A N HOUR LATER, MIKE ENTERED the wardroom for dinner. Riley and Swede appeared to be in an intense discussion. The other officers listened without interrupting. The XO came into the wardroom and took his seat, the accepted signal to begin the meal.

"The captain's asleep," the XO said. He unfolded his napkin. "We'll send some food up to his cabin later." The other officers maintained the captain's pattern of mealtime silence

The exchange of odd glances between Riley and Swede caught Mike's attention. After their third set of glances, Mike considered asking Riley for an explanation. On a hunch, he listened instead.

"How do you think this will play out?" Swede's matter-of-fact question came across as part of an ongoing conversation. Swede set his napkin aside and nodded to Riley.

"You mean the investigation into today's incident?" Riley said in as casual a manner as Mike had heard in a long time.

The XO's head snapped up, his mouth open. A wide-eyed gaze flashed to Riley, then to Swede. He raised his napkin and slowly wiped his mouth. Head cocked, he paused. His glare settled on Riley, the forgotten linen napkin fell to the deck.

"What investigation?" the XO said with chin raised toward Riley, a gesture that might have been a challenge from anyone else.

"We fired on a commie train," Swede said before Riley could reply. "We witnessed the shoot-down of our plane in the fire fight. We steamed into enemy fire when Mike took us in close to rescue the pilot. I suppose his initiative might be worth a commendation under normal circumstances." The XO leaned forward and opened his mouth as if to speak.

"Yeah," Riley joined in, "but these weren't normal circumstances. Any investigation board will find out right away that the captain pulled Mike's OOD qual some time ago. You and the captain didn't believe he was qualified. If not qualified, they'll want to know why you stationed him on watch as OOD. Serious questions will be asked. An investigation's inevitable, don't you think?"

Riley's performance merited at least an honorable mention.

The XO's eyes scanned the other officers at the table then alternated between Riley and Swede.

"That too, I suppose," Swede said. "But, if I were investigating this one, I'd be thinking along a different line. For example, first I'd want to know why the captain assigned an unqualified officer as OOD on the bridge with the ship at battle stations. Next I'd want to know why the XO permitted an unqualified OOD to order the pilot's recovery. With the captain out of commission, we all know the XO should have been on the bridge taking command. I'd want to know where you were, XO, in the middle of combat action."

Swede paused his unhurried analysis. The other officers nodded in near unison. Swede seemed to expect a response from the XO.

The XO, mouth open, jerked his head from officer to officer. He paused, raised his coffee cup but set it down again without drinking. The steward brought coffee at the XO's signal, but midway Riley's negative headshake sent him back to the wardroom pantry.

The XO leaned over to pick up the napkin he'd dropped. Riley winked at Swede across the table.

The XO sat up and wiped his mouth with the napkin. His gaze continued to shift back and forth between Riley and Swede. He glanced around the table at the silent, intent officers.

"What are you talking about?" the XO said. "You know where I was. I had to help the captain, uh, to make sure he was okay."

"Guess we better expect to do some serious explaining after we get back to Yokosuka," one of the officers said. The XO's head swiveled as his eyes darted to the speaker.

"The admiral is bound to ask for a report," another officer said. "I expect we'll see a message to start the process any time." He turned to Mike. "Have any come in yet, Mike?"

Mike recognized the ploy.

"Not yet," he said. "Pops is on the lookout. He'll let me know pronto when the admiral's message arrives."

The XO sat silent, his dinner unfinished. His hand wiped his mouth several times.

"You know," Riley said, "I guess it's inevitable that the admiral will ask why the captain let Mike stand OOD watches for the entire last month if he wasn't qualified. Sure we're shorthanded, but not that shorthanded. Hell, in a worst case even the XO could have stood a top watch."

Heads turned to the XO. His hand made another quick swipe across the pencil mustache. He raised his empty coffee cup, studied it, and set it down again.

Swede winked at Riley and flashed a glance to Mike.

"If I were you, XO," Swede said. "I'd warn the captain about what to expect as soon as he's coherent, and I'd reinstate Mike's OOD qual before the admiral asks some touchy questions."

"I'm curious what sort of story you and the captain will have for the investigators," Riley said straight-faced. The XO's eyes shifted to his plate for a moment. Mike struggled to conceal his smirk.

"I'd better check on the captain," the XO said. He tossed his napkin on the table and left the wardroom.

Riley and Swede exchanged a thumbs-up.

Mike huddled at the fold-down desktop in his stateroom, a blanket around his shoulders. Would he ever be warm again? The past month's mind-numbing watches had sapped his energy. The turnover of the northern patrol assignment to a Canadian Frigate the day before had been uneventful and swift. His intent to write to Carol cooled faster than the tepid coffee on his desktop.

"I wonder…" Riley said as he brushed aside the curtain to Mike's stateroom.

He looked at Mike for a moment, then flashed a smile and slapped Mike on the shoulder.

"Hey, cheer up, Sport," Riley said. "Don't let that pig slop from the XO get you down. You did the right thing. We all know it."

"Thanks," Mike said. He appreciated Riley's friendship and support. "That doesn't change things, though."

"Don't be too sure," Riley said. "The XO's in a sticky corner. We all know he should have stayed on the bridge and taken command. He knows it. The captain will know it, too—when he recovers. Neither of them can afford to push for court-martial. We'd all have to testify." Riley pulled a fresh cigarette from his shirt pocket. He lit it, took a long puff, then turned and sat on Mike's lower bunk.

"You won this one, Kid," Riley continued. "The XO may be slime, but he ain't stupid. Neither is the captain. My guess is you can forget any court-martial."

After Riley left, Mike patted the insignia pouch in his pocket. Despite the XO's threat, the pilot rescue registered as a high point, one of the better things he'd done aboard *Bartley* regardless of how the captain or the XO might deal with the situation later. Flight training might be in jeopardy but he would not give up his dream. He'd acted properly. He'd saved a life. If he'd been the man in the water, he would have wanted to be picked up without delay. His father would have been proud that he had acted as he did.

The XO's court-martial threat fought for prominence in Mike's brain. It contested with his anticipated chat with Ensign Bill Carey, the rescued pilot. Carey's injuries weren't serious and he rested in the upper bunk in Riley's stateroom. Doc Webster had said he'd given the pilot something to sleep.

Carey's presence offered Mike an unexpected opportunity to learn about the pilot's mission and about flying from a carrier. This wasn't likely to happen again soon. More than ever Mike wanted a flyer's life. He had to admit, however, his months on *Bartley* had led him to better appreciate his father's experience.

The next night, after turnover of the bridge watch, Riley asked Mike, "Did you talk with Carey yet? He's up and around now."

"I tried to chat with him in the wardroom for a while before lunch," Mike said. "We didn't get much chance to talk though. The XO kept horning in with petty crap for me to do."

"I chatted with him for maybe five minutes before dinner," Riley said.

"What did he have to say?"

"Did we get any important messages today?" Riley asked. The change of subject puzzled Mike. Riley never asked about message traffic. Okay, he'd play along. "Not unless they came in the last ten minutes," Mike said in a flip way to let Riley know he was on to his tricks. "Pops said the afternoon stuff was routine. Why?"

"Oh," Riley said, "I figured we might get something important. I suppose you know that the admiral is Bill Carey's uncle." Riley twisted his mustache and grinned.

23

BARTLEY HAD MOORED AT THE Yokosuka Naval Base pier the previous afternoon for supplies and shipyard installation of a sonar system upgrade. Mike refreshed his coffee and was midway through reading the third of five letters from Carol when Riley stormed through the wardroom door.

"Finally," Riley shouted. He slammed the door and headed for the coffee server. "Thought those jokers were blowing smoke when they promised the gear to us today or tomorrow. First time they've been on time that I can remember."

Mike, Swede, and the second division officer looked up. Each had been catching up on their mail.

"What's up?" Mike said. The exuberant comment came as a welcome contrast to Riley's recent frustration with the ship's sonar equipment.

"The new sonar gear really is here. I've seen it," Riley said. "The shipyard crew will pull the old units today and tonight then start the new installation tomorrow." He poured a cup of coffee and joined the men at the table.

"How long will that take?" Mike said. He hoped *Bartley* could stay alongside the Naval Base pier for several days. Their brief in-port stay would give him an opportunity to shop for gifts for Carol and the baby. *Bartley's* schedule contained nothing yet about returning to the States. Would he make it home for Christmas? Not likely.

"I talked with the shipyard supervisor," Riley said. "His best guess is they'll have the gear swapped out and tested in seven or eight days, maybe sooner. Underway tests after that."

"No rush," Swede said. "I ain't thawed yet."

A week later, Mike strolled the main deck before breakfast in anticipation of getting underway for the post-repair sea trials of the sonar upgrade.

He'd told Carol that things were almost back to their depressing normal. By their second day in port the captain had recovered, was mobile with a slight limp, a small bandage on his left cheek, and as grumpy as ever, if not worse.

Mike hadn't told Carol of the XO's threat of court-martial. He expected the captain to take some action as soon as he recovered. Almost a week had passed but the topic hadn't surfaced in any fashion. Riley had told him to forget it but Mike couldn't chalk it up to more XO bluster.

The bridge duty rotation plan assigned Mike the morning 0800-1200 officer-of-the-deck watch. The damp, November chill and dense fog found its way through his several layers of clothing more easily than the wind and snow showers had during the past five days. Testing would be an interesting change. *Bartley* could return to her regular fleet assignment the next day if the tests were successful.

Captain Cavallo conned the ship from their pier-side mooring out into Tokyo Bay. Once clear of the shipyard, he turned the conn over to Mike and climbed into his pedestal chair on the bridge, opened his paperwork folder, and appeared to ignore all else.

Mike risked an XO chewing out for interrupting when he went to the navigator's table to check their position on the XO's plot. The XO ignored Mike and stared at the fog. Back at the conning station, Mike headed *Bartley* south for the forty-five minute transit to the test area, a reserved sector of southern Tokyo Bay.

A half-hour into Mike's OOD watch, Riley stepped out of the sonar shack forward of the open bridge and ambled to the starboard wing. His broad mustache-topped smile signaled that his sonar equipment functioned once again.

"Can't wait to get to the testing area," Riley said to Mike and Brooks. "The tech rep we snagged from the shipyard says the preliminary tests check out great. Having the gear working again makes this a sunny day for me, despite the damned fog."

"When we go outside for the higher-speed tests," Riley said to Brooks, "notice the two white anchor buoys at the net's entrance. Those babies are huge, over twenty feet in diameter. They used to be the hinge points for the old gates that allowed passage through the anti-sub nets."

"I don't follow you," Brooks said, head cocked, a suspicious squint in his eyes. "Will they be a problem to us?" Mike chuckled to himself about Brooks' caution. He'd received his share of Riley's teasings since joining the watch team.

"The Japs installed a fence of inter-linked metal rings, like chain mail, across the Tokyo Bay entrance during World War II," Riley said. "They had to do something to keep our subs from sneaking in and shooting up their shipping. Hundreds of white floats support the net. They're attached at something like thirty-foot intervals. After the war, the Japs removed the entry gates but those big white anchor buoys are still in place."

"How long are the Japs going to keep them there?" Mike asked.

"Who knows?" Riley continued. "A barge rigged with floodlights to mark the entry gate at night is tied to the southern buoy."

"When you said nets," Brooks said, "I thought you meant fishing nets and were pulling my leg again." The comment brought chuckles from Riley and Mike.

"You'll see when we get there," Riley said and returned to the sonar shack.

Fifteen minutes later, Riley stuck his head out of the sonar compartment's hatch forward of the open bridge.

"Sir, we're ready to start the sonar testing," he said to the captain.

"Mister Kinkaid," Cavallo said, "give Mister Riley whatever he needs for the tests." He followed Riley into the cramped sonar control compartment.

Mike had an uneasy feeling. Tokyo Bay was a busy place, good weather or bad. The heavy fog at the naval base had become erratic with large, dense patches in the southern test area. He scanned the sea around *Bartley* then checked the radar for other shipping. Nothing to be concerned with. Would the reduced visibility, and varying speeds it demanded, interfere with the sonar testing? Mike hadn't thought to ask Riley.

"Figured I'd check out the new equipment," Powell said to Mike when he came to the bridge. Powell scanned the surrounding fog, checked *Bartley's* heading and the radarscope.

"We're going too fast," Powell said to the XO standing at the plotting table. "Ten knots is too much for this visibility. I recommend we slow down."

The XO looked at Powell, his face emotionless. "That's up to the captain," he said and went back to his plot.

When the captain stepped from the sonar shack moments later, Powell repeated his worry, only to be brushed aside. At the port wing of the bridge, Cavallo pushed the XO aside as well.

Mike's uneasiness grew. The captain glanced at the chart, but not at the radar. Surely he could see how the fog restricted their visibility.

"Increase your speed to fourteen knots, Mister Kinkaid," Cavallo ordered and settled into his bridge chair, soon immersed in paperwork again.

Mike paused for a moment. His duty as OOD, responsible for the safety of the ship, obliged him to offer his own caution although he expected to be ignored as Powell had been.

"Sir," Mike said. "I recommend we slow down, not speed up. This fog is thick. We won't be able to stop in time to avoid a collision if a fishing boat pops up."

"Do as you're told, g'dammit." Cavallo glowered at Mike, the telltale eyebrow active.

Uneasy, Mike stepped to the port wing of the bridge, and checked the radar display at the navigator's station. He estimated that his visibility through the fog couldn't be more than a quarter mile, often less, and showed no signs of improvement. He repeated the circuit. What had he missed?

Riley jumped out of the sonar compartment hatch and peered around. His sudden appearance and agitated scan of the surrounding water worried Mike further.

"What's the problem?" Mike asked.

"No problem," Riley said. He joined Mike and Brooks on the starboard wing of the bridge. "System's working great," he said in subdued tones. "It shows the sub nets the way it should. Shows them too damned close, though. No point in hugging the nets." Riley glanced at Cavallo, still busy with his papers. "I'll tell him."

"Captain," Riley said, "recommend we move farther up the bay. We don't want to tangle with those nets."

The captain stared at Riley with a frown, lips pursed. Cavallo's eyebrows twitched twice.

"We're okay here," Cavallo said. "Get on with it."

"Sir, everything's working up to specs and no detectable leakage in the dome," Riley reported. "We've done all we can and stay under the fourteen-knot limit for this op-area. We need some higher speed runs for the last five tests, maybe up to twenty-seven knots if we can," he said, tension evident in his voice. "I recommend we go out the gates to the outer bay to finish."

Cavallo cocked his head and turned away. Riley paused as though expecting approval or further direction. After a time Riley shook his head then joined Mike and Brooks across the bridge.

"As usual, no comment from the old man," Riley said. "Don't know what he plans to do."

"Mister Kinkaid," the captain looked up from his papers and ordered, "Head for the entrance. We'll go outside for the last tests. Riley, let me know when you're ready." He bent over his paperwork again.

Riley ducked back into the sonar shack.

Mike shared a glance and a shrug with Brooks. The captain was back in form, grumpy, rude, impatient, and apparently none the worse for his fall. The contrast with his predecessor, Captain Clark, grew more dramatic by the day. Cavallo's behavior flaunted all the leadership principles Mike had learned in his midshipman training. Why had this man been given a command?

Although the fog had become less dense, Mike estimated visibility to be between a quarter to a half mile at best. None of the net's white supporting floats, each at least twice the size of a bathtub, could be seen through the fog.

"Left standard rudder," Mike ordered. "Come left to new course 068. Make turns for eight knots." His order for an easterly heading would parallel the net barrier and point *Bartley* toward the opening to the outer harbor.

"Mister Kinkaid." The captain laid his papers aside and said to, "Why are you slowing?" The grumpy tone couldn't be missed.

"The speed limit through the gates is eight knots, sir," Mike replied.

"I know that, g'dammit." The captain shifted in his chair. "What's your heading?"

"We're coming left to 068, sir," Mike said, checking the compass to confirm their left turn. "I'm putting us in position to turn south and transit the net gates."

"Dammit, Kinkaid," the captain said. "Do I have to do everything myself? Turn to the outbound heading of 176. Can't you read your charts?"

"Sir, it's too soon," Mike said. "A turn to 176 now will drive us into the nets."

"Do what you're told, g'dammit." The captain jumped down from his pedestal chair.

A brief twinge grabbed Mike's stomach. He'd have contested the order on the spot if it had been anyone but the dictator captain. Why was the man so damned unwilling to listen? He'd received sound advice from knowledgeable men. Mike's uneasiness grew.

"Sir," Powell said. He laid his hand on the captain's arm. "Mike's right. We need to stay on this heading longer before we turn."

"G'dammit, you two," the captain yelled and flung Powell aside. "I said come right to new heading 176. Now carry out your orders." Powell's eyes widened.

The captain pushed Mike and Powell away from the voice tube. "This is the captain," he yelled to the helmsman. "I have the conn. Come right to heading 176."

"Coming right to new course 176, sir," the helmsman in the wheelhouse replied.

"No, don't, Captain," Mike yelled. We'll—"

From the sonar compartment's hatch Riley yelled, "Captain, we're too close. Turn back or you'll ram the nets. We're too damned close."

Hands on hips, the captain glowered at Riley. "What is this, a mutiny, g'dammit?"

Mike stole a quick glance at the radar repeater. Three large blips jumped off the screen at him. He peered ahead. The two huge anchor buoys emerged through the fog with the companion net-tender barge attached to the nearest one.

"Sir," Mike shouted and pointed, "the barge and the buoy. We're going the wrong way. Come left or we'll ram the nets."

Cavallo ignored Mike.

"Mister K," Tucker called, "bow lookout reports the big white buoy and barge dead ahead, sir."

Powell grabbed the captain's arm and repeated Mike's warning. The captain shrugged off Powell. Cavallo mumbled something and stepped to the opposite side of the bridge. Had the mumble been an order?

"Captain Cavallo, we need to turn," Mike called. "Now, sir."

Safe navigation of the ship was the XO's responsibility. Mike expected him to warn the captain as well. The XO, head down over his chart, didn't move. He gave no sign that he understood the situation and made no effort to intervene.

The nearest anchor buoy and the attached net tender barge, clearly visible now, were less than two-hundred yards directly ahead. At this speed they had fifteen, maybe twenty seconds, before they would collide resulting in serious damage to *Bartley*, the buoy, and the net tender.

Powell, arms waving, ran to the captain and yelled, "Captain. Come hard left. You'll ram the nets on this heading."

Mike's anger surged. Would the ever-obstinate captain accept Powell's warning? Should he intervene and give the order even though Cavallo had the conn? *Bartley* drove toward imminent collision.

The captain finally looked to where Powell pointed. He stared for a moment as though transfixed, then screamed, "Left full rudder, g'dammit. All engines emergency back full. Sound collision quarters."

Bartley's momentum drove her toward the barge and buoy. The twin propellers slowed to stop, reversed, then, in full power, made a frantic effort to halt *Bartley's* advance. The vibrations from the backing engines at full power made the entire ship shake like a high-speed run over a potholed country road. Mike hadn't experienced an emergency backing order before and wasn't prepared for the violent heaves and *Bartley's* prolonged shudder. He grabbed a stanchion to keep from falling. He could hear shouts from below, steel doors slamming shut, men running, all somehow tempered by the fog. The ship, like a willful child, resisted all efforts to stop or turn.

With the engines now in full reverse, slowing *Bartley* yet unable to stop the collision, the disaster unfolded before Mike.

The sound of the loud, jarring impact, like a fast car hitting a steel wall, was somehow less severe than Mike had expected. The wrenching screams of metal-on-metal that followed immediately, however, came as a total surprise. *Bartley's* sharp bow cut the barge's mooring lines like a giant razor. *Bartley's* forward motion stopped as though snagged by the nets.

Mike lost sight of both the barge and buoy. They thumped and rumbled along the hull and sounded as though *Bartley* was taking heavy damage. The barge reappeared adrift on the port side about twenty feet away, apparently undamaged. Mike glanced to starboard. He couldn't see the white anchor buoy.

A momentary, stunned silence enveloped the bridge. No one moved. No one spoke for what seemed an eternity. The captain's stubborn disregard of the offered help left Mike angry, his fist flexing. Why had the old man failed to heed the many warnings?

Mike expected an order from Cavallo, who, immobile on the port wing of the bridge, stared at the fog-shrouded water. Just what went on in his head?

Mike couldn't hesitate while the captain snapped out of his stupor. He was OOD, responsible for the ship and its crew even though Cavallo had taken the conn. He had to act if the captain wouldn't. *Bartley* could have been seriously damaged. Had there been any injuries? He needed answers.

"All engines stop," Mike ordered through the voice tube to the wheelhouse crew. The engines quieted. He spun back to the captain ready to respond to orders. Cavallo remained motionless and silent.

Mike flashed a quick glance at the XO leaning over the navigator's table, his shoulder twitching. The XO's eyes were fixed on the captain like a marionette waiting for his strings to be pulled.

"Mike," Brooks called. "The anchor buoy. We punctured it. It's partly submerged and sinking."

A hundred yards away one of the net's smaller floats bobbed a few inches above the surface through the now thinning fog. The floats closer to *Bartley* were underwater. The collision must have severed the anchor buoy from the net it supported. They'd created a major safety hazard. The damage had to be reported to the Japanese harbormaster.

Seaman Tucker relayed to Mike a growing flood of reports from *Bartley's* damage control and repair parties. Soon the squawk box added to the noise level. All spaces remained watertight with scattered minor damage and no personal injuries. Sonar reported that its equipment continued to function with no detectable damage. Mike's apprehension eased.

Powell grabbed the radiophone to inform the harbormaster of the collision.

"Sir," Powell said to the captain, "Harbor Control says the barge crew's routine replacement team left about thirty minutes ago. They'll check the anchor buoy and report to the harbormaster after they have a look-see. Nothing more we can do here. Recommend we return to the pier."

"Mike," the vacant-eyed captain said, "take us back to the pier." No bluster or anger in his voice this time. Shoulders slumped, he left the bridge.

❋

After he turned over the watch, Mike lingered in the wheelhouse and contemplated what entries to make in the ship's log. He refilled his coffee cup from the quartermaster's pot nearby and downed half of it in a couple of swigs, still angry at the captain's failure. The pause helped calm him but not enough to remove the anxiety. It had been his watch, his responsibility. What entries should he make? The quartermaster's log lay open on the tabletop. It contained all the routine entries, *Bartley's* course, speed changes and the times for each. A key entry read: 1039 Captain takes the conn.

At intervals Mike paused to write some of the non-routine items on scratch paper before entering the edited version into the logbook. What he wrote had to be accurate and clear. His entries might come back to haunt him and the captain. An investigation of the incident was inevitable. Although the captain gave the crucial orders, Mike remained responsible for all that happened during that watch. *Bartley* had disabled Japanese national property. The incident could become sticky. The captain would be held accountable. Short of a fluke, Mike would be, too. No way around it. Should he record that *Bartley* suffered minor damage? The reports from the crew were incomplete. The full extent of *Bartley's* damage wouldn't be known for days. He recorded what he knew. At least there were no casualties.

24

"HERE'S SOME GOOD NEWS FOR a change," Mike said five days later. All hands had enjoyed the brief in-port respite for the sonar upgrade. They expected the admiral's inquiry into the net incident and remained curious about what would follow.

"New orders. Captain hasn't seen them yet." Mike handed a just-received message to Riley. "I figured you'd like to read this before I show it to him. We're reassigned to the patrol force that guards the waters along Korea's western coast. Don't see what our role is though."

Riley took the message copy, read through it twice, handed the message back, then pulled a cigarette from his pocket and lit it.

"Get underway in the morning?" Riley said, an inquisitive squint in his eyes, his head cocked. "What about the investigation? Unless someone has made a mistake, those orders look like the admiral has resolved the net incident." Riley paused and took a lengthy drag on his cigarette. "Wonder what the outcome was? Anyway, we won't have to hang around here answering questions."

"I wonder if that means we can put the incident behind us." Mike said.

"I asked Powell about it this morning," Riley said, then took a long drag on his cigarette. "He's surprised nothing's surfaced. Not a word since the captain met with the admiral again. I can't imagine the old man getting off with only an ass chewing. We may never know if the admiral chose administrative action over tying us up in port and pressing on with a formal investigation. It has to be a marker on the old man's record in any case." Riley scowled at Mike and twisted his monster mustache. "You haven't kept any messages from me, have you?"

Mike shook his head. The message traffic contained nothing new. His OOD qualification hadn't been questioned so far, but a further inquiry seemed inevitable. Complete exoneration in the collision seemed unlikely but he could hope. His letters to Carol hadn't mentioned the incident. Better to wait until he had something definite to write to her. And there was the XO's threat of court-martial. He hadn't heard any more about that, either. Hell, he had been doing his duty in both the pilot recovery and the net collision. No need to apologize. His father would have agreed.

After an uneventful three-day transit from Yokosuka, *Bartley* had dropped anchor at sunrise in the fleet anchorage offshore from the port of Inchon on South Korea's northwest coast. Mike leaned on the rail where he could watch the activity below. The captain, the XO, and Lieutenant Powell left in the motor whaleboat headed for the admiral's force flagship anchored nearby. The admiral's message that morning simply said come for a mission briefing. What would *Bartley's* new mission be? Would the ship join a carrier task group as before? Mike hoped he'd seen the last of the mind-numbing, independent coastal patrols.

"That was a pretty short visit to the flagship," Riley said over a cup of coffee after the captain's return. He pulled out a fresh cigarette. "Our new assignment can't be too complicated. At least Cavallo took Powell along this time. Powell will tell us what's going on."

"There hasn't been any new message traffic that would give us a hint," Mike added. His curiosity grew.

The captain, true to form, offered no details about *Bartley's* new assignment. Riley's impatient probe at lunch prompted a frustrating response from the captain: an inshore patrol.

"What the hell's so secret about a patrol, anyway?" Riley said to Mike after lunch. "Why won't that old bastard open up and tell us where we're going and why?"

"The whole crew's fidgety," Mike said. "Pops told me they don't trust the old man after he signed us up for the indefinite extension out here. Don't blame them."

Later, Riley stepped into the radio shack and motioned to Mike. "Powell wants to see us," Riley said. "He has news from the admiral's intelligence officer."

Mike jammed his unsorted messages into a folder, grabbed his parka, and trotted after Riley to the CIC spaces on the deck above.

"Our first patrol in this new assignment begins tonight during the 2000 to 2400 watch," Powell began. "Who has the CIC watch tonight?" The controlled anger in Powell's voice surprised Mike. Everyone accepted Powell as the voice of reason and sanity, seldom ruffled.

"I do," Riley answered. "It's Mike's turn for frostbite tonight," he added in his jovial manner

"I thought you two had the afternoon and mid-watch cycle," Powell said. He slid his glasses down his nose and peered over the upper rim.

"We needed a change," Riley said, "so we shifted the cycles. Mike and I have the eight to twelve from now on. The captain didn't object."

"Where do we patrol?" Mike asked. He peered over Powell's shoulder at the chart table. Curiosity mixed with a tinge of apprehension.

Powell scratched his head, and rubbed his chin. A scowl creased his brow. The pencil in his hand tap-danced a nervous jig on the plotting table chart before them.

"Same mission," Powell said. "We look for mine-layers again. The admiral's staff told us floating mines have appeared again after the recent break in the weather."

Why was Powell angry? His behavior puzzled Mike. What made this assignment so different?

"What's the problem, boss?" Riley asked.

Powell studied at the chart and bounced his pencil for almost a minute before he answered.

"Apparently the Gooks are using the same tactic we ran into before. They take advantage of the tides and the currents to float their mines along the coast toward the fleet anchorage area," Powell said. His pencil traced a northward path on the chart's transparent overlay. "Makes our job tougher."

"What about subs in the area?" Riley asked.

"No subs," Powell said. "Water's too shallow."

"How shallow? We have good water for this run, don't we?" Riley asked.

"Most of it," Powell replied. "The staff briefer on the flagship told us this area has some serious tide ranges. Up to twenty-six feet last year they said, but usually less. Shouldn't be a problem. If we stay on our proposed track, we stay in deep water."

"Where do we patrol?" Mike moved around the plotting table for a better view of their planned route.

Powell ground out his cigarette in overkill mode, leaving tiny shreds of tobacco in the ashtray and muttered something. Was Powell's angry scan of the compartment a search to see who might overhear their conversation?

"Mission planning is my job, understand?" Powell glowered at Riley, then at Mike. His barely-controlled anger added emphasis to his words. "Not this time, though. The old man did this one all by himself. He must think I can't lay out a simple patrol track." Other officers respected Powell's judgment. Mike hadn't previously observed Powell question the captain's decisions.

Riley's squinting eyes and uplifted chin telegraphed concern.

"I don't like the way he's laid out this one," Powell continued. "Told him so this afternoon. 'Do it my way,' he said. He won't listen. Riley, take a look at this."

Powell pointed to a heavy line on the chart's overlay. The route the captain had chosen formed a reverse block letter "C". The long leg would take them northward at ten knots for about three hours along an inner channel that varied between three and five miles wide. A long, narrow island would be to port for about three-fourths of the leg. The main coastline, and the few fishing villages and coves indicated on the chart, would be to starboard.

"With this plan we don't go near these fishing villages where we could expect to find boats... along here." Powell's pencil pointed the chart. "And, dammit, all we have are these old Japanese admiralty charts. They're supposedly the best available. They're vintage 1926. Twenty-five years old, dammit. To top it off, the old man has decided to make this first patrol at night. That's stupid, especially when we have a choice. Floating mines are hard enough to see in daylight as you well know. Impossible at night. He just won't listen."

Riley's narrowed eyes and slight headshake revealed that Powell's out-of-character demeanor bothered him, too. Powell's considerations in selecting a patrol route made better sense than the captain's.

"And here," Powell indicated the patrol track's northern-most point, "he puts us right under the guns. Why so close? We're looking for mine droppers, not medals."

Riley's eyebrows shot up and Mike's stomach tensed.

"Wait a minute, boss," Riley said. "What's this about guns?"

Mike had been trying to read parts of the chart across the table to get a better feel for what he would deal with in his upcoming watch. The mention of guns snapped his attention back to Powell.

"In our briefing on the flagship, the admiral's intelligence officer told us some of the enemy's heavy guns were reported along the coastline bluffs," Powell said. His pencil tapped the chart around the top of *Bartley's* proposed northern leg. At that point Mike would face a peninsula and would have to make an approximate ninety-degree turn west to keep the ship in deep water.

"The admiral's staff didn't have an exact position for the guns," Powell added. Mike wasn't comforted by the uncertainty in Powell's reply

"I'm not keen on getting shot at, you know, boss," Riley said.

Mid-afternoon Mike took a brief stroll on deck to quell a growing anxiety. Alone in open water, the frigid scene, windless, no land in sight, and solid overcast increased his unease. He hustled to the radio shack for a cup of warm coffee hoping it would cheer him.

Mike went to the bridge earlier than usual for his 2000-2400 watch as OOD. That gave him time to get night adapted and to once again review the inshore patrol track *Bartley* would travel. A quick check of the navigator's chart showed no changes to the planned patrol. He hoped the extra sweater he'd added under his parka would keep him warm on what promised to be another bitter cold watch.

Instead of following his normal routine, Mike did not examine the radarscope before relieving the watch. He avoided the touchy XO and his dominance of the vital navigation instrument. The XO prided himself on his accurate navigation. He didn't tolerate interference from anyone but the captain. The XO's abrupt actions and mumblings, as he took range and bearing measurement of the southern end of the nearby island, raised Mike's curiosity. The XO's uncharacteristic mutterings as he converted his radar readings to his chart confirmed that he, too, was apprehensive about their mission.

A dead calm had set in around lunchtime. The skies held a low overcast. Mike scanned the cloud cover for breaks. He couldn't see stars. A quarter moon, invisible through the misty haze, would set in twenty-five minutes. He shook his head. Fishing boats would be hard to spot even if in clear moonlight. These were lousy conditions to search for any mine-dropping boats.

The presence of big guns, supposedly in range of their intended path, worried Mike. *Bartley* would transit the patrol track with all lights blacked out, a near impossible target at night. But, if mines had already been dropped, he and his watch team wouldn't be able to see them floating in the dark water. Why had the captain insisted this first patrol be at night? Had anyone challenged the captain on his decision? The XO and Powell should have at least. Maybe they'd get a chewing out for the effort, but it would have been the right and professional thing to do.

Mike followed the familiar turnover ritual and assumed the OOD watch from Lieutenant (JG) Davis five minutes early.

"Has the captain been up here yet?" Mike asked. The watch turnover usually included information on the captain's whereabouts. Davis hadn't offered the information. "Where is he?"

"Don't know, Mike," Davis said. "I haven't seen him. Last I knew he was in his cabin. Check combat. He might be down there. I expect he'll be up here before we turn north, anyway."

Seaman Tucker also relieved the bridge phone-talker early. Tucker waited to the side between the conning officer's station and the navigator's table, within earshot of any activity on the cramped open bridge. He pulled his knit cap down around his head and over the bulging earphones of the sound-powered phone rig he wore. His nod to Mike indicated his readiness.

Ensign Brooks came onto the bridge a minute later and set his coffee cup on the shelf behind the windscreen. He looked around the bridge and glanced at the surrounding waters. A noticeable shiver coursed through his body.

"Damned quiet up here tonight," Brooks whispered to Mike after the JOOD turnover ritual. "You feel it? Spooky."

"Combat says the captain's in CIC, Mister K," Seaman Tucker reported. "Just walked in. Isn't he supposed to be up here?"

"Thanks, Tuck," Mike replied. "I thought so, too. He should be up here later."

Mike called through the voice tube to CIC and received Cavallo's permission to turn north at the scheduled time, beginning the longest leg of the patrol. His stomach tightened as he ordered the turn at 2005. The turn to port, around the nearby island's southern end would begin the patrol's longest leg, and drive *Bartley* into unknown and dangerous water. Something didn't feel right.

Mike reviewed his responsibilities for the watch in addition to the routine. At its northern end, the three-hour and ten-minute leg could put the ship under the enemy guns. Then Mike would turn to the west to follow the planned track. All seemed simple enough.

Mike shivered, imagining what could lie ahead. *Bartley* might intercept fishermen dropping mines. How would they deal with the fisherman? Suppose they did find a mine, or more than one? What if they hit one? He tapped the emblem in his pocket.

"Bridge, conn," Mike called to the quartermaster in the wheelhouse. "Pass the word. Set readiness condition three. Do not sound the klaxon. We want to stay quiet and dark tonight."

The possibility that *Bartley* might encounter enemy gunfire from shore batteries had flashed throughout the ship earlier in the day. Mike was surprised but reassured when the crew made all the ship's compartments watertight in half the usual time. The crew needed no urging to man the key defensive stations.

"Pass the word to all topside watch standers to check for lights," Mike said to Seaman Tucker. "I want to be at absolute darken ship. Nobody smokes. No lights. No exceptions."

"Aye, aye, sir," Tucker said. Soon he added, "All stations report the ship's dark, Mister K. Nobody can see a damned thing."

"That's the way I want it," Mike said more to himself than to Tucker.

"Mister Brooks," Mike ordered, "check the wheelhouse, the lookouts, and signal bridge. Make sure they're on their toes."

"It's eerie," Brooks reported after he returned. "The crew is more than ready. Everyone's on edge, waiting. No one moves who doesn't have to. Nobody's talking either, only whispers. The helmsman asked me if the Gook gunners could see or hear us. I told him no."

Mike wandered the bridge at intervals to look for light leaks. He shared Brooks' apprehension. Were they facing combat? Maybe he had an overactive imagination. If the Gooks had guns near the northern turn, could their fire reach the ship? He tried a violent headshake to clear his brain of the image of enemy shells hitting the ship.

"Seems quieter than usual," Brooks confided in a whisper about an hour after the turn to the north. "None of the normal chatter. I don't like this, Mike. Do you suppose those guns could reach us if we stayed on this track?"

Mike shrugged but didn't reply.

The sky had become more haze than clouds, diffusing what dim light came from the stars. In reply to Tucker's frequent queries, the lookouts reported that they saw nothing beyond the ship. The dim red glow of the dials on the bridge instruments added to Mike's uneasiness, an eerie sensation he couldn't identify or dismiss.

Ensign Brooks paced across the narrow bridge. He stopped at alternate wings to listen and to peer in silence into the darkness on either side.

"All I hear, other than our machinery noise, is the lookouts' reports," Brooks said. "I can't see a damned thing."

Mike limited his reply to a nod.

"Suppose any mine droppers are out there tonight?" Brooks asked.

Mike shrugged again.

The XO paced the bridge whenever he wasn't busy with his navigator's plot or on the phone with the captain in CIC two decks below. Their apparent disagreement on the ship's position rattled Mike.

"Sure wish the captain would at least let us turn on the surface search radar to get a fix," were the XO's first words to anyone on the bridge since the start of the watch. "He can leave the air search off if he wants. It wouldn't help now anyway. I don't like dead reckoning navigation in these waters."

In disbelief, Mike stopped breathing for a moment. The radars were off? He hadn't checked the radars after he came on watch. He should have.

"Have you asked him?" Mike said.

The XO shrugged and went back to his charts.

"Why did he turn off the radar?" Mike called to the XO, frustrated by the XO's unwillingness to question the captain. Why was he so afraid of the old man, afraid enough to put us all in jeopardy?

"Don't know." The XO looked away. "I guess he doesn't want the radar's search signal to be detected and reveal that we're out here." He stared into the blackness and wiped his face.

Seaman Tucker pulled Mike aside. "I've been thinking, Mister K. What if we do run into one of them Gook boats? If the radar's off, how do we find 'em if they don't show some lights? And if we do find one, how will we catch him if we can't see him? Hell, if they dropped mines like before, we might run right into one of them suckers. We were damned lucky it was daylight last time."

"Guess I don't have answers for you, Tuck," Mike said. Good questions. Tucker's concern reinforced his own. How would he deal with a mine-dropper if he encountered one?

Mike tapped Brooks' shoulder and pointed to the sky. "Look. We've moved out from under the worst of the haze. I can see stars again."

"Yeah." Brooks gazed to port where the island should be, then to starboard where the mainland should be, all distant, unseen shores. "Can't see any land though, or any boats either, unless we run over one. You sure we're okay? On track I mean?" He motioned toward the XO. "The XO's chatter with the captain has me wondering. I'd hate to hit one of those rocks."

Bartley soon emerged from under the last of the haze and into a clear sky. Ahead, Mike could see the intense black ridgeline of the east-west promontory ahead defined against the faint, starlit sky.

"The top of the ridgeline is moving up," Mike said ten minutes later. "It's blocked some of the lower stars we could see a few minutes ago."

"I see it, too." Brooks pointed to the loom of the peninsula ahead. "I'm sure it's not our imagination. What do you think? Should we tell the captain?"

Mike checked the clock. Six minutes to go before the planned course change. Why not make it now? The turn point had been the captain's arbitrary selection. Nothing magic about it as long as the ship could alter course safely. The charts showed clear, deep water to the west. The ship had passed the northern end of the island to the west ten minutes earlier. He could come left at any point into open water.

"We're getting damned close, Mister K," Tucker said, insistent this time. He pointed to the looming land. "You sure the XO knows where we are?"

Mike stuck his head into the navigator's hut. He confirmed his next course. The dim red light showed the XO's latest plot of *Bartley's* position but offered no clues that he could use to judge the ship's distance from the promontory ahead. His gut insisted the ship was closer than the XO's plot indicated.

"Take a look ahead, XO," Mike said. "The clouds have cleared. I can see the land ahead against the backdrop of the sky. Can't make out what exactly. Doesn't matter. We're closer than your plot shows. Too close."

The XO glanced ahead. He shook his head then looked back at Mike as though he expected Mike to elaborate. He bent over his chart again before he picked up the phone to the captain.

"Sir," the XO said, "the cloud cover's lifted. Hasn't helped much. Mike thinks he can see the promontory ahead, but I can't... okay... behind our intended track... okay, yes sir, delay our turn five minutes."

Mike checked his watch.

The XO shook his head again and returned the phone to its mount on the bulkhead.

Mike strained to pick out any detail in the landmass ahead. Why did the XO's plot disagree with what he, Brooks, and Tucker saw? All three of them could see danger looming ahead. Why in hell wasn't the XO more concerned? They could safely turn left any time. What made the captain think he had a better picture of their position? If nothing else, Cavallo should come to the bridge and see for himself.

"I don't like this at all," Mike said. "A five-minute delay could put us aground."

"I agree," Brooks said. His strained voice revealed their collective, heightened tension. "We're way too close. Don't screw around. Turn, now."

The peninsula's ridgeline had become a well-defined, solid black silhouette that appeared to climb faster against the backdrop of the starlit sky. Mike knew the movement wasn't his imagination. Everything convinced him that *Bartley* confronted an unknown shore and probable disaster. The shore could be beach or rocks, maybe cliffs. Mike's mind filled with a vision of *Bartley* driven into a rock wall. With disaster imminent unless he turned, Mike moved to the XO's chart table.

"XO, we're too close to the promontory, closer than your plot shows," Mike said. "We need to turn. Now."

The XO looked at Mike without comment.

"The chart shows plenty of open water to the west for the next leg," Mike persisted. "Unless we come left now we'll run aground, head on. We can't wait longer."

The XO squinted into the blackness ahead. He shook his head yet again. "No, we'll turn when Captain Cavallo says," the XO said. A nervous hand wiped his face.

Mike gritted his teeth, and muttered, "Don't hesitate. Don't rely on the XO. Protocol be damned. Tell Cavallo yourself."

Brooks, standing at Mike's elbow, said, "I agree. We can't wait."

Mike called the captain through the voice tube to CIC with the same warning. He heard no response from Cavallo or anyone in CIC.

Mike's mind jumped to a new plateau, calm, in control even though an inner instinct insisted collision or grounding was imminent. Move into open water, out of danger. Head west now.

"Bridge, conn. Left full rudder, come to new course 273," Mike ordered four minutes and twenty-five seconds before the captain's modified time. The new course should put the ship in clear, open water. Mike tapped the small gold emblem in his pocket. The captain could hang him if he chose to do so, but this was the right move now. Eager nods from both Tucker and Brooks supported Mike's decision.

"What the hell are you doing, Kinkaid?" The XO yelled and grabbed Mike's arm. "Why are you turning early?" He bolted back to his chart table and muttered to himself.

Mike ground his teeth. The ship heeled into a turn to port. His stomach tightened. Had he turned soon enough to avoid disaster?

"Rudder is left full, sir," the helmsman's routine call came through the voice tube to the bridge. "Passing 355 to new course 273." Mike held his breath. He expected an immediate, irate call from the captain, or countermanding directions through the voice tube. He'd failed to follow Cavallo's standing orders. He'd turned without permission. His OOD qual could be in jeopardy. But, he had to turn. He listened at the voice tube. The only words he heard were the helmsman's reports. Tucker announced the turn over his phone circuit.

"Good move, Mister K," Tucker said after his report, unmistakable relief in his voice. "Let's put them guns behind us."

"I hear breakers, Mike" Brooks screamed and pointed from the starboard wing of the bridge. "I see them, too. And some rocks. Oh, God, we're close. Hang on."

Mike kept his death grip on the binnacle. Tight-jawed, he glanced at the all-too-slow swing of the compass as *Bartley's* turn to port continued. He was helpless to do more. The impact would come at any instant, a grinding collision, the ship sinking, men crying for help. Mike envisioned himself, detached somehow, a passenger on a fateful trip, able to observe, but unable to control the events to follow.

"Steady on new course 273, sir," the helmsman called through the voice tube from the wheelhouse.

Mike's knees trembled. Sweat rolled down his neck. His grip on the binnacle eased when he recognized the familiar, slight wallowing sensation of the ship again steady on course.

The three of them had been right. *Bartley* had turned too close to the promontory, closer than either the captain or the XO had plotted. The ship must have progressed farther north along the track than anyone had known. His course change had averted grounding head-on. A shudder accompanied Mike's realization. Thank God he turned when he did.

Some of the larger rocks in the area loomed above the ocean's surface ahead, menacing distant forms of black-on-black. Where was the ship exactly? He had to keep *Bartley* in deep water.

Mike pictured the chart in his head. He searched for a large, distinctive rock in the shape of a tailor's thimble. Without radar, the pinnacle would be their principal navigation reference after the turn to the west. But, he'd have to rely on an eyeball-search to spot it without radar. The chart said the rock rose forty feet above the surface and should be off the starboard bow now that the ship had steadied on the new westerly course.

"Anyone see the pinnacle? I don't," Mike said to Brooks and Tucker.

"Don't see it either," Brooks said from the starboard wing of the bridge. "I can see some dark things in the distance to starboard, probably smaller rocks. They're too small to be the pinnacle though."

Astern, the peninsula retreated. The ridgeline appeared to move lower against the sky's backdrop at a discernible rate but not fast enough for comfort.

"We came too damned close for—"

"Over there," Tucker shouted and pointed off the port bow. In the distance, Mike saw the unmistakable black outline of the tailor's thimble.

Mike stopped breathing. His fists flexed. Why was the pinnacle off the port bow? It should have been to starboard on this heading. That distinctive rock had to be the one shown on the chart, the only one in the area. A silent message screamed in his brain. You turned too late. You're north of where you should be. You're in danger. Get back to open water and onto the planned track. Now.

"Continue your turn. Come left to new heading 230," Mike ordered to the helmsman. Would the turn be enough? Did they have clear water ahead on that course? He'd give almost anything for working radar.

Mike visualized how to regain their desired track, much as he'd visualized his moves in his chess games with Riley. His brain urged another turn south into the water clear of rocks. Put the pinnacle on the starboard bow. It's still too far away to be a collision threat, but that margin won't last forever on this heading.

"Come left to new course 210," Mike ordered.

The ship's bow moved left, southward toward deeper water, but the pinnacle rock's bearing didn't change. What's wrong? An inner sense warned Mike.

The chart showed shallow water to the northwest of their position. How close were the shallows? He didn't have time to find out. Instinct told him to get into deeper water fast. Turn farther south. Turn now.

"Left full rudder," Mike ordered. "Continue your turn. Set new course to 160."

Mike glanced at the XO expecting him to intervene. The XO, trance-like, silent, gripped the support strut of his navigator's hut.

"Rudder is left full," the helmsman responded. "Continuing left to course 160, sir. Passing 195."

The pinnacle rock appeared to drift to their right slower than Mike wanted, but at least in the desired direction. *Bartley* had passed through this area, west of the island, earlier in the afternoon while they headed for the starting point of the patrol. Deeper water lay ahead on the new southeast heading. Mike's tension eased. In a few minutes they would regain the planned track.

Bartley's bow raised out of the water... then Mike fell forward...

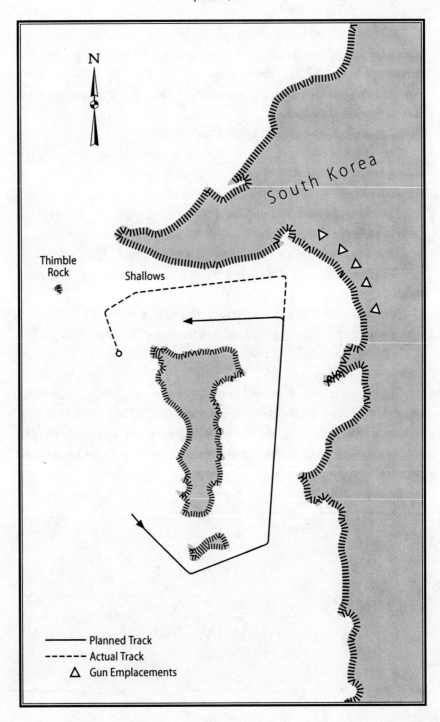

25

EVERY HEARTBEAT SENT HAMMER BLOWS to Mike's head. Why was he on his knees? Had he imagined that an invisible hand had reached down from the heavens, lifted *Bartley* from the water, dropped her, and impaled her on a rocky beach?

Mike stumbled to his feet, still dizzy, a steadying grip on the nearby stanchion. The bullet's scar in his shoulder throbbed. His fingers discovered his parka's newly torn left sleeve then brushed the telephone handset that dangled from the holder.

He looked around the open bridge at the others. Brooks sat on the deck, his back to the bulkhead, rubbing his eyes. Seaman Tucker, silent and unsteady, struggled to stand. He grabbed the coaming rail to steady himself then adjusted the sound-powered phone set that had fallen around his neck. The XO gripped the plotting table supports as he rose to his feet with great care. He gawked at Mike, mouth open, speechless, his hat on the deck.

Mike gasped. The sudden stop, the shriek of metal scraping, and the crazy vibrations throughout the ship finally made sense. *Bartley* had hit something underwater. The ship's forward momentum had pulled *Bartley* farther onto the obstacle that now held her. That would explain the rumble and grinding sounds that resembled dragging a heavy metal garbage can over pavement. All forward motion had stopped despite the engines' efforts to push the ship onward. *Bartley* was aground.

Mike's heart pounded. He had to act. He could attempt to back free from whatever held the ship, but a backing order might rip away the hull plates. That could sink her. He couldn't allow *Bartley* to be stranded for who knew how long. The captain should be here.

"Emergency all back full," Mike called into the voice tube to the wheelhouse chose to reverse engines. "Sound collision quarters." The order to the crew to seal off the ship should prevent or at least minimize flooding.

Bartley vibrated and flexed to a degree Mike had never believed possible while the engines struggled to pull the ship from her captor. The propellers revved up to full. Mike couldn't detect any movement at first. Then the ship inched backward in short jerks and bumps as though Poseidon himself fought to hold the ship captive. High-pitched, metal screams and underwater rumbles broadcast *Bartley's* struggle. The sounds created a chilling picture of hull plates being torn off. Had he made the wrong decision?

The ship flexed like an anguished fish on a hook. The screeching stopped. A settling sensation followed. Was this a preliminary to sinking? Mike strained to identify clues. *Bartley* settled into a calm sea and appeared to remain afloat.

His mind raced. He needed answers. What damage had the ship suffered? Where? How much? What about injuries or casualties? Was she still seaworthy? How about flooding? Was sinking still a possibility? How imminent?

The initial damage reports to the bridge came one-by-one over Seaman Tucker's sound-powered phone circuit. Minor reports came at first, some falls and bruises, gear tossed from lockers, and dishware spilled in the galley. Soon the information overload challenged Tucker's ability to keep up and maintain circuit discipline.

The captain scrambled onto the bridge. "All stop," he ordered to the helmsman through the brass voice tube. In moments the engines slowed their throbbing, then silence. A motionless captain appeared to listen while the ship drifted, but he said nothing more. An ominous quiet blanketed the bridge once the thrashing propellers had stopped.

The XO stayed at his plotting table, his eyes locked on Captain Cavallo. Seaman Tucker's stage whispers repeated to Mike the information he continued to receive from the damage control parties.

Mike waited for orders from the captain, ready to respond. What went through the old man's mind? As OOD, Mike should take some action if the captain wouldn't.

Mike's analysis of *Bartley's* condition seemed to come unbidden from some automatic region of his brain. The reports so far hadn't described an imminent threat of sinking. The ship wasn't listing, or settling by either the bow or stern, as he had feared.

"Sir," Mike said to Cavallo, "damage control central reports number one fireroom is flooded. The lone man stationed in the fireroom, Seaman Bradford, isn't accounted for. Number two fireroom is dry with minor damage. Mount One's forward magazine has some flooding. It's coming through the hull plates. Emergency pumps are staying with the flooding so far, but they're not gaining on it. Sonar reports their gear is out. No fires reported. Some falls and bruises, but no serious injuries."

"XO, get the chief engineer up here," Cavallo ordered.

Mike had the uneasy feeling some other action should be taken, but couldn't determine what. Letting the ship float with the tide seemed irresponsible. He and Riley hadn't discussed a circumstance like this.

"How about the missing man?" the captain asked as the chief engineer stepped on to the bridge. "What's his name?"

"Seaman Bradford, sir." The jacketless chief engineer mopped sweat with a rag. "Haven't located him yet. He's one of the new men, sir. He had the cold iron watch alone in the fireroom. It's flooded now."

"So, where is he?" the captain asked. Cavallo's quiet, conversational manner surprised Mike. The usual, grumpy bluster had disappeared. He seemed genuinely concerned with the missing man's welfare.

"Don't know, sir," the chief engineer said, still panting after scrambling up from several decks below. "Held a quick muster. Accounted for everyone else. It's possible he didn't get out."

"Do we have any way to tell if he's still in the engine room?" the captain asked.

"We've opened the access hatch, checked the water level. Compartment's full," the chief engineer said. "No sign of Bradford, sir. We don't have any way to search for him. Nobody on board is a qualified diver.

Unless Bradford got out fast, well, I'm afraid it doesn't look good."

The captain stared at the chief engineer for half a minute, waved his head from side to side, straightened his back and focused on the XO.

"XO, account for all hands," Cavallo ordered. Quiet resolve replaced the normal bluster, almost apologetic. "Check every man. Call me immediately when you find Bradford." He turned to Mike.

"You have the conn, Mister Kinkaid." The captain's order, given without the usual negative growl, surprised Mike. "We'll stay at collision quarters until I order you to secure. Tell Powell to draft a report and meet me in my cabin." The captain's finger tapped the XO's chest. "Set a course back to the anchorage." Cavallo said in his normal gruff manner. "And stay in deep water this time."

The captain reset the normal steaming watch with the exception of the damage control parties that worked to contain the flooding. After he was relieved as OOD about 0045 Mike settled in the wheelhouse to write the log for the watch. He tried to focus on his task despite the turmoil in his head. The weight of his actions and the probable end of his dream to fly fought for dominance over his attempt to concentrate. The possibility that he had caused another man's death remained at the edge of his mind demanding recognition. But, if he hadn't turned when he did, more would be dead.

The quartermaster's detailed record of the events of the watch included every course and speed change, the time of each action, and who had given each order. Mike offered silent thanks.

The events replayed in Mike's mind during the hour spent writing the log, normally a ten-minute task. The words must record an accurate picture, as was the case in the net collision. An accident of this magnitude, with probable major damage to the ship, could not escape investigation. An examination would probe for ambiguities, inconsistencies or mistakes. Three times Mike reviewed what he'd written. All were clear statements, none misleading or irrelevant.

Mike half-filled a mug of coffee from the wardroom and stumbled, exhausted, to his stateroom. The night's events continued to cycle through his mind. Riley entered Mike's stateroom and found him at his desk, staring at the bulkhead. A tablet with random notes lay on Mike's pull-down desktop.

"Can't sleep either?" Riley said.

"Haven't tried." Mike beat a pencil on the tablet. "Thinking about what happened. Making some notes."

"Me, too." Riley sat on Mike's bunk. He rested his chin on bridged fingers. He yawned then massaged the back of his neck, patted his shirt pocket, and pulled out two folded sheets of yellow tablet paper. Riley blinked several times, rubbed his eyes, glanced at the sheets, and tossed them in Mike's wastebasket. "No need to keep these any longer."

"Wait. What's that?" Mike said.

"My notes from the watch," Riley said. "My log's done. Don't need them anymore, I guess."

Neither spoke for several minutes. Mike's pencil continued to tap before he straightened up. He fished Riley's notes from the wastebasket and laid them next to his own.

"I should have turned sooner," Mike said.

"Agreed," Riley said as if emerging from his own fog. He stretched, and shook his head several times as though to chase the fatigue. "I noted the old man's plots and listened to his chatter with the XO. A simple navigation job got away from them. They couldn't agree on our position. And, as usual, the captain wouldn't listen."

"Why did the old man turn off the radar?" Mike's anger surged. "We had a working radar. We steamed in dangerous and unfamiliar waters at night. Dammit, what valid reason did he have to deny us our best tool for safe navigation? That's not only stupid, it's criminal."

"I tried to reason with him," Riley said, "Turn on the surface search radar for a few seconds at least so we could get a quick fix." He shook his head in slow, deliberate swings. "He wasn't buying. He said we'd give away our position. Guess he was worried about Gook guns on the bluff."

"No guns, right?" Mike said.

"Right," Riley said. "I'd say the staff's info was bum dope. Our troops cleaned out all the Gooks along this part of the coast some time ago. If any guns were on the bluffs, they had to be dummies or leftovers."

"Or, if some Gook guns were up there," Mike's raised arm waved toward a phantom cliff, "they had no way to know we were in the channel." Mike's exchange with Riley had brought new energy and buried the drowsiness.

"I vote no guns," Riley said.

"How could they see us?" Mike added. "We were blacked out. Couldn't see a damned thing. Not a light showed the whole watch. We were too far away to be heard, too. No chance we'd be fired on."

A moment later Riley's head snapped up, wide-eyed. "Hey." He jabbed a finger at Mike. "You remember Powell's comment about the tidal action and the strong currents mentioned in the admiral's briefing? That has to be the answer. Why didn't I think of it before?" He thrust a finger at Mike again. "Where were we in the tidal cycle?"

"I didn't think to ask Davis during the watch turnover," Mike said. "That's not info we normally keep track of. Maybe we should have."

The tides had to be the explanation. No other scenario made any sense. A strong northerly flow would explain the navigational difference. Mike had failed to note the conditions in his log entry. He couldn't go back and add it now. Maybe it wasn't important. It could be if Riley's hunch was right.

"C'mon, think about it," Riley said.

Mike stood, and tossed his jacket onto the upper bunk. He bent three times to touch his toes to get his blood flowing. The fog in his head cleared and he dropped back into the cramped stateroom's single chair.

"I suspect we had an ebbing tide, a northerly flow?" Riley said. "That might account for being farther north than we plotted, and... Oh, hell. We'll never know. Guessing games don't get us anywhere."

Riley's idea made sense. Mike cringed at the realization that he, too, should have considered the effect of the tides. Had either the captain or XO made allowance for currents?

Mike leaned his chair back against the locker, legs outstretched. The more he considered Riley's premise, the better he liked it. The captain or the XO, maybe both, probably didn't know what the currents were either. The topic hadn't been mentioned in any conversation he'd heard. Unknown currents, or misjudging their strength would explain their plot differences.

"Before this is over," Mike said, "there'll be more questions than I want to think about. We need to write down all our ideas, what we saw, what we did, you know, stuff we don't put into the log. That way we'll have everything we might not remember later. Put down who said what and when. Record the details, things we'll wish we remembered when the questions start coming."

Mike's energy returned. He reached for his cup and took a sip of the cold coffee.

"Hang on to these." Mike returned Riley's discarded notes. "I can't see how we can avoid some serious questions. We better be prepared."

Riley stuffed the notes into his pocket. He looked at Mike. "Any word about Bradford?"

Mike shook his head. Please let the missing seaman be found. His gut told him otherwise. An innocent man may have died even though an early turn had likely saved others. He cringed at the possibility that this incident, like his earlier man-overboard rescue, would also become a frequent, unwelcome nightmare.

26

BARTLEY RETURNED TO THE FLEET anchorage off the South Korean coastal city of Inchon. The admiral's message had ordered Captain Cavallo, the XO, and Powell to report to him in person. Mike was relieved not to be included on the whaleboat that shoved off headed for the force flagship across the choppy sea. Some sort of discipline would come soon enough and now that the admiral was involved, it would likely be more than a chewing out.

In the radio shack Mike sorted through old messages. Pops came in and told him of the buzz among the crew about the extent of the ship's underwater damage. The sonar equipment didn't respond. The crewmen had been able to limit flooding in the forward ammunition storage magazine, but the pumps couldn't lower the water level. The destroyer tender that served as both the admiral's flagship and mother hen to the anchored fleet provided some help. A diver was inspecting the underwater hull, but the tender wasn't equipped to make repairs. Mike's depression grew with each bit of bad news.

When the whaleboat returned, Mike, Riley, and many curious crewmembers searched for clues. How soon would they know what lay in store for *Bartley*? The hull needed a shipyard and soon. How long would the repairs take? Any chance the ship could get temporary repairs and head home to San Diego? He hoped that, for a change, the captain would break his habitual, dour silence. The entire crew deserved to know their fate without delay.

The captain, the XO, and Powell remained mum. The crew's wild rumors grew, most of them pessimistic. Mike remained tense waiting for confirmation.

Mike began a letter to Carol, but trashed the first page. He had nothing conclusive to tell her, and what he did know would only cause her worry. Instead, he glossed through the day's message traffic unable to concentrate. Riley wandered into the radio shack and pulled up a chair.

"I suppose you know about—" Riley started in a subdued tone.

"Bradford?" Mike said. His throat tightened for a moment. "Can't find him. He didn't make it."

"Don't take it so hard," Riley said. "We had an accident. You did what you had to do."

Mike shuddered. He couldn't suppress the recurring image of a young man's body afloat in the blackness of the flooded fireroom. He didn't know Bradford. He probably hadn't even seen him. What a hell of a way to die.

"No word yet on what happened with the admiral," Riley said. He shifted in his chair and pulled out a cigarette. "I tried to pump Powell. He won't talk either. When will it be our turn to answer to the admiral?"

"Don't know," Mike said. "I'm in no rush."

"Today's lunch had to be one for the books," Riley said. "Like eating in a morgue. I don't ever remember a meal when no one spoke a word. And such grim faces."

The next morning Mike and Riley, along with several other officers, assembled in the wardroom for an initial damage report by a member of the admiral's staff.

"We recommended to the admiral," the short, bald staff officer said in emotionless tones to open the briefing, "that you go to the shipyard for a better inspection and repairs. We've already sent our preliminary damage report to them." He flipped through some papers in his folder.

"The admiral has ordered," the staff officer continued, "that a formal Board of Investigation be convened to examine the grounding." Mike and Riley exchanged glances. "The board will conduct their fact-finding aboard the British ship *HMS Ladybird*, the joint area flagship. They're in Sasebo. They'll meet with you after you arrive. The shipyard there will give the damage details to the investigators once they get you into dry dock."

Mike tried to quiet the pounding blood in his head. The situation grew more serious with the staff officer's every word.

Bartley's chief engineer scribbled on his note pad. The XO twisted in his seat but said nothing. Mike looked around at the officers at the table. All waited for the captain's reaction. So far, Cavallo remained impassive.

"Here's the damage we found," the staff officer checked his note pad. "You have a gaping hole under the bow. Your sonar's gone, stripped from the hull by whatever you hit. You lost the sonar's guts, too. The impact damaged the area around the forward magazine. You'll have to continue pumping until you get into the shipyard. We'll provide a spare portable pump before you leave the anchorage."

Mike glanced at Riley. The slow shake of Riley's head and his frown added to Mike's anxiety. Perhaps the damage was more serious than the loss of the sonar.

"You have about a ten-foot split in the hull on the port side," the staff officer said, "about four inches from the keel. The flooding in your number one fireroom is from that break. And, ah, you've been briefed about the drowned man?"

Mike resented the staff officer's insensitivity as if Seaman Bradford were a piece of broken machinery. He clamped his jaws shut and glared at the staff officer. Bradford was a man. Doing his job. An innocent victim.

"Your keel is damaged. Needs a closer look," the staff officer continued. "A couple of inches more and you would have broken her back."

Mike cringed. He'd come close to sinking the ship. How many men would have been lost? He hadn't realized how close until now.

The staff officer flipped through more papers. "You're not combat ready in this condition. You're damned lucky the damage wasn't worse. The shipyard in Sasebo is expecting you."

"When can we leave?" Captain Cavallo said. He had sat through the briefing stone-faced, without comment or question. Unlike the XO and Powell, he had taken no notes.

"It's up to the admiral," the staff officer said. "I'd wait for better weather if I were you. I'd recommend an escort, too. Rough seas can be dangerous. Don't know how much flexing this tub can take in its condition."

Another wave broke over *Bartley's* bow and drenched the bridge with spray. The admiral had denied the captain's request for an escort, claiming an imminent fleet operation couldn't spare a ship to accompany them to Sasebo. *Bartley* had no choice but to steam alone through the heavy seas.

Mike ducked below the windscreen. The ship fought for survival in a storm that labored to sink her. Would the next wave be the killer, the one too powerful for *Barley's* ruptured hull to withstand? Even with speed limited to eight knots, the damaged ship groaned with each swell she struggled to ride over. She screamed in pain as each wave flooded her bow.

Were the ship's protests like the death groans of a dying animal, or was his imagination working overtime? How much punishment could the ship take before disaster struck?

Mike's bridge watch team, cold and wet from the fierce wind and rain, huddled wherever even the slightest protection from the storm could be found. Mike read the expressions on each haggard, sleepless face. All aboard believed, as Mike did, that *Bartley* wouldn't reach Sasebo. If the ship floundered, no nearby ship could save them in the fast-moving storm. As a precaution, Mike had stationed a radioman around the clock at the ship's emergency radio.

Mike calculated they were in their twentieth hour on a course southward toward the Sasebo shipyard on Kyushu, Japan's southern island. No changes to course or speed were planned. This time, the usual chatter on a quiet watch was limited to abbreviated, routine reports.

"Mister K," Seaman Tucker shouted over the wind, "Damage Control Central reports they checked all watertight hatches again like you ordered. The ones by the forward magazine have to stay open to handle the flooding. They're barely holding their own. Even the portable pump is working full time, our last one." He pulled the drawstrings of his parka's hood to close it around his face. He put his back to the wind and spray. "Will we make it, Mister K?"

"Don't know, Tuck," Mike said. He didn't want to sound pessimistic for Tucker's sake, but he held little hope. "Guess this is a good time to talk to the man upstairs."

If the ship flooded and sank with no other ship nearby, his radio gang would probably get out an emergency radio signal, but the chance of finding survivors in this weather would be slim at best. Life vests had been distributed to all hands. He shook his head to chase the images of a sinking ship and drowning men.

If something did happen to *Bartley*, how would Carol know? If he didn't survive, how would she cope with his loss? And the baby. His child might never know its father. Carol would have to raise the child on her own. What insurance or support would the Navy provide to her?

Mike slept little after the watch. The ship's tormented pitch and roll threatened to toss him from his bunk. A pillow over his head failed to muffle the relentless screech of the port propeller's shaft bearing. That damage hadn't been included in the diver's abbreviated underwater inspection. What else had the inspectors missed?

Mike's bridge watch the next morning matched the torment of the night before. Mike, Brooks, and Tucker huddled against the frigid spray's onslaught each time *Bartley's* bow dug into one more enormous wave. The screeching that had terrorized all hands through the night had ceased after the captain ordered the engineers to lock the port shaft during the 0400-0800 watch. Thereafter, *Bartley* steamed with a single shaft, one working fire room, and one working engine room, only half their engineering plant. Slow flooding persisted in the forward magazine spaces. Mike offered a silent prayer that the ship had escaped further damage. They had no reserve.

The captain roamed the bridge in silence for the third time since Mike's watch began. What went through his mind? Cavallo had avoided eye contact and not said a word to Mike or anyone on the bridge during those brief appearances.

Mike sympathized with the tired damage-control crews who worked around the clock to pump water from the flooded magazine and shore up the leaking hull. The ship's slow progress tested the strength of *Bartley's* thin hull, the crew's limits, and their determination to survive.

"Combat, conn," Mike called into the squawk box. "Any surface contacts on the radar? I can see a couple hundred yards at best up here."

"Nothing," Riley replied. "And how about avoiding those potholes, Mike? Everyone down here is either hanging on or puking."

"At least you're dry," Mike replied.

"Tell the captain I've secured the air search radar," Riley added. "The antenna's hanging up with all this bouncing around. Nobody's flying in this damned storm anyway."

"Bridge, aye," Mike said. "I'll tell him."

Midway through the watch, the wind shifted around to the ship's port beam. The change caused *Bartley* to roll dangerously in the wave troughs. Mike insisted the others on the watch team maintain a firm grip on a stanchion or other support, or risk a serious fall. A modest change in sea state followed and permitted *Bartley's* one operating propeller to stay below the surface most of the time, even though the rain and wind attacked without letup.

The phone buzzer startled Mike. He had drifted into a mental fog. Angry with himself, he rolled his shoulders, grabbed the handset and turned his back to the wind and rain. He put his right hand over his other ear to dampen the wind noise.

"Bridge. Kinkaid," Mike answered.

"Chief engineer here, Mike. Here's what I told the captain. The backup pump in the forward magazine has died. Don't know about a fix yet. The main pump is holding up okay. Don't know how long it will last. Can you stay on this course for another hour? Longer if you can. That will give us a better chance to fix the backup pump."

"The next course change isn't until tonight at 0130, then it's direct to Sasebo harbor's outer buoy. We should spot it about sunrise," Mike said, "if we hold together..."

27

MINUTES BEFORE SUNRISE, *BARTLEY* REACHED the outer marker of Sasebo harbor. The storm had passed leaving scattered low clouds. The quiet harbor slept. The early morning sun cast shafts of gray and silver, revealing the frigid harbor scene as though etched on polished steel.

Bartley's safe arrival in port did little to erase Mike's depression. No telling how long the ship would be forced to stay there if many of the more than thirty ships in the harbor also needed repairs. Would *Bartley* be given priority? How long before they would be interrogated by the Board of Investigation?

Mid-morning, Mike took two cups of coffee to Riley's stateroom.

"Any word yet?" Riley asked. A dead cigarette hung from his lips. His desktop ashtray overflowed.

"Powell says all the dry docks are full." Mike stifled a yawn. He unzipped his jacket and slumped in Riley's spare chair. "We'll have to sit here. Don't know how long."

"The crews trying to contain the leaks in the forward magazine are beat," Riley said. He ground out the cigarette. "They're doing their best to stay ahead of the leaks. I sent my sonar team to give them some rest." Riley rummaged through a wardrobe drawer and pulled out a new cigarette pack.

"I overheard the chief engineer's report to the captain," Riley said. "The shipyard will send another pump and a team to try a temporary patch on the leak in the magazine. They'll send a diver, too."

A sudden twinge in Mike's stomach threatened loss of his breakfast.

The diver would retrieve Bradford's body. His coffee cooled untouched.

Later that afternoon, four of Bradford's shipmates carried his body, zipped in a dark green body bag, to a stack of wooden palettes on the fantail arranged to serve as a temporary bier. The engineering gang and crewmen not on watch assembled to honor their shipmate's farewell.

Mike forced himself to participate in the impromptu ceremony. The man he'd never met, maybe had never seen, lay in an undignified, rubberized wrapper.

Both the captain and the XO had gone ashore to the shipyard. Since *Bartley* didn't have a chaplain, Lieutenant Powell, the next senior officer on board, bowed his head and led the assembled officers and crew in a brief prayer. All hands rendered a salute to their comrade, as two of the men lowered Bradford into the ready launch.

Mike realized he would always remember that frigid scene. New clouds blanketed the skies into a premature sunset while shipmates rendered their last farewells. Cold and blustery winds anointed the somber shipmates with the first wave of freezing rain.

"Read this," the XO said and thrust sealed envelopes at Mike and Riley at a breakfast of hotcakes and sausage on their fifth day in Sasebo. "Come see me if you have any questions."

In Riley's stateroom, Mike read from his letter, "Report to the flagship *HMS Ladybird* at 1030 tomorrow to appear before a formal Board of Investigation for questioning as an interested party regarding the grounding of *USS Bartley* on 22 November, 1951."

"Mine says 0930," Riley said. "Otherwise it's the same. Looks like it's about to hit the fan." His shoulders slumped. His usual half grin hadn't been seen in days.

Since the grounding, Riley shuffled and seldom finished sentences. He had mentioned once that he expected the incident would cost him his promotion to lieutenant and the chance for a Navy career. Mike's burden grew with the knowledge.

"Guess we better tell the XO that we're supposed to report to the flagship tomorrow morning," Mike said. "I'm sure he knows why." Would the XO give him some clue on what to expect? He wouldn't ask. The XO didn't need another excuse to harass. Besides, no one on board had ever encountered a formal Board of Investigation.

Mike rapped on the XO's doorway, Riley behind him in the passageway. Papers shuffled inside but no one replied. Mike knocked again then drew aside the heavy green curtain to the XO's stateroom.

"Yes?" The XO looked up from the paperwork on his desk. A twist at the corner of his pencil mustache revealed the trace of a malevolent smirk.

"Sir, about those letters you gave us," Mike said. He didn't try entering the stateroom. He'd learned this technique minimized the probability of a tantrum. "We're supposed to report to the flagship tomorrow morning before a formal Board of Investigation. Request permission to leave the ship in the morning to testify."

"Permission granted," the XO said. He shuffled papers on his desk for a moment before continuing. "Come see me after you return. I'll have some questions for you both." His pause and a longer-than-usual stare, warned of impending harassment. Finally he returned to the papers on his desk.

"Oh, Kinkaid." The XO's call, undisguised irritation in his voice, stopped Mike a few steps down the passageway. "Hold on a minute."

Mike paused before returning to the doorway. Now what? Another menial task?

"You ever hear of the tin can *USS Dunleavy*?" The XO's left hand tapped the book repeatedly. Shoulder ticks warned of more probing.

Mike steeled himself. Had he revealed any emotion at the mention of his father's ship? Instinct told him to play dumb.

"Why?" Mike said keeping his voice neutral. "You asked the same thing once before?"

The XO's quick right hand swiped across his pencil mustache. His gaze alternated between Mike and the book as though contemplating his next move. Some mutterings Mike couldn't understand followed by a shake of his head that dismissed Mike.

Mike headed to his stateroom and gestured to Riley to follow. He tossed his cap on the upper bunk, his left fist flexing.

"The XO's weasel enough to make my case look even worse," Mike said. "Here's his chance to discredit my OOD qualifications, maybe more."

"Oh, come off it, Mike," Riley said. "You made the right move and we all know you did." He pulled a cigarette from a pack in his desktop and lit it. "The entire watch team will testify. They'll get the same story from everyone. The board isn't stupid."

"I guess you're right, but I don't trust him," Mike said. "We better take our notes with us tomorrow. You never know what they'll ask."

The next morning Mike and Riley huddled in the ship's whaleboat. Both wore their dress blue uniforms, overcoats, and scarves. The frigid, twelve-minute trip across Sasebo's choppy harbor took them to the British headquarters ship, *HMS Ladybird*. The British vessel served as the flagship of the Sasebo, Japan area Joint US/UK Naval Command. The gray-green British flagship reminded Mike of an ocean liner, squat and ungraceful. From the whaleboat she looked dour, uninviting.

Clouds, like a field of gray boulders above, threatened rain, maybe even snow if the temperature dropped a degree or two. Silent and huddled against the weather, Mike's mood mirrored the dark skies. Once again he exhausted all the possible outcomes that might result from his testimony to the board. None offered any promise of reprieve. His order to turn early had saved *Bartley*. Mike stood by his decision even if it meant court-martial and the end of any chance to fly for the Navy.

Riley stated their business to the British officer of the deck. British protocol and ceremony fascinated Mike. He had studied their naval tradition: crisp, sure, and colorful. Memorable were the impressive snap of salutes, the spotless quarterdeck area, and the watch team at rigid attention. Intriguing as it was, the British Navy's ritual didn't ease Mike's apprehension.

A British seaman escorted Mike and Riley along an interior passageway and up one deck. *HMS Ladybird's* interior lacked *Bartley's* narrow passageways, low overheads, and exposed pipes and wires. *Ladybird's* wider passageways almost gave the feel of a luxury ship. Mike could walk without having to duck his head.

On the upper deck, Mike was surprised to see Seaman Tucker and

Quartermaster Manelli walking toward them. The men stopped their conversation in mid-sentence on seeing Riley, Mike, and their escort. Both flattened their backs to the passageway bulkhead to permit the three to pass.

"What are you two doing here, Tucker?" Mike stopped to ask.

"Last night the XO told us to come over here at 0800 and talk with some captains about the grounding, sir," Tucker said. An upbeat, high-energy attitude usually defined Tucker. This morning both he and Manelli appeared glum, even angry.

"We can't talk to you about what happened though, sir," Manelli added. "They ordered us to keep our mouths shut."

Mike glanced at Riley's raised eyebrows.

"Who gave you that order, Tuck?" Riley asked.

"The old captain, the balding one. Ham-something," Tucker said. "Don't remember his name. You going to talk with him, too? Better be careful, sir. He's madder'n hell about something. Told us we was lying. I don't cotton much to that, you know."

Mike's curiosity increased. If he were conducting the investigation, he would question the two seamen, too. Tucker and Manelli had played key roles in the incident. They had witnessed the actions and had recorded details, timing, and orders given that night. Maybe this captain Ham-something had pressured them. Both wouldn't hesitate to tell the truth.

"Okay. Thanks, Tuck," Mike said. "Carry on. We'll see you later."

The British escort led Mike and Riley up one more deck and into a small compartment. Three chairs, a coat rack, and a wall-mounted telephone comprised the room's amenities. The deck and the walls, the same dull gray-green color as the ship's outer hull, oozed a somber atmosphere.

In the barren and windowless office, Mike and Riley stashed their scarves in topcoat pockets then hung them and their caps on the rack before sitting. Riley broke the silence first.

"Our outhouse back on the farm had more charm than this place," Riley said. "Even had a catalog." Mike appreciated Riley's effort to lighten the tension.

"Five minutes to go," Riley said after a glance at his watch. He reached for his cigarettes but stopped with Mike's warning headshake.

"You could be in there more than the hour allotted in those letters," Mike said. "I don't like the idea of cooling my heels here while you're facing the brass." Sitting alone with his mental turmoil for an hour or more seemed like a premature prison sentence. Think positive said an inner voice. Maybe it will go fast.

"Let's meet on the quarterdeck after I'm through," Mike said. "We can go back to the ship together and compare notes."

Riley nodded agreement.

The door to the meeting room opened revealing a portly Navy captain in dress blue uniform. His ruddy complexion emphasized his white-fringed baldness. Mike and Riley jumped to attention.

"We'll be with you in a minute," the captain said and left through the outer door.

"Looks like too much coffee to me," Riley said still standing at attention. "He must be the one Tucker mentioned." Both resumed their seats. Ten minutes later the captain returned.

"Mister Riley?" The captain said.

"Yes, sir." Riley said as both officers jumped to their feet again.

"Come in here with me." Riley followed the pudgy officer into the adjoining room.

After they had entered, a second captain, tall and red-haired with a touch of gray, leaned through the doorway. "Sit down and relax," he said to Mike. "We'll be a while. You're next." Mike flinched at the ominous tone.

Mike stretched his legs and wiggled his toes. He scratched his head, although he didn't itch. He rubbed his nose. The hands on his watch needed permission from some reluctant, superior power for each tick. The waiting room felt like a holding cell. He listened to perhaps catch bits of conversation but the air flow through the ventilating system offered the only sound. This had to be how a caged animal felt. No. More like a Roman gladiator anticipating the arena.

After half an hour Mike pulled out his notes. He would need to be sure about all the events and the details. The board would want details.

Ages later, Mike's watch indicated Riley had been with the board for an hour and ten minutes. How much longer—

The meeting room door burst open. Riley strode out, face flushed, scowling. The red-haired captain followed.

Mike tensed, alert for a clue from Riley.

Riley grabbed his overcoat from the rack. "I'll meet you at the quarterdeck, Mike," Riley snapped on his way out.

The captain returned to the meeting room and closed the door behind him.

Whatever had happened in the next room had to have been serious. Five minutes passed before the same red-haired captain opened the inner door and motioned to Mike.

"In here. You're next," he said and returned to the room ahead of Mike.

28

MIKE'S RIGHT HAND TAPPED HIS father's emblem hidden in his front pants pocket. Chin up, he stepped through the doorway to stand at attention before the board. The room, smaller than he expected, was about four times the size of the tiny waiting room. The stale odor of cigars lingered, their haze dulling the air. A table covered with a dark green, heavy-weave cloth dominated the space. The balding captain sat at the head of the table. Two other U.S. Navy captains sat along either side, the red-haired one and a slight, hawk-nosed one. A sailor sat at a small table in the corner.

"Ensign Kinkaid, correct?" the portly captain said.

"Yes, sir," Mike said locking eyes with him.

The officers on either side were mannequins compared to the heavy-breathing, paper-rustling, captain. Mike clenched his fists to counter his internal tension.

The captain pointed toward an empty chair at the far end of the table. His eyes followed Mike's walk to the chair.

"I'm Captain Hamilton," the man said. He paused. Then he nodded at each of the officers. "This is Captain Everson," on his left, slight and pale, "and Captain Michaels," on his right, the one with red hair. Neither acknowledged the introduction.

Mike sat erect, both hands in his lap, ready for the worst. Instead, Captain Hamilton shuffled his papers, sorting them into three piles. Captain Michaels poured fresh coffee for three from a carafe, none for Mike.

Captain Hamilton looked up, paused for a moment as if studying an opponent. He ran his hand across his white-fringed head then leaned forward.

The atmosphere in the room, an unexplained closeness, screamed to Mike that his fate had already been determined. If true, it made little difference how he testified. He would tell the truth and trust that the testimony of Riley and the others would support his own. He'd made the right move turning *Bartley* early. It had saved the ship. And yes, it did result in the death of one man. But, he'd never know how many others were saved by that turn.

"Grounding a warship and the loss of a man's life are serious matters." Captain Hamilton stared at Mike, unblinking. "I want to stress, this is a formal investigation of the incident. You have been designated an interested party. We're here to get the facts, the details of your involvement."

"Yes, sir," Mike replied, head held up, sweaty hands now clasped in his lap, eyes locked on Captain Hamilton.

"A detailed record of these proceedings with the questions we ask and the answers you give will be part of the official record." Captain Hamilton nodded toward the yeoman recorder in the corner. "Do you understand, Mister Kinkaid?"

Mike caught an element of anger in the captain's statement. Why the anger? This meeting was supposed to be an impartial inquiry, not a pre-judgment.

"Yes, sir," Mike said. He'd have to be careful with his words. He couldn't afford to let his own temper show.

"Based on what we find," Hamilton continued, "we'll recommend appropriate action to the admiral. Charges could be brought against you that could result in a court-martial. I warn you again that your testimony will be part of our report, every word of it. You will be notified if this board recommends further action in regard to your involvement."

Mike needed no elaboration. The faces of the two other captains remained impassive.

"Please raise your right hand, Mister Kinkaid," Captain Hamilton said. "Do you solemnly swear the testimony you are about to give is the truth, the whole truth, and nothing but the truth?"

"I do," Mike said. He was tempted to gulp but stifled the urge.

Mike's narrow, low-backed chair wobbled as he moved. He crossed his legs at the ankles. The seat didn't fit his two-hundred pounds.

Captain Hamilton opened with questions about Mike's background, experience, and training. The red-haired captain to Mike's left, took his own notes. The one on Mike's right didn't move. He seldom even blinked.

"Mister Kinkaid," Captain Hamilton said, pushing aside his papers and leaning back, his words drawn out in an apparent attempt to set a less-formal tone, "we've read your log entry for the watch when *Bartley* ran aground. We've also read the CIC watch officer's log." Hamilton pointed to the folders in front of him. "We have spoken with other members of *Bartley's* crew about the incident. We also have the preliminary diver's report of the damage. Those findings will be updated once *Bartley* goes into dry dock for repairs."

Captain Hamilton lurched forward in his chair.

Mike recoiled at the abrupt movement. He'd expected gentlemanly behavior, an objective examination of the facts. Instead, theatrics were at play, perhaps an attempt at intimidation. Okay. He'd stand his ground. He had nothing to hide.

"Did Captain Cavallo issue any orders to you or to Lieutenant Watkins, your XO, about the ship's movement?" Hamilton challenged in a strong, command voice. "Any changes to *Bartley's* course or speed?"

"Yes, sir," Mike replied. He'd keep his answers simple and direct. "He approved our turn to the north at the beginning of the watch."

"What I'm looking for is any changes made on that northern leg. Did Captain Cavallo order one or more changes to your course or speed, even minor ones, a change of a turn or two in speed perhaps, or a degree or two of heading?" Captain Hamilton's raised voice warned of a growing impatience. "In short, did he direct you to change the ship's course or speed in any manner at any time in that northern leg? Your log contains no such entry."

"No, sir." This didn't seem like the time to elaborate.

"Did you make any turns or speed changes without Captain Cavallo's knowledge or permission?"

"No, sir," Mike said, "except the turn at the top of the northern leg. I told Captain Cavallo I was turning and why. I didn't wait for his permission."

"We understood Lieutenant Watkins and Captain Cavallo maintained separate plots of the ship's position." Captain Everson, the small one, spoke for the first time. His voice carried the chill of cold steel. "Am I correct, Mister Kinkaid?"

"Yes, sir," Mike said. "I didn't know the captain kept his own plot in CIC until Mister Riley told me—"

Captain Hamilton pounded the table.

"Am I to believe you were a casual observer in this process, Mister Kinkaid?" he said, a skeptical note in his loud voice. "You were the OOD were you not? Were you simply a passive onlooker?"

The question's implication stung. A deep breath, longer than normal, gave Mike time to think before he answered.

"Sir, our orders have always been to stay out of the XO's navigation business when he's on the bridge. We give him the info or help he asks for. Otherwise, we stay out of his way. We had no reason to ask what the captain was doing in CIC."

Captain Hamilton sat back in his chair.

"Mister Kinkaid," Captain Michaels said, "Did you at any time have any reason to suspect the ship's plotted position was in error?"

"Yes, sir." Mike didn't miss Michaels' more congenial tone.

"Tell us about it, please," Michaels said.

"After Captain Cavallo turned off the radar, we were—"

"What?" Captain Hamilton lurched forward, his ruddy complexion flushed. "What's this about turning off the radar? When did that happen?"

Caution rang in Mike's mind. This can't be news to the board. Riley would have told them the radar was off and Cavallo and the XO had already given their testimony.

"Captain Cavallo ordered CIC to shut down the surface search and air search radars after we turned north," Mike said in as unemotional a tone as he could manage.

"Why?" Captain Hamilton leaned forward with his question.

"I don't know, sir," Mike said. Don't let them fluster you.

Captain Everson slapped the flat of his hand on the table and said, "You were in restricted and unfamiliar waters. You'd set darken ship condition on a moonless night. Why in hell would he turn off the radar?"

"I can't answer that, sir," Mike said.

"You can't. Or won't?" Everson challenged.

"I don't know—"

"When did you learn the radars were off?" Everson laid both palms on the table.

Mike took a deep breath. The questions were coming too fast. Think before you answer. Don't let them trip you.

"The XO told me about midway along the northern leg," Mike said in as deliberate a manner as he could muster.

"What did he say?" Everson challenged.

"He said he wanted the captain to turn the surface search radar back on," Mike answered.

"Did he ask Captain Cavallo to turn the radar on?" Everson's tone changed as though he was hearing something for the first time.

"I don't know, sir," Mike said. "He didn't tell me."

"What concerned Lieutenant Watkins?" Captain Everson said.

"He didn't say," Mike replied, "only that he and Captain Cavallo disagreed about our position."

The volume and tempo rose with each succeeding question. All three captains leaned forward now in their chairs intent on the exchange, like a football team in the huddle.

Mike's discomfort grew. He needed a drink of water.

"How often did Lieutenant Watkins plot your position?" Captain Michaels asked, his freckled forehead wrinkled with a frown.

"I don't know," Mike said, alert to a possible change in tactics.

"So you were on dead-reckoning navigation for the entire northern leg, correct?" Captain Michaels continued.

"Yes, sir," Mike said.

"When were the radars turned on again?" Michaels paused to make another note on his tablet.

"Sometime after I came off watch," Mike said. He should have recorded that item in his notes.

"Your log doesn't mention that the radars were off," Captain Michaels said. "What else did you leave out?"

Mike flinched. What else had he missed?

"I didn't record the tidal data," Mike said. What would they make of that admission?

"Why?" Captain Everson interrupted.

"We don't put that information in the OOD's log," Mike replied. "Besides, I didn't know the tidal conditions when I wrote the log. I don't think anyone knew."

"Again, why not?" Captain Hamilton unclasped his hands and pointed a finger at Mike, his voice rising. "Did you attempt to find out about the tides or prevailing currents at any time before or during the watch? Did you ask the off-going OOD?"

"No, sir."

"I'll ask you again," Captain Hamilton said, his voice louder still. "Why not, Mister?"

"Tide and current information hasn't been a part of our watch turnover procedure, sir," Mike said. Was that a required part of an OOD's log on other destroyer-type ships?

Captain Everson's white-knuckled fist struck the table, rattling the coffee cups.

"Did Lieutenant Watkins say anything to you about tides or currents?"

"No, sir," Mike said.

"Were either Captain Cavallo or Lieutenant Watkins on the bridge when you relieved the watch?" Captain Hamilton said.

"The XO came to the bridge while I was relieving the previous watch," Mike replied.

"And Cavallo?"

"In CIC, sir," Mike said.

"Why wasn't he on the bridge?" Captain Hamilton shouted. "Isn't the bridge his usual combat station?"

"Riley, I mean Mister Riley and I figured the captain would be on the bridge for the patrol," Mike said. "We were both surprised that he chose CIC instead."

"When did the captain arrive on the bridge?" Hamilton shifted in his chair, his fists flexing as though having trouble containing his temper.

"A minute or so after we grounded," Mike said not sure where the questioning was headed.

Hamilton sat back in his chair with a deep sigh. He shared eyebrow-raised, questioning glances with the two other captains.

"You're telling us he wasn't on the bridge at any time on your watch until after the grounding?" Hamilton's question lacked the earlier anger. He leaned forward to rest his elbows on the table, his chin on paired fists.

Mike caught the tone and gentler change in manner, and studied Hamilton for signs of entrapment.

"Yes, sir," Mike said. "He was not on the bridge until after we grounded." The scratching of the yeoman's recording provided the only sound.

"Let's go back to this radar situation," Captain Everson said in a conversational tone. "I understand the surface search radar was off during the patrol. Am I correct?"

"Yes, sir, or, I mean, no, sir," Mike said. "The surface search was on when I came on watch. The XO was checking range and bearing to a nearby island at the time."

"Explain, please," Everson said, now with a tinge of anger.

"The radar repeater on the conning bridge is in the navigator's hut," Mike said. "We were passing close to an island to port when I relieved the watch. I didn't interfere because the XO was busy working with the radar to check our position."

"So you didn't confirm that the surface search radar was operating, correct?" Captain Everson said.

"Correct, sir."

"Go ahead," Everson said with a wave of his hand.

"About two hours into the northern leg," Mike said, "the XO told me that Captain Cavallo had ordered both the surface and air search radars turned off after we turned north."

"Did you consider," Captain Hamilton asked, his rising anger apparent, "shutting down the radars to be a normal or prudent action under the circumstances?"

"Hell no, ah, sorry, sir," Mike said. "No, sir. The radar is always on when we're underway, except this time." Mike's disquiet grew at the tennis-match-like exchange of questions and answers.

"The quartermaster's log doesn't have an entry about securing the radars," Michaels said. "The CIC log entry recorded at 1956 reads, 'The captain ordered all the radars turned off.'"

"You told us earlier," Hamilton said, "that Captain Cavallo ordered the radars turned off. Were you told why, by anyone, at any time?"

"No, sir," Mike said.

"Any ideas?"

"With the radars off," Mike said, "we wouldn't radiate and maybe tip off our position to any enemy guns on the bluffs."

"Were any enemy guns on the bluffs, Mister Kinkaid?" Captain Everson's demeaning tone made clear his doubt.

"I don't believe so, sir." Why were the captains angry and apparently getting more so? He flexed his fingers out of sight below the table.

"Did you have any indication your position was other than along the planned track?" Captain Hamilton said.

"The XO told me his plot disagreed with Captain Cavallo's plot," Mike said forcing himself to remain calm and give thoughtful answers. "Since he didn't say by how much, I figured the difference wasn't significant, except at the northern end of the leg. The entire watch team agreed we were approaching too close to shore."

Captain Hamilton sat back in his chair and took a swallow of his coffee.

"What was your thinking before you made the turn to the west," Hamilton's words resumed a conversational tone, "and later to the south, and why you turned earlier than planned?"

Mike related the sequence again, how the haze cleared, how he could identify the loom of the peninsula ahead against the backdrop of the star-filled sky, and his conviction of the ship's imminent grounding. He included his own misgivings, and his attempt to get approval for an early turn into clear, open water.

"I see." Hamilton took another swallow of his coffee. "The loom of the land against the starlit sky? Did anyone else on the bridge make the same observation?"

"Yes, sir, Ensign Brooks and Seaman Tucker," Mike said. "Both agreed with me. I told the XO. He glanced ahead for a moment but went back to his charts. He didn't indicate if he saw the movement or not."

"I see." Hamilton said again and leaned back in his chair, his arms folded across his chest. "You said the black-on-black image led you to believe you were too close to the land."

"Yes, sir," Mike said.

"What type of shoreline did you have ahead of you when you initiated the turn," Hamilton asked, "and how close did you come to it?"

"I don't know," Mike said. "The charts don't contain shoreline information either."

Captain Hamilton scowled. "Let me ask you again. Do you have any idea how close you came to the shoreline?" He shook his finger at Mike.

Mike's head inched back before he steeled himself to be still.

"We were damned close," Mike said fighting a welling anger, both hands now flat on the table. "Brooks and Tucker both yelled that they heard breakers. They saw rocks moments after I started the turn." Mike's words came faster. His volume grew. "They were scared as hell. Based on their yelling, I expected to hit. And, no, I didn't see the rocks. They can tell you what they saw."

"So," Hamilton said, "you initiated the turn earlier than planned because you believed the ship to be in danger of running aground, in this instance, head on."

"Yes, sir," Mike said. They didn't seem to believe him. Why? Riley, Brooks, and Tucker would have told them the same thing. Did they think we were all liars?

"Did you notify Captain Cavallo and Lieutenant Watkins that you intended to turn early? More to the point, did you receive permission, Mister Kinkaid?" Hamilton's question became an accusation.

"Well, ah, yes and no, sir," Mike said recalling his actions. "I called my turn to combat. Tucker passed the same word to combat on his circuit for backup. I know the XO heard the call. He stood a couple of feet away by the navigation table and watched me when I gave the order." Mike had the captain's attention. "For the second part of your question, no, I didn't get permission. We faced an emergency."

"Why didn't you follow Captain Cavallo's order, Mister Kinkaid?" Hamilton said, leaning forward, his eyes in keen focus.

The question stunned Mike.

"What order?" Mike asked. There hadn't been one.

"We understand Captain Cavallo countermanded your turn order and told you to maintain your original course and speed," Hamilton said. "Why didn't you obey his order?"

Mike sat rigid. He regarded Captain Hamilton, his heart pounding. He searched his memory. Had he missed a countermanding order from Cavallo? No. Riley would have… Dammit. No. No such order was given. He had to maintain control here. Could he keep his voice calm and deliberate?

"Captain Cavallo didn't give any orders," Mike said in slow and distinct words, like bullets fired at Hamilton. "He didn't say anything. Neither did the XO."

The three officers, grim-faced, seemed to expect more.

"Are you telling us you didn't hear Captain Cavallo's order, Mister Kinkaid?" Hamilton emphasized the word "hear."

"If he gave such an order," Mike answered in the same deliberate manner, "I didn't hear it. No one else on the bridge did either."

"If you had heard the order," Captain Everson said, "would you have followed it?"

Surprised by the question, Mike reacted with a short intake of air.

"I refuse to answer your question, sir." Mike's head pounded from the rise in blood pressure.

"You what?" Everson snapped. "I asked you a question, Mister. Let's hear it."

"I respectfully decline to answer your question, sir," Mike said exhaling. He clamped his jaw so the anger in his head wouldn't spill out. Why weren't they considering that his early turn saved the ship? Did they intend to make him the scapegoat because he was the junior man in this fiasco?

"Why won't you answer us?" Captain Everson persisted.

"The question is irrelevant, sir," Mike said. "You told me this meeting wanted facts, not guesses." He could feel the anger threatening his belly. "No order was given. I won't deal in speculation." His anger caused each succeeding word to be louder than the last.

"Look, young man," Everson continued, his voice raised to match Mike's, "we're not playing games here. This is a formal proceeding. You will answer my question, understand?"

"Believe what you want, Captain Everson, but I'm sure Riley told you the same thing." Mike, head raised and chin thrust forward, returned Everson's stare. He had done the right thing. He would not knuckle under for any damned captain.

Captain Everson's gaze didn't waver for what, to Mike, seemed an eternity

"Let the record show the witness refuses to answer the question," Everson said to the yeoman recording the proceedings.

"Have you considered the consequences of your actions, Mister?" Captain Everson said.

Mike filled his lungs and held his breath to retain his wavering self-control. He leaned forward in slow motion, his eyes locked on the penetrating stare that had pinned him to his chair moments before.

"Captain," Mike said fighting to keep his words civil, "what makes you think Captain Cavallo, or anyone, gave such an order? Did any of the others on the watch team hear such an order? Or any order?"

"Mister Kinkaid—" Captain Hamilton attempted to interrupt, but Mike ignored the cautionary tone.

"I sure as hell didn't," Mike said, "because Cavallo gave no order. My turn saved the ship. And, if you want to speculate, what if I hadn't turned when I did?"

"Mister Kinkaid." Captain Hamilton yelled as he jumped up, toppling his chair.

Mike's anger propelled him to his feet too, on the verge of insubordination. To hell with it. They wanted the truth. Let them deal with it.

"*Bartley* would be a pile of junk smashed against a Korean cliff," Mike said in a near shout, "and more than one man might be dead. Yes, I've considered it. I should have turned even sooner."

"Sit down, Mister," Captain Hamilton bellowed and slammed his fist on the table spilling one of his piles of paper. "You're out of line. I won't tolerate any further outbursts. Understand?"

Mike hesitated for a moment then grabbed his fragile chair and sat with care. His hands balled into white-knuckled fists out of view in his lap. The room took on an electric silence, the only sound the yeoman's scratching.

Captain Hamilton righted his chair and resumed his seat. He reached for a document, read part of it then closed his folder. He rubbed his chin.

"Have you discussed the testimony you've given today with either Captain Cavallo or Lieutenant Watkins?" Captain Hamilton said in a congenial manner. The question and the change in tone surprised Mike.

"No, sir. Was I supposed to?"

Captain Everson stifled a brief chuckle, the first break in his dour demeanor. Captain Hamilton covered a slight grin. Their humor confounded Mike.

"No, I wanted to be sure these were your words and recollections," Hamilton said, "and to be sure you hadn't been influenced by a conversation with either of them. Have you discussed the grounding with anyone else?"

"Yes, sir," Mike said. "Mister Riley and I talked several times."

"How about with any others of the bridge watch team?"

"No, sir," Mike said.

"Any more questions, gentlemen?" Captain Hamilton asked the captains.

Both men shook their heads.

"Mister Kinkaid." Again, Hamilton fixed Mike with an intense stare reminiscent of the look Mike remembered as a child when scolded by his father. "I don't know if we'll need to talk with you again. I reiterate that this has been a formal inquiry. Although you are designated an interested party, you are not charged with anything at this point. Whether your status will change remains to be seen. We'll make our recommendations to the admiral."

Mike tried to comprehend the board's abrupt end. Was he off the hook? Or, did the captain mean they'd already decided and couldn't tell him yet?

"If the admiral decides to pursue this incident," Captain Hamilton added, "a court-martial may follow. If a court is convened, you may be charged. You would also be required to testify under oath. Until then, you are not to speak with any of the other watch standers, in particular Captain Cavallo or Lieutenant Watkins, about our questions or your replies. I can assure you it's in your best interest to keep your mouth shut. Do you understand?"

"Yes, sir."

"Mister Riley has been ordered to remain silent, too," Hamilton added. He waited for questions from the other captains. Two heads shook no. "Thank you for coming this morning, Mister Kinkaid. You're dismissed."

Mike left the meeting room. He fought an urge to kick something as he put on his overcoat. His instinct said the board had already made their decision. Guilty. That meant they'd send the case to court-martial.

Where had they picked up that crap about countermanding orders from Cavallo? But, had an order been given? Had he missed it? Had he ignored it in the anxiety of the moment? If he'd missed or somehow ignored it, he had no defense. His career had ended before it had begun.

Mike's mind fought the whirlwind of questions. How could he refute the charge other than through the testimony that the others must have already given to the board? If the board didn't believe him, whom would the court believe? And if he did face a court-martial, how could he explain it to Carol? He knew she would support him because she loved him. But a court-martial would put flight school out of the question and would end his Navy career. What else would he do then, with a new wife and a child to support? Dammit, not guilty. That turn saved the ship and saved lives.

Mike and Riley rode the motor whaleboat to *Bartley* in glum silence. The charge of disobeying an order dominated Mike's brain. How long before he learned the board's official decision?

Riley put his hand on Mike's shoulder after they crossed *Bartley's* quarterdeck. "We need to talk," he said. He made no attempt to hide his anger.

"In your stateroom," Mike said, "after I report our return to the XO." He headed to the XO's stateroom.

The XO looked up from his stack of papers.

"Reporting back aboard, sir." Mike said.

"What did they want?" the XO asked as Mike turned to leave.

Mike hesitated, debating whether to reply or leave. Captain Hamilton had warned him to keep mum. The XO knew damned well what they wanted. He'll try to worm out something to help his own case.

"They asked about the grounding." Mike wanted to leave.

"So, tell me about it." The XO wasn't going to quit.

Mike stopped with one foot in the passageway.

"Sorry, sir. I'm under orders not to talk to anyone about the session, or the incident."

"Sure, but it's okay to talk to me about it," the XO said, trying to sound friendly.

Mike's stomach tightened. He wouldn't grant the bastard a clue.

"Sorry, sir." Mike walked down the passageway, fists clenched. A minute later, Mike threw his hat on Riley's upper bunk.

"Why the hell didn't you tell me?"

"Tell you what?" Riley spun around from the washbasin, towel in hand. "Ah, let me guess. It was—"

"You know damned well what I mean," Mike shot back. "Where did you get off telling them a damned lie about the captain countermanding my turn order? He never did and—"

"I didn't." Riley bunched the towel up as if to throw it at Mike.

"The hell you didn't," Mike said, then he studied Riley. No. Riley wasn't the one.

"They asked me the same thing," Riley said. "I told them Cavallo didn't give an order, any order. I told them I stood right next to him the entire time until he raced up to the bridge after we grounded."

"So where did they get the idea?" Mike said. He owed Riley an apology. "I damned near messed my shorts when they came up with that business about a countermanding order." He slammed his fist on Riley's desktop. "Dammit, there wasn't one."

"Same thing happened to me." Riley tossed his towel on the upper bunk. He motioned Mike to sit in the spare chair. He reached in his shirt pocket and fished out a cigarette but didn't light it. "I'm convinced our inquisitors think we're lying. If they believe you disobeyed an order, it makes their job easier. Don't they understand your early turn saved the ship?"

Mike remained standing, but his balled fists relaxed.

"I thought the brass were on a fishing trip or trying to set me up," Mike said. "Don't think so now, looking back at it. Someone told them that damned lie, someone they'd already talked to. And they believed it."

"Think about it," Riley said. "Who'll benefit if the board can be convinced that the captain countermanded your decision to turn?"

29

WHILE *BARTLEY* HAD FACED AN indefinite wait for drydock space in Sasebo, an unexpected vacancy at the Yokosuka Naval Base promised faster repairs so the ship had limped north. The ship had been quickly imprisoned in the dry dock, and the preliminary damage inspections completed. The hull repairs and the sonar replacement required an eight-week purgatory confining *Bartley* until well into the new year. Going home to Carol was further away than he'd expected.

Life quickly became trying. Lethargy crept into Mike. Finding something of interest to include in his letters to Carol became more difficult each day.

Eight days in, Pops took a phone call while Mike and Riley were reviewing a new classified document in the radio shack.

"Yes, sir. He's here. Both are. Yes, sir." Pops paused and studied the phone, his lips pursed, eyes narrowed. In slow motion, he hung the handset back into its wall mount. "That was the XO." He pointed to Mike then Riley. "He wants you two in the wardroom now. He didn't say why."

"What do you suppose he wants this time?" Mike said. He gathered the classified document, and returned it to the safe.

"Beats me." Riley stretched and reached for his coffee. In mid-swig he stopped. "Wait." He pointed a finger at Mike. "The board, you know, our three captain prosecutors from Sasebo. They weren't due here until tomorrow. You don't suppose…"

Mike preceded Riley into the wardroom and paused mid-step. All three captains from his board of inquisition, as he viewed the threesome, sat around the table with Captain Cavallo and the XO. Only Cavallo's head remained down.

"We're here earlier than expected," Captain Hamilton said and ran his palm over his balding head. He waved to his fellow board members, Captains Michaels and Everson, who sipped coffee. "We lucked into an Air Force flight. Too bad you didn't stay in Sasebo. We wouldn't have had to prolong this investigation."

Mike flinched at the portly Hamilton's brusque manner. He'd carried a secret hope that the questions about the grounding were at an end.

Captain Cavallo finally looked up from the document he'd been reading, removed his glasses, and folded the papers.

"So, let's get on with it," Hamilton said. "We don't have much time. We have a hop back to Sasebo this afternoon." He pointed to Mike. "Kinkaid, we'll start with you. Let's go up to the bridge where you stood your watch." Cavallo and the XO rose to join Mike and the three captains.

"Sorry, gentlemen." Captain Hamilton raised his hand. "We want to talk with each man one at a time. I'll let you know when we're ready for you." He pointed to Riley. "We'll call you when we're ready to check out CIC."

Mike led the way to the open bridge above the wheelhouse. A thick, chill overcast hung low over the harbor. He shivered at the cold wind that blew off Tokyo Bay. The light jacket he wore below deck would suffice for maybe five minutes of semi-warmth in this frosty air. He hadn't had time to grab his parka from his stateroom.

The three captains nosed around the open bridge. Hamilton's examination of the instruments at the primary conning station was no more than a glance before he hunched behind the windscreen. Everson, the dour one, walked the breadth of the bridge, wing to wing, twice as if making some measurement. Mike had no idea what he expected to see. Michaels seemed to focus on the vicinity of the navigator's space and the adjacent radar repeater. He scribbled notes on his small notepad.

"For some reason I'd pictured your bridge to be larger," Michaels said with an arm-waving gesture. "Where is this navigator's hut you referred to in your testimony? I don't see it."

"Over here." Mike took the four steps to the port wing. "The table top and blackout cover are stowed while we're in port. The plotting table folds down between the radar repeater and the bulkhead, here." Mike gestured to show the movement. "The shipyard has the blackout canopy for repair."

"I see what you mean about not much room on this bridge." Captain Michaels folded his arms across his chest against the strong breeze and also backed behind the windscreen.

"Show me the voice tubes you say you used, Mister Kinkaid," Captain Hamilton said. He pulled his jacket's collar closer together.

Mike's jaw tightened. The voice tubes were unmistakable. Hamilton had baited him. His gut screamed caution.

Mike put his hand on the pair of three-inch diameter brass tubes at the center-front of the bridge. He pointed to matching pairs located on each wing.

"The left tube of each pair goes to the wheelhouse," Mike explained. "The right tube goes to CIC."

"Where were you standing when the ship grounded, Mister Kinkaid?" Captain Everson said.

"Right here, sir," Mike said, taking his usual place at the conning station.

"Where was Lieutenant Watkins at that time?" Captain Everson said.

"Over there." Mike pointed at the navigator's area.

"Where were the other watch team members?" Captain Michaels said.

"Brooks and Tucker stood on the starboard wing," Mike pointed, "over there."

"When they heard breakers and said they saw rocks?" Captain Everson interrupted. He made no effort to hide his skepticism.

"Yes, sir." Mike caught himself flexing his fist. Why were they interested in dumb things like where everyone stood?

"Kinkaid, were you here at the voice tube to combat when Captain Cavallo ordered you to maintain course and speed?" Captain Hamilton's booming voice carried the same threat Mike remembered from the earlier questioning. Mike locked eyes with Hamilton.

"Captain Cavallo gave no order," Mike said. The words were louder than he intended. He lowered his voice. "I ordered the turn here, where I am right now. I didn't move from this spot until the impact."

"You're not going to own up to it, are you?" Captain Hamilton said.

"Get off it, Captain." Mike's snap response now matched Hamilton's volume. "Cavallo gave no countermanding order… to anybody… at any time."

Hamilton locked eyes with Mike, his pale eyes squinting. He chewed a lip.

"Let's go below to the wheelhouse, away from this wind," Captain Hamilton said. He stopped on the top step of the ladder. "And Kinkaid, tell Riley we're ready for him in CIC."

Thirty minutes later, Riley plopped into the chair next to Mike's desk in the radio shack. "Glad that's over. Don't know what their visit accomplished, though."

"Me either," Mike said. He slid his papers aside and passed the ashtray to Riley. "How'd your session go?"

"Hard to say," Riley said. "Lots of the same questions they fired at me in Sasebo. Where'd the captain and each of the crew stand? I'll be damned if I know why. Maybe they figured I didn't hear the supposed order. Hell, CIC is tiny. You could damned near touch any other watch stander. I showed them the radar consoles and the DRT plotting table, how we made the settings, things like that."

"Same thing happened to me," Mike said.

"I told them to forget it," Riley said. "Cavallo didn't say a damned word after you called your turn. He heard your call and just looked at me. He didn't appear angry or anything. He ran to the bridge after we hit."

"They won't give up," Mike said.

"There's something else you ought to know," Riley said. "The small, steely one, Everson, didn't seem quite so sure of our guilt for a change. Hendricks and Collins were in CIC when we walked in. They stayed out of the way until, right at the end, Everson asked the Hendricks if he'd been on the watch when we grounded. Hendricks said he and Collins were on duty during that watch. He told them he didn't hear Cavallo give a countermanding order. Collins said the same thing."

"Have our hangmen talked with Cavallo or the XO yet?" Mike said.

"The board stayed in combat but shooed out Hendricks and Collins, and told me to get Cavallo. I think he's talking with them now." Riley stroked his mustache. "They're a hard bunch to figure. I agree with you, though. They're convinced you caused the grounding and that I contributed. Wish I knew what they asked Cavallo and the XO."

"More important," Mike said, "what answers did they get?"

30

MIKE ATTEMPTED TO MAINTAIN A positive outlook on the investigation despite the depressing visit of the board's captains three days before. Had their visit helped or hurt his case? The incoming message traffic had contained nothing new regarding the investigation. The ship's captivity in the frigid and gloomy dry dock hadn't helped. *Bartley's* repairs had progressed as the shipyard had predicted, the only element Mike considered good news.

After lunch Mike entered the radio shack for his routine visit. Pops Dietrick's eyes weren't twinkling.

"There you are, Mister K," Pops said. "We've been looking for you."

"What's the problem?" Mike asked.

"The XO's steaming about something."

"Nothing new there," Mike said. "What happened?"

"When Fingers was delivering the message traffic he heard the XO talking loud in his stateroom like maybe he had somebody in his stateroom with him. When Fingers knocked on the bulkhead and pushed open the curtain the XO was alone.

"What messages did you give him?" Mike asked. "What turned him on?"

"Fingers never gave him the messages," Pops said. "He started yelling. Didn't make sense to Fingers. Then he wants you in his stateroom immediately, and how Fingers had better make damned sure you are."

"How long ago?" Mike asked, wondering what he would be chewed-out about this time.

Pops looked at the clock and said, "Maybe ten minutes."

Mike rapped on the bulkhead at the XO's stateroom, brushed aside the frayed, green curtain, and stuck his head in.

"You wanted to see me, sir?" Mike said.

"You bet your ass I do, Mister," the XO said, his voice a near shout. "Get in here."

Mike stepped into the stateroom and stood at attention, silent, his jaws and fists shut tight. The stance provided a perverse benefit, a way to pique the XO and at the same time make sure he didn't do or say anything stupid.

The XO grabbed a paper from his desk and waved it at Mike.

"Just what did you tell the board?" the XO said, almost as a shout. "Your little game lit another fire under them. The board grilled the hell out of me. Captain Cavallo too." His volume grew. "The captain's boiling. He thinks you told them something. We need to know what it was." He wiped his mouth with every second phrase. "Enough of your schoolboy games, Mister. Let's hear it," the final words a scream.

Mike searched his memory for anything he might have said to the board members to spark this tirade.

"I didn't say anything I haven't already told you," Mike said. "I showed them the bridge layout and where we stood when we grounded. We weren't on the bridge five minutes. What did they ask you, anyway?"

"None of your damned business," the XO snapped at normal volume and wiped his face again. "The admiral's orderly just delivered this letter," the XO said waving the paper. "The captain got one too. What in hell did you tell those people? Why does the admiral want to talk with me again, anyway? You screwed up, not me." The XO's words became a shout. His face had turned an ugly, splotchy red. Waving arms punctuated his statements. "What lies did you feed them? I demand to know."

The XO appeared to have lost control. Mike stayed beyond reach of the XO's flailing arms, the XO's worst temper display yet.

"Dammit," the XO said and slammed the letter onto his desktop. He shook his fist at Mike. "Speak up, Mister."

"I showed them around the bridge," Mike said with as little emotion as he could manage. "I told you before, we didn't discuss the grounding."

"That's all?" The XO said louder. "I asked what did you tell them? Answer me." Mike didn't retreat.

"I've answered you as best I can, sir," Mike said. A faint flush of enjoyment at the XO's frustration tinged Mike's growing anger, one of his rare chances to counter the months of belittling harangues.

"Dammit, Mister," the XO jumped up, the shoulder tick in action. His chair toppled backward to the deck. "This is gross insubordination. Do you understand you're refusing to follow a direct order?"

The XO paused, dropped his arm, his hand no longer a fist, but continued his heavy breathing. Heavy perspiration stained his collar and armpits.

"Okay, enough," the XO said. He righted his desk chair but didn't sit. "If you won't answer, consider yourself confined to the ship for the indefinite future. When you decide to tell me what you told the board, I'll consider lifting your restriction. Not one minute before, understand?"

Mike stifled a chuckle at the sight of spittle oozing from the corner of the XO's mouth. With guilty pleasure he enjoyed the XO squirming.

"From now on, Mister, you must have my express permission every time you want to leave this ship." The XO shook his finger at Mike, his face flushed and sweating. "No exceptions. And if I'm not here to give you permission, you stay on board. Understand? And I'll let you off the ship only for your comm duties or to make a head run on the pier. Nothing else. You hear?"

Mike's tactic to remain silent during the XO's tirade had worked.

"How about your letter?" The XO grabbed the paper off his desk again and waved it at Mike. "Didn't you get a letter like this to report to the admiral?"

"No mail came for me today, sir," Mike said.

"The captain's ready to explode." The XO's voice cracked and the volume dropped as his rant evolved into a plea. "He wants answers before we talk to the admiral tomorrow. I don't have any."

The XO's phone rang.

"Yes, sir. Right away, Captain." The XO grabbed his cap and scurried past Mike.

31

Two days later, Mike received the XO's permission to leave the ship after convincing him that a classified document run to the base communications center was overdue. He needed the exercise so he deliberately took the long route past the parade ground and the red brick hospital to the gray cement block admin building where the pubs were kept. After his return, Mike sat next to Riley at the table in the radio shack while both entered the several document changes Mike had picked up.

Pops motioned to Mike for a private talk. He pointed to the passageway outside the radio shack and nodded for Mike to follow him. Pops' out-of-character behavior piqued Mike's curiosity.

"I don't do this with the captain's personals, you know," Pops said. He held a message form to his chest. "This time it's different. You need to know about this one."

Mike took the captain's message from Pops and read:

Priority 221452Z JAN
Personal for Commanding Officer.
  Immediate additions to flight training pipeline required to
  fill current and projected shortages. Officer volunteers
  of class of 1951, qualified and previously promised flight
  training upon commissioning, are urged to reapply subject
  to concurrence of unit's commanding officer. Ensign Michael
  A. Kinkaid, 515045/1100 eligible for immediate transfer.

Expect detach on or before 20 Jan 1952 to report to Chief
of Naval Air Basic Training, Pensacola NLT 7 Feb 1952.
Advise.

"Thanks Pops," Mike said. He had to fight a tightened throat "I don't believe this is happening. This better not be one of your jokes."

"We know how much you want to fly, Mister K," Pops said with a wide grin. "Hope this message is your ticket."

"Let me have this for a minute before you take it to the captain," Mike said.

Pops' eyes twinkled. "It's never been out of my hands, Mister K. Understand?"

Mike let Pops precede him into the radio shack. Inside, he motioned to Riley to step out into the passageway.

"You haven't seen this, understand?" Mike handed the message to Riley.

Riley stroked his mustache as he read the message over a second time. "I don't believe it, Mike. You're sure this isn't one of Pops' tricks?"

"We'll need a new chief if this is a trick," Mike said.

Mike's letter to Carol lay unfinished on his desk. Several times over the previous two days he had considered sending the good news to her, but each time he reconsidered. The next mail would carry the good news to her once the captain's approval had left the ship. Riley had warned him to avoid raising anyone's curiosity. Now he could easily endure his confinement to the ship. He'd be on his way to Carol and Flight School in Pensacola in days.

Mike swung around from his desktop when Pops stepped into his stateroom without knocking, Riley a step behind. Pops' gloomy expression raised Mike's curiosity.

"What's going on, Pops?" Riley asked. "Why the long face? And why did you drag me along?"

"Captain said no, Mister K," Pops said, his expression glum. "Sorry. I tried to stall his answer to Washington, but the XO got on my back to confirm that the message had been sent."

"What message?" Riley and Mike said in unison.

Pops handed the message to Mike.

"The XO drafted the message," Pops said. "The captain signed it without a change,"

Riley looked on to read it, too.

PRIORITY
TO: CHIEF OF NAVAL PERSONNEL
SUBJ: RELEASE OF ENSIGN MICHAEL A. KINKAID 515045/1100,
USN
REF: YOUR 221452Z JAN
ENSIGN KINKAID RETAINED ON BOARD AS PRIMARY INTERESTED
PARTY IN GROUNDING INCIDENT NOW BEFORE BOARD OF
INVESTIGATION. ANTICIPATE DISCIPLINARY ACTION TO FOLLOW.

32

THE FOLLOWING WEEK THE MAIL brought two letters for Mike. He grinned. Despite the negatives of dry dock living, at least the crew enjoyed more frequent and reliable mail service.

The first letter on pink onionskin, from Carol, included some details about her job at the university library, the concert she attended with sister Lisa, and a weekend visit with her mother. And as always, a plea for Mike to come home or to give her information so she could plan. She knew, though, that the deployment remained indefinite. Her latest visit to the doctor confirmed all was well with the baby and her general health.

Lisa, Carol's older sister, had sent a pale blue airmail letter. Mike hadn't expected to hear from her. He barely knew her. He checked the postmarks. Lisa's letter had been mailed three days after Carol's.

Mike read Lisa's first paragraph then stopped breathing for a moment. He noted her large flowery, handwriting. Why hadn't she sent a telegram or asked the Red Cross to contact him? Shaking hands held the sheet.

Minutes later Mike motioned from the doorway to Riley in the operations department office. Riley grabbed his foul-weather jacket, and followed Mike to a sheltered spot on deck.

"What's the problem?" Riley said while he held up his collar against the chill breeze. A finger pointed to the blue sheet in Mike's hand. "Problems at home?" Riley asked.

"Worse than that," was all Mike could choke out.

"C'mon," Riley said and led Mike to the wardroom where he poured two cups of coffee. He motioned Mike to continue to Riley's stateroom.

Mike regained some of his composure after he'd downed half his coffee.

"It's Carol," Mike said. "She's in the hospital." His jaw muscles worked. Clenched fists rattled the paper in his hands.

Riley's palm-up gesture motioned Mike to continue.

"This letter is from Carol's sister, Lisa," Mike said after a moment. "She wrote it five days ago." He paused again, scratched his nose with his sleeve, and moved his mouth as though trying to speak. He handed the pages to Riley.

Riley glanced at the first sentence, put aside his coffee, and read:

Dear Mike.
Carol's in the hospital resting and may not be able to write for several days. The baby is fine."
Carol fell at the library while carrying some books. Nothing is broken, but she sprained her back and her right leg. She's in some pain but they gave her medicine to control that. The doctor insists that she stay in bed for at least a week, then get physical therapy. Mother and I have decided she shouldn't go back to work with the baby due in about two months. We don't want her to fall again. As soon as she is able to get around I'll take her to Mother's.
We hope you are home soon. One of us will write again within a few days. I'm sorry this will be slow reaching you but I don't know a fast way."

"Her letter took five days to get here," Mike said, his anger fighting a growing fear. "Why the hell didn't she send a telegram? I told Carol

230

how to contact the local Navy office and the Red Cross. They know how to get word to me."

"How about an international phone call?" Riley said. He leaned forward, elbows on his knees. "At least let her know you got the information. I've never tried. Tough to get a line, I'm told."

"Okay, or how about a telegram? How do I do that?" Mike said. He had to let Carol know he'd learned of the fall. Even more important, he needed to hear more about her condition and the baby's.

"You have an address?" Riley said.

"Carol could be at her mother's place or at Lisa's. Maybe she's still at the hospital."

"Maybe the Red Cross office could help," Riley said. "Let's give that a try."

"Do you suppose I could get emergency leave?" Mike shook his head and raised his hand before Riley could speak. "Guess I know the answer without asking. Not a chance."

"Right," Riley said. "After what's happened, you're the last one the captain or XO would give a break."

Mike read the letter for the third time. He pounded his fist against the bulkhead, chin on his chest. He could not help Carol. After a moment, he bowed his head and returned to the chair. He should be with Carol to talk with her, reassure her that he loved her, and let her know he supported her. Thank God the baby was okay.

"Write out what you want to say to Carol," Riley said, "and I'll get it over to the Red Cross office for you. I'll ask the Seattle office of the Red Cross to find her hospital and get the message to her."

Mike, paused, wrestling with what to say in a telegram. It had to be brief. On the back of a message form he scribbled the cryptic words: Lisa's letter received, wished he were with her, and much love. He gave the note to Riley then shook his hand.

"Thanks. I'm going to try for emergency leave, anyway," Mike said. "The worst the XO or Captain can say is no."

"Lots of luck," Riley said. His voice held little hope.

"Come in," the XO said after Mike knocked. He glanced up then scowled. "What do you want, Mister?"

"I need to talk with you, sir," Mike said.

"So, talk." The XO's belligerent attitude foredoomed the request. Nevertheless, Mike had to try.

"I request emergency leave, sir," Mike said, standing at attention.

"You what?" the XO said. The sudden flash of surprise fast became a gloat. "Fat chance, Mister. Leave for what?"

"My wife's taken a serious fall," Mike said. "Her sister's letter came today." Mike held up the blue sheet but didn't expect the XO to read it. "She's in the hospital. She's seven months pregnant. I need at least a week at home. Riley and Pops can handle the comm job while I'm gone as long as we're stuck here in the dry dock. We get our message traffic through the base communications office anyway. I need to leave tomorrow."

"What a crock of bull, Kinkaid," the XO said. "You stay aboard while this investigation continues, understand? You're the prime cause of all our troubles. I don't care if your wife is dying. Request denied."

Mike held his temper. This was not the time to vent.

"I want to talk to the captain about this, sir," Mike said. He took a risk asking to go over the XO's head. He had to try. It might work. It was possible the captain would see things differently.

"Over my dead body, Mister," the XO shouted and pounded his fist on his desktop. "You're out of line to even suggest going to the captain without my permission. Get the hell out of here with your crybaby story. You can't go. And don't forget that you're restricted to the ship until I say otherwise."

Mike didn't hesitate. Already restricted to the ship, facing imminent court-martial, even severance from the service because of the grounding, what could he lose? What more could the captain do? If the XO wanted to push insubordination for going over his head, Mike already lived with all the XO's restriction options.

Mike rapped on the captain's cabin door. He raised his fist for a second knock but heard Cavallo's "Come in" growl. The captain leaned back in his desk chair, slid his glasses down his nose and waited for Mike to speak.

"Sir, I need to talk with you," Mike said.

The silent captain frowned at Mike. His apparent anger forewarned Mike that his effort was pointless.

"Sir, I request emergency leave. My wife's sister just wrote. My wife had a bad fall. She's in the hospital. She's seven months pregnant." Mike held out the letter. "I need to be there. I want to leave tomorrow."

Mike expected an immediate outburst. Instead, the captain locked eyes with him and made no effort to take the blue sheet. His eyebrow danced a jig. An interminable moment passed before he spoke.

"Did you talk to the XO about this?" Cavallo asked, through clenched teeth.

"Yes, sir," Mike said.

"And what did he tell you?"

"He didn't approve."

"Then why the hell are you coming to me?" the captain bellowed. "You're not leaving this ship."

33

A DEPRESSING CHRISTMAS AND NEW Year season had passed without ceremony in *Bartley's* prison-like, dry dock existence. Mike scoured every incoming messages but each day passed without mention of the investigation. The Japanese shipyard workmen continued *Bartley's* repairs, the only bright spot.

Mike had pictured his first Christmas with Carol. They had so much to celebrate and plan for with the baby due in less than two months. If Cavallo hadn't extended *Bartley's* deployment, Mike would have been home with Carol. The small gift he'd sent her wouldn't make up for not being together.

A week after New Years day, Mike set his mail on one of the two gray metal desks in the ship's operations department office, then dragged the spare chair next to Riley's desk.

"Anything new from the board?" Riley said, "But then, I guess we shouldn't be expecting anything so soon. They're probably enjoying the holidays while we sit here and freeze." Mike hadn't counted how often he and Riley had exchanged a similar conversation since the three captains' visit.

"Nothing," Mike said. "The captain and XO have been up to the admiral's office a couple of times, Pops tells me. Maybe they know something?"

"You can bet neither will say a word to us even if they do," Riley said. He ripped the cellophane wrapper off a fresh cigarette pack, removed one, tapped it on the desktop, and lit it. The glance he gave to Mike after a long draw contained none of his usual good humor. "Good news is pretty damned rare these days," Riley said through a cloud of smoke.

"Well, maybe." Mike said. He selected one envelope from the small collection he'd brought and pushed it toward Riley. "Take a look. It's a new notice from the Bureau of Naval Personnel. Came in the morning's mail. Go on. Take a look. This might be my chance."

Riley squinted at Mike in his familiar, inquisitive way before he read the new notice, subject: Flight Training.

"Hmmm. I see," Riley said after he'd read the first paragraph. "Are you really going to face the old man after the grounding? You know that stubborn bastard won't give you the time of day now that his command is in jeopardy. No way he'll approve any request of yours. Remember, he already blocked your emergency leave request. Then there's that message to Washington telling them you're in a pending investigation. Unless lightning strikes, you're going to end up this tour with a court-martial, or at least officer fitness reports that will sink any future promotion, let alone any chance to fly." Before Mike could reply, Riley raised a cautioning hand and shook his head. "Yeah, I know. You're going to guts it out despite what I say, right?"

Mike grinned. He knew he could count on Riley to help.

"You think about it," Mike replied. "I'm sitting here on my ass waiting for the axe to fall. I know I'm destined to fly, somehow. This in-port period might be a chance to get the required flight physical. Whether or not I get the captain's approval is moot. At least the flight request letter will get to Washington saying I'm still qualified. Like you said, maybe lightning will strike. But, I'm not going down without a fight."

Riley grinned and read the document, this time in more detail.

"So, they've changed the requirements for flight training applicants," Riley said. "You don't need to be OOD qualified anymore, I see." He threw a questioning glance at Mike. "Doesn't make much difference in your case, but the fact that you have your OOD qual might work in your favor."

"Right," Mike said. "I passed the written test for flight training last spring. Don't have to take it again." Mike gestured at the page, urging Riley to read on.

"You'll need a recent physical." Riley ground out his cigarette in the desktop ashtray. "The base hospital can handle it."

"A flight surgeon has to examine me," Mike said. "Pops checked the base hospital for me. They don't have one assigned. They told him they're only assigned to carriers and air stations, not to the hospitals out here."

"Any airfields around here?" Riley stroked his mustache. "Wait a minute. How about a carrier? *USS Valley Forge* pulled in last night. I understand she'll be here for maybe five or six days for some repairs."

"Bingo," Mike shouted. "I should have thought of the carrier. *Valley Forge* is sure to have a flight surgeon."

"What's to lose?" Riley said. "You won't need the XO's permission to pay him a visit. Routine comm business, you know." He twisted his mustache.

Mike grinned at Riley's gambit to create some counter-XO intrigue. He snapped back to reality when Riley added, "Don't let the XO know what you're doing. Until we get answers about the investigation, no telling what he might do."

"You notice anything else?" Mike pointed to the paper in Riley's hand.

Riley scanned. He wrinkled his brow and shook his head.

"The old flight training directive required me to complete a normal sea duty tour before I could re-apply," Mike said. "That's two years in my case."

"So...?"

"That requirement's been scrubbed."

"So, what else?" Riley said.

"The application needs the captain's approval."

Mike found Riley alone at the coffee service when he walked into the wardroom that afternoon after his visit to *USS Valley Forge*.

"No luck," Mike said, anticipating Riley's question.

"They won't test you?" Riley took a sip of coffee then tilted his head sideways to motion Mike toward his stateroom for a private chat.

"They have two flight surgeons," Mike said. He sat in Riley's spare chair, setting the coffee cup on the desktop. "One doc left last night on emergency leave back to the States. No idea when they'll get a replacement.

No one there could tell me where the other doc was or when I could see him. I'll have to chance another visit when I can escape the XO."

"We aren't leaving this stinking dry dock until our sonar dome is replaced anyway," Riley said. "Try the carrier again."

"And," Mike said, "I understand *Valley Forge* is sticking around, too, until their catapult and some other gear is fixed. Maybe eight to ten days. Might be sooner."

The next day Mike overheard Pops tell a radioman that he planned to visit *USS Valley Forge* to look up an old shipmate. On a hunch, Mike motioned to Pops to step out on deck.

"If you're headed for *Valley Forge*, Pops, would you do a favor for me?" Mike said. "I need to set up an appointment with the carrier's Doctor Collins sometime before *Valley Forge* leaves."

"Sure, Mister K." Pops eyed Mike and stroked his beard. "He knows about this, does he?"

"No," Mike said. "Tell him I need a physical."

"You okay, are you?" Pops cocked his head. "You can visit the base hospital anytime, you know. XO can't stop you from doing that."

"No, I need to see Collins," Mike said. "Just between you and me, Pops. I need a flight surgeon. No other doctor." He knew he could depend on Pops to keep mum.

"Be glad to," Pops said. He grinned and added under his breath as he turned away, "You're bound to fly, aren't you?"

Mike grinned inwardly. He'd suspected that Pops knew of his dream although he'd never directly spoken to him about it. Guess that was why guys like him are Chief Petty Officers.

Pops returned to the radio shack after lunch and motioned to Mike to step outside.

"Sorry, Mister K. Your doc wasn't aboard," he said. "The chief in the carrier's sick bay said Doctor Collins is helping at the base hospital while the ship's in town." Pops lowered his chin and looked at Mike with what Mike regarded as a cautious concern.

"And by the way," Pops added, "I think you need to do a run to the classified pubs office to pick up our stuff, ah, soon, say tomorrow about 1400."

The now pseudo-concern in Pops' eye piqued Mike's curiosity. This didn't appear to be more of Pops' practical jokes. Mike had learned to respect the leprechaun in Pops after being the target in a couple of Pops' tricks. What's the game this time? He'd play along. He needed a chuckle, anyway.

"Why a pubs run?" Mike said. "I picked up changes for only two pubs on the last run."

"Let's put it this way," Pops said. The sly twinkle crept into his eye. "I urge you to make a run, say tomorrow at 1400." Pops pulled a small pill bottle from his pocket. "And when you're there, since you'll be just across the parade ground from the hospital, I need a refill on these blood pressure pills. They should be ready at the base hospital pharmacy."

"Okay," Mike said. He took the bottle, grinned and winked, still suspicious of Pops' request. "What game are we playing this time? And, I don't need to visit the hospital. The duty radioman can collect your pills on one of the daily comm center runs. You're getting a little old for this sort of thing, aren't you, Pops?" But, he'd play along.

Mike checked his watch the next day and grabbed the classified publications pouch but stopped when Pops waved at him.

"You on your way, sir?" Pops asked.

"Yes. You need anything else?" Mike said.

"Yes, sir," Pops said. "When you visit the hospital for my pills would you drop this off? I found some pictures I'd promised an old shipmate, Chief Lukens. He's assigned there in the hospital. We served together on the *USS Springfield* during the war." Pops handed Mike an envelope. "Turn left at the hospital check-in counter. He's in the third office on the right."

"Is this another of your practical jokes, too, Pops?" Mike said.

"No, sir," Pops said with a rumbling chuckle and wide grin. He patted Mike on the shoulder. "Not this time."

Okay, anything to take his mind off the investigation. The more he thought of it, a visit to the hospital might give him a chance to contact Doctor Collins. It was worth a try.

Mike prepared to leave the ship and steeled himself for the next episode in the XO's vendetta. He knocked at the XO's stateroom.

"Request permission to go ashore, sir," Mike said.

"Where are you off to this time, Mister?" The XO scowled when Mike entered the stateroom. "Seems to me you spend too damned much time ashore but not enough on board tending to your duties."

"Making a run to the base comm center, sir," Mike said. "Classified updates."

"Didn't you just make a run, what was it, three days ago?" the XO said.

"New stuff, sir," Mike said.

"Okay," the XO said with a wave to Mike. "Report to me when you're back aboard."

No classified documents or changes waited for *Bartley* in the communication center's classified material control section, and Chief Lukens wasn't in his hospital office when Mike arrived. Okay. Pops had suckered him again. What sort of joke had Pops arranged for him this time? Mike could see four men in the long hospital corridor. None looked old enough to be a chief petty officer.

"Mister Kinkaid?" came a voice from behind him. Mike wheeled around. A chief petty officer approached and held out his hand. "Chief Lukens," the man said to introduce himself. "Good afternoon, sir. Follow me please."

Mike hadn't expected a trip through the hospital if that's what Pops had up his sleeve. Some past pranks had been more sophisticated. Maybe Pops was losing his touch?

Chief Lukens led Mike along the corridor. Around the corner they entered the second door on the right.

"Have a seat, sir," Chief Lukens said. "The doctor will be with you in a minute."

"What's this about, Chief?" Mike said. A doctor? He hadn't come to see a doctor. What had Pops dreamed up this time?

"Chief Dietrick asked me to see you," Mike said. "I was to give you this." He handed the envelope to Chief Lukens.

"Oh, thanks," The chief said taking the envelope. He caught Mike's eyes. "I gather Pops didn't tell you?" Chief Lukens said. "I'm not surprised. That's Pops for you. We've arranged—oh, here's Doctor Collins now."

"Good morning. Understand you need a flight physical," the man in white coat and stethoscope said as he approached. He smiled and held out his hand. "Kinkaid isn't it? Okay, let's check you out."

Doctor Collins followed the same procedure Mike remembered from his flight exam the previous March. The doctor asked the same questions and led Mike through the same coordination exercises. The exam seemed every bit as thorough as the previous one but speedier.

"Okay, Kinkaid," Doctor Collins said thirty-five minutes later. "You passed. The blood and urine tests will be ready tomorrow. I don't expect any problem. We'll send the results to Washington by the weekend." He signed the medical form and gave a copy to Mike. "Go ahead and put in your request letter to Washington, but don't delay. This physical exam expires in sixty days."

34

S O, HOW'D THE EXAM GO?" Riley said when he stepped into Mike's state-room. The upbeat lilt in his voice revealed that he'd already guessed the good news.

Mike put down his pen and smiled at Riley.

"I passed." Somehow voicing the outcome crystallized the fact, but his words didn't carry a rush of excitement.

"In that case why so glum?" Riley said. "I figured you'd be all smiles."

"Well, I have some problems," Mike added.

"Dammit," Riley said, "You collect them like flies around the pigpen, don't you?" He took his usual seat on Mike's lower bunk and pulled out a cigarette. "No joking. You did pass, didn't you?"

"The physical does a Cinderella act in sixty days," Mike said. "If I don't get the letter to Washington by then with an approval endorsement with the captain's signature, I'm dead."

"I don't know what to tell you." Riley scratched his belly. "You knew the XO would fight you. What about the other problem? You said there were a couple."

"Have you checked your mail?" Mike said.

"Nothing." Riley said. "Don't expect any. Why?"

"I didn't get one either," Mike said.

"You mean a letter from Carol?" Riley asked.

"No," Mike said. "It's just that the XO got a letter from the admiral," Mike said. "He said one came for the captain too. He said we were sup-posed to get one, too."

After lunch, Mike sat at his stateroom desk going over his draft letter to Washington requesting reassignment to flight training. In his imagination he piloted one of the many planes he'd watch land on the carrier during *Bartley's* plane guard assignments.

Fingers came in interrupting the reverie, and dropped off the folders containing the afternoon's messages for Mike's review.

"Nothing important in this bunch, Mister K," Fingers said.

Ten minutes later, after he'd gone through the messages, Mike gathered the material on his desk and headed for the radio shack via the captain's cabin. Captain Cavallo had insisted that his message copies be in a special folder arranged in a specific order and that Mike personally deliver them. On any other ship the duty radioman would deliver them. If the captain wasn't in his cabin, he was to leave the message folder on Cavallo's desk. Mike chalked it up to another of the old man's aberrations. Since the captain wasn't in his cabin, Mike followed the routine.

The next morning, Captain Cavallo stormed into the wardroom for breakfast and slammed a handful of papers on the table. The papers knocked his rolled napkin in the silver metal ring to the deck. He glowered at the seated officers, mumbling. The captain gulped half a cup of coffee and raised his cup for an immediate refill before the steward brought his usual scrambled eggs and side of sausage. Mike and all the officers had become accustomed to Cavallo's grumpy behavior. This morning he surpassed grumpy.

Mike folded his napkin and, following the accepted protocol before rising, looked at the captain and asked to be excused. Only then did he realize the man had been staring at him with a trace of a malevolent grin.

"So you want to be a flyboy." The captain's bellowed words came as a challenge, not a question.

"Ah, yes, sir," Mike stammered.

Cavallo's eyebrow twitched. The narrowed eyes revealed a sadistic pleasure in the exchange.

"Denied, dammit," the captain hollered. His fist pounded the table in a single blow. Several cups and dishes rattled. "I won't approve your letter, now or ever."

"But why, sir?" Mike steeled himself to hide his flash of anger. "I've passed all the tests. I've qualified as OOD. You said yourself a couple of weeks ago I've done my comm job well."

"Doesn't matter," the captain said. "You'll complete your tour on this ship if I have my way, dammit. We'll let Washington decide what to do with you afterwards." He lifted his empty coffee cup, glanced at it, then slammed it into the saucer. Both shattered. "Flight school, huh? That's a stupid move. I won't support it. Forget it."

"Navy Regulations, Article 1156, requires you to forward requests like this, even if you disapprove, sir," Mike said. "At least send the letter to Washington so they'll know I'm still qualified and a volunteer."

"Don't quote Navy Regulations to me, you smart-ass college punk." Cavallo's chair toppled when he jumped up. He shook his fist at Mike, an uncommon gesture for him. "You'll stay aboard as long as I have command of this ship." He slammed the wardroom table again. "You'll stand your watches and do your job with the rest of us. I don't want to hear any more about it. Understand?" The captain grabbed his papers and left the wardroom, a muttered comment lost when the door slammed behind him.

How had Cavallo learned of the letter? Mike had shown it to no one. He'd left it on his desk unfinished.

"Why did you go to Captain Cavallo without coming to me first?" the XO screamed from his place at the table. "You know better than to go to him behind my back, Mister. What in hell was he talking about anyway?"

"My request for flight school," Mike said. "I drafted a request letter yesterday. It's still on my desk. I have no idea how Cavallo learned about it."

"Why didn't you follow proper procedures? The XO's shoulder tick had begun to emphasize every fourth word. "You college kids never learn discipline. You'll follow procedures or I'll make your life miserable, understand?"

The XO looked around the room at the hostile officers' faces. "Nothing goes to Captain Cavallo without my approval first. That's an order." He, too, stormed out of the wardroom.

Mike glanced around the table. Only Riley really knew the story. Mike realized he owed his shipmates an explanation.

"I drafted a request for flight school," Mike said. "It's still on my desk. I didn't say a word to the old man."

Later, Mike delivered the morning message folder to the captain's empty stateroom and picked up the folder he had left there the afternoon before. He detoured to his room before going on to the radio shack and tossed the captain's folder on his bunk. The folder hit the edge of the bunk. Message copies cascaded onto the deck. His draft letter to Washington lay on top. "No" was scrawled across it in red.

Mike slumped into his chair, head on his chest for a moment. He must have been careless. How'd his letter get to Cavallo? No excuse. He raised his head to Carol's picture on his desk. Maybe this misstep would be a setback, but it didn't have to be the final word. He'd followed the rules. He'd stand his ground.

An hour later Mike carried a new, completed flight school request to the XO's stateroom to follow protocol seeking his approval first. He braced for the expected explosion.

"You don't listen very well, Mister," the XO said. He ran a hand across his mustache and settled back in his chair. "You heard the captain. Have you forgotten he already told you he wouldn't approve it?"

"I heard him," Mike said. "Not approving and not sending are two different things. He's required by Navy Regulations to forward the letter, even if it's with his disapproval. I expect him to follow regulations."

"How stupid can you be, Kinkaid?" the XO lurched forward and shook a finger at Mike. "First you run this ship aground and probably wrecked the captain's career, and mine, because of your incompetence. Then, you whine about emergency leave with some trumped up excuse. And now you want me to support another dumb stunt. Maybe we should let you go. If we're lucky, you'll kill yourself and save us all a lot of grief."

Mike's flexed fists helped diminish his anger. He hadn't expected the XO to agree. He'd followed procedures in bringing his application letter to the XO first. He'd go to the captain next, regardless. What did he have to lose at this point?

Despite the tirade, the XO initialed the paper and handed it to Mike with a gloating grimace.

"Fat chance," the XO said, "but go ahead."

Minutes later Mike presented the request to the captain for signature. The XO's "recommending disapproval," clearly visible. He laid a second sheet that quoted the relevant passage from Navy Regulations on the desk as well. The captain grunted, ignored the Navy Regulations extract, and signed the disapproval endorsement. He looked up at Mike, his eyebrow fluttering at full speed. He shook the letter at Mike.

"The XO was right," the captain said. "You aren't qualified. No discipline. You're a loser. You'll never be promoted while I have command." He tossed the page at Mike and waved him away. "Now, get the hell out of my sight."

After dinner, Mike handed an envelope to Pops addressed to the Bureau of Naval Personnel, Washington D.C. He made little effort to mask his frustration. Even with the captain's signed disapproval endorsement, the letter would at least tell the Navy Department he continued to be a qualified volunteer. He couldn't give up the fight.

"Pops," Mike said, and handed him an envelope. "Have the duty radioman drop this off at the base post office tonight when he makes the evening message run."

Pops nodded and gestured a thumbs-up to confirm he knew what the envelope contained.

"Fingers, take care of this for Mister K," Pops said, "and see that it gets out in tonight's mail.

Mike sat at his desk, staring at the bulkhead, his brain in turmoil. How would Washington treat a request burdened with a pending court-martial?

35

THE RAIN AND WIND HAD stopped during the night, leaving a thick fog shrouding Tokyo Bay and the shipyard. Mike strode three extra laps around the deck to battle his depression. He rehashed his situation in an endless search for a way to escape the XO's vendetta, return to Carol, and somehow get orders to flight school. Each exploration came to the same conclusion. He had no choice but to complete his tour on *Bartley*, and do his best to stay out of trouble. The request for flight training was doomed to failure. He'd stay alert in the meantime for any new avenue to achieve pilot training. Maybe the gods would relent and allow *Bartley* to return home before their baby's birth.

Tired of walking and worrying, Mike skipped breakfast and went to the radio shack for some of Pops' Poison. Pops met him, a message envelope held against his chest as though it contained classified information. He tipped his head in a motion for a private chat in the outer passageway. His expression gave no hint of whether the message brought good or bad news. He handed the envelope to Mike.

"For the captain," Pops said, expressionless for a moment, then stepped back into the radio shack.

Mike gulped when he read the brief message. He detoured into the operations department office to find Riley. Riley needed to see the message, too. The captain could wait.

Riley nodded his understanding when Mike beckoned him to follow him out on deck.

"It's hit the fan." Mike said handing the envelope to Riley.

Riley scanned the message and scratched his head. "I wondered how long this would take." He dangled the change-of-duty orders for Captain Cavallo between two fingers as if it were offensive trash. The message to Cavallo read:

> "WHEN RELIEVED, REPORT TO COMMANDER CRUISERS-DESTROYERS PACIFIC FLEET IN SAN DIEGO, CALIFORNIA FOR DUTY."

Mike looked to Riley to see his expression. Riley motioned to Mike to sit in the spare chair. How long before similar terminating orders for them followed?

"Here's how I see it," Mike said. He leaned forward, elbows on his knees. "The captain's orders are way too soon to be normal rotation. Hell, he's been in command, what is it, not even six months?"

"It's just what I predicted," Riley said and stroked his mustache. "The Navy doesn't show much tolerance."

"I've heard about the no tolerance thing for commanding officers," Mike said. "This was a major incident with serious damage to the ship and loss of life. Do you see any extenuating circumstances to make this an exception?"

Riley glanced at the brief message again. "No clue about his assignment here. Wonder what it'll be?" He fingered a fresh cigarette from his shirt pocket, lit it, and sat back momentarily staring at the bulkhead.

"To think that bastard extended us so we could sit on our butts freezing in dry dock," Riley said.

"If Cavallo's orders are the first shoe to drop," Mike said, "do you think we'll see orders for the XO too?"

"And we're next," Riley replied. He ground out the cigarette and returned to the paperwork on his desk. Mike's stomach tensed at Riley's words. What was in store for them?

Message orders in hand, Mike ambled along the narrow passageways in no hurry to present the bad news to the captain. He didn't know what reaction to expect. He rapped on the captain's door. His uneasiness persisted. A brief sense of guilt flashed through his gut. One man had died, and another man's career had probably ended because of the grounding. The captain's premature loss of command was an expected outcome. Mike almost felt sorry for him. But, in the Navy's eyes the captain was in command, and therefore responsible for whatever happened to the ship and its crew.

"What is it?" the captain growled, and slid his glasses down his nose. "Can't you see I'm busy?"

"Special message for you, Captain," Mike said, and handed him the envelope with the message form inside. "A personal."

Captain Cavallo adjusted his glasses, opened the envelope and appeared absorbed in reading for the better part of a minute. He flipped the page over as though to look for a continuation on the back. He didn't move for a moment, no expression. He returned the message to the envelope and placed it on his desk under an anchor-shaped paperweight.

"I'll take care of this," the captain said. He waved to dismiss Mike.

"Mister K," Pops said and handed Mike his morning cup of Pops' Poison. "The whole ship's buzzing. You hear any of it yet?"

"No," Mike said. He gulped down some of the strong brew and set the cup on his mini-desk. "Hear any of what, Pops?"

"Scuttlebutt's running wild everywhere from the bilges to the open bridge. Can't keep secrets on this bucket. The crew wants to know when the captain will be relieved. They're bugging me and the other radiomen. Hell, we don't know either." He set the messages that had come in during the night beside Mike's cup. "I've heard some wild stories," Pops continued, "about who might be the new captain, wild guesses about his background, too, like, would he be a real tin-can sailor? Stuff like that." Pops picked up the pot to refill Mike's cup, and added, "And I'm wondering if he'll be a stubborn and domineering SOB like Cavallo?"

Later that afternoon, Mike handed Captain Cavallo another personal-orders message. A Lieutenant Commander Richard Torrance was to report to *Bartley* as commanding officer, the message the entire crew had anticipated. No dates were specified.

"Special message for you, sir," Mike said. "Any special handling with this one?" He waited.

Captain Cavallo read the brief message. He shook his head, laid the sheet on his desk and waved Mike away without answering.

By the time Mike returned to the radio shack, Torrance's name had become common knowledge throughout the ship.

Three days later, the petty officer on watch at the quarterdeck phoned the radio shack for Mike, the day's duty officer.

"Sir, Lieutenant Commander Torrance came aboard a couple of minutes ago. I've escorted him to the wardroom. He wants to see the captain or the duty officer."

An agitated Mike scrambled down the ladder from the radio shack to the wardroom. This hurried welcome would make a damned poor first impression on a new captain. Why hadn't the ship been notified of the new captain's expected arrival? Captain Cavallo or the XO should have been on the quarterdeck to welcome him aboard.

When Mike entered the wardroom, he noted a slim man with a deep suntan and receding, rust-brown hair. Mike's instinct flashed a positive signal at the broad smile and the twinkle apparent in the man's eyes.

"Welcome aboard, sir. You must be Lieutenant Commander Torrance," Mike said. "I'm Ensign Kinkaid, today's duty officer. Both Captain Cavallo and the XO are ashore. Sorry I wasn't at the quarterdeck to meet you. We didn't have any word when to expect you." The men shook hands.

"Don't worry about it, Kinkaid," the man said. "They had me scrambling for a while." He didn't elaborate. "How about showing me around while we wait for Captain Cavallo? Lead on."

After a brief tour of the bridge area and CIC, Mike led Lieutenant Commander Torrance through the hatch to the radio shack.

"Attention on deck," Pops called to his radiomen and jumped to attention. All eyes scanned the newcomer.

"I'm Lieutenant Commander Torrance," the new captain said. He extended his hand to Pops without waiting for Mike's introduction. "You must be the Pops that Mister Kinkaid has told me about. He tells me you run a great team."

Torrance shook hands with each man in the radio shack. He

asked every radioman about their duties, how long they'd been aboard *Bartley*, and the name of their hometown. Mike grinned at the unmistakable contrast between the personalities of the old and new commanding officers. The radiomen shared looks of astonishment and pleasure. Mike didn't miss Pops' broad grin and thumbs-up gesture as he followed the new captain out of the radio shack

Lieutenant Powell, *Bartley's* operations officer, hosted Torrance and a small group of officers including Mike and Riley over coffee in the wardroom after a brief tour of the ship. The new captain told them of his recent hospital stay while recovering from injuries incurred when his ship suffered crippling damage in a typhoon the previous summer. He kept the story of the tragedy brief, but said several men had received major injuries.

A half-hour into their conversation, Captain Cavallo entered the wardroom. Lieutenant Commander Torrance, introduced himself, and extended his hand to Cavallo. After a half-cup of coffee, Cavallo invited Torrance to join him in the captain's cabin. The others lingered around the table to compare first impressions.

"I wonder what Torrance will hear," Mike said, "about the harbor net collision and the grounding?" Mike said. More to the point, what would the new captain hear about Mike and Riley and their roles in the incidents?

Before the evening meal, Lieutenant Commander Torrance left the ship to return to his temporary room at the naval base's Bachelor Officers' Quarters. The ship buzzed with rumors and first impressions, although few of the crew had met or seen the new captain.

The XO fidgeted and toyed with his meal through the silent dinner that evening. He wiped his miniature mustache twice as though about to speak, but held off each time. After a deep sigh, he rolled his napkin, put it in the silver napkin ring, and leaned forward. A significant shoulder tic followed.

"Captain," the XO said, "have you and Lieutenant Commander Torrance discussed when to schedule the change of command, sir?" The eyes of everyone at the table shifted to the captain.

Cavallo ignored the question and didn't look up from his plate of corned beef hash.

"We have things to prepare," the XO said, "like inventories and condition reports." He spoke faster, his anxiety evident. "We need to get started on fitness reports for all the officers, too. I'll get the assignments out tonight. We need to set a time for the ceremony and figure out where to hold muster for all hands out of the weather."

The captain continued his meal appearing to ignore the XO. Mike ground his teeth when he recalled the flurry of paperwork the XO had imposed on all the officers in late summer when Captain Clark had been relieved. Would they go through that again?

The captain leveled a baleful stare at the XO and chewed his last bite. He drained his coffee before he answered.

"Tomorrow." The captain's eyebrow twitched.

On the quarterdeck the next morning, Mike covered for Riley as the day's duty officer while Riley kept a dental appointment at the base hospital. Mike took the phone call from Captain Cavallo at 0915.

"Have someone pick up my gear and take it to the pier," Cavallo said. "Also, get a base taxi to take me to the BOQ. I'll be at the quarterdeck in about twenty minutes." Mike replaced the phone. The XO had come up beside him.

"Kinkaid, make an entry in the log," the XO said. "Lieutenant Commander Torrance took command effective 0900 this morning."

"No ceremony?" Mike said, surprised at the abrupt transition. It was better this way. Cavallo wouldn't be missed. Torrance had accepted the commanding officer's title of Captain and Cavallo would be history.

The XO shook his head.

Lieutenant Commander Cavallo and now-Captain Torrance walked together to the gangway ten minutes later. The two shook hands without comment. Lieutenant Commander Cavallo, following the traditional quarterdeck ritual, turned aft to face the flag, rendered a salute, and crossed the gangway to the rim of the dry dock. He turned left along the walkway to the waiting taxi without a look back.

"Thanks, Kinkaid," Captain Torrance said to Mike. He strode toward the hatch off the main deck, tapped the XO's shoulder as he passed, and said, "Let's talk."

Mike relished the frigid morning's pristine sunshine, clearing weather at last. A chill, early-February breeze chased fast-fading remnants of scattered clouds. *Bartley's* repairs were complete. Only the final underway testing of the new sonar installation remained before they would rejoin a carrier task group.

Mike and *Bartley's* excited officers and crew welcomed their freedom after eight weeks in dry-dock, no longer forced to endure the inactive, depressing, and hospital-like, live-aboard experience. The shipyard had provided fresh water and electricity service. However, because the dry-dock lacked sewage connections, the men had endured two months of frigid trips to a cluster of outhouses about two-hundred yards from the ship. All aboard had served their penance.

The first underway OOD watch again fell to Mike, after Captain Torrance had introduced a more rational watch rotation plan. Mike now had his own watch team with Ensign Brooks as his assigned JOOD.

At the shipyard's signal that all was ready for *Bartley's* exit, Mike expected Captain Torrance to assume the conn and get the ship underway from the flooded drydock himself as Captain Cavallo had done. Instead, the new captain motioned to Mike to proceed with the delicate backing maneuver as conning officer.

Mike gasped in astonishment at the captain, momentarily stunned at his good fortune. Mike's chest swelled in silent exhilaration at Captain Torrance's acceptance of his qualification, even though he hadn't been able to observe his ship handling skills. Inspired, Mike executed a flawless exit maneuver.

"Nice job, sport," Riley said when *Bartley* had cleared the dry dock. He whispered to Mike, "Almost like you knew what you were doing." He twisted his mustache, grinned, and continued to the sonar shack.

36

BARTLEY'S ACTIVITIES FOR THE WEEKS after they rejoined the task group fell into the familiar pattern of round-the-clock steaming, anti-submarine searches, and related drills. Mike liked best *Bartley's* assignments to plane guard station where he had a front row seat when planes landed. Bad weather had made some of the carrier's flight operations particularly intriguing. It remained a mystery how the pilots were able to fly in the dark during heavy storms, and land on the carrier's often-pitching deck. Someday he would learn to do it too.

After an afternoon watch, Mike followed his usual routine and stopped by the radio shack to check on messages. Message traffic had been light for several days. In particular, nothing they'd received related in any way to the progress of the investigation.

"Mister K," Pops grabbed Mike's arm when he entered. "This schedule change just came in. Those bastards won't leave us alone."

Pops thrust a message form at Mike. He stood with hands on his hips, and bounced up and down on the balls of his feet while Mike read. He hadn't seen Pops this agitated before. The long deployment had shortened tempers for all the radio shack crew.

"Oh hell, not that damned northern patrol again," Mike said as he read the message. Images of the last patrol, the boredom, the miserable weather, the train shoot incident, and pilot rescue flashed through his tired brain.

"Have you checked the dates?" Mike said looking up at Pops.

"We get eight days in port after this current underway period," Pops danced as though standing on hot steel, his arms waving. "Then it's back to Siberia again, dammit. When will it be our turn to go home?"

"Okay, I'll take this one to the captain," Mike said.

How would he explain another delay to Carol? Patrolling the purgatory of Korea's northeast coast again meant at least a month's delay before *Bartley* could be ordered home. Carol's impatience and plea for his return couldn't be missed in her latest letter. Their baby was due soon.

Lieutenant Powell, who usually received schedule updates, wasn't in the ops department office when Mike entered, but he found Riley deep in paperwork.

"Don't throw away your long johns," Mike said. "Take a look at this." He tossed the schedule change on Riley's desk and slumped into the spare chair.

Riley read the message but remained silent for longer than Mike expected. Riley stroked his mustache then shook his head.

"Has the captain seen this yet?" Riley asked.

"I'm headed his way," Mike said, "but figured you should see it."

"Damn," Riley said. "Why pick on us again?" He stabbed a finger at Mike. "You don't suppose the admiral has a soft spot in his heart for you because you snatched his pilot nephew out of the water, do you? Remember, when you were on Cavallo's short list for court-martial? The admiral's commendation message to Cavallo about the rescue saved your butt."

"If he liked us so well," Mike said, "how come we go into purgatory again?"

"By the way," Riley said and reached into his shirt pocket for his cigarette pack, "I've been meaning to ask you." He lit a cigarette, returned the pack to his pocket, and leaned back in his chair. "I haven't heard of any more of your set-tos with the XO lately. You just not telling me, or has something changed?"

"You haven't noticed?" Mike said, irritated by Riley's roundabout way of getting to the point.

"Would I ask if I had?" Riley said.

"He's pulled his old stunts a couple of times," Mike said, "but only when Torrance isn't around. He shut up quick yesterday when the captain came into the wardroom during an XO eruption over a routine message. It looks to me like the XO's staying clear of the captain, for a while anyway."

"Don't count on it," Riley said.

37

"MISTER K," FINGERS SAID. HE shook Mike again. "Wake up, sir. It's important."

"What's up?" Mike said and rubbed his eyes. He swung his bare feet onto the cold steel deck. A quick glance at his watch showed forty minutes after midnight. He'd been asleep less than an hour.

"Pops wants to see you, sir," Fingers said. "Says it's urgent. You gotta get up."

Still groggy, Mike slipped on his clothes and reached for his parka. Whatever had come up had to be serious for Fingers to be so agitated. Pops hadn't called him to the radio shack before, not even once. His sleepy mind could think of no reason for the urgency. All the communications functions had been running well.

Pops held out a cup of his strong brew to Mike who took it and waited for an explanation of the early wakeup call. Pops' pursed lips and steady gaze were unexpected. He usually had a smile. This had to be serious. Mike looked at Fingers. Fingers looked away.

"Why the hell did you pull me out of the sack in the middle of the night, Pops?" Mike said. He sipped the coffee.

Pops held out his hand to Fingers, palm up. Fingers opened a drawer, withdrew an envelope, and handed it to Pops.

"A special message, Mister K. For you." Pops offered Mike the envelope, the special type reserved for Red Cross messages.

Mike flinched. His shaky hand reached for the envelope. Red Cross messages passed through the Navy communications system were not common. More often than not they conveyed unpleasant messages. The last one received several months before notified one of the radio-men of his mother's death. Is Carol okay? The baby's due. He removed the message.

To: Ensign Michael Kinkaid, USS Bartley
From: Seattle Office, American Red Cross
Karl Alan Kinkaid six pounds seven ounces born 4:12 a.m.
March 7, 1952. Carol and baby well. Lisa sends.

Speechless for several minutes, Mike ignored his tears. His mind spun. He'd promised to be at Carol's side when the baby was born. He offered a silent prayer for her forgiveness and his baby's continued good health. How much longer must he wait before he could hold her and the son he'd dreamed about, a son named for his revered father?

"Thanks, Pops," Mike whispered. The three men clinked coffee mugs in a salute to the baby. "Good news for a change."

Minutes later, Mike flipped on Riley's stateroom lights and yanked off his covers.

"Get up, you dumb Irishman," Mike yelled. "It's time to celebrate."

38

For Mike, *Bartley's* mission supporting the carrier task group became mind numbing. Much as he tried to keep his problems buried in the back of his mind, they captured his attention all too often. The baby, Carol's health, the deployment without end, and the unresolved outcome of the grounding investigation all swirled in his head. Worst of all, he could do nothing to resolve any of them.

Surely by now he and Riley would have learned of the investigation's findings. The admiral's decision should be imminent. It could bring court-martial for Mike, Riley, and the XO.

While on plane guard station on the carrier's last night of flight operations, Mike spent the first hour of the 2000 to 2400 bridge watch coaching Brooks on the intricate ballet of maneuvering the ship. The unseasonable shifting winds required the carrier to make frequent changes in heading to keep the wind down the flight deck for the landing planes. Mike and Brooks kept busy maneuvering *Bartley* to maintain the proper position behind the carrier.

"I think I'll watch this air show one more time before we head in tomorrow," Captain Torrance said as he stepped from the ladder onto the open bridge. He climbed into his pedestal chair and set a hot cup of coffee on the coaming. "You've watched this flying game for some time, Mike. Are you still sure you want to fly from a flattop?"

"Yes, sir," Mike said, no longer averse to showing his enthusiasm. "Haven't changed my mind."

"Uh-mm," the captain muttered and sipped his coffee.

Mike spent the next forty-five minutes intent on the several course and speed adjustments needed to keep *Bartley* in position. Brooks responded well to the maneuvering tips Mike provided, tips Mike had learned from Riley over the last several months.

The XO came to the darkened bridge with some papers for the captain's review. Almost immediately the first plane landed for the carrier's last recovery cycle of the evening. Instead of leaving the bridge, the XO stepped behind Mike near the fire control director station, a spot Mike and Brooks had long referred to privately as the XO's bitching station.

A prickly sensation found its way to the back of Mike's neck. He walked across the bridge to the radar repeater in an effort to shake the feeling. A check of the bearing and range to the carrier confirmed *Bartley's* position: precisely on station.

The XO didn't leave.

Mike moved to the binnacle to check their course and speed. Everything checked. He crossed to the starboard wing of the bridge. Seaman Tucker followed. Brooks remained by the binnacle to monitor their heading.

The XO watched but didn't move.

"Looks to me like you're off station, Mister Kinkaid," the XO said loud enough for the captain to hear. "Sloppy ship handling," the disdain in his voice evident.

"I checked it, XO," Mike said in an equally loud voice. "We're on station, right where we should be."

"I said it doesn't look right," the XO repeated. "Check your position again, Mister Kinkaid."

Mike strode across the deck and checked the radar repeater again. A squawk box call to CIC confirmed his readings.

"Combat confirms we're on station, XO," Mike said through clenched jaws.

He wanted to say, "Get off my back, you jerk. Come check our position yourself if you think I'm off. We're exactly where we should be and have been on station the entire watch. Go below, you jackass, and tend to your papers." Instead, Mike clamped his mouth tight in the realization he had almost spoken the insolent words aloud.

"Still doesn't look right to me." The XO accompanied his criticism with an audible chuckle he meant to share with the nearby captain.

Mike gritted his teeth. He tried to take his mind off the XO's petty tyranny. Why didn't the captain step in and stop this harassment?

Moments later the carrier turned without telling the task force in advance, a constant irritant to the smaller ships, but part of their job. Mike recognized the movement by the change in the relative position of key lights on the carrier. He noted Brooks nodding at the trick Mike's coaching had pointed out.

"Right ten degrees rudder," Mike ordered.

Brooks relayed the order to the helmsman through the voice tube and received the helmsman's confirming reply.

"Why are you turning, Mister Kinkaid?" The XO's voice carried an unmistakable sneer. "You told me you were in position."

"The carrier's turning, sir," Mike said eyes on the carrier.

"They haven't announced a turn, Mister Kinkaid." The XO exploded with a gleeful snort and moved closer. "Your imagination is getting ahead of you. Another dumb move—again. Now all you've done is get out of position."

"I can see them turning." No "sir" from Mike this time, fists now clenched.

Four minutes later, as the carrier steadied on its new course, Mike ordered, "Steady as she goes," to match the carrier's move. Brooks relayed the order.

"Sir," Seaman Tucker said, "combat reports the carrier announced the new recovery course is 184."

"Very well," Mike replied, and checked *Bartley's* heading. His course change estimate had caused him to overshoot by two degrees, well within normal tolerance, but one more excuse for XO harassment.

"Come left to 180," Mike ordered. Brooks relayed the order.

Mike clenched his teeth. He counted under his breath how many seconds would pass before he'd hear another XO bitch. Twenty-two seconds was all it took.

Mike, fists still clenched, fought to keep his anger in check. He shot a quick glance at the captain. Why didn't he intervene? Why didn't he stop the XO's interference? Captain Torrance watched the landing aircraft. When the XO resumed his badgering, Mike and Brooks exchanged raised eyebrows and slight nods toward the XO.

"You didn't gauge your maneuver very well for a qualified OOD, Mister Kinkaid," the XO said, louder this time. "Can't you do better? You're out of position again like I said, Mister Kinkaid." The XO moved to the starboard wing of the bridge and faced the lights of the carrier in the gloom ahead. "Check it, Kinkaid," he said.

Mike took the five steps to the radar repeater. His death grip on the instrument provided no relief. He focused on the carrier's lights to calm his growing anger before examining the radar display. *Bartley* was seventy-five yards farther behind the carrier and on bearing, well within tolerance for station keeping.

"Add four turns, Mister Brooks," Mike said ordering a small increase in *Bartley's* speed. His fists flexed. "We're on station, XO." Again, he did not add the customary "sir."

"Have you checked with combat?" The XO's tone confirmed his enjoyment in taunting Mike. He stepped back to his bitching station.

Mike nodded to Seaman Tucker who recognized their private signal to make the routine call to CIC for a position crosscheck.

"Combat confirms we're on station, sir," Tucker reported.

Once again Mike checked the range to the carrier on the radar repeater.

"Drop four turns, Mister Brooks," he ordered to resume the speed required to maintain their position.

"Pretty sloppy ship handling again, Mister Kinkaid." The XO said, unquestioned derision in his words. "I think we qualified you too soon."

Enough. Mike spun around. Two slow and menacing steps put his face within inches of the XO's.

"You say my ship handling is deficient," Mike said in lowered tones. "Why don't you relieve me? Apparently you can do better." Mike's nose moved a millimeter closer with each deliberate, tension-filled word. "Do you relieve me, sir?" Mike didn't restrain the urge to spit out the "sir."

The XO took a quick step back. The move put his back against the cold steel bulkhead, the base of the fire control station. His head swiveled as though to determine what had stopped him.

Mike matched steps with the XO. The sight of the cowering XO disgusted him. This man was Naval Academy trained. How had he ever gotten a commission? Why had the Navy promoted him, and recalled him to active duty? Surely his past fitness reports had recorded his failures.

"Don't get smart with me, Mister," the XO said, an anxious note in his voice. "I'll have your ass."

"Do you relieve me, sir?" Mike repeated, staring down at the shifting eyes. The XO stammered, unable to offer an answer before Mike leaned closer. "I asked you a question." Mike's every word spoke intensity and authority. "You say you can do this job much better. Do you relieve me? Do you have the watch? Sir?"

Mike whipped the lanyard over his head and pressed his binoculars, the badge of the Officer of the Deck, against the XO's heaving chest. He stared down into the XO's eyes now a hand's width away.

"Uh, of course not," the XO mumbled. His hand moved across his face. He attempted to shout, but his quivering voice produced a raspy, "Get back to your job, Mister." He coughed. "This is insubordination." The XO paused to catch his breath. "Consider yourself on report, Mister, on report."

Mike did not yield. He did not step back.

"I understand I am not relieved," Mike said, struggling to keep his words professional. "Is that correct?" Before the XO could reply, Mike added, "As OOD, I am in command of this ship's operation while I'm on watch. You are interfering with the safe conduct of the watch. Relieve me or get off my bridge." Mike leaned closer to the XO.

The XO shrank. His head snapped left and right in a search for an escape. He squirmed.

"You are interfering with the watch, sir." Mike's low-pitched words, spoken louder but with deliberate self-restraint, carried ominous overtones. "Leave my bridge. Leave now." Mike took a half-step back and, in an ultra-slow motion, his right hand rose from his side.

From the corner of his eye, Mike saw the captain step down from his pedestal chair. He ignored the movement.

"Mike," Ensign Brooks called and waved in an attempt to signal Mike. Mike didn't respond to Brooks' call, either.

"Enough, Mister Kinkaid," Captain Torrance said. The captain's iron grip on Mike's shoulder spun him around. "Get back to your duties."

At the captain's touch, Mike's instinct said attack. He stopped, his arm half-raised, the captain's face inches away. Stunned, Mike gaped into the captain's unblinking eyes. Although his arm lowered, Mike's balled fists didn't relax. He needed a deep breath to regain his composure before he could answer.

"Yes, sir," Mike replied. He regretted his folly, seconds too late. Why hadn't the captain stepped in earlier before he'd made a real ass of himself? Had he been insubordinate? No question. Had he been provoked? Sure, but what difference did that make? He'd threatened a senior officer.

Mike's anger spiked at the look of relief in the XO's eyes and satisfied grin at the captain's intercession. Dammit, the captain had let the XO get away with this. He saw the whole thing. Why did he tolerate the XO's harassment in the first place? Why did he support that bastard?

The XO ducked, slipped past Mike, and scampered across the deck to the ladder leading to the wheelhouse one deck below. Mike almost followed then froze, mindful of the captain's order.

The XO paused on the ladder's third step and called to Mike.

"I'll get you for this, Mister," the XO gasped. "You're on report, Mister. On report."

Rigid, jaws and fists clenched, Mike shook with anger.

"Mister Kinkaid," Captain Torrance said from behind Mike.

For a moment the words didn't penetrate.

"Mister Kinkaid." The voice, louder this time, spoke authority. Mike spun toward the voice.

"Yes, sir," he said, with an effort to maintain a respectful tone.

The captain tilted his head as though to judge Mike through new eyes.

Mike steeled himself, angrier with his own behavior than with the XO. Accept it. The bastard won this round. The XO's harassment had goaded him into stupid behavior, and in the sight of the captain. He had no acceptable excuse.

Captain Torrance crossed the bridge to the ladder. He paused and looked back at Mike, stern-faced. "Yes you were provoked, Mister Kinkaid. Doesn't matter. I don't tolerate insubordination."

His mind in turmoil, Mike stood frozen. The episode had soured what had promised to be a good relationship with the new captain. His father would have been more than disappointed. If a chance for flight school had ever existed, it was dead now.

39

RAIN FROM A FAST-MOVING COLD front caught up with *Bartley* and followed her into Tokyo Bay the next morning. The ship moored alongside the Yokosuka Naval Base pier one hundred yards from their earlier dry dock confinement. Mike carried the previous day's messages to his stateroom for his routine review. Midway through the first stack, Riley threw the stateroom's entry curtain aside as he burst in.

"Dammit. Aren't you ever going to learn?" Riley said in a near shout. "I hear you lost it with the XO last night and right under the captain's nose as well. You and your big mouth are in real trouble this time. What the hell happened?"

Mike's head turned toward Riley then snapped back to the messages on his desk. What was the best way to answer Riley? He had probably heard an exaggerated version of the incident. Mike's fingers appeared to search through the pile of messages.

"Another XO harassment session," Mike mumbled.

"The word around the ship is that your "session" as you call it, was way more than one of your frequent little dust-ups," Riley said. "The story's all over the ship. You screwed up. When will you learn to keep your damned mouth shut around that jackass? Now let's have it. What exactly happened?"

Mike had tried to be an exemplary officer, to be the man he knew his father expected him to be. He had excelled, earned early and full qualification and the respect of his radiomen and fellow officers. Now his damned temper had blown it all. Riley's unexpected criticism smarted, but the words were mild compared to Mike's internal torment. He continued to flip through his message pile and pretend to read, too ashamed to acknowledge the deserved reprimand. Maybe Riley would leave.

"Dammit, Mike," Riley hollered. "I'm talking to you." Riley stood hands on hips.

What help could Riley offer now? He'd only heard the scuttlebutt, the product of the ship's rumor factory. Even if Riley listened to Mike's version of the encounter, nothing would change.

"What happened?" Riley asked again, his voice demanding straight answers and no nonsense. "I can't help if you clam up on me. Now, let's hear it."

"What difference does it make?" Mike's retort matched Riley's volume. "You want me to be a good boy and say, 'yes, sir,' and 'no, sir?' Am I supposed to bow down and do whatever that buffoon says, like one of the first-year plebes he hassled at the Naval Academy? Dammit, I'm not a plebe. I'm a commissioned officer. I do my job and do it damn well, too. I'm not out for praise, just..."

"You got it out of your system, now, do you?" Riley said. He hadn't moved a muscle or even blinked during Mike's flare-up. Mike squirmed under the intense gaze.

"Okay. Sit down," Mike said chastised. He nodded toward the bunk. He shoved his papers aside and the ashtray to the desk's edge so Riley would light up and give him a moment to get his thoughts together.

Riley didn't budge.

Chagrined, Mike looked down at the deck for a moment before he spoke. He lifted his chin, looked at Riley, and related the highlights of the incident.

"Anything else?" Riley crossed his arms. "I want the whole story."

"You won't let up, will you?" Mike said.

"Keep talking." Riley's eyes continued to pierce Mike.

"I knew the captain would give me hell after the XO left the bridge." Mike sat back in his chair and pursed his lips. "I deserved it." Somehow, admitting his guilt eased his anxiety. "Instead, the captain said he knew I'd been provoked. Said it was no excuse. Said he didn't tolerate insubordination."

"It's about time you accept the facts." Riley sat on the bunk and leaned forward, elbows on his knees. "The XO has a bug up his ass. He blames you for his brother's death. He won't drop it. This can't go on."

"There you are, Kinkaid," the XO's voice startled Mike. The XO stormed into the stateroom brandishing a paper at Mike.

"Enough of your insubordination, Mister," the XO hollered. "Last night was the last straw. You can't dodge this one. The captain saw it all."

The XO ran his hand across his pencil mustache and paused as though he expected a contrite response from Mike. The XO's shoulder tic returned. His hand wiped his face again. Brow furrowed and chin up, he took a step toward Mike.

"Listen to me, you. See this?" The XO waved the paper at Mike. "You're on report. Gross insubordination. You threatened a senior officer. There are witnesses. You're restricted to the ship until the captain deals with you. You're confined to your stateroom, except for meals and your duties. You can bet your precious fitness report is going to read like crap after this. You'll never be promoted. Understand?"

Pressure built behind Mike's eyes and tightness gripped his stomach. He balled his fists. Riley's unexpected grip on his arm cautioned him.

"I want you to know I've got your number." The XO pulled an envelope from his pocket and shook it at Mike. "Your father killed my brother. I checked. Got confirmation in this morning's mail. Your dad was Lieutenant Commander Karl Kinkaid, *Dunleavy*'s captain when the ship went down in 1943. My brother was a crewman on *Dunleavy*. He died in the sinking."

"Wait a minute," Riley said raising his hand in a stop command.

"Wait nothing," the XO said to Riley. The paper rattled in his shaking hand. "I've got the truth at last, Kinkaid. Are you going to deny it?"

Angry, Mike leaned forward, his eyes locked on the XO. Riley pulled at Mike's arm. Mike took a deep breath, paused and accepted Riley's restraint. Anger wouldn't solve anything. He'd take another tack.

"Your brother's name was Frank Watkins, right?" Mike said in a tone lacking anger despite his pounding heart.

A flash of surprise widened the XO's eyes. His chin came up. "How'd you know?"

"Was he a chief quartermaster?" Mike strained to keep his voice calm.

"So you did know after all. I knew it." The XO threw out his chest and flashed a gleeful, victorious grin.

"What makes you think he died in the collision?" Mike did his best to keep anger from his voice.

"Pretty damned obvious, isn't it?" the XO said. "He never came home. I never got another letter from him. Nobody would tell me what happened."

"What did you find out?" Riley said.

"What's it to you?" the XO sneered at Riley.

"Frank didn't survive," the XO said. "I dug into the records and learned about the sinking."

An idea flashed in Mike's mind. "When did you learn of his death?" he said.

"What does that have to do with it? I'm his only family. The Navy sent me a telegram the day before my fall classes started at the Academy."

Mike made a deliberate effort to slow his words and lower his voice. He had to maintain control.

"I met your brother Frank in the hospital in late March 1943 while my father recovered from his injuries," Mike said.

Mike hadn't anticipated the emotional release his words produced, as though he had left a dark cave and stepped into brilliant sunlight. Suddenly he was calm and in control. Maybe now the XO would back off. But the man continued his stunned gaze, spittle easing from the corner of his mouth. A hand wiped his face.

"That's a damned lie," the XO yelled. "It's not possible. Frank went down with the ship in January 1943."

"I attended the ceremony," Mike continued in the same controlled tone. "I talked with your brother."

"What ceremony? What the hell are you talking about, Mister?" The XO's voice grew louder with each statement.

"The ceremony where my father pinned a medal on your brother for his lifesaving efforts when the ship sank," Mike said

"How could that be?" the XO shouted. He stopped as though thinking. A violent negative headshake followed. "He died in the collision and sinking."

"You're wrong, XO," Mike said. "How else would I know his name? I met him. I shook his hand. Frank saved my father's life. He saved several shipmates. He earned the medal. If he died at sea sometime later, I'm sorry."

"You're lying to me, Mister." The XO's words came as an angry bellow. "If he did all those things, how come I never heard from him again? How come I didn't hear about the medal?"

"Your brother survived the sinking, XO." Mike's assurance grew. "He told me what happened."

The XO stiffened. He glared at Mike. His free hand wiped his face. His hands shook as if he held a live electric wire.

"Dammit, Kinkaid. I don't believe you," he screamed. "You're lying to me because I found you out." A violent shudder racked his body. "Why in hell should I believe you anyway?"

Instinct prompted Mike to stay with the calmer tone, although he wanted to strangle the XO. Again, Riley squeezed his arm. Mike got the message. Can't let this get out of hand. He would continue the reasoned approach.

"Think about it," Mike said. "The collision happened in January. You said you weren't notified of your brother's loss until late summer. That's over six months later. Have you considered the time difference? I don't know what your brother did after I last talked with him. He told me he had orders back to sea."

Perspiration dripped from the XO's brow. He swallowed several times and wiped his ashen face.

"I don't believe you," the XO said in a sudden, anguished cry. "You're lying to me, dammit. You're trying to cover for your old man. Well, it won't work with—"

"Just a minute," Mike said opening a drawer in his stateroom desk. He drew out a small leather case, shuffled through the contents, and extracted a worn and faded photograph.

"This is the last picture I have of my father. I took this photo at the medal award ceremony." He handed the picture to the XO. "Is this man standing next to him your brother?"

The XO gasped slack-jawed at the picture. His hand and the picture shook.

"Good morning, Captain," Riley's startled voice said.

A stern-faced Captain Torrance stood in the doorway. He studied the three officers in turn, his brow furrowed. His eyes settled on the XO.

"What's going on?"

The XO stared at the captain for a moment longer. His shoulder tick resumed a life of its own. He swallowed twice and again wiped his face.

"Uh, well, sir, uh, I was putting Kinkaid on report for last night," the report form shook in his hand, "and, ah, I confined him to the ship until you can deal with him, and…"

The captain reached for the report form.

"I see. Anything else?"

"Uh, well," the XO stuttered, "ah, no, sir."

Mike plucked the photo from the XO's other unresisting hand. The captain's unblinking eyes, under a furrowed brow, locked on the XO.

"I'll deal with this later," Torrance said, motioning with the XO's report form.

Mike and Riley exchanged a glance at the captain's unexpected intensity. Torrance stuffed the XO's report form in his hip pocket. He pulled a folded message form from his shirt pocket. Something had changed, but what?

"I have something we need to discuss, now, Gene," the captain said to the XO. "Come up to my cabin." He walked away down the passageway. The XO followed. He didn't look back. Mike and Riley exchanged raised eyebrows.

"How much do you think the captain heard?" Mike said.

"Don't know," Riley said. "Maybe most of it. I didn't hear him coming."

"What is it about me, Riley? Do I attract trouble?" Mike searched Riley for answers. Why hadn't the captain spoken to him? Was he in more trouble than he'd thought? "Every time I turn around I dig my hole deeper. Last night on the bridge, and now here."

Riley didn't answer. He picked up the photo of Mike's father and studied it. He shook his head and laid it back on the desktop.

Mike's relief at telling the XO the true story died as fast as it had blossomed.

"I expected to feel better after I told him the truth," Mike said. "He doesn't believe me."

"Even with the picture," Riley agreed.

Mike shook his head.

"How long before the captain hangs me?" Mike said and slumped into his chair.

40

MIKE AWOKE EARLY AFTER A restless night. While he shaved and dressed, an uneasy feeling, one he couldn't identify, persisted. Breakfast offered no appeal, so he skipped it and made his visit to the radio shack. The ominous feeling wouldn't leave him while he followed his ritual, reading through the night's message traffic. A mental note reminded him to re-check the messages later on the chance he might have glossed over an important item.

A brief chat with Pops and a second cup of Pops' Poison didn't alter Mike's mood. Still anxious, he left the ship for his periodic visit to the base communications center to collect any new classified publications and updates.

Five minutes into the half-hour walk, he remembered that he had neglected to get the XO's permission to leave the ship. He'd followed the protocol on past runs to the comm center. Today he'd forgotten. Too late now to avoid another XO blow-up. He wouldn't go back and ask.

The brilliant late-winter sun had replaced the fast-moving cold front. The sun's warmth and the half-hour walk helped ease the tension Mike had been unable to quiet.

At the communications center the new publications shipment had to be unwrapped and each document logged. He glanced at his watch. He'd been gone over two hours.

The XO wasn't in his stateroom when Mike stopped by to report his return. Odd, the stateroom didn't have the usual tidy stack of papers on the desk. Maybe he'd gone ashore. Mike hustled up the ladder and along the boat deck passageway toward the radio shack to stow his documents. Unexpected laughter and loud chatter came from the radio shack.

Mike stepped through the shack's hatch and stopped short. The space held his entire twelve-man radio gang, all sharing some excitement. Three or four radiomen normally occupied the shack when *Bartley* was under-way, only one or two when in port. Why were they all there? Pops and the other radiomen behaved like kids waiting to open a Christmas present.

"What's going on here?" Mike asked, scanning his excited crew.

Pops pushed through the gathered radiomen, spilling some of his coffee in mid-stride, and reached up to grab Mike by the shoulder.

"You know about the XO, don't you, sir?" Pops said.

"What about the XO?" Mike said, confused by the hilarity.

"You're not going to believe this, Mister K," Fingers said. His uncharacteristic wide grin surprised Mike.

"The XO left the ship with all his gear about ten minutes ago," Pops said. "You missed him. They didn't have much time for a turnover."

"Turnover?" Mike didn't track what Pops said. "Who are you talking about?"

"Lieutenant Powell," Pops said. "He's our new XO." Pops held out his hand to Fingers. "Let me see those message orders."

Fingers opened the captain's private message folder and handed the top message to Pops.

"This came in yesterday. I gave it to the captain right away. He said he'd deliver it to the XO himself." Pops handed the paper to Mike. "I would have let you see this one first, but these orders required special handling, for Captain Torrance only."

Mike read the brief message.

"To: Lieutenant Eugene A. Watkins, 312025/1105 USNR
On receipt, Detached. Report to Commander Cruisers/
Destroyers Pacific, San Diego, California for processing
and release from active duty..."

Mike's stomach lurched. He and Riley had expected orders for the

XO, but not immediate detachment and termination from active service. The board's findings remained unknown, but the evidence was clear enough. Both Captain Cavallo and now the XO had received quick and career-ending treatment. He felt a pounding in his head. Were he and Riley next? When?

Mike handed the orders back to Pops. Fingers snatched the phone on the first ring.

"Yes, sir. He's here. Yes, sir. I'll tell him." Fingers' furrowed brow raised Mike's curiosity. Fingers hung up and said, "Mister K, the captain wants to see you in his cabin," he glanced at the bulkhead clock, "in twelve minutes."

Mike had known his career would end some time although he hadn't expected to serve less than a year. He tried to shake his apprehension. Maybe the captain wanted to talk about something else. Relations with Captain Torrance had been good until the recent incident on the bridge with the XO. He'd done his job well and stood good watches. No mistakes. The radio gang performed well. All his reports were in.

But, all that didn't matter. The dust-up with the XO had to be Torrance's number one topic. Maybe he deserved a chewing-out. No. The XO's orders and immediate detachment sent a clearer message. The Navy would deal with Ensign Kinkaid next.

"Captain wants to see us, together," Riley said as Mike passed through the wardroom on the way to his stateroom. At the far end of the deserted table, Riley showed none of his usual good humor. Mike' hopes sank. "Both of them" could only mean one thing.

"What's the problem?" Mike said, stalling. This could be it. He had no choice.

"Don't know. Looks serious." Riley downed the last of his coffee. "Our new XO's up in the captain's cabin with him now."

"Hold on." Mike needed a moment to think. "Let me check for any messages for Torrance that the duty radioman may have left on my desk." He knew there were none, but needed time to think.

Mike returned to the wardroom. He braced himself for the bad news. His mind had long ago exhausted all the possible outcomes. None were positive. He had done his duty to the best of his ability. Was Riley to get the axe too?

"Okay. Let's go see the old man," Mike said. His words sounded more confident than he felt. He led the way to the upper deck, to the captain's cabin.

Mike paused before the door and reached to pat the gold emblem in his pocket before he knocked. The emblem he always carried was missing. He stopped breathing in a flash of panic. Where had he put his father's emblem? He tried the other front packet. Not in his hip pockets either. What happened to the emblem?

"What's the matter?" Riley grabbed Mike's arm and spun him around. "You okay?"

Mike gulped, shook his head, and gasped. "Nothing," he choked out. "Tell you later."

Mike's pulse pounded. The time had come time for the axe to fall. He couldn't avoid the inevitable. He'd done his duty. He'd made his case to the board as best he could. He owed no apologies. Shoulders back, head up, Mike rapped on the captain's door.

Instead of the usual call to come in, the captain opened the door.

"You wanted to see us, sir?" Mike said standing at attention

"Yes. Come in," the captain said. He waved them into his cabin then sat at his desk.

The two officers entered the cabin, closed the door, and stood at attention. Lieutenant Powell sat across the desk from the captain.

"I won't be long, gentlemen," Captain Torrance said, his usual pleasant smile missing. To Lieutenant Powell he said, "I guess we can log this as a good day and a bad day."

Captain Torrance moved a small pile of papers on his desk before he focused an unblinking look at Mike, then Riley. An eternity passed before he spoke. He raised the papers in his hand as though prepared to read aloud. Instead he put them back on his desk then looked again at Riley, then at Mike.

"It's been obvious to me since I've come aboard that you two are the best of friends. Because you are, it's appropriate for you to share what I have to say to each of you."

The captain's words were business-like. Mike could read nothing in his manner. Neither anger nor humor there. Sweat formed in Mike's palms. Powell, the new XO, revealed nothing.

The captain picked a paper from the pile on his desk and scanned it for a moment. His eyes lingered on Riley then shifted to Mike. His expression didn't change.

Mike searched the captain for a sign, even a hint of the usual telltale wrinkles at the corners of his eyes, some indication of his normal, upbeat mood. Nothing.

"I suppose it's customary to pass along the good news first." A smile edged its way onto his mouth. "I am aware of *Bartley's* recent incidents, and that you both risked indictment in the grounding. Before I reported aboard, I reviewed the investigation's preliminary report. I think you've seen how the Navy deals with false testimony."

Mike's stomach tightened. What false testimony? Whose?

"I know you've been anxious about the effect of the grounding on your career, Riley," Captain Torrance said. "I'm not permitted to show you the documents," he motioned to the papers on his desk. "The good news is I am permitted to say you have been removed as an Interested Party in the grounding incident. Your conduct was correct and appropriate. Your involvement will be erased from your permanent record. The slate is clean."

A quick rush of relief filled Mike. Riley's ear-stretching grin doubled the size of his monster mustache. Until this moment Mike hadn't recognized how heavy a burden Riley had carried. But, the flush of delight dissolved in an instant. Why did the captain mention only Riley?

"I have a letter received this morning from the Bureau of Naval Personnel in Washington." Captain Torrance selected the top paper on his desk. "Given the significance of the content, it's appropriate for me to present this to you in person." He handed the single page to Riley. "Congratulations, Lieutenant."

The captain's reference to good news and bad news flashed through Mike's mind. The good news first, he'd said. Riley's was first. His was next.

Riley scanned the paper. "Well I'll be damned," He said in a hushed voice. He handed the letter to Mike.

"Promotion to Lieutenant," Mike exclaimed, pleased at Riley's unexpected but welcome advancement. Mike extended his hand to Riley. "And long overdue if you ask me."

"Better yet," Riley said and twisted his monster mustache, "It's backdated to August. That's a nice pay raise."

"One more thing," the captain added. "With Lieutenant Powell as our new executive officer, the operations officer billet is vacant. You're next senior and best qualified on board. As of today you're our new operations officer, Lieutenant."

Riley's eyes flared in surprise. He rubbed his mustache again and flashed a broad grin at Mike.

"I want you to stay aboard, Riley," the captain continued. "If you agree, I'll send a message to Washington to have you extended for a normal tour in the operations officer billet. The assignment will serve you well when you apply for a regular commission. I urge you to send that application soon. The timing is in your favor."

"You're on, Captain," Riley said. A wink followed his grin. He shook hands with the captain, then Powell.

Captain Torrance picked up the next paper from the stack on his desk. Mike's eyes darted between the captain and Powell searching for some hint of what was next. He examined this near-expressionless captain who he admired. The words about the good news coming first hammered his brain. His father's advice that you cannot escape responsibility resounded in his head.

Mike's resolve returned with a shake of his shoulders, chin up, his view locked on the captain. He forced himself to stand taller, ready for whatever he might hear.

"Mike," the captain said glancing at another paper taken from his desk, "as I told Riley, I'm aware of how uneasy you two have been about the outcome of the grounding investigation and its impact on your careers. I've read all your testimony. This letter, also from Washington, closes a difficult chapter for you and reflects how the board evaluated your actions in a perilous situation. I think you better read this." The captain handed a letter to Mike.

Mike's shaking hand reached out to accept the paper, his throat tight enough to prevent speech. He steeled himself for the inevitable disappointment. He reached with his other hand to tap the gold emblem in his pocket, but winced when he remembered its disappearance. He was on his own now.

Mike looked to Riley then Powell before his eyes settled on the words on the letter in his sweating hands.

> FROM: CHIEF OF NAVAL PERSONNEL
> TO: ENSIGN MICHAEL A. KINKAID, 515405/1100, USN
> SUBJ: CHANGE OF DUTY
> WHEN RELIEVED, DETACHED. PROCEED TO CHIEF OF NAVAL AIR
> BASIC TRAINING, PENSACOLA, FLORIDA FOR UNDERGRADUATE PILOT
> TRAINING CLASS 5-52. REPORT NOT LATER THAN 16 MAY 1952...

Rockets went off in Mike's head.

"Congratulations, Mike," Captain Torrance said and stood to shake Mike's hand.

Mike, mouth half open, was unable to express the turmoil in his mind. A quick glance at Riley caught a wink and an ultra-wide grin.

"The board assures me," the captain continued, "that you have been fully exonerated because of your sound judgment and prompt action to save *Bartley,* and your straightforward testimony in the investigation."

Mike felt an inner flush. His worry that the incident would jeopardize any chance of flying had vanished. The incident was history, unrecorded history as far as his career was concerned. He wouldn't have to contend with a career black mark.

The captain reached across his desk and touched a separate pile of papers. "Mike. Your actions in the net incident were prompt and correct as well. That incident, too, is history. Your slate is clean."

Mike shared a grin with Riley. Powell's eyes held a rare sparkle.

"Oh, and yes," the captain added with a tilt of his head. "I imagine you wondered about my earlier reference to bad news."

Oh, no. What had he overlooked? Was he rejoicing too early?

"The bad news is," the captain continued, "with your departure, *Bartley* will be losing a damned good officer and ship handler. The entire crew will miss you."

Mike took a minute to understand. A warm glow flowed through him. The past weeks of anxiety seemed to melt away to become history. He offered a slight nod of thanks to his father for watching over him. He hadn't needed the good luck emblem.

"There's one more thing, Mike," Captain Torrance glanced at Powell and added. "I want you to know I'm aware of the issue with Lieutenant Watkins. I served my first assignment as Ensign on *Dunleavy*. I knew your father as a superb officer and leader."

Mike felt a flush at the captain's compliment. Why hadn't he mentioned earlier that he had served under Mike's father?

"I also knew and respected Chief Watkins," the captain continued. "I transferred to another ship before the fatal convoy. Many of those lost were friends. I'm certain your father would be proud of the fine officer you've become, Mike. Good luck in your flying, and, enjoy your new family." He laid the papers on his desk. "Thank you, gentlemen, and congratulations. I'm proud of you both."

Each officer responded with a warm "Thank you, sir" and shook hands with Captain Torrance. Riley and Mike exchanged grins, then turned to leave.

Mike's swirling mind didn't register that Powell was speaking until Riley grabbed him and pulled him back into the cabin.

"We have some business to attend to," Powell said.

"Mike, there's the matter of your relief," Captain Torrance said. "I can't let you go without a replacement. We have to have a communications officer."

Apprehension hit Mike. He knew about the Navy-wide officer shortage. Finding another officer to replace him as communications officer approached the impossible. Only two of the six ensigns ordered to the ship had reported aboard. Several vacant billets remained. Without a replacement on board, his coveted orders might melt away like spring snows.

"We have an idea we want you to consider," Powell said. Nothing in

Powell's demeanor offered a hint. "Can you train Ensign Brooks in your job in, say, six days?" Powell asked.

Brooks? Six days? Mike didn't understand. He understood his obligation. He would turn over his duties to someone able to handle the job when he left, whenever that might be, and for whatever reason. On previous bridge watches Brooks had talked about his interest in the communications officer duties. Sure, he could train Brooks, but what had six days to do with it?

"Yes, sir," Mike replied. "Brooks could do the job. We'll get together, go over details, do a classified document inventory, and check him out on the crypto procedures. He's quick."

"In six days?" the captain said.

Mike expected some explanation. A sense of frustration grew.

"I don't understand," Mike said. "What's important about six days?"

"Mike," Powell said, "You know the latest schedule has us underway for another northern patrol in six days. If you came along, we wouldn't be able to detach you until we got back, maybe thirty to thirty five days later. You're due for some leave, and since you have to be in Pensacola in May, you might miss your required reporting date. We can detach you in six days, before we depart for the patrol. We can, that is, if we have someone to fill your shoes by then."

Mike looked at Riley's grin. He imagined his own smile must be at least as broad. Both the captain and Powell chuckled.

"Captain, there's only one valid answer," Mike said. "Brooks will be ready."

The captain pulled out the upper drawer in his desk. He removed a dark blue box slightly larger than a cigarette pack.

"Mike, here's something else you've earned. The yeoman delivered this to me with yesterday's mail." The captain shot a wink at Riley. "I understand the crew calls you Deadeye. Pops explained to me how you came by the name, and how a Navy officer earned a Purple Heart. Congratulations." He opened the lid to expose the Purple Heart medal and handed the thin, blue box to Mike. "I'm sure your father is proud."

Thank you, sir," Mike said, "I hope you're right." He flashed a broad grin as he held out his hand to Torrance and accepted the box.

Mike followed Riley into the passageway and closed the door to the captain's cabin. He grabbed Riley's arm a few steps outside the captain's cabin and spun him around.

"You got the message, didn't you?" Mike said. "The XO. It had to be the XO."

"What message? What about the XO?" Riley said with a searching frown. "What are you talking about?"

"The captain's comment about false testimony," Mike said. "It explains everything. But whose false testimony, right? Not ours. Could be Cavallo, but my guess is the XO. Maybe both?"

"Had to be the XO. It fits." Riley stroked his mustache. "Explains his frenzy, too. They were on to him."

"And Cavallo must have gone along with him," Mike added. "Remember we wondered why the board didn't question us further, but the captain and XO had several sessions."

Twenty minutes later, washing his hands at the basin in his stateroom, Mike jumped when Riley and Fingers entered unannounced. Mike still reeled from the meeting with the captain.

"A present from the crew," Fingers said. He laid on the desktop an envelope with Mike's name scrawled across it. "You've earned this, Mister K."

Mike dried his hands and tossed the towel onto the lower bunk. He didn't understand. He opened the unsealed envelope. It contained two copies of his request for flight training that Captain Cavallo had forwarded to Washington weeks before as disapproved. What was special about that? Neither Riley nor Fingers offered a clue. What were they driving at?

Riley's attempt to hide his grin confused Mike. Riley nodded again toward the documents in Mike's hand. Okay, he'd play along. He scanned the first sheet with Cavallo's disapproval endorsement. Nothing new there. He looked at Riley again expecting some explanation.

Riley nodded again and pointed to the letters. The second sheet was identical. Almost. Mike gasped. The endorsement at the bottom of the second copy, above Cavallo's signature, read "recommending approval."

Mike's quick glance at the first sheet confirmed the wording difference. He cocked his head at Riley waiting for some explanation.

A twinkle crept into Riley's eye.

"The crew sends their best wishes, Deadeye," Fingers said flashing one of his rare smiles. "Seems we had a small mix-up with the mail that day." His fingers wiggled as though he were signing something.

Mike's mouth dropped at the realization of what had happened to his letter to Washington. Riley rested his hand on Fingers' shoulder. Fingers' grin continued.

"Thanks," Mike said and shook Fingers' hand.

Riley's cigarette lighter transformed the evidence to ashes in the ashtray. Mike grinned.

The last of Mike's papers fit into his smaller bag next to his rubber-banded collection of Carol's letters. The drawers in the stateroom's desk and wardrobe cabinet were empty. Brooks, standing behind Mike, had agreed to acquire the cold weather clothing Mike no longer needed.

"Guess that's it," Mike said after a brief, final scan of his stateroom. "Time to head home." Their shared grins confirmed Mike's eagerness to be on his way, and Brooks' pleasure at inheriting Mike's stateroom and new assignment as *Bartley's* communications officer. Brooks picked up Mike's small leather bag and followed.

Riley led the way down the inside passageway, through an empty wardroom, and onto the main deck. Mike followed carrying his vintage B-4 bag. At the quarterdeck, he stopped at the sight of the men gathered there. He looked at Brooks, standing a step away, for some explanation. Brooks grinned and nodded.

Fingers stepped forward from the assembly, took Mike's bag from him and proceeded to the gangway. Another radioman took Mike's smaller bag from Brooks and followed Fingers. The two radiomen continued to the pier and sat the bags next to a base taxi.

Mike's throat tightened at the unusual gathering. Many other officers had detached before without ceremony. Why were the officers and crew turning out for his departure?

"Move it, Mike," Brooks said. "It's cold out here and I don't have all day." Mike caught the teasing in Brook's voice.

Captain Torrance, Lieutenant Powell and Riley waited for Mike at the quarterdeck. Pops and the entire radio gang stood at attention behind the captain. A major portion of the crew assembled behind them. The officers had lined up in two rows to form a corridor for Mike to pass through to the quarterdeck.

"Attention on deck," Captain Torrance ordered. "Hand salute." All hands saluted Mike following the captain's lead. Each officer offered best wishes as Mike strode between them to the quarterdeck.

"Request permission to leave the ship," Mike saluted and said to the captain in keeping with the traditional Navy ritual.

"Permission granted," replied Captain Torrance who returned Mike's salute. Mike shook hands with Captain Torrance, Lieutenant Powell, and Riley. "Thanks" was all he could croak out to the other officers. He waved to his radio gang and the collected crew. Mike faced aft, rendered a salute to the flag to complete the Navy ritual then stepped onto the gangway.

The ship's bell rang, two dings, a pause, followed by two more. Riley's voice announced over *Bartley's* 1-MC public address system, "Deadeye departing. Godspeed, shipmate."

THE END

LaVergne, TN USA
10 December 2010
208256LV00005B/94/P